MAD MARIENNE

KATELYN YATES

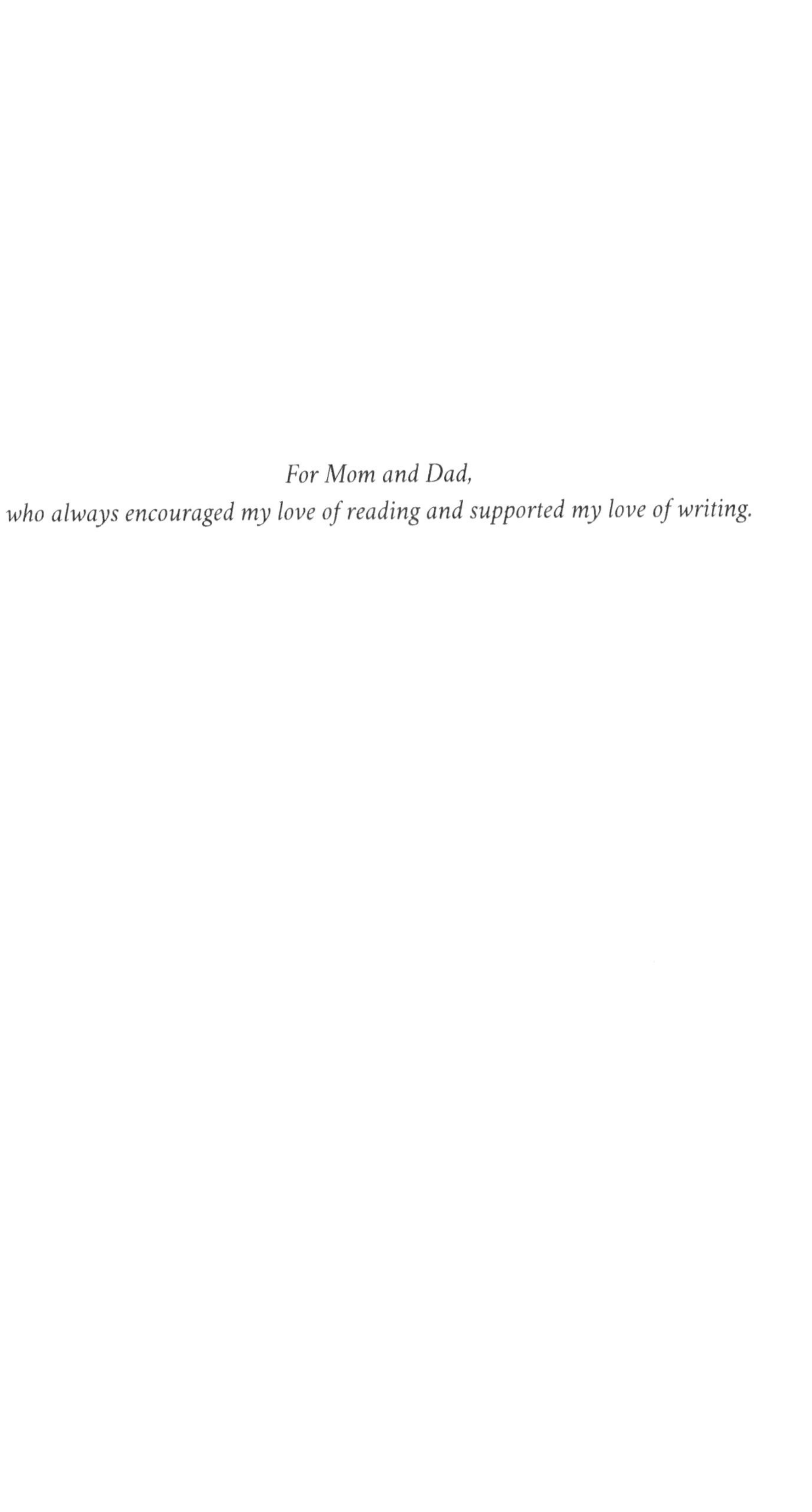

For Mom and Dad,
who always encouraged my love of reading and supported my love of writing.

PROLOGUE

MAY 26, 1897

This wasn't the first time Marienne had run away, but she vowed it would be the last. She sat in the pub tucked deep in an alley in the back streets of Naples, her hands wrapped around a cheap glass of wine, heart still pounding. No one had batted an eye when she entered and ordered her drink—although only eighteen, she looked older. But her distinctive deep red hair cascading down her back, perfectly curled in ringlets, was easily recognizable to those who were undoubtedly already searching for her. She only hoped they wouldn't think to look somewhere so crowded and frequented by the working class.

As she sipped her wine to calm her racing pulse and thoughts, Marienne studied the automatic liquor dispenser that hissed with compressed air just behind the bar. Copper piping wound around the brick wall, and spigots hooked up to bottles of various shapes and colors, waiting patiently for the bartender to turn the right knobs to mix a perfect drink. The large metal lion head above the bar slowly opened and closed its jaws, occasionally blinking as gears whirred and clicked just out of sight, the sound drowned out by the late night crowd. The lion head shimmered with the telltale glitter of luma.

Marienne glowered at her drink. She had always wanted to study the mysterious luma, but not like this.

Not by being betrothed to Luma Baron Prescott.

"It's a perfect match," her father had said earlier that evening. "We're lucky that out of ten Luma Barons in the world, one is not only a mere four years older than you, but that he also thinks you're quite the striking match. It's an opportunity we can't afford to pass up. The British Luma Baron and the Italian ambassador joining their families will benefit everyone."

"Everyone except me," Marienne muttered into her glass as she took another drink. She hated Prescott, as she hated her father. They sat in the parlor discussing marriage arrangements and her dowry as if she wasn't there.

As if she was just another company asset to be traded.

"*Pardonnez-moi*, may I sit with you?"

Marienne tore her gaze away from her wine to see a French boy about her age with eyes as blue as the sea and hair as golden as the weak electric light around them.

"You're welcome to sit here," she answered, "but I won't be staying much longer."

"Somewhere else you want to be?" he asked as he sat down, placing his own glass of amber liquor on the table.

"More like somewhere I don't want to be," she said quietly before taking another sip of wine. She listened to a few bars of the music crooning from the phonograph, relishing the bubbles of anticipation in her chest. There was no other feeling like an escape, and this would finally be the one that worked. It had to be.

"My name's Robert," the boy introduced. He pronounced his name the French way, with the emphasis on the second syllable and omitting the last letter.

"Marienne," she returned with a smile. Her name, too, was French, although half her ancestry was Italian. "Do you often spend your time in seedy pubs?"

He shook his head. "Today's a rare occasion where my feet are on solid ground. I thought I would celebrate the docking of our airship."

Marienne's green eyes lit up like sparks. "You seem young to be working on an airship. Unless you're indentured?" Her eyebrows rose.

Robert smirked. "My captain pays me. I'm a valued member of the crew."

"Sounds to me like your captain is irresponsible, trusting one so young."

"He might be reckless, but James is hardly irresponsible. It takes a lot to run a lightning-chaser."

Marienne leaned forward, all other thoughts fleeing from her mind. "A lightning-chaser! Does that mean you work with luma?"

Robert shook his head. "We're paid by Luma Barons for the lightning, but they won't tell us why. Honestly, that's the most boring part. It's sailing into storms at the height of their rage that makes a man feel alive." His eyes and smile flashed as he took a drink, noticing how Marienne hung on his words. "But I suppose if you were just leaving, I don't have time to tell you about any of that."

She glanced at the door, then the clock, a frown creasing her brow. "I suppose I could stay for one story," she said dismissively.

Hours passed as Robert told her story after story of the storms he had flown into, of the crackle of lightning surrounding him, and the resounding thunder that vibrated deep in his bones. He told her about the crew, and his eccentric captain, James. As he listed off all the places he had been, Marienne sat back with a sigh.

"It sounds like a dream," she admitted. "Being able to travel anywhere."

Robert leaned towards her, an idea forming in his mind. "If you could go anywhere in the world, where would it be?"

"The sky," she said dreamily. "Forever. I would never come down."

"But if you did have to dock," he pressed. "Where would you go?"

"Spain. Don Quixote has captured my imagination."

"We regularly stop in Spain," Robert said, his voice rising in excitement. "And we travel all around the world. My captain takes women as well as men; I'm certain he would let you on!"

Marienne's eyes grew wide. This was it—the escape she had

dreamed about. "You think so? On an airship… I could make my own decisions."

"You'd still have to follow the captain's orders," he reminded her.

"Perhaps for a time," she said archly, suddenly appearing much older. "Until I can get my own airship and be my own captain. Then I will truly be free. But it could all start tonight." The stars danced in her eyes.

Robert stood and offered his hand. Marienne took it and they ran out of the pub, out to the night and the empty streets. The chill wind tore at her curls and stung her cheeks, but she didn't care. Soon she would be flying! Flying away from her old life and everything she hated to a sky endless with possibilities!

Robert led her through the airship docks where enormous balloons bobbed lazily, dark shadows against the dark sky. Anchors tethered them to the ground with massive claws and cables that glinted in the moonlight, but Marienne didn't have time to admire them or even guess which one might be her new home. Robert tugged her along, past the last airship.

"Did we pass it?" she asked.

He shook his head. "We dock somewhere special. Hurry, just a few more blocks!"

But as they rounded the corner, Marienne's hand slipped out of his. He stumbled a few more steps before he could stop himself. When he turned around, his attention was fixated on her horrified expression; he did not see the trio of well-dressed gentlemen advancing from the shadows until they had caught hold of her. Though their words sounded soothing and gentle, their grip was tight.

Marienne threw a frantic glance at Robert and desperately called his name. "Help me!"

He ran back to her, but the largest of the men blocked his way. "You will have nothing more to do with this young woman," he commanded, one white-gloved hand gripping his cane tightly.

Robert shuffled to one side to see Marienne thrashing wildly, her arms pinned behind her back. One of the men said in a low voice, "I have the chloroform, but I hope it doesn't come to that this time."

"You can't take her!" Robert shouted.

"I believe you were the one about to take her," the large man in front of him responded. His tone was deep and dangerous, but calm as a windless day. "Her father wants her home. Run along and we'll have no more trouble."

As the man turned away, Robert's hand curled into a fist. With a cry of rage he struck at the man's back.

Too quick for him to see it coming, the man slapped Robert on the cheek so hard it left a stinging red imprint. Robert raised his fist again, but before he could strike, a hand gripped his arm tightly. He turned to see his captain, James.

James dragged Robert off into an alley and hissed a quiet reproach. "What were you thinking?" His face held the kind of stern expression Robert had always expected a father to make.

"She needs our help," he begged.

Marienne shouted his name again. Robert flinched at the sound, and closed his eyes as her voice was cut off with a muffled yelp. He took a shuddering breath that didn't seem to fill his lungs at all.

"We could have saved her."

CHAPTER 1

NOVEMBER 27, 1904

Serving the British Luma Baron should be an honor, but Katherine dreaded it. The tea set rattled in her hands as she entered the Emerald Parlor. She hadn't served anyone of this high status for two years, and the humiliating result of that incident replayed in her mind. *You had only started as a maid then,* she reminded herself, trying to dismiss the memory. It clung to her consciousness like a stain, scalding shame burning her cheeks. She glanced at Alexander Castle, the master of the Luma Baron's country manor just outside of York—her master for the past two years. *It's not as if I have improved much.*

"But surely there must have been other offers in the past five years," Mr. Castle insisted, entirely engrossed in his conversation.

"Plenty." Luma Baron Prescott sat back and licked his wide lips. "But none that would grant me half as much political gain as Ambassador Santorini's daughter. And she was a beautiful woman. I said I would marry her, and I must—"

He was interrupted by the crash and clatter of breaking porcelain as Katherine and the tea set tumbled to the floor together.

"Clumsy girl!" Mr. Castle spat.

"I'm—I'm sorry, sir," Katherine stammered as she picked herself up off the ground, careful not to cut herself on the sharp edges of shattered cups. She smoothed the skirt of her pale yellow uniform, now stained with tea. "I did not see your foot there."

"Is this how you run my house when I am away?" the Luma Baron asked. His cold blue eyes pinned Katherine to her spot. She dared not even breathe.

Mr. Castle frowned. "Of course not, Antoine. It's only this one. Not certain why she was chosen to serve us. I've tried disciplining her, but she never quite seems to learn." He fixed his dark gaze on her as well, and Katherine shrank.

She didn't know what to do, or where to look. Beads of sweat prickled on the back of her neck. Her fingers twitched, but she couldn't move under those judging eyes, so she pinched at the pale yellow fabric of her skirt.

Luma Baron Prescott sighed. "I suppose we can't expect all of them to be competent, that's just statistics. Well, girl, why aren't you cleaning it up?"

"Sorry!" Katherine piped. She dropped to the floor so quickly that she planted her palm on the sharp corner of a fractured saucer. Her breath hissed through her teeth, but she had been given an order. So she set her jaw, wrapped the wound in a cloth napkin, and picked up the pieces. Some of them grew slick with the few drops of blood that seeped through the makeshift bandage. But she refused to bleed on the dark green carpet, which was already soaked through with tea and cream. *I'm going to be punished for this mistake*, she realized with a shudder. *Best not to make it worse.* Sugar cubes crumbled between her fingers as she tried to pick them up.

"You can't even clean up your own mess properly," Mr. Castle sneered. But he made no other comments as he watched her laboriously place each piece of shattered porcelain onto the tray.

His silence did not ease Katherine's anxieties as she stood obediently, waiting to be dismissed. *Why can't I just do things right?* Her left hand stung where it had been sliced, crying out for a real bandage instead of a tea-soaked rag, but Mr. Castle expected her to follow protocol.

He glanced down at the carpet. "You've missed one."

She followed his gaze. A fragment of white porcelain, no larger than a grain of rice, sparkled in the deep green carpet. With a grimace of pain, she set the tray on the floor, added the errant shard to the pile, and resumed her position awaiting his approval. Mr. Castle nodded imperiously.

"Throw the broken tea set out. Tell Martha to prepare more tea and serve us. Then you may dress your wound, and return here to clean up the rest of your mess."

Katherine nodded. Tears pricked at the corners of her eyes from the pain in her hand, but she turned away quickly and scuttled from the room so he wouldn't see. As she left, she heard Mr. Castle apologizing to Luma Baron Prescott for her behavior and inviting him to another room of the house.

On her way to the kitchen, Katherine passed Martha and told her that she needed to prepare more tea. The other maid glared scathingly at her as she continued down the hallway as fast as she could without spilling any of the broken pieces off of the tea tray, trying to ignore the familiar expression. The shards of ceramic rattled on the tray, as if to chorus the words pounding in her head: *useless, useless, useless.* She unceremoniously dumped the broken tea set into the garbage bin, wishing that erasing her mistake could be so simple.

Once her hand was hastily bandaged, Katherine returned to the Emerald Parlor and began mopping up the spilled tea. She heard soft footsteps behind her and her muscles tensed, but she did not turn around until he said, "Little Mouse, I have a task for you."

"Yes, Mr. Castle?" She stood and faced him, gripping the dripping rag tightly so her fingers wouldn't twitch.

"The replacement gears for the laundry should have arrived in town, and the automaton cat is low on oil again. I need you to fetch these for me. Perhaps I would be willing to forget today's incident if you were to negotiate the price down to, say, two-thirds of asking?"

Katherine fought to hide her panic. The most she had ever negotiated was a quarter off of the asking price. But to avoid punishment for breaking an entire tea set? *Just do what he says. When I follow the rules, I am safe.* "I will try. I'm sorry, sir, but I have not finished cleaning."

"I'll have Eleanor finish up here. You go on ahead. I want those gears by supper, so the rags you stained can be washed as quickly as possible."

"Yes, sir." Katherine frowned at the thought of Eleanor cleaning up her mess. *One more person to hate me.*

As she passed by Mr. Castle on the way out of the room, he caught hold of her arm in a vice-like grip. "You aren't going to let that little scratch on your hand keep you from repairing the laundry tonight, are you? Because you know I need you. You're the only one here who can fix the machines around the estate. You've never messed those up. Not once."

She couldn't help the surge of pride that rushed to her chest. "Thank you, sir. I'll fix it tonight."

"Good. Now go, before I rub luma into your hand." He released his hold on her and she quickly obeyed, her heart pounding. Rumor had it that putting luma into your blood bound you to a person, and she hoped that one day she would escape this house and Mr. Castle.

CHAPTER 2

Katherine closed the kitchen door behind her, hand still stinging as she gripped the doorknob, then began to walk the path towards town. She had barely cleared the corner of the manor when a sharp whistle demanded her attention. Luma Baron Prescott stood next to an automobile with a sour expression. The raised hood of the vehicle obscured the top half of another man who muttered to himself as he stared at the machinery inside.

"Girl—what was your name?" Luma Baron Prescott called.

"Katherine, sir." She bobbed into a wobbly curtsy, and secretly hoped that he wouldn't remember her.

"Alexander tells me you're good with machines," Prescott continued as if she hadn't spoken. "My automobile won't start and my driver can't find the problem. Let us see if you are better at fixing machines than you are at serving tea."

Katherine's face flushed, but she responded, "I certainly am, sir. My father taught me—"

Prescott interrupted her with a dismissive wave of his hand. "Yes, yes, let's not waste time with your personal history. Get to it."

The man behind the hood of the automobile straightened and gave Katherine a relieved look. As she approached, he said in a thick Irish accent, "Thank you, miss. I can't seem to find the trouble. She just wouldn't start. She was fine coming here yesterday, though."

Katherine nodded, only half listening as she stepped into place and inspected the orchestra of metal that fit together to form the engine. Why wouldn't it play its symphony? As she leaned over, her short brown hair slipped out from behind her ear and obscured her vision. She frowned as she tucked it back again. It would be easier to tie it back with a ribbon if it were longer, but Mr. Castle said it looked better chin-length, so that is how it stayed.

She studied the orderly tangle of machinery, trying to recall the last time she had looked at an engine. Over two years, since Mr. Castle wouldn't allow her to work on anything so important as the automobiles or the generator that powered the mansion. *If I do a good job here, perhaps I can have more opportunities to practice*, she thought excitedly. But it had been so long, could she remember...

"There!" She cried out triumphantly when she saw the problem. "The starter is out of alignment. Did you hit a large pot hole or bump on the way here?"

"As a matter of fact, we did," the driver said. "Just outside of Leeds."

Katherine nodded. "And you wouldn't have noticed anything was wrong until you needed to start the automobile again. It's an easy fix," she assured the Luma Baron. "I just need to get my—I mean, the tools." She turned and trotted back the way she had come, satisfaction quickening her step.

It would have been faster to use the main entrance, but that was something that Prescott certainly would have told Mr. Castle, and he would not tolerate it. Katherine shuddered at the thought. *Although it isn't as if he's always so awful.* Her mind turned to how he had told Prescott that she was good with machines. *And I wouldn't deserve the punishments if I wasn't so bad at everything.*

Katherine sighed as she opened the door to the basement, then jumped back as a small brass figure streaked past, followed closely by a larger, silver shape. She watched with fascination as the estate's automaton cat crouched, its amber glass eyes following an autorat that scurried in a serpentine pattern across the hall. With the rhythmic clicking of coils and springs being released and a mighty groan of creaking joints, the automaton cat pounced. It snatched the autorat up in its jaw and, with a swift snap of sharp metal teeth, severed the struggling mechanical vermin's head from its body. The autorat went limp with a soft whirring of gears ticking down, like a heartbeat stopping. Even though she had seen this exact scene play out a handful of times before, Katherine still marveled at how these two machines behaved so similarly to the creatures they resembled.

"Good girl, Millicent," Katherine praised the 'ton cat as it trotted to her, joints still squeaking. Its yellow glass eyes glinted with luma as it deposited the autorat's body at Katherine's feet. She picked it up and inspected it.

The receptacle in its belly shimmered with the pale gold light of luma. Katherine turned it over in her hands, watching the soft, sand-like particles shift. She hadn't seen luma in its raw form since her father had died, and it still filled her with an acute sense of wonder. When added to machines, luma enabled impossible, marvelous things. But no one knew exactly what it was.

Of course, the fact that she was holding it meant that the autorat had gotten into one of the basement's luma supplies, intending to take its plunder back to its master. Millicent did her job well, and Katherine patted her head again before she walked down the basement steps. Millicent followed, creaking all the way, her yellow glass eyes scanning for more autorats.

Along the far wall of the basement, a large, complex machine stood as stately and impressive as an admiral. Katherine paused to admire it. To her, this was the real commander of the house: the generator. It regulated all the mechanical components of the household, and proudly reported the temperature, pressure, and other mechanical levels on dials and gauges crammed across every square inch of its metal surface. Two chutes protruded from one side: one for coal, and another for luma, but the supplies for both were kept behind a locked door. Pipes and wires extended out, behind, and up from the generator, into the walls, and throughout the manor.

It was the only machine in the manor forbidden to her.

She shook herself out of her reverie. Luma Baron Prescott was waiting for her, and she couldn't let Mr. Castle catch her lingering here.

Katherine stood on her tiptoes to reach the shelf where the tools were kept, then placed the autorat body inside the toolbox. She would show it to Luma Baron Prescott— he would know what to do with the luma. And perhaps she could keep the autorat to tinker with later.

As she left the basement, Katherine's foot caught on the top step, and she tripped, her knees hitting the floor painfully and the toolbox scattering its contents before her. She watched in horror as the autorat body hit the hardwood floor, the glass receptacle cracking and rolling in a neat arc, leaving a trail of fine, shimmering luma in its wake.

Heart pounding, she frantically picked up the tools and placed them haphazardly back in the box. In the basement there was a special scraper designed to gather all the minuscule particles into a dustpan. If she cleaned up quickly, no one would have to know.

Footsteps approached from the end of the hallway and Katherine froze. In a moment, Mr. Castle loomed over her.

"You spilled luma?!" he roared.

"I'm sorry—it was an autorat, and… accident," she whimpered in a small voice.

"Do you have any idea how much that costs? No, of course you don't," he sneered. "If you did, you wouldn't be here, trying to pay it off with all of your repeated mistakes! The cost of this will be added to your debt."

Katherine flinched. She needed to escape. "I'll clean it up."

"No you won't." His voice was low and cold, and it chilled Katherine's blood.

She had to leave, *now*. "Luma Baron Prescott is expecting me to fix his automobile." She picked up the toolbox and waited, muscles tense, to be excused.

"Go."

She breathed a sigh of relief and started down the hallway.

"You'll be sleeping in the garage tonight, Little Mouse."

Katherine stumbled, but kept walking. "Yes, sir." Her fingers twitched against the metal handle of the toolbox. The garage would be cold with winter coming on, and she knew from experience how the thin and scratchy canvas tarps failed to provide any warmth. And with the added debt from the luma... When would she ever escape this place?

Fixing the automobile was as easy as Katherine had anticipated it to be. She eased the starter back into place and tightened the bolts holding it in. The driver started the car and it hummed to life; music to Katherine's ears.

"There you go!" she said with a smile. But her pride could not erase the guilt she felt for the mistake with the luma. She placed the tools back in their box, but before she could pick it up, Luma Baron Prescott spoke.

"You were going into town, weren't you?" he asked. "As a thanks for fixing my automobile, you may ride with me. I have some business in town, and I have delayed you from your task."

Katherine stopped. Was this a trap? It seemed too nice to avoid the mile and a half walk to town. But it would be unheard of for her to refuse. Not only was he a Luma Baron, but he was also the man she was indentured to. Mr. Castle was her master; Luma Baron Prescott owned her.

"Thank you, sir," she said, settling into one of the leather seats. "That's very kind."

"And this way if anything happens to the engine, I have you with me already."

"That's very prudent of you, sir." She sat stiff, hands folded in her lap and eyes down, afraid to put even a hair out of line. So far Luma Baron Prescott had not shown any sign of a temper like Mr. Castle had, but Katherine knew that each man had his limits. She did not want to find out what his were.

"Of course it is!" The Luma Baron gazed out the window at the bare-branched trees and clear blue sky. "You know, when my father discovered luma, I was a mere five years old. I was raised to lead the British Luma Company, and I have made it what it is today. When my father passed ten years ago, critics questioned if I—the first to inherit one of the ten existing luma distribution companies—would successfully continue the legacy or if it would be absorbed by the French Luma Baron. Robillard!" His face wrinkled with a disgusted expression as he said the name. "But I proved them all wrong, and look at the British Luma Company today!"

"It's very successful, sir." She frowned.

"You have something on your mind," Prescott observed, turning away from the window. "You may speak freely."

"I was just wondering about luma," she said, relaxing at his words. "If we knew more about what it was and where it came from, perhaps we could understand more about how it works and why some inventions succeed and others fail."

Luma Baron Prescott's face bloomed a deep shade of red. "Those kinds of questions will get you into a lot of trouble," he growled. He pointed a stubby finger at her. "I'll let you off this once with a warning, trusting that you aren't a spy digging for trade secrets. But if I catch even a whiff of you poking your nose where it shouldn't be, I'll sell you off to pay your debts, and your brother, too."

Katherine shrank at his words, crossing her arms over her chest and pinching at her arms. But at that last part she sat up. "You know where Ethan is?" She hadn't seen her brother since they were indentured two years ago.

"Even if I did know exactly where he was, what makes you think I would tell you? Remember that I own you both, and I expect top service and strict obedience or I may have to adjust the amount of money you're paying off each day." Prescott turned back to the window, the conversation clearly over and the atmosphere in the automobile soured.

Katherine's heart sank to her stomach. She didn't know the rate that Ethan was paying off their debt, but if her actions reduced that amount they would both be indentured for much longer. When she had first come to the estate, she had calculated that she would be there for about a year and a half, but some of her mistakes had cost her "wages" for the week, extending her servitude. She shuddered at the thought of spending another year or more with Mr. Castle.

Relief washed over Katherine as they entered the town. The automobile parked on the main road by the luma distribution center, where Prescott entered without a word. The driver tipped his hat at Katherine, who gave him an apologetic smile back. She walked down the road toward the mechanist's shop, admiring the way the afternoon sun lit up the stained glass window on the steeple of Saint Stephen's church. She had always admired the window, which depicted the saint's vision of heaven. The sun lit up the whites and yellows in dazzling brilliance that shone like luma.

A dark blur spread like ink in water across the light in the window. Puzzled, Katherine turned to see thick black smoke trailing behind a rapidly approaching airship. As it passed overhead, Katherine joined the chorus of gasps around her, barely audible above the roar of the engine. She gasped not only from its obvious distress, but also in awe at such a magnificent vessel; its sleek hull shone in the sunlight, with a large, wine-colored balloon struggling to hold it aloft as it veered towards the woods on the outskirts of town.

As those around her muttered about the ship's mechanic taking care of it, Katherine bit her lip. Something in the deep, mechanical rumble rattled in dissonance, like a dying man's last breath, and no self-respecting mechanic would have let that sound go on for long. The ship would soon crash.

I'll just take a look, she promised herself as she ran towards the trail of billowing smoke. *Like with the automobile, it won't take long. I'll still be back to fix the laundry.*

CHAPTER 3

Katherine's breath came in painful spurts by the time she reached the airship, and she leaned against a tree for support. She had left the town far behind, much farther than she had anticipated, but the thought of the ship and crew in trouble had kept her following the smoke. The airship appeared to have landed safely, the anchors firmly attached to thick tree branches, but the hull still leaked thick black smoke.

Up close, the airship was even more spectacular. Unlike many other ships, the hull of this one tapered towards the bottom, like a mariner's vessel, and even had something shaped like a bowsprit at the prow as if designed to cut through more than air and clouds. *It must be a pleasure cruiser*, Katherine thought. No practical cargo airship would be designed so extravagantly. As she crept closer she spotted burgundy-painted letters along the side: *Vincenzo*.

Katherine glanced behind her, towards where she knew the estate —and Mr. Castle—waited for her return. Her heart dropped as she realized how much time she had spent reaching the airship, and her fingers twitched as she thought about Mr. Castle's demand that she fix the laundry tonight. But the ghost of his warning was drowned out by some vehement swearing in a female voice.

A woman paced the ground beneath the airship, cursing anything within her imagination, at first under her breath, but soon her tone grew loud enough for those watching her from the deck to flinch. Katherine watched her in almost as much awe as she had regarded the ship. The woman wore breeches and boots like a man, and her corset sported coat-tails while still highlighting her full, curvy figure. The woman's hair spread out from her face in a wild mass of curls that did not extend past her chin, and was the same deep red shade as the balloon holding the airship aloft. Katherine tugged at the ends of her own hair: chin-length, straight, brown. Plain. Mr. Castle insisted she keep it this length, but she could not imagine anyone telling this woman how to style her hair—or commanding her to do anything.

"And may autorats ingest every drop of your earnings!" the woman bellowed to the deck. She turned to face Katherine so quickly that her curls tumbled around her face. She fixed Katherine with cat-like green eyes. "And now we have attracted curious locals. Brilliant." The woman strode towards her.

"I think I can help," spilled out of Katherine's mouth. She clamped her lips shut, immediately wishing she could retract the words.

The woman raised a single eyebrow. Katherine was surprised to find that she wasn't much shorter than the woman in front of her. Her presence demanded respect.

Katherine swallowed and tried again. "I saw the airship crashing. I came to see if everyone was okay."

"Do you really think you can help us? You're young." The woman's tone was direct, not sneering like Mr. Castle and not pleading. Her feline eyes stared deeply and unblinkingly at Katherine, daring her to attempt deception.

Katherine nodded, heart pounding. "I'm nineteen. My father worked as an engineer and mechanic on the air docks in London. Abraham Whitehall. He taught me everything he knew, and let me join him for jobs since I was twelve." She did not admit that all she had worked on for the past two years had been light bulbs and stoves.

The woman looked Katherine over with no attempt to hide her judgmental expression. "He wasn't one to pay off his debts," she observed, looking pointedly at Katherine's pale yellow dress—the color of servitude to a Luma Baron.

Katherine bristled and the tips of her ears burned. "He did the best he could!" she shouted. "And if you think so low of those who have to borrow from greedy Luma Barons simply to stay in their own business, then good luck finding someone to repair your ship!" She turned to leave, feeling as if as much steam were pouring from her as from the airship.

A hand on her shoulder stopped her.

"You got spunk, kid. I admire that." The smile on the woman's face was amused and proud. "Come aboard, take a look."

The fight left Katherine like helium leaking out of a balloon, leaving shame behind. "I'm sorry," she said as she followed the woman towards the airship. "I don't know where that came from."

"You defended your father, and yourself. It was good! And impressive that you stood up to me. I'm Marienne. I captain this fine vessel." She couldn't keep the pride out of her voice as she gestured to the *Vincenzo*.

"This is yours?" Katherine couldn't say why she was surprised. Command seemed to come naturally to Marienne.

As she drew closer to the *Vincenzo*, the excitement of being aboard an airship once again built inside her. The simple machines at the estate could never satisfy her the way real engines could. Even the automobile engine paled in comparison to an airship. Her stomach lurched familiarly as she climbed the rope ladder towards the deck. Her left hand stung beneath the bandage, but it was easy to ignore when compared to her anticipation.

She hadn't been on an airship since her father died. He used to bring her along to his jobs, though he would never let her do any of the actual work for his clients. Instead he talked her through what he had done. Afterwards, she would practice in his workshop.

Katherine could not let Marienne know this was her first time actually repairing an airship herself. She found comfort in reminding herself that everyone who had known her praised her for being a good mechanic. Even Mr. Castle.

"Our last mechanic left us very suddenly six weeks ago," Marienne explained once they stood firmly on the deck of the ship, her voice cutting through Katherine's thoughts. "So we had to improvise. Our radio operator offered to try to keep the ship in running condition until we got a new mechanic. He did such a good job, I was hoping I wouldn't have to hire anyone new, but today proved that wrong."

The texture of the deck was rough enough that even Katherine's simple boots didn't slip—at least, when it was dry. She couldn't be sure her feet would stay planted once the airship went through a cloud. *What are you thinking?* she scolded herself. This was simply a repair job, then back to the estate to fix the laundry. Her stomach plummeted at the thought.

Katherine avoided the gazes of the crew members, setting her sight firmly on the floor and letting her hair screen her face from them as much as it could. Marienne led her down into the belly of the ship, down a hallway with metal floors and beautiful dark wood walls peppered with nicks and dents.

"Here we are," Marienne announced.

A heavy door made of metal still leaked tendrils of smoke, even when closed, and a high-pitched rhythmic chirping sound pulsated from the room. Marienne frowned and, pulling her sleeve over her hand, yanked open the handle. A wave of heat and humidity assaulted Katherine as a cloud of steam and smoke enveloped her.

"Marienne!" A man's voice echoed through the metal-filled engine room, straining to be heard over the chirping. With a metallic whine, sunlight poured into the room, blinding Katherine as the smoke poured out of ventilation grates.

Katherine blinked until the sun-spots disappeared, but the room was still hazy. She could see outlines of various machine parts—the main engine, the coal chute, the climate control unit—but some shapes were unfamiliar to her and she couldn't make out the details yet.

"Bert, return to post!" The man said in a commanding tone. An automaton bat circled the engine room, chirruped once, then settled itself on the ceiling. The man then turned back to Marienne. "I don't know what went wrong."

"It's alright, Todd," Marienne responded. "I am really to blame. I should have hired someone new the moment Nathaniel was gone. But we have a volunteer here to take a look." Marienne stared at Katherine expectantly.

"I'm Katherine," she said, a little too late. "I'm sorry for not introducing myself earlier."

A voice crackled through a panel set into the wall by Katherine's head, causing her to jump. "Captain, you're needed on deck."

Marienne frowned. She took Katherine by the shoulders and studied her face. "Can I trust you?"

Katherine, heart pounding, nodded.

"Good. Todd, keep an eye on her. I'll be back soon."

As Marienne left, the sound of her boots echoing through the halls, Katherine acutely felt the beads of warm moisture on the back of her neck and arms, even though most of the steam had seeped out of the engine room. Todd tugged on the ends of his tight curly hair, and Katherine wondered if he felt as nervous as she did. It seemed Marienne took all the confidence with her. But he smiled jovially, his cheeks dimpling.

"I heard you've been keeping things running around here," Katherine started. "Have you had much training in mechanics?"

He shook his head. "Just what I've picked up from being curious. Let me show you where the trouble started." He moved across the room with an awkward gait, and Katherine thought he was limping. But when he moved past the engine, she realized that the rhythmic thumping she had taken for a broken mechanism had actually been the sound of the crutch he leaned heavily against for support. His left trouser leg was knotted at the knee, the space below it empty.

Katherine gasped, then felt her ears grow warm. "I'm sorry, that was rude of me."

Todd only smiled sympathetically. "It's always a shock the first time," he said in a subdued tone. "Lost it in the Aerocorps several years ago. Come on." He perked up and waved her over. "The smoke started over here."

She followed him to a machine just off to the side of the main engine, a hinged panel on one side hanging open. "Oh, no wonder!" she exclaimed. "This is the cooling unit. If something goes wrong with this, the whole thing overheats. Then you have a mess of problems. It's a good thing you landed in time."

Todd nodded. "Once I realized something was wrong, I alerted the captain and helmsman so they could land as soon as possible. I couldn't really see what the matter was," he admitted. He grabbed a lantern off the workbench and held it up for her.

"No kidding," Katherine muttered as she looked inside the unit. A mass of gears and a few electrical wires greeted her, cobbled together to cut corners and make do without parts that the unit had lost some-where down the line. Katherine wondered if some of the pieces had been salvaged to repair other parts of the engine. "Who was your mechanic?" she said more to the engine than to Todd. "He ought to be ashamed of himself, leaving a machine looking like this."

She turned to him. "I'll be able to more clearly see what's wrong if I can use your lantern and gloves, but I will need you to do the actual repair." She held up her bandaged hand.

His brow furrowed as he handed her leather gloves too large for her. "I'm sure I can follow your instructions, but are you alright?"

"Just an accident earlier," she said, trying and failing to force levity into her tone. Once she was done with this job, she would have to return to the estate. Mr. Castle would be livid at her detour, but she pushed the thought from her mind as she tugged the glove on over her bandage.

Katherine took a deep breath and plunged into the maze of mechanics inside the cooling unit. The shadows shifted around her as she adjusted the lantern. Looking around, she shook her head at how each part had been doing more than it should have to make up for what was missing. "If I was the mechanic on this ship," she muttered, "the first thing I would do is to get everything in proper order again."

"What was that?" Todd called from behind her.

"Just wishful thinking," she replied with a sigh. She pushed a couple wires out of the way and noticed a gear that looked out of place. Well, more out of place than any of the other piecemeal parts. When Katherine reached out to touch it, it fell down with a clatter. After several struggling attempts in the oversized gloves, she managed to pick up the gear with a wry smile.

Content that she now knew the problem—and its solution—she extracted the upper half of her body from within the machine. Handing back the gloves, she reported, "There's a fan in the corner that needs room to blow. This gear was blocking it." She held up the offending piece. Small spots of rust had formed on some of the teeth.

"It was just a matter of unblocking the fan, then?" Todd asked. "You fixed it?"

She shook her head. "I wish it was so simple, but the gears in there have not been placed at random. Everything is all mixed up inside." She frowned and patted the side of the machine, as if comforting a sick child. With eyes closed, she thought about what she could do to fix the airship now and have it last long enough for them to buy the parts they needed for the cooling unit to remain in functioning condition. At last she took a deep breath. "Okay, I have an idea. Do you have any extra gears? We'll need about two or three."

Todd showed her a box on the workbench that housed a collection of gears of all sizes, metals, and degrees of rusting. She found some rods to thread through the gears and anchor them to the metal side of the machine. With a sigh, she breathed a silent apology to the airship. As beautiful as it was on the outside, it deserved a much better running engine. The *Vincenzo* deserved someone who would take care of it.

Katherine now held the lamp up as she directed Todd where to solder the rods to the metal plating, and which gears to place where so that they fit together snugly enough to turn. She was amazed at his balance as he knelt with only one leg, but she tried not to stare. Once the job was done, the fan had enough room to move and cool down the machine. Katherine nodded with satisfaction.

"That should hold you for some time," she said. "But I think you should get a real mechanic soon. I'm sorry," she added hastily. "I'm being rude again."

"I'm not offended," he said with a smile. "Like I said, I only know what I've picked up. As for a mechanic…" He looked towards the door, and when Katherine followed his gaze she saw Marienne standing in the doorway. How long had she been there?

"Correct me if I'm wrong," Todd continued, "but I think we've found our new mechanic."

Katherine's heart sank as Marienne nodded. She had probably gone down to the village and found Devin Toomer, the mechanic who came to the estate whenever the generator needed maintenance. As hard as she had tried to deny it, Katherine had begun to hope that she could stay on the *Vincenzo* and work in the engine room every day, restoring the mess of machinery to what it should have been. Katherine looked down at her pale yellow dress. She should have been back to the estate hours ago, repairing the laundry.

She nodded and said in a resigned tone, "I'll be going, then."

"Katherine." Although Marienne did not raise her voice, her tone demanded attention. "Who are you indentured to?"

"Luma Baron Prescott," she stammered.

The captain's brow furrowed and her gaze drifted towards the open grates as if she could see outside. "His estate is closer to London, if I recall."

"His main estate is," Katherine answered. "But this is his summer cottage. It's currently under the supervision of his cousin, Alexander Castle." She attempted to remain as polite and neutral as possible, but her voice broke when she said the name of her master.

Marienne returned her piercing gaze to Katherine. "You hate it there." It was not a question.

"I'm sorry," Katherine whispered. "I must go." But even as she walked the few steps to the door, she knew her heart would remain firmly welded to the engine room.

"Why?"

Marienne's question stopped Katherine in her tracks. She turned to face the captain, too many protests on the tip of her tongue to choose only one. Yet she remained silent as Marienne continued.

"I have a grievance against Prescott, and it seems to me he has enough maids"

Katherine's eyes widened as Marienne's meaning sank in. "You want me to stay? To run away with you?"

"If you can keep this ship in the air, you have a place with us." Marienne smiled.

The offer seemed too good to be true. Katherine opened her mouth, wanting to agree, but Mr. Castle's voice rang in her head. *Fix the laundry tonight, so you can clean up your mistakes.* She crossed her arms over her chest and her twitching fingers began to pinch and pull at her arms.

"I'm sorry, but I can't. It would be illegal for me to leave my servitude. I've done all I can here, and it's past time for me to return to the estate. Thank you for letting me work on your airship."

Marienne pursed her lips in disappointment, but nodded. "I can't say I understand nor agree with your decision, but I will respect it. Let me walk you back to the deck."

With each step, Katherine's heart sank more and more. She had spent less than an hour in the engine room and it already felt more like home than the estate she had lived at for the past two years.

When they reached the deck, Katherine noticed that a small crowd of onlookers had gathered, their expressions in various states of concern, curiosity, and desire to take advantage of an unfortunate situation. She spotted Luma Baron Prescott and her stomach lurched as she shrank back. If he saw her here, he would inform Mr. Castle, and there was no telling what her punishment would be for deviating from his orders.

Marienne leaned over the railing and shouted down, "I already told you, we're not in need of any more assistance, so return to—" She cut off abruptly as her face blanched.

Luma Baron Prescott's face, already red from indignation, turned a violent shade of purple when he saw the captain of the ship.

Marienne's jaw tightened, but she wasted no time. "Nyx, take us up! NOW!"

From below, Katherine heard Luma Baron Prescott scream, "Marienne de Santorini, I demand you return my ship at once and come down here this instant!"

"Katherine, pull up the rope ladder!" Marienne shouted.

Katherine hesitated. If she followed the order, she could not return to the estate. Mr. Castle would be furious.

"Do it now!" The desperation in Marienne's voice and the fact that Luma Baron Prescott had almost reached the rope ladder made the decision for her. Katherine cranked the winch that smoothly retracted the rope ladder just as Prescott snatched for it, his hand closing around empty air.

"I will find you!" he bellowed. "I will send every airship in my control after you! There will be no place of rest, no dock for this airship that is not in my power to bring you back to me!"

The *Vincenzo* ascended, causing the end of the rope ladder to swing wildly until it was fully retracted. Katherine's short-cropped hair whipped in the wind, and the hem of her yellow dress beat against her calves as the airship lifted higher and higher. The treetops shrank and her view expanded as the world spread out in front of her like a living map, complete with birds flitting around at eye level and miniature people walking around on the ground. But as she saw the estate in the distance that she detested so much, Katherine stumbled back, bumping into Marienne.

"I'm sorry," she said, "but I believe I've just been kidnapped."

CHAPTER 4

"*R*obert!" Antonio called out as a handsome blond man entered his shop. "You should have radioed me to announce you were coming. I would have hidden my best fabrics!"

Robert grinned and embraced his old friend. "That is exactly why I did not, *mon ami*. And I wasn't sure myself if I would dock in Prague this month."

"You still fly that old junker?" Antonio stepped back to his counter where he sorted bobbins of thread while Robert perused the styles displayed on mannequins throughout the store. Shaking his head, the shopkeeper continued, "You should settle down, open yourself a nice, stationary tailor's shop... just not anywhere near me!"

"Ah, but then how would I bring the exotic fashions of the world to my adoring customers?" Robert rubbed the linen of a ruffled russet blouse on a mannequin, imagining how it would look in sapphire or emerald. The style would lend itself beautifully to a peacock-inspired gown, but browns were much more popular in Western Europe right now. He would have to travel far to sell it, or wait for Carnival.

Antonio's deep laugh resounded through his shop. "Exotic fashions? Does what you're wearing count?"

Robert looked down at his simple yet classic white shirt with puffed sleeves, jade vest and well-cut black trousers. In contrast, Antonio's waistcoat sported tails that drooped nearly to the floor, a cravat that jutted out of his chin like a turkey wattle, and a well-sculpted top hat. He glittered all over with brass chain trim and cogwheel accents.

"What I wear is necessary for my lifestyle. No amount of helium would lift that ensemble, my good man!"

Antonio laughed again, and Robert moved on to browsing the shelves and shelves of fabric wrapped neatly into bolts.

"I've got something new you'll like," Antonio said, pulling a bolt of fabric out from behind the counter. "Wasn't sure if I would hold on to it for you too long, but you came at just the right time—it was delivered the day before yesterday."

Robert reverently took a corner of the fabric in his fingers. It shimmered with luma, a subtle effect on the cream-colored satin. "It's perfect," he whispered.

Antonio beamed. "I knew you'd like it. How much do you want?"

"All of it."

The shopkeeper's eyes widened. "That's—"

Robert calmly took several bank notes out of his pocket and handed them over. "Is that enough?"

Antonio counted through them, then grunted. "I'll get your change. How do you manage to afford this?"

"Business has been good." Robert flashed a grin.

With a shake of his head, Antonio gave Robert a few coins. "I swear, I never even see anyone go into your airship when it's docked."

"I'm simply respecting your wishes and not setting up shop near you!" Robert opened the door to leave. "Keep an eye out for pastels, they'll be the next big thing, mark my words! And thank you for the satin!" He exited the shop, admiring how the luma in the fabric shimmered. It would look even better in the glow of firelight.

Yes, it was perfect. It would look stunning on her.

As he approached the airship docks, Robert's admiration shifted to his airship. The *Madness* was an outdated warship with a few modifications, including his sewing workshop added to the back of the hull. However, the airship still sported guns and cannons, which he had always told Antonio was in case of sky pirate attacks. He never told him that the *Madness* was the one doing the attacking.

The first mate, Landreau, came out to meet his captain on the gangplank. "We've sold all the luma, sir," he reported in low tones.

"Excellent. Let's hope it makes it to someone who can do some good with it." Robert glanced towards the International Luma Distribution Center with a distasteful glare. Ever since Marienne had explained to him how Luma Barons intentionally inflated the price of luma, Robert had made luma harvesters his sole targets.

"And how are we on supplies for the Revel?" Robert asked.

"Here they come now." Landreau pointed to the crew members driving a rented cart laden with barrels of fine liquors. As they began to unload, Landreau turned his attention to the bolt of fabric tucked under Robert's arm. "Looks like you found something good, too."

"Indeed I did!" Robert proudly showed off the satin and how it shimmered in the sunlight. "Take it to my workshop, will you?"

When the first mate took the bolt of fabric, he frowned. "Is this luma-infused?"

"But of course! Only the best for my clients."

Landreau sighed. "It's a good thing we had a large haul this run. Robert, you know I respect you, but you can't keep spending so frivolously. It's getting more and more dangerous to attack Luma Barons. I am asking—no, *begging* you to please take money as payment for your work this time."

Robert forced a brilliant grin, but could not hide the chagrin in his eyes. "Where would the fun in that be?"

"Getting paid." When Robert did not react, Landreau shook his head and took the bolt of expensive fabric on board.

With Landreau gone, Robert could now watch the bustle of activity around him with spirits as high as a helium balloon. He turned his charming smile at the sound of heeled boots approaching behind him to see a lovely young woman with coppery curls walking down the gangplank.

"Rachel!" he called to her. "Come, my darling! We alight at sundown!"

She shook her head. "I'm not coming."

Robert deflated. "Not coming?"

"No, I…" She looked at the *Madness* longingly. Lovingly. Then, shaking herself, she continued. "I'm staying here."

"But why? I thought you liked sailing the sky." Robert's ocean-colored eyes betrayed his heartbreak as he searched her expression.

"I did. I loved… all of it! Even the raids and the storms. But I can't do it anymore." She closed her eyes. "I can't pretend to be Marienne."

Robert's spirits crashed. He wanted to protest, to say she wasn't a surrogate or stand-in, that she was enough just the way she was. But the words wouldn't come.

Rachel whispered, "I saw how you looked at her last year at the Revel. You never looked at me that way. I can't go through that again."

"Where will you go?" he croaked.

"I'm staying here." She glanced around with a small smile. "I actually just got a job with a seamstress, simply by saying I had learned from you. So thank you for the experience. And thank you," she gave him a kiss on the cheek, "for the experiences."

As she walked away, Robert felt as if a hole had opened up in the metal plating of the *Madness*. He wished he could say it was because he loved Rachel, but in reality it felt like this every time someone left his crew. It always felt like the airship wasn't complete without them. He knew that for months he would still expect her to be there, calling out for her until Landreau would remind him that she had left. He saw it all play out so clearly because it had already happened to him so many times before.

People left him. Sooner or later, they always left him.

CHAPTER 5

Katherine watched the estate shrink as the airship carried her further away. The tumult of emotions was too much for her to sort out, but she was aware that relief was among them. Behind her, Marienne paced the deck agitatedly. Katherine was surprised to find that the captain looked even more upset than she had when the airship had been leaking smoke.

Marienne turned and saw Todd standing on deck. Rage etched into her face, she stomped towards him. "This is your fault!" she shouted. Katherine flinched, but she didn't notice. "Two places! Out of the whole world, only two I refuse to visit and, devil take my soft heart, I make an exception for you!"

"I was not going to miss my goddaughter's christening!" Todd retorted. He adjusted his crutch to stand a little taller, challenging Marienne. "You also wanted information, and we got it!"

"Rumors!" Marienne pointed towards the woods where they had anchored, the landscape fast retreating. "And now Prescott has seen me! He knows to look for the *Vincenzo* now, and he won't stop! You know he won't stop."

Katherine watched, fascinated. Was Marienne… scared?

Todd said in a low, soothing tone, "We'll figure it out. We always have."

Marienne sighed and her gaze drifted towards Katherine. The captain straightened, regaining her composure, and said, "Will you please join me in my quarters?"

Katherine timidly followed her through a door set below the control room, her trepidation melting away as she marveled at the simple elegance of the quarters. The back wall was entirely made up of windows with thick, velvet curtains drawn to either side so that the room was illuminated with soft evening light. In front of the windows squatted a plush sofa, and to the right stood a four-poster bed with curtains drawn. At the foot of the bed a grand piano patiently waited to be played.

Marienne immediately moved to the piano and plucked out a three-note arpeggio in the high register. "I must apologize. I gave you the choice to stay with us or return to your servitude, and even said I would respect your decision, and now I have gone back on my word."

"I admit, I was shocked at the turn of events." Katherine blushed. "I'm sorry, that was rude."

A sigh and an eight-note scale up, then down. "No, I was the rude one, stealing you away like that. If you still want to return to the estate, I can drop you off in London with enough money for a train and cab to get you back. But…" She took a deep, shuddering breath, "I cannot take the *Vincenzo* back to that estate. What was Prescott even doing there?" The last part she said mostly to herself, but Katherine couldn't answer even if she knew.

Her own thoughts were wrapped up in the possibility of returning. Her stomach plummeted at the thought. Mr. Castle would know she was gone by now, and when she returned he would have had plenty of time to think of a suitable punishment. She began pinching at her forearms.

Marienne turned from the piano to observe Katherine. "Do you really want to go back?"

"Want to?" There was something about Marienne that invited

candor, made it easy to tell the truth. Katherine shook her head. "No, I don't want to. But I have to."

"Why?"

"Because I'm indentured." Katherine gestured to her dress. "If I don't return, my debts won't be paid. And it's illegal. If I stay, we'll both be criminals."

Marienne's cat-like green eyes bored into Katherine as her fingers rested lightly on the piano keys. "Have you ever made mistakes as a maid? Broken something, spilled something, offended the wrong person?"

Katherine looked away, the pinching increasing intensely, pain and red marks erupting erratically across her arms. How did she know?

"Has Prescott ever added those mistakes to your debt?"

Squeezing her eyes shut against the shame, Katherine nodded. Marienne obviously wouldn't want her now, knowing that she was so useless. Who would?

"That's illegal."

Katherine's eyes flew open and she stared at the captain, but Marienne was softly playing another arpeggio.

"If the actions of an indentured servant cost a company money or assets, the company must pay for the damages unless it can be proven that it was deliberate sabotage. But Prescott is so powerful, no one is willing to challenge his practices." She glanced at Katherine. "I'm willing to bet that you've already paid off your debt, if you've been there more than a year."

"I've been there two years," she said softly.

Marienne continued, "Stay with us and I'll pay you. What you do with that money is your decision. You've got," she glanced at a clock on the wall, "three hours to decide. At that point we'll be out at sea and I won't be turning around."

Katherine shook her head. "I still don't think I can stay. My brother is also indentured. If I leave, what will happen to him? I can't just leave him in that situation. I might never see him again."

"Then rescue him."

Katherine gaped at Marienne, but there was no hint of humor in her expression. She was not only serious in the suggestion, but sincere in her belief that it could be done. "How?"

With a shrug, Marienne said, "That's something you'll have to figure out, if you decide to join my crew." She turned again to the piano and played a minor chord deep in the lower register. She resolved it to a major chord before continuing. "I'll help if I can, but be aware that the safety of my crew takes priority. I sincerely hope you'll stay with us. For your sake as well as ours." Her perceptive eyes flickered to Katherine's hastily bandaged hand. "No matter your decision, I recommend you go see Rose, the ship's surgeon. She'll see to that cut."

"Yes, ma'am," Katherine said. She curtsied, then flushed at Marienne's grimace. "I'm sorry, it's a habit." She hastily left the room and nearly ran into Todd, who hovered just outside of earshot at the door.

When he saw her, his shoulders relaxed. "How are you holding up?"

"Marienne told me to see Rose. I'm sorry, but I don't know where she is. Could you show me to her?"

"Of course!" He led the way eagerly, and as they made their way below deck he glanced over at her. "Did Marienne say anything else?"

"I have three hours to decide if I want to stay or return."

He frowned. "That's not much time."

They plunged back into the relative darkness below deck. Todd's crutch thumped against the scuffed wooden floors, and Katherine couldn't help but notice that the dark red paint on the walls was flaking and peeling in places. It was a magnificent ship, but was in desperate need of maintenance.

"Here we are," Todd announced, pushing open a door. Inside, two rows of metal-framed cots lined the walls to the left and right, leaving a walkway down the center. Towards the back of the brightly lit room, a counter stretched halfway across the space, laden with supplies. The top of a chest of drawers could be seen behind the counter, with a simple wooden chair sitting sentry next to the chest. Rose stood by the counter, labeling a bottle of clear liquid.

She looked up as they entered and smiled. "Marienne radioed down to tell me you would be coming in. Katherine, was it?"

She nodded and almost dipped into a curtsy again, but stopped herself in time.

"Come, sit down," Rose invited as she stood and placed the bottle down on the counter. "Todd, Marienne said you should go back to the engine. I can take care of our guest."

He glanced at Katherine, then, seemingly satisfied, left. Rose had a gentle manner that instantly put her patients at ease. Katherine felt comfortable here, and she would feel even better knowing that Todd was watching the engine. She would never forgive herself if something went wrong.

She doubted Marienne would forgive her, either.

"Now, let's take a look at this hand of yours." Rose unwrapped the bandages carefully.

Katherine winced at how they pulled at the sticky wound that had not yet scabbed over completely. To distract herself, she asked Rose, "How long have you been a part of the crew?"

"I joined right after Nyx," she answered with a chuckle. "That would be about a year after Marienne started flying. Nyx has a tendency to jump into conflict headfirst, and so Marienne thought it might be a good idea to find someone to patch up the first mate." Rose frowned at Katherine's hand. "This wound looks angry. How did you get it?"

"I cut it on broken porcelain." Katherine looked away.

"That would explain these shards. Hold still." She turned and grabbed a pair of tweezers from the counter. "Were you able to apply antiseptic before wrapping?"

"No." The fingers on Katherine's right hand twitched, and she started to pinch at her leg. She winced slightly at the little twinges of pain as Rose plucked out the shards, trying hard not to think about how they got there and the humiliation she had endured. "What is it like, flying with Marienne?"

"Always an adventure," Rose said distractedly. "I don't see too many injuries, though. Usually altitude sickness for those still getting used to being up so high, and the occasional lightning shock or burn. Some scrapes here and there, but except Nyx, not too many get into any serious danger." She sat up with a satisfied sigh. "That's all of them. Now I'm going to disinfect it, so you will feel some stinging." She daubed some liquid onto a cloth and patted it against the cut.

Katherine inhaled sharply, her breath hissing between her teeth as pain flared in her palm.

"I know," Rose soothed. "But I'm done now. Just need to wrap it and you'll be on your way." She smiled at Katherine. "You've been a good patient."

"I'm sorry for not properly taking care of it."

The surgeon was quiet as she wrapped Katherine's hand in fresh bandages. "You're a mechanic, right? That takes attention to detail, and a sharp mind. If you injured your hand, you wouldn't be able to work with it anymore."

"I'm not a mechanic, I'm a maid."

Rose looked at Katherine with gentle brown eyes, but her tone was direct. "If you were a mechanic and not a maid, would you have cleaned up your hand right away?"

Katherine saw in Rose's eyes an understanding. She knew, instinctively, that Rose was really asking if she had been prevented from bandaging her hand properly. Just as Rose would know, instinctively, if she tried to lie about it.

Looking away, Katherine said, "It was my fault." Her fingers twitched, sending a stab of pain into her left hand. "I'm sorry, but I should go back to the engine. Thank you for seeing to my hand."

As Katherine stood to leave, Rose said, "If the situation you left is worse than the one you find yourself in, I would call that a rescue."

MARIENNE'S FINGERS flew across the keys automatically in a quick-tempo song. Her mind whirled dizzyingly around and around, like a cyclone that focused on one spot: Prescott. Prescott proposing, Prescott showering her with gifts, Prescott holding her too tight while dancing, Prescott complimenting her beauty. The way he cut her off in conversations, never listening to what she had to say. The way he would berate his indentured servants. The way he saw only how he could use people to further his profit and prestige. Or how he actively encouraged the illegal and inhumane practices of his luma harvesting company, bragging about it to his business associates while Marienne endured their grating laughter at yet another lavish dinner that she could not enjoy, knowing that she was as much prisoner to him as those who were indentured to the company.

Three knocks sounded on Marienne's door, interrupting her thoughts and her song. She sighed and called without rising, "Come in, Nyx."

The first mate entered, closing the door behind her, then leaned on it, arms crossed. Marienne felt her gaze as she continued playing, the movement of her fingers across the keys doing little to quell the turbulence in her chest.

After nearly a minute of silence, Marienne said, "Aren't you supposed to be at the helm?"

"Beth's taking over for a bit. I heard you yelling at Todd. Are you going to tell me what that was about, or are you going to keep avoiding everything?"

Suppressing a sigh, Marienne continued to play her song, trying and failing to distract herself. She and Nyx were kindred spirits, which worked very well when running a ship together. However, it also made it hard for Marienne to hide her feelings from her first mate. She opened her mouth to try to speak, but the words caught in her throat. Swallowing, she tried again. "Prescott was there. He saw me." Her fingers slipped and she played a wrong chord, the sour sound hanging in the air like acrid smoke.

Nyx frowned. "That's... a problem. What are we going to do about it?"

"I don't know," she admitted in a whisper, fingers hovering over the piano keys.

Nyx walked over and placed a hand on Marienne's shoulder. "You don't have to decide right now," she assured the captain. "We're on our way to the Revel. Whatever you decide can wait until after that."

Marienne stiffened, regaining her composure. The Revel. The one time a year she allowed herself a holiday and celebrated with friends —with other airships like hers. If Prescott was following her, they would all be sitting ducks. Should she cancel the festivities?

"Thank you, you are dismissed," she said stiffly to Nyx. She did not look at her first mate; she could not bear to see the hurt expression that she knew was on her face. "I have much to consider at the moment. And please be aware that we have a guest aboard."

"I saw her," Nyx said as she paused at the door, one hand on the knob. "Do you think she'll stay?"

Marienne stared out the large windows at the English countryside drifting past. "We shall see."

CHAPTER 6

Now that the smoke and steam had cleared out of the engine room, Katherine could identify and observe each machine housed there. She set to work running diagnostics immediately in an effort to prevent any mechanical surprises that could put her possible escape to an abrupt end. Todd eagerly showed her around and answered every question he could.

For a while, she sat and watched the engine, the crankshafts pushing the sixteen pistons up and down like so many beating hearts. It was the heart of the ship, thrumming rhythmically as it breathed life into the entire airship. She closed her eyes, lulled by the music of it. It creaked a little and had some minor rattling, but she could hear nothing concerning when it came to the engine. If it hadn't been on, she would have lovingly patted the copper siding. Even though she hadn't been on the *Vincenzo* long, it felt like being home.

Adjacent to the engine sat the cooling unit that she had fixed—although she feared the repair was only a temporary solution. Climate control pipes and gauges stretched along the wall between the door and the venting windows, the pipes disappearing into the ceiling to wind throughout the ship. It reminded her of the generator back at the estate, but somehow felt more friendly. Clinging to the ceiling above the engine, the automaton bat hung silently.

"Bert will alert you to any mechanical failures he can detect," Todd explained, pointing to the automaton. "His eyes use infrared light, and he has supersonic hearing. Usually he will catch something before it becomes serious, and he's trained to hit the intercom button," he pointed to the speaker set into the wall. "That way, no matter where you are on the ship, you'll know to come. He has different vocal patterns for different problems, but I haven't memorized them. The manual is somewhere over there." He gestured vaguely to the workbench.

As Katherine moved around the engine towards the workbench, she saw another piece of machinery that caused her to squeal with joy. "A helium purifier!" She immediately dropped to her knees to inspect it, hands fluttering over the smooth brass exterior.

"How did you miss that earlier?" Todd teased. "What did you think this enormous pipe going through the ceiling was for?"

"I thought it was central heating," she admitted. "I didn't realize it went all the way to the balloon. Of course!" She put a hand to her forehead. "The pipes in the middle of the deck! I thought they were for supplying more helium, but I didn't realize how! Last I had heard this was only theoretical."

"Luma made it possible."

She nodded, opening the panel and looking inside. Unlike the other machines, this one was in perfect condition, and sparkled with luma. Katherine breathed deeply the scent of metal, oil, and fresh air. But, as she closed the panel, her grin disappeared and her mood dampened. She turned back to the workbench and sat down.

Todd sat next to her, studying her face. "What's got you down?"

"I'm sorry, I shouldn't concern you," she said, blinking away the distant expression. "I was only thinking."

"Want to tell me what you were thinking about? I'm a great listener," he urged with an innocent grin.

She shrugged. "So many people found what they were searching for with the help of luma, and they changed the world. But so many others didn't. What did the inventor of the helium purifier have that my father didn't?"

"More time, more resources, more funding, along with other things," he answered. "Take your pick. The way I see it, luma is a tool, just like anything else. And when it comes to invention, you can use your tools and intellect as much as you can, but you also need a healthy dose of luck. And besides," he smiled, "if things hadn't happened the way they did, I wouldn't have met you. And I think that's a pretty good outcome, don't you?"

"I'm still not sure if I'll stay," she reminded him, glancing around the engine room. Her heart wasn't in the words, though, and her arguments seemed pale and flimsy when compared to the machinery in front of her. She felt alive here, more alive than she had felt for years.

"Oh, something tells me you'll fit in just fine around here. I've never seen anyone as happy as you are with these machines. Except maybe Nyx when she's found a new weapon." He shook his head at her quizzical look. "You'll meet her later. The point is, you love it. You hated your old life—if you didn't, you wouldn't even contemplate staying with us. You found a way out. Take it," he encouraged. His dimples appeared as he smiled.

Katherine admired how openly he spoke to her. He had such an honest face, she doubted he said any of it for Marienne's benefit or as a ploy to get her to stay. Before she could respond, the speaker in the wall crackled to life and Marienne's voice filtered through.

"We are approximately ten minutes from London. Katherine, have you made your decision?"

She stood and walked over to the intercom. Under the speaker were two buttons, one red and one black, and below them was a series of buttons numbered 0 through 9. Next to the intercom was a yellowed piece of paper that gave the call number for each room on the ship. She glanced at Todd.

"The black one will call back the room that just called you," he instructed.

Katherine pressed the black button, then hesitated. Thoughts of Mr. Castle, the engine, the estate, the *Vincenzo*, Marienne, and Todd swirled in her mind like a dizzying nickelodeon. But when she glanced at Todd, and he smiled at her with those dimples, she felt confident for the first time in two years.

"I'm staying."

Todd beamed as Marienne responded, "Glad to hear it. I think you'll find you belong here. You should come up and meet more of the crew." The speaker shut off with a click.

"Come on," Todd encouraged, offering his free hand for her to take. "You heard Marienne, let's go to the deck."

Katherine took his hand and followed him out of the engine room.

As they moved down the hallway, Todd pointed to an open door. "That's the radio control room. I'm there most of the time." When she slowed to glance through the door at the radio equipment inside, he laughed and said, "Come on, there will be time enough for you to tinker later."

Katherine emerged onto the deck and gasped. "It's night time? Already?"

Todd chuckled. "Didn't realize your first day on an airship had passed so quickly, did you?"

"I'm surprised I wasn't even hungry." Her stomach growled and she blushed. "I'm sorry, I was mistaken."

"Good thing I saved some food for you, then." Katherine turned at the sound of the voice behind her. A woman stood with a bowl in each hand, the moonlight glinting off her blonde hair as if strands of luma shone in her spiky ponytail. She was taller than Todd, and her short sleeves showed off her lean biceps. But what intrigued Katherine the most was the arsenal of weapons she wore on her person. Two guns were strapped across her back, and a pair of swords sat at her hip. A short knife was strapped to her thigh, but at that point a bowl of soup was shoved in Katherine's face and she had to stop counting.

Aromatic steam wafted up from the soup, and a soft biscuit bobbed in the middle invitingly. Katherine took a few greedy bites before Todd led her to a bench where they could sit down and eat. The woman followed them.

"I'm Nyx," she introduced. Suddenly Todd's earlier comment made sense, and Katherine looked at him, hoping to convey her under-standing. "I'm the first mate on this ship, and frankly that means you'll be dealing with me more than Marienne, so we should get acquainted. Marienne's already told me everything she knows about you."

I'm sure that's more than I think, Katherine thought, recalling Marienne's discerning green eyes. She doubted little escaped their notice. She shivered, and not entirely from the thought. Although the soup warmed her throat and stomach, the night air blew cold against her arms and legs.

Nyx frowned. "You should get a coat. Did you bring one?"

Katherine shook her head as Todd said, "We kind of kidnapped her, she didn't exactly have time to pack."

Nyx turned and called to a stocky man, "Clyde, go grab one of the spare coats, would you? Smallest you can find," she added, glancing at Katherine. "I don't think we've had anyone as small as you on board before. Finding clothing could be tricky."

"I'm sorry I've become an inconvenience."

"You're not," Nyx countered. "Without you, we'd likely still be grounded." She frowned at the thought, then shook her head. "The previous mechanic left some things behind that we've just been keeping in storage. Beth's pretty handy with a needle, she could maybe alter it for you. You don't mind wearing trousers, do you?"

Katherine shook her head. "Easier to work in. If I never see this dress again, it would be too soon," she added, looking down at her pale yellow maid's uniform.

"You need gloves, too," Todd reminded. "Nyx, do you think she should go to Robert?"

Nyx pursed her lips. "I'll bring it up to Marienne, but we're not planning on seeing him until the Revel. Ah, thanks Clyde." The man handed Katherine a dark blue wool coat.

When Katherine put it on, the sleeves extended past her hands and the hem of the coat fell around her mid-thigh. It was warm, though, and she buttoned it up gratefully. "Thank you, Clyde," she called out. The man waved at her.

Her dinner finished, Katherine moved to the railing of the ship.

She gazed out into the inky night at the city lights that faded into the distance, looking like stars that had fallen to earth. She turned her attention to the sky, and gasped. Stars surrounded the airship, enveloping everything in tiny particles of light, like silver gears revolving around each other as they slowly spun the sky around and around.

"They're beautiful, aren't they?" Todd said as he joined her.

"They're so much brighter up here," she breathed. "I mean, that's impossible, but—"

"No, you're right." He chuckled at her incredulous look. "Katherine, do you know what luma is?"

CHAPTER 7

"What is luma?" Katherine frowned at the unexpected question. "It's highly debated. Concentrated aether, glitterdust, magic, a hoax. It depends on who you ask."

"But do you know where it comes from?" Todd watched eagerly for her response.

Luma Baron Prescott's anger burned fresh in her mind. "That's a dangerous question," she said, echoing his words. "All anyone knows is that it comes from the sky. You could get into trouble for trying to know more."

"Trouble?" Todd's expression turned to one of concern. "For knowledge? From who?"

Before Katherine could answer, something deep within the belly of the ship rumbled. "Is that the engine?" Her voice rose in panic, but the words were drowned by the metallic whine of large gears moving.

Looking over the side of the railing, she spotted masses of leather stretched across a skeleton of metal poles like a bat's wing. She knew an identical wing unfurled from the other side of the airship.

"Are we coming up on turbulence?" she asked, concern coloring her words.

But Todd laughed, loud and jovial. "Those aren't stabilizers," he said. "That's just a falsehood the Luma Barons have spread. These," he gestured to the wing below them, "are what collect luma."

Katherine gazed down in awe. A crackle of electricity ran through the air, raising the hairs on her arms, even though there wasn't a cloud in sight.

"Lightning," he explained. "It runs down the poles, see?" He pointed to where the metal sparked with jagged flickers of pale light. "Now watch." He directed her attention up to the stars.

Katherine gasped, unable to believe what she saw. An indistinct, nebulous cloud of luminescence gathered, falling from the stars and pooling on the leather wing until it drifted down the sloping poles into the hull of the ship, visible more from the darkness it left behind. The luma looked like sunbeams until it touched the leather, at which point it seemed more familiar to Katherine, like sand made of light. She watched the luma roll easily down the length of the wing towards the ship, her attention fixated on the glittering, shining, precious luma pooling below her in a greater amount than she had ever seen.

"I don't... understand," she admitted. She felt as if lightning had coursed through her body, leaving her limbs tingling. The gleam of light danced behind her eyelids as she blinked.

"The stars aren't as bright in London, are they?" Todd beamed. "That's because the sky over major cities has been harvested so much that it has little to give anymore. The stars have less light there."

"But that's—"

"Impossible?" He shook his head, his curls bouncing. "Luma's an impossible thing. It's starlight, Katherine."

Starlight. She gazed out at the night sky, eyes and mouth open in awe and wonder. Starlight pulled from the heavens around her—the most influential scientific discovery of the century, and it had always been there, surrounding every airship, visible from every corner of the world on any cloudless night.

Her head snapped sharply to look at Todd. "This is illegal." Her voice was flat. "Luma Barons protect this information and this resource, and you're up here taking what you want so you can —can—"

"Sell it on the black market."

Katherine turned at the sound of Marienne's voice behind her. "You're…"

"What?" The captain advanced slowly, the lamplight reflecting off her green eyes threateningly. Katherine backed up against the railing. She was trapped. "What are we, Katherine? Out with it."

"You're pirates." Her voice came out in a squeak; a small gear that needed oil.

Marienne stopped. "Yes, there are some who call us as much. But I have no need to explain myself to you. You, who voluntarily ran away from your servitude."

"After you kidnapped me!"

Marienne pursed her lips. "You had the chance to leave. You didn't take it."

"You didn't give me all the facts!" Katherine retorted, surprising herself with her boldness. Even when arguing against Marienne, the captain's confidence was infectious. "You didn't tell me you're running an illegal luma harvester." She glanced at Todd, and his brown eyes wordlessly pleaded with her. But she couldn't do what he wanted. "I'm sorry, but I would like to resign."

"I'm afraid it won't be so simple," Marienne said. "We cannot turn around and go back to England. And now you know too much about me for me to let you go." Her tone wasn't threatening, merely matter-of-fact, but it did not calm Katherine's fears as Marienne drew a knife from her belt. She held it up and watched how it glinted in the starlight. "A Luma Oath should do."

Katherine gasped and heard the sound ripple around her. Many members of the crew had gathered around them and she squirmed, but not only from the attention. She spotted Nyx, whose expression was unreadable. Beside her, Todd frowned.

Finally finding her voice, Katherine said, "That's just a rumor, though, isn't it?"

"If it is, then you have nothing to worry about," Marienne replied archly. "But would you really take that risk? The luma in your veins wouldn't bother you unless you lead the law or Prescott to us."

Katherine gulped. She wondered if any of the other crew members were kept here against their will, bound by an Oath. But she couldn't bring herself to search their faces. She couldn't tear her gaze away from that knife, reflecting the luma drifting through the sky as if it were already coated in the substance, ready to slice through her skin. If she swore an Oath, she was bound until Marienne died... or Katherine broke the Oath. If that happened, the luma would rush to her heart and stop it. *I make so many mistakes, how could I avoid accidentally saying something I shouldn't?*

A Luma Oath was impossible. It had to be rumors. But a glance at Todd's tight-lipped expression brought his words to mind: "Luma is impossible." Some still considered it to be magic.

She gaped at Marienne, stammering without a sound, her mouth opening and closing like bellows. Who was this woman? Where had the understanding, kind, gentle woman who tinkered on the piano gone, and who was this ruthless, callous captain standing in her place?

Todd stepped forward, his crutch breaking the silence by scraping against the rough deck. "Does she have to decide now? The next time we dock will be the Revel, and that's two weeks away. Give her some time." His tone was soothing, not begging, and Katherine was surprised at his negotiation. "It's been a long day for all of us, with more unexpected twists than I think any of us would like. Let's not tempt fate further by rushing her into a decision we may regret." He looked over his shoulder at Katherine, who managed a grateful smile.

To Katherine's surprise, Marienne sheathed the knife with a nod. "This will be a trial period, for all of us. You'll continue as our mechanic until after the Revel. We will treat you as a member of the crew." She swept a warning glance over the crowd, searching for any protest, any sign that one of her own would contradict her. Satisfied, she turned her attention back to Katherine. "For all intents and purposes, you're one of us for now. If you and I are not completely satisfied with the arrangement by the end of that time, you can stay grounded."

Katherine nodded. The arrangement was more than reasonable.

But Todd's expression turned angry as he blurted, "You can't just leave her behind after the Revel! That's no place for—"

"Don't tell me what I can't do!" Marienne turned fierce, her words like darts slicing through the night air. "I'm being more than generous as it is." She drew herself to her full height and regained her composure. "Besides, nothing has been decided yet. I suggest you return to the engine room. If anything breaks on this ship under your watch, I might kick you off somewhat sooner than agreed."

Katherine obeyed. Todd began to follow her, but she shook her head with a mumbled apology. Guilt settled into her stomach as she saw the hurt and concern on his face, but other emotions already filled her. Too many for her to sort out, the mixed-up feelings made her feel like a balloon filled with too much helium—stretched thin and ready to pop.

When she returned to the engine room, she pulled her bed out from the wall, almost wishing that tears would flow so that she could relieve the pressure in one fit of emotion. Wrapping herself in the blanket, she stared at the thrumming engine.

"You're like me," she whispered. "All jumbled up inside, and just wanting someone who understands to make it all better."

CHAPTER 8

NOVEMBER 28, 1904

"I think you owe me some explanations," Katherine said as Todd entered the engine room. She had already begun to think of it as her room.

"And a good morning to you too," he said with a half-smile that revealed his dimples. But he still tugged nervously on his curls. "Did you sleep well?"

"As well as I could," she replied curtly. Her dress was rumpled and she already felt dirty for having worn it overnight.

"Nyx is finding some clothes for you," he said, as if he could read her mind. He moved to inspect the engine.

Katherine frowned in irritation. She had already inspected the engine this morning. She had found a mostly-empty notebook on the disorganized workbench and started writing down major improvements that needed to be made to the machinery. She had started marking the most important with a star, but gave up after she realized that one entire page had been marked as such.

"Why didn't you tell me you harvest luma?" she demanded.

Todd tugged on his curls and stared at the engine. "I was afraid you wouldn't want to stay," he admitted. "And, as Marienne said, if you chose to leave you had no incriminating evidence against us." He finally turned to her. "I know it's a lot to take in, but haven't you ever wondered why Luma Barons are so secretive about luma? Why they're the only ones who can sell it?"

Once again Katherine's thoughts turned to her conversation with Luma Baron Prescott. She did want to know more about it, but his rage was seared into her memory. "It's still illegal."

Todd opened his mouth to counter, but Nyx walked in with a bundle of clothes, interrupting him. "Here's one of Nathaniel's old shirts," the first mate said. "And a pair of trousers I scrounged up from storage. They're the smallest I could find, but here's a belt just in case." She handed the bundle of clothing over to Katherine. "And Todd? Get out of here. Don't be a creep." She smirked as she left.

Todd rolled his eyes at Nyx's jab. "I'll be in the radio room. Let me know when you're ready for some breakfast and I'll show you where the galley is."

Katherine nodded and closed the door behind him. As she dressed, she found herself grateful for the kindness that Nyx and Todd had shown her. She shook her head against the thought, cinching the belt tight. They were still criminals. She couldn't get wrapped up in this business, no matter how kind they were.

She found Todd in the radio room, and stopped to look at the equipment, but her stomach grumbled loudly. Todd laughed. "You'll get to see the machines in good time," he promised as he stepped out into the hallway.

When they arrived at the galley, Katherine saw that about half the crew sat inside. Although only a couple looked up at her as she entered, Katherine acutely felt the presence of each of the dozen people. Her pulse whispered in her ears and she wanted to run back to the engine room and hide among the machines. But Todd steered her towards a buffet-style counter that opened directly into the kitchen. A rail-thin woman stirring a giant pot waved at her, and Katherine timidly waved back.

"That's Beth," Todd said. "The ship's cook. We all take turns helping her out with cooking and cleanup."

Katherine spooned some porridge into a bowl and grabbed a slice of buttered toast. She sat down next to Nyx, who was eating alone. "This isn't your usual sky pirate ship," Katherine observed, looking around at the circular tables, crystal chandeliers, and wide windows that showcased the Atlantic ocean stretching out around them. Most sky pirate ships were utilitarian, either merchant or military vessels for their cargo holds and weapons. But this was an elegant and somewhat small vessel.

"Noticed that already, did you?" Nyx snorted.

Her sarcastic tone earned her an elbow in the ribs from Todd. "Perceptive," he praised. "This ship was originally designed to be a pleasure cruiser. A sky-yacht, if you will."

"What happened?" Katherine pressed.

"We stole it."

"From Luma Baron Prescott?" She recalled his shouted demands that Marienne return the ship to him.

Todd frowned. "That was a long time ago."

She let the subject drop, sensing that he didn't want to discuss it anymore. Katherine wracked her brain, trying to remember how to make polite conversation. It had been too long since she had needed to; the other maids at the estate ignored her most of the time, and the rest of the time they were complaining about having to clean up her messes. "Um, Nyx, where are you from?"

"Doesn't matter." The first mate reclined, putting her hands behind her head. "I changed my name and I'm never going back. I didn't like who everyone wanted me to be, so I ran away, joined Marienne's crew, and now I do it all. Up here, you can be whoever you want, do whatever you want," she said with obvious relish.

Katherine shook her head. "I don't want to be anybody else. Just me. At least, who I was. Before my father died." *Before Mr. Castle.* She pressed her thumb against her injured hand. Could she remember how to be that person, or had she been erased completely?

She blinked and realized that her porridge was growing cold and less appetizing. She took a bite anyway, if only to avoid the gaze of her companions. Their expressions were all too familiar to her by now:

curiosity mixed with pity. Even though his life had meant everything to her, she didn't like to talk about her father's death.

"I'm needed on deck," Nyx announced abruptly. "You should come up, too, when you're done eating. Get away from the machines a bit and get some fresh air."

"But I like the machines."

"You need sunshine, Gearhead."

Katherine rolled her eyes, but finished her breakfast hastily. Even though it was cold, she ate all of it—wasting food seemed a sin when resources were limited. She placed her bowl in the tub with the rest of the dirty dishes and followed Todd up to the deck.

As they emerged onto the deck of the ship, Marienne called out: "Catch him! He's in big trouble!"

Katherine snapped out of her melancholy reverie to find something flying straight at her. It was metallic and reflected the bright morning light in dazzling flashes. Todd reached out with his free hand to snatch at it, but missed as it deftly dodged out of the way. Katherine held up her hands to shield her face, but the thing turned upward and flew over her head. She turned around to watch it as it soared around the deck, dodging everyone's efforts to stop its flight. The sun spots burning in her vision prevented her from seeing it clearly until Marienne whistled.

The sharp, shrill sound immediately brought it to attention and it landed obediently on the deck.

Katherine gasped. "Another automaton!" She rushed forward, reaching it at the same time as the captain, who picked it up and placed it on her arm. Katherine shrank back.

"This is Nikolai," Marienne introduced. She noticed Katherine's hesitance, and held the automaton falcon out. "Go on," she urged. "I know you want to." She smiled invitingly, with no hint of the ruthlessness she had displayed the previous night.

Katherine didn't want to risk Marienne's wrath again, but the automaton enchanted her. She stroked his copper feathers, each one etched with an intricate swirling pattern and attached to tiny hinges that allowed them to ruffle or catch the wind. His head, which had been tucked close to his chest sheepishly, now rose with a proud arch of his neck, accompanied by a soft click and whir of gears. She leaned closer to look at his deep blue glass eyes, illuminated with a spark of luma. "He's beautiful," she whispered.

"He's mischievous," Marienne added in a tone that was equal parts exasperated and fond. "He's caused a leak in the refrigeration unit in the hold. It will require your attention, and possibly some luma."

"What happened?" Todd asked.

"Nik saw an autorat. What more do you need? If you don't want to be living on rations of jerky and hardtack for the next two weeks, I suggest you get down there and fix the problem!"

"Yes, Captain," Todd said.

Before she obeyed, Katherine paused and asked, "Did Nikolai get the autorat?"

Marienne grinned. "Yes, he did."

Katherine nodded. "Good boy." She turned and followed Todd down to the hold of the ship. As they hurried through the hallways, she noticed he was frowning. "What's wrong?"

"There's food in the hold for the Revel," he said, tugging on his curls. "But Marienne didn't mention it at all, only the food for us. Why?"

"What is this Revel? You've mentioned it several times now."

"It's a big party," he explained, then hesitated. "We meet up with some other crews and celebrate whatever winter holidays everyone celebrates."

"Other pirates, you mean," she said in a flat tone.

"Not all of them. James is a lightning-chaser, so he's legitimate. The only illegal thing he does is sell to us."

Katherine stopped and crossed her arms over her chest. "I shouldn't help you. I shouldn't care about the food for people like…" She paused. She had been going to say "people like you," but as Todd turned to her with deep brown eyes, the only word that came to mind was *honest*. Todd had been kinder to her in the past two days than anyone had in the past two years.

His honest eyes turned weary. "Marienne has asked us to do this together. Please, I can't do it alone."

She nodded and they continued down the hallway, his words sticking like sharp fragments of wire in her heart. Especially that "please."

Once in the hold, Todd led her to the metal refrigeration unit in the corner. Katherine lingered behind him, staring in awe around her at the hold. The room was long and wide, but the ceiling was low, giving it the illusion of being smaller than it was. Most of the room was filled with metal barrels of luma, but before she could observe any more, Todd urged her towards the steel door at one end of the hold that contained the refrigeration unit.

When she opened the door, her cheeks stung as steam sparkling with frost and luma hissed out of a pipe. "Todd!" she shouted.

"I've got it!" He stepped past her, his crutch sliding on the slick floor, but he moved confidently.

Katherine watched with equal parts concern and admiration as he tugged on his leather gloves and turned the valve. If it weren't for the knotted up trouser leg and his ever-present crutch, she would never have guessed that he was missing a limb. The ghost of an idea began to conceive in her mind, the barest skeleton of a blueprint already sketching itself out... But she shook her head and forced herself to focus on the task in front of them.

She cautiously moved closer to observe the damage, now that Todd had turned off the flow of water. It seemed that the autorat had begun to chew through the pipe to get at some luma inside, and when Nikolai caught it his beak or talon had gouged through the metal. "It should be a simple patch job," she remarked. "But we have to work fast to get it done before the food starts to thaw. There's scrap metal in the engine room, right?"

Todd nodded. "And welding tools. I can go get them."

Katherine shook her head. "I'll go. I should start getting used to the layout of the ship. Can you check for any other damage and autorats?" He nodded as she left. Making her way towards the engine room, her thoughts drifted to the idea she had had earlier. It began to solidify in her mind, taking on more definite shape and igniting a familiar warm spark in her chest. She hadn't had the chance to tinker in a long time, and this would be the biggest project she had ever undertaken.

But as she reached the engine room, she realized that she would only see that project to completion if she stayed as a part of the crew. She sighed as she searched the cluttered workbench for scrap metal, welding tools, and the special tinted goggles. It seemed that she could be truly happy here. But it was wrong. What these people did was wrong, and sooner or later they would be punished for it. She knew that all too well, and she didn't want to be around when it happened. She had endured enough punishments.

The frost had already begun to drip by the time Katherine returned, and she frowned. "Find anything else?" she asked.

Todd shook his head. "I moved the food away from the pipe, so it won't melt when we weld it."

"Good thinking." She smiled at him as she handed him the metal and welding tools. He would have to take care of the rest, as she still lacked gloves, and she couldn't even watch as there was only one pair of goggles. She wished she could be the one to actually do the patch job. As much as she enjoyed figuring out the solutions to problems, she loved working with her hands most of all. It frustrated her that the lack of gloves restricted her from much of the actual mechanics.

"We also need to add some luma back into the coolant," Todd said as he stood. "I'll go to the engine room to do that. Gloves," he said, holding up one hand and wiggling his fingers. "When I'm done, I'll radio you to turn the valve back on."

Katherine nodded, noting the speaker set into the wall by the door. She wasn't happy with the arrangement, but understood its necessity. She hadn't had the chance to personally work with luma, and she itched to try it. She paced the room, rubbing her arms to rid herself of goosebumps, and cursing her lack of work clothes.

At last Todd's voice crackled through the speaker. "It's ready, Katherine! Turn it on!"

She obeyed and watched the pipe carefully to make sure the patch was secure. It held, and she smiled. Working together, she and Todd made a good team.

CHAPTER 9

NOVEMBER 30, 1904

R obert pulled the needle through thick navy brocade, gold embroidery thread following behind. The jacket sleeve had sat unfinished for weeks, and the deadline for this commission was fast approaching, but his thoughts still strayed to a different project. The sketch sat next to him on the desk, one he had made long ago with Marienne in mind. The luma satin would be perfect for it.

But instead he embroidered the jacket. He couldn't bring himself to make the dress, not yet. The hole Rachel had left had yet to heal. And if he presented the dress to Marienne, how long would it take for her to leave him too? He loved her—everyone knew it—but he could not bring himself to act on those feelings. Because every time someone left him.

"Captain," Henri's voice crackled through the speaker in Robert's workshop, startling him as he pulled the thread taut. "Radio call for you from the *Vincenzo*. It's Marienne."

Robert paused in his embroidery. Marienne calling him personally? It must be important. "*Merci*," he said into the speaker set into the wall next to him. "Patch her through."

A couple seconds of silence allowed Robert to resume his work, then a burst of static followed by Marienne's alto voice—smooth as silk and rich as velvet, even through the mesh of the radio speaker.

"Robert?"

"*Bonjour.* To what do I owe the pleasure?"

"I'm not coming to the Revel." Words stiff as felt.

The needle slipped and pricked his finger. He immediately wrapped it in his handkerchief to keep from spoiling his project, but his thoughts raced elsewhere. "Why?"

"I had to tell you. I was supposed to bring some food, so if you could stop and pick up the extra, I'll send James with money to repay you next time I see him."

"You didn't answer my question." Robert leaned his head against the wall next to the speaker, as close to her voice as he could get.

Silence, thick and heavy like wool.

"Prescott."

Robert's breath hissed through his teeth. "What has he done?"

"It's what I did. He saw me. He still thinks I belong to him and now I'm..." Her voice nearly faltered, but when she spoke again her words were harder than before. "I know it's only a matter of time before he catches up to me. I cannot in good conscience lead him to... the others."

Robert couldn't breathe. First Rachel and now Marienne? Who else would leave him? He could not imagine a Revel without her there. She livened up the atmosphere with merely her presence, and they would exchange stories around the blazing fire. No one else had a sharp enough wit to contend with James' quips, or was bold enough to tell Robert he had had too much to drink and was making a fool of himself. Her lovely alto voice would fill the night with some sultry song that others would dance to, but Robert would sit by the fire and watch it reflect in her red curls and alluring green eyes.

"I'll also need to move to a new collection circuit." Marienne's curt voice cut through his reverie like freshly sharpened scissors into cotton. "This one's become too predictable. He'll—"

"No!" Robert finally found his voice. A Revel without Marienne would be torturous, but for her to change circuits? He would never see her again. That would be unbearable. "Stop. Just…" He took a shuddering breath and ran his uninjured hand through his hair. "Stop and think."

Her voice was infuriatingly calm as she said, "I have been thinking. If Prescott catches me, that's the end of it. All of it. I'm willing to do anything to keep that from happening."

Even leave me behind? Robert thought. *Like everyone else.* "Come to the Revel."

"I told you I can't. They could be following me right now."

"So what if they follow you? Marienne, the island will be crawling with pirates! People who would gladly fight a Luma Baron's airship, especially for you."

"But—"

"Please." She paused and he filled the silence. "If you have to change circuits after that, fine," he lied, "but at least say a proper goodbye. Not like this. Besides," his gaze turned desperately to the sketch on his desk, "I have a gift for you."

Marienne sighed. "Fine. I'll come to this last Revel."

"*Merci.* I can't wait to see you."

As the radio clicked off, Robert unwrapped the handkerchief from his finger, wondering how he could possibly prepare himself to say goodbye to Marienne.

Or, perhaps, how he could convince her that he wouldn't have to.

CHAPTER 10

"So Marienne convinced him that she was a world-class masseuse!" Todd could barely contain his infectious laughter. He sat on the workbench in the engine room, having been kicked out of the radio room so Marienne could make a private call. Katherine listened intently to his stories of his adventures with Marienne while she worked on cataloging the inventory of spare parts scattered around the workbench.

"And he believed her?" She looked up from sorting wrenches to look at Todd incredulously.

"Hook, line, and sinker! And despite never giving a massage before in her life, Marienne lulled him into such a trance that she slipped the key right off his neck. He never suspected a thing!"

"And the guards just let her free you?"

"After that start, Marienne was confident she could get away with anything. She waltzed in like she owned the place, wearing her best superior expression." Todd arched his eyebrows in imitation, eliciting laughter from Katherine. "She said I was pardoned by the governor and no one even questioned her!"

She shook her head. "Unbelievable." But a smile played on her lips as she returned to cleaning the grease off the wrenches. "You never did say why you were locked up in the first place."

He leaned back, adopting a different attitude, now that the story was over. "Oh, this was right after we took command of the *Vincenzo*, and we didn't have titles for the ship in Marienne's name yet. I had been watching the airship and wasn't clever enough to claim to be Prescott when questioned."

Katherine frowned and worked harder at a stubborn grease spot. "I almost forgot that you're pirates," she said in a low voice.

Her fingers twitched whenever she thought of how many rules she was breaking. Mr. Castle was undoubtedly outraged at her behavior. She shut her eyes tight against the thought of what he would do to her once she got back.

Todd studied her thoughtfully. "Why does it bother you so much?"

"Laws are there to keep people safe. You're breaking the law and endangering people. Like me." She scowled at him.

"Some laws are written by those in power simply to keep themselves in power."

A shiver ran down Katherine's spine, but she shook her head. "When I follow the rules, I am safe from harm and punishment."

They sat in uncomfortable silence, the only sound between them the thrum of the engine.

At last, Todd said, "One more story for today."

Katherine picked up another wrench, grateful for the change in subject and eager to hear the story.

"Before I met Marienne, I joined the Aerocorps. It had been my dream to fly, and my family's expectation that I would join the military. It was the perfect career."

Katherine glanced at the knotted up trouser leg, sensing that this story would not be funny and lighthearted like the last one.

"During training, we were doing an exercise in aerial combat. A cannon misfired and some shrapnel hit my leg. I requested medical aid, but my captain demanded that I complete the training first. When it was all over, my leg had become infected. Amputation was the only option."

Gone was the jovial, bright mood that had lightened the engine room only minutes before. A somber, subdued tone filled the room like smoke.

"My career was over. I was sent home before I even finished training, all because of the rules someone in charge had set. Because they hurt me instead of protecting me." He shook his head. "I thought that was the end for me. Who would hire a cripple to fly on an airship? But then I met Marienne." A grin lit his face; a candle in the darkness.

"She let you come with her," Katherine said.

He barked a single laugh. "She *needed* me to come with her. As much as she wanted to fly, she had no idea how, and my training came in handy. She gave me a second chance. By breaking the law." Todd held Katherine's gaze for a few seconds before sliding off the workbench and leaving the engine room.

As his step-thump rhythm faded down the hall, Katherine sat alone amongst the machinery. His words echoed in her mind, lingering like the buzz after an electric shock: *his rules hurt me instead of protecting me.*

CHAPTER 11

DECEMBER 17, 1904

Katherine tugged on Todd's leather gloves and knelt next to the clattering machinery that rested along the outside wall of the engine room. The fingers of the gloves stuck out nearly an inch past her own, but it would have to do since Todd was busy at the helm. She couldn't let the gloves stop her from working. For the past three weeks she had noticed how every time the *Vincenzo* hit turbulence, something along the wall rattled terribly—it had even woken her up a couple of nights. But in her cursory assessment of the machinery in the engine room she had found nothing immediately pressing along the outer wall, and so had shifted her attention to other, more demanding machines. Minor malfunctions could easily add up to disaster in the air.

With those repairs finished and the main mechanisms safely out of danger, she now listened intently from one metal casing to the next, trying to isolate the rattling noise. *There.* She paused at the combination humidity condensing and water purification unit, lightly touching its casing with her too-large gloves. She could feel in her fingertips an off-beat vibration, like a dancer who doesn't know the correct steps.

"Luckily, you are not a machine that will cause us to crash," she said as she twisted the handle and swung open the casing, exposing the machinery inside. A sudden, intense rush of air tugged at her hair and clothes, sucking them towards a small tube set in the back of the unit. From above her head, Bert chirped loudly. Katherine scrambled back and fumbled along the side of the casing until she found the switch to power down the machine.

The loud suction stopped, and with it Bert's alarm, leaving the comfortable thrumming of the engine and Katherine's rapid heartbeat in its wake. She sighed in relief.

Foolish girl! Mr. Castle's voice chastised. *You should have known better. Perhaps if you stuck to what you know instead of playing at runaway, you wouldn't embarrass yourself like this.*

Katherine frowned. The further she flew from England, the more she feared returning to the estate. So much time had passed, surely Mr. Castle had thought of a particularly terrible punishment for when she returned.

That is, if she chose to leave the *Vincenzo*.

Katherine tugged the gloves on as tight as she could and plunged once again into the inner workings of the humidity condenser and water purifier. The entire left side of the unit was taken up by a water tank—the product of the machine's work. The tube that had been suctioning at her—behaving itself now that the valve was closed—connected to the outside of the airship, pulling in moisture from the atmosphere as the ship sailed through the sky. Or, at least, it did when the door was closed. Once Katherine had opened the casing, the pressure change had caused the flow of suction to reverse. But when functioning properly, the machine was a welcome addition to the engine room. The collection and purification was a slow process, however it helped provide more water during long journeys, which in turn could be used for other machines or—in an emergency—to wash or even drink.

Hands and eyes moving methodically, Katherine scanned the individual machine parts for the source of the rattling. The noise had stopped, now that the *Vincenzo* sailed smoothly again. Experimentally, she tapped against the side of the machine and heard a responsive buzz. She repeated the process until she had isolated the sound to the purification module. With a frustrated grunt, she grabbed the lantern and brought it inside the unit so she could see into the shadowy corners.

With careful movements, she opened up the purification module. The machinery inside sparkled with luma and Katherine breathed a silent thanks to Todd for letting her use his gloves. This luma was fresh—not the kind infused during the smelting process of each individual part, but the kind periodically added through the chute into a machine to coat the mechanisms. Another tentative tap on the side of the unit and the answering rattle brought her attention to a bolt on the side. Katherine held up the lamp to investigate.

The problem wasn't with the bolt, but with the nut that held it in place. A small fracture, only visible by the rust that ate through the metal plating, had formed and loosened the nut slightly. She pulled a wrench out of her tool belt and began to twist the nut, only to have it snap in half at the first turn. With a frown, she picked up the two halves and pulled herself out of the machinery.

Everything on this ship is two steps away from completely breaking down, she thought, staring at the broken nut in her gloved hand.

As she walked towards the workbench to find a replacement, Katherine tripped over the lantern. She stumbled, but managed to catch herself by grabbing on to the side of the humidity condenser, a strange pain pressing into the scab on her palm.

The switch clicked on.

Katherine watched in horror as the suction tube activated, and with the purification module still open, sparkling grains of luma funneled frantically through the small opening and out into the open air as Bert screamed his alarm.

Fumbling with the oversized gloves, Katherine struggled to flip the switch off. Once the rushing of air and chirping of the automaton had stopped, she stooped to assess the damage.

Not a single sparkle of luma remained in the purification module.

Katherine's heart sank to her stomach. *I've done it again,* she thought as she stared at the dull, empty machine. She winced at the memory of Mr. Castle's thunderous roar: *You spilled luma?!*

What would Marienne do?

As her fingers twitched, Katherine felt the hard metal of the broken nut still clutched tightly in her hand. She stood and walked to the workbench, feeling as if she were wobbling on a tightrope-thin resolve. *If I can fix it and no one finds out, perhaps she won't get mad*, she thought.

Carefully laying the two halves together, Katherine dug through the recently organized tray of nuts to find one in the correct size. She tossed the broken one into the scrap bin before returning to the humidity condenser and water purification unit to finish the repair. Once the nut was securely in place and her tapping confirmed no more rattling sounds, Katherine went to the storage closet in the corner of the engine room.

The closet housed any large necessities that didn't fit on the workbench: coal, luma, oil, and grease, among other materials and items. Sheets of scrap metal for large repairs leaned against one wall, jangling slightly as she opened the door. Katherine reached for the jar of luma on the shelf above the coal box, only to find it empty when she brought it down, the small rubber scoop rattling inside.

"No!" she exclaimed in despair. Todd had warned her earlier that they might be low, but he had not told her what to do in the event that it was completely gone. She placed the jar back on the shelf, fingers twitching so bad that she almost dropped it. She peeled off the large gloves and stuffed them into a pocket on her tool belt, then left the engine room to go ask Todd where she could get more luma, pinching her arms along the way.

But I don't have to tell him why, she resolved as she walked out onto the deck.

Muffled voices in loud, angry tones drifted across the deck, and Katherine scurried quickly up the stairs and into the control room, where Todd stood at the helm. He grimaced as the voices shouted over one another before subsiding into grumbling. Katherine looked at the floor and realized that they were directly above Marienne's quarters—the source of the argument. Although the tones were loud enough to be clear, the words themselves were indecipherable.

"What's that about?" she asked, not sure she wanted to know the answer.

"Marienne and Nyx," he said with a sigh. "They get like this sometimes. Always makes it awkward for whoever is steering at the time. Which is usually me."

Katherine pinched at her arms, unable to ignore the nagging feeling that she was the subject that the captain and first mate argued about. Todd alternatively kept the helm steady and checked the various instruments set into the controls in front of him, leaning the stump of his leg onto a stool for support, his crutch waiting patiently against a wall. After a moment he glanced at her, a grin flashing across his face. "What brings you up here? You can't be done tinkering for today, it's not even dark yet!"

The pinching fingers paused, still painfully holding on to her skin as she remembered her terrible clumsiness and its devastating results. "I need luma. The jar is empty."

"Oh, it is? I'm sorry, I didn't mean to leave you without it. You can get some more from the hold. There should be a barrel marked for internal use. I would show you if I wasn't on duty right now. And normally I would ask Nyx to, but..." He winced as another bout of shouting began. "Given the circumstances, I don't think you should interrupt."

Katherine nodded and left the control room, feeling less sure about herself than when she went in. She slowed as she passed by the door to Marienne's quarters.

The door opened.

"I'm allowed to have secrets from you!" Marienne's voice carried clearly across the deck.

"Not if it involves the crew!" Nyx retorted from the doorway. "But since you're too stubborn to realize that right now, fine! Have it your way." She slammed the door behind her. Glancing around the deck, Nyx's gaze fell on Katherine.

The first mate was seething, her expression as turbulent as a storm. Katherine ducked and ran down below deck to the hold. Expressions like that always meant trouble for whoever got caught in their path.

Katherine paused at the door that led to the hold, her hand resting on the brass doorknob, the familiar sick feeling in her stomach. She had never been in the hold by herself before—only with Todd when they fixed the refrigeration unit. Was she really allowed to? Todd had said she could… well, implied as such. But sometimes she didn't know she had done something wrong until it was too late, and Mr. Castle caught her. He lectured and punished, despite her protestations that she didn't know any better.

You should know better, his voice echoed in her mind. She shut her eyes against it, but it continued, *And you would know better if you were smarter. But you wouldn't have to be smarter if you just followed directions without mistakes all the time.*

Katherine opened her eyes with a frown. "You're not here," she whispered, and she pushed open the door.

"What are you doing?"

Katherine screamed and whirled around to see Nyx standing behind her, watching curiously. "I… I'm sorry," she stammered as her fingers twitched. She examined Nyx's face, searching for any hint of the fury she had displayed just moments before on the deck. "I must have gotten lost."

"No you didn't." Nyx smirked as she said it, but the expression wasn't malicious. She was… amused? She tapped the brass doorplate that clearly read "Hold," and said, "You want to go in, don't you?"

Katherine hesitated. Was this a trap? A ruse to lure her inside and then tell Marienne she had been where she wasn't supposed to be? What would Marienne do then?

Nyx turned from the open doorway. "You coming? I thought you wanted to see the luma."

"Actually, I need some luma to complete repairs on the humidity condenser and water purifier," Katherine stammered as she followed Nyx into the hold.

When she had come with Todd, she hadn't paid much attention

to the rest of her surroundings. Now, soft yellow light from electric lamps illuminated the hold, revealing a wide, low-ceilinged room that stretched from port to starboard, and nearly from stem to stern. Along each of the two outside walls, a long, rectangular flap like a mail slot—for now firmly closed—extended along the length of the hull. Below it, unfamiliar, circular metal caps sat at intervals. *Those must be for collecting luma*, Katherine thought. The refrigeration unit jutted out from the stern wall, a large room in its own right. She touched the door lightly as she passed, hoping the patched pipe still held. As she followed Nyx through orderly rows of barrels that took up most of the hold, Katherine was overwhelmed by the decadence of the sheer volume of luma surrounding her.

"What was wrong with the water unit?" Nyx asked as she squeezed past a couple of close-set barrels.

"Just some annoying noise," Katherine admitted. "A loose nut. It actually fell apart in my hand."

"You broke it?" Nyx exclaimed, whirling around suddenly.

Katherine shrank back. *She can't know that I spilled luma, too*, she thought frantically. Her fingers pinched.

A grin split Nyx's face. "I'm impressed. Didn't think you had that kind of strength." She patted Katherine on the arm.

"It was completely rusted," she tried to explain, but Nyx shook her head.

"I'm teasing, Gearhead. So you thought you would top off the luma in the machine while you were at it?" she asked as she patted a barrel.

Katherine nodded absently, simply agreeing so that she wouldn't have to admit to her mistake. But she was distracted by the large black letters painted on the side of the barrel that proclaimed in serious font: INTERNAL. But other scribbles around the label said things like: "This means you can use it—unless you're Clyde" and "First Mate gets privilege." One small note reminded "Todd—if the jar is low, refill it."

"Wasn't there luma in the engine room storage?" Nyx asked as she twisted open the lid. She rolled her eyes when Katherine shook her head. "Todd didn't pay attention to the supply, *again*. Go grab that glass jar off the shelf over there, would you?"

Katherine obeyed, tugging on Todd's gloves before bringing the large jar to Nyx, who used a rubber-coated trowel to scoop the luma out of the barrel and into the jar. Katherine leaned as close as she dared, admiring the sparkling golden light that glittered from the barrel, reflecting off of Nyx's beaming face.

"There's so much of it," Katherine breathed.

"We get about four barrels each collection," Nyx said casually, twisting the lid onto the jar, now that it was nearly full. "We have to keep one every twenty, for ship maintenance and sometimes crew wages, if they choose. Here," she handed the jar to Katherine. "You can bring back the empty one when you're done with repairs."

"When my father was experimenting with luma, he would bring home a handful every month or so," Katherine said softly, holding the jar up to her face and twisting it so she could watch the luma sparkle and glow. It was more than her father could ever have afforded. She shook her head, unable to comprehend becoming so accustomed to the precious commodity she held in her hands.

"That's one of the many problems with luma barons," Nyx said as she fastened the lid back onto the barrel of luma. "Can you imagine how even more advanced technology would be if everyone had access to luma?"

"If Marienne knows how to collect it, why hasn't she taught others?"

Nyx walked over to the outside wall of the hold, motioning Katherine to follow. She pointed to a metal tube set into the wall, shut tight with a small round cap. "The supports for the wings are hollow, so lightning can run through them, see? But it won't work with just any metal—this is a special alloy, and Marienne can't figure out what it is without destroying it." She shrugged. "Only luma barons can authorize this alloy being used in airships, and those who make it have to sign a nondisclosure—or so Marienne says. Rumor has it that they might even be bound by a luma oath."

Prescott's words repeated in Katherine's mind: *Those kinds of ques-*

tions could get you into a lot of trouble. A shiver ran down her spine. "I really shouldn't know this," she said hastily. Her voice was flat and she looked away from the fascinating instruments set into the wall.

"Why?" Nyx studied her. "In case you go back? I guess you're stuck with us, then!" Her grin disappeared when she saw Katherine's dismay. "That was a joke. Of course we want you to stay with us, but only if you want to. Go on, get back to your repairs."

Katherine walked out of the hold at a subdued pace, clutching the jar of luma in her gloved hands and thinking hard. *Do I want to stay?* The question had hung over her for three weeks, but now somehow it felt sudden and real. As she walked into the engine room, an unconscious smile spread across her face. *I love these machines*, she thought, not for the first time. *Although they need a lot of care, I want to provide it.* She retrieved the scoop from the previous luma jar in the closet, resolving to return the empty jar to the hold when she got the chance.

First, Katherine checked to ensure that the purification unit cover was closed tightly. Satisfied, she scooped a careful measure of luma into the chute, then closed the humidity condenser and flipped the switch. The machine hummed contentedly, no hint of the irritating rattling. A surge of pride ran through her and Katherine patted the side of the machine fondly.

As she placed the full luma jar on its shelf, the speaker in the engine room crackled to life. "Katherine," Marienne's voice echoed, bouncing off the machinery. "I would like to speak to you on deck, please."

Katherine's limbs grew cold. Had the captain found out that she had lost luma? Or was this the result of her argument with Nyx? The empty jar would have to wait. Katherine had learned from her years on the estate that it was best to come when summoned, no matter what she had been doing.

CHAPTER 12

Katherine joined Marienne at the railing. Her stomach felt as if they had hit turbulence, though the airship sailed smoothly through the clear skies. Nikolai sat on the captain's shoulder and fixed Katherine with a glass eye, then bent his head down for her to stroke. She found it amusing, since there was no way he could feel her touch. *He must simply like the attention,* she decided.

"We land in two days," Marienne said, her green eyes fixed on the horizon. "Nyx tells me you're in need of new clothes. There will be a tailor present at the Revel, but if I am to pay for your new wardrobe, I need to know that this is an investment." She fixed Katherine with a sidelong glance.

Katherine turned away, and her gaze fell to where Todd, now off-duty, bantered with Nyx about something that had happened long ago in Ireland. His laughter carried across the deck, and Katherine smiled. She rubbed the scab on her left hand— it had nearly healed now. The incident in the emerald parlor seemed so far away, almost as if her entire time at the estate had been a horrible nightmare, and she had now awoken. The thought of Mr. Castle never reaching her again made her feel as light as helium.

But her mood plummeted as she realized that she was still making clumsy mistakes. Surely Marienne wouldn't want her to stay if she knew about the luma Katherine had spilled.

"You wish to say something," Marienne said in that firm tone no one disagreed with. "Speak your mind."

Too ashamed to face her captain, Katherine turned away. Nikolai whirred, offended and confused that she suddenly stopped her affections. "I'm sorry, but I'm not good enough for this position." She glanced back at Marienne, afraid of her reaction.

Marienne narrowed her green eyes at Katherine, who felt like the captain was seeing through her. Shrinking back, Katherine wished she could retreat to the engine room, but Marienne's gaze pinned her in place.

"I am curious to know why you think so. From all reports from Nyx you have acclimated fairly well to life on the airship, and Todd won't stop talking about all the improvements you've made to the engine."

Katherine flushed at the idea that Todd spoke so highly of her. "I disagree. I make mistakes. I..." She hesitated. Marienne deserved to know about the lost luma, but if Katherine didn't tell her, would she find out anyway? Mr. Castle always had—somehow, he always knew that Katherine had made another mistake or mess. The punishments were worse if she had tried to keep her mishaps secret.

The words rushed out before she could lose her resolve. "I lost luma! It was sucked out of the water purifier. I'm sorry!" Katherine watched Marienne anxiously, muscles tensed for the inevitable explosion.

The captain's face remained mildly curious. "Was it an accident?"

Tentatively, Katherine nodded. Of course it was! Why would she intentionally waste the most precious resource on earth? But accident or no, the result was the same. The punishment was the same.

"Have you learned how to avoid repeating this mistake in the future?"

Katherine thought for a moment, the question taking her off guard. She could be more aware of where she placed the lantern, taking care that it wasn't in the path of where she needed to go. She could close the water purifier casing before standing to avoid accidentally spilling luma. She could also devise a cap to go on the suction tube made of leather to avoid anything being sucked out of the airship if it were accidentally turned on while the casing door was open. At last she nodded.

"Then I don't see why one little mistake should disqualify you from a job you so clearly enjoy."

"But I wasted luma!" Katherine protested.

"A scoop of it," Marienne said with a dismissive wave of her hand. A sly smile teased across her face. "In case you haven't noticed, we have plenty to go around."

Katherine returned to petting Nikolai as she struggled to understand Marienne's casual attitude concerning the matter. Would there really be no further consequences to her mistake? Not even a dock in her pay? Something inside of her suddenly felt like a misaligned gear gently easing back into place, causing others to turn and the whole to function properly.

The *Vincenzo* was home.

She belonged here, a feeling she hadn't known for two years. Todd laughed loudly, and Katherine smiled. The people here cared about her. How could she possibly ever consider giving that up to return to the estate, to Mr. Castle?

The only anchor that remained to that life was Ethan.

"Did you mean what you said about supporting my search for my brother?"

"I don't say things I don't mean," Marienne assured her, once again gazing at the horizon. "But please understand that the safety of my crew comes first."

Katherine nodded. Perhaps she would find him. Or perhaps she would pay off their debt. But she couldn't do that if she went back to Prescott's estate. The punishment for running away alone would likely add years to her debt. Nyx's words echoed in her mind: *up here, you can do anything.* She could even save her brother.

"I would like to stay," Katherine said at last.

Marienne turned to her, an enormous grin on her face. "Wonderful! I'm glad to hear it! Tell Todd to call Robert about the clothes. I'll discuss payment with him at the Revel."

"Yes, Captain."

Marienne flashed her one more smile before striding towards the helm, her tall boots clacking against the deck. Katherine felt as though she should feel the familiar guilt, thick and heavy in her stomach—she always did when she made a mistake. But it wasn't there. She hoped that meant it was the right decision after all.

CHAPTER 13

Robert worked furiously at his sewing machine. The Revel was less than a week away now, and he was still working on the second sleeve of Marienne's dress. It was a simple design, but he had other commissions to do as well. All that was left was to attach the sleeves to the bodice and embellish them with scarlet ribbons. It would be done in time. And it would not be a parting gift.

He snipped the thread and held the sleeve up for inspection. The indigo velvet made a nice contrast to the cream-colored satin that hung on a dress form in the corner. Any and all arguments to convince Marienne to stay that he had thought of so far seemed weak to him, and almost all of them came down to *I don't want you to go.* And he could not offer to follow her. She would despise the offer, and accuse him of trying to control her or tie her down. Besides, he had ground-based clients he was obligated to.

As he pinned the sleeves to the body of the dress, a call on the speaker interrupted his tangled thoughts. "Captain, it's the *Vincenzo.*"

Marienne? "Patch it through."

After a few seconds of static, a male voice called out, "Robert?"

"Todd, my boy!" Robert grinned, but couldn't help the twinge of disappointment he felt. "How are you doing?"

"I'm well! Marienne is doing well, too."

Robert rolled his eyes. He wasn't going to ask, but it was nice to know.

"We've got a job for you," Todd continued.

"I hope it's tailoring, because it's too close to the Revel for me to target a haul for you." The sleeves pinned on, he slipped the dress off the form and draped it on his work table, then picked up the unfinished coat sleeve. He would have to continue the dress later, but hated idle hands while talking.

"You know Marienne wouldn't hire you for a mark."

"I don't know you wouldn't," Robert countered, pulling the gold thread taut. "What's the job?"

"We've got ourselves a new mechanic—"

"Engineer!" a female voice called out from the background.

"A mechanic who fancies herself an engineer."

Robert smiled at the lighthearted teasing tone in Todd's voice. Fondness, perhaps, or admiration. Robert knew all too well how Todd felt about this new mechanic-engineer.

"Keep it up and I'll turn off my intercom and you won't be able to talk to me while I work!" she huffed.

"Okay, I'm sorry!" Todd laughed. "Anyway, Robert, she needs some work clothes. Do you think you could take some time during the Revel to make her some?"

"Perhaps," Robert said. "I'll be arriving in two days. Do you know when you'll land?"

"We'll be there a day after you."

"If you can stay perhaps two days after the banquet, I can make a week's worth of clothing for your new *mademoiselle*."

"Thank you, Robert!" the woman's voice piped through the speaker again. "I'm sorry to make you work during your holiday."

"*Mais non, de rien*," he responded with a shrug he knew she couldn't see. "*Mais*, what is your name?"

"Katherine. Sorry I didn't introduce myself sooner."

"Until we meet, then, Katherine."

Todd added, "Payment will be discussed in person, as per Marienne's wishes."

"*D'accord*," Robert said. He knew Marienne hated owing debts, but perhaps if he demanded something unusual she would have to delay changing circuits until she paid him. He grinned at the ingenious idea. "I'll see you at the Revel."

"Isn't it amazing that the radio can carry such clear transmissions at great distances?" Katherine babbled eagerly. She sat in the radio operator's chair while Todd sat on the counter next to the equipment. "Robert's airship is a full day ahead of us—so far that we can't see it on any of our scanning equipment, but with the right code we can talk to him as if he's in the room with us! Not only that, but because of this switch box," she pointed to a small device set into the wall, "you can move the call to any room on the *Vincenzo*! Isn't that fantastic?" She beamed at Todd.

He chuckled. "I suppose. This technology has been around for a while, though."

"I know," she nodded. "The radio was one of the first inventions enhanced with luma. The increase in communication really helped connect the world! We've experienced an incredible technology boom because of the spread of ideas, and it can all be traced largely back to this humble but incredible piece of technology!" She blushed and looked away. "I'm sorry, I get really excited about machines."

"You don't have to apologize. I like hearing you talk about machines." He smiled. "I'm really glad you decided to stay."

"Me too." She smiled back at him, but it quickly faded. "I just wish I knew how to help Ethan."

"Who?"

"My brother," she sighed. "He's still indentured. I don't know where he is. We were separated when we were indentured, and I haven't even heard from him for the past two years. I don't know what will happen to him now." Her breathing sped up as her mind raced. Her fingers twitched. "What will they do to him, now that I've run away? Have I pushed all of my debt onto him? I made so many mistakes, added so much to my debt… I—"

"Hey, look at me," Todd soothed. He took her trembling hand in his. "Breathe. Slowly now."

She obeyed, turning her shallow, shuddering breaths into deep, deliberate ones. But the fear remained. "What have I done? Enslaved him for my own freedom?"

"There's a lot we don't know about your brother's situation right now," Todd admitted. He kept his voice soft and even. "We don't even know where he is. Is there a possibility he could have finished his servitude?"

Katherine shook her head. "Our debt was shared. If he paid it all off, I would have been freed too. If I hadn't made so many mistakes it might have been paid off by now." Her fingers twitched in Todd's grasp. "What if the only way I can see him again is by going back?" She choked on the words, shutting her eyes tight against the thought.

Todd's expression hardened. "We'll find a way to help your brother. I promise. Look at me." She did, hazel eyes large and bright with unshed tears. "I promise we will find him. But you won't do it by going back. I'll do what I can to help you find your brother, but if you go back, life will be worse than before. And you'll have the added torment of knowing you had the life you wanted, the job of your dreams, and gave it up."

She nodded. "You're right. I think… I belong up here." She looked around the radio room and smiled. It wasn't nearly as exciting as the engine, but she still loved the simple machines.

Todd breathed a sigh of relief. He noticed that she did not pull her hand away from his. "I think you'll like the Revel," he said at last, trying to change the subject to something lighter.

"Where is it?" she asked. "When Marienne mentioned leaving me there, you got really upset."

"It's on a deserted island in the Caribbean. Not big enough to put on the maps, and only accessible by airship, due to dangerous reefs surrounding it. But it's beautiful and has lots of trees to anchor to."

"Just not somewhere you would want to live," she noted. "You seem to have quite the influence on Marienne."

"We've been in this together from the beginning," he said with a shrug. "We stole this airship together, she and I. I've always been grateful to her, so I treat her with the respect a captain deserves, and she looks out for me. But I've also known her the longest, so I can tell when she needs some guidance."

Katherine glanced at the knotted-up trouser leg and chewed her lip thoughtfully. Todd had never seemed unhappy with his condition, and he navigated the airship flawlessly. But the idea that had lodged in her mind refused to budge and fleshed out with more details and logistics. Where to place gears, what metals to use, and luma. She would need luma.

It was one of the reasons she decided to stay: Marienne allowed her crew to take some luma instead of their wages if they wanted. When she combined that with Todd's friendship, the possibility of finding Ethan, and her fear of Mr. Castle, she could think of no reason to return.

"So, Katherine," Todd's voice and grin brought her back to the radio room, and she realized she was still holding his hand. "Are you ready for the Revel?"

CHAPTER 14

DECEMBER 19, 1904

"*N*ow *that's* a pirate ship!" Katherine said as they approached the *Madness*.

Todd flashed a grin at her, then returned to focusing on his balance as they walked across the sandy beach. Every year he forgot how difficult it was to navigate with his crutch, but he wanted to be with Katherine when she met Robert. The French captain had a large personality, and Todd didn't want her to feel uncomfortable around him.

"It's a junker," Marienne snorted. "He bought it from an Aerocorps surplus auction."

"That explains the militaristic design," Katherine continued. "Probably a late 1880's model, possibly early 90's, but that's only if it has the luma infused navigation system, which isn't likely given that the helm is at the front of the deck."

Todd grinned admiringly at her torrent of words. He liked it when she talked like this, even though he sometimes had a hard time following along.

"What's that on the back of it, though?" she asked. "That's not standard design."

"That would be Robert's workshop," Marienne explained. The sun glinted off large windows that wrapped around the extra room, making it impossible to see inside. "He commissioned it especially for his tailoring work."

Marienne ascended the rope ladder first, and Todd told Katherine to go next. "They don't have a fancy lift like the *Vincenzo* does," he explained. "So I have to go last."

She nodded and ascended the ladder. He smiled as he thought of how much time she had spent examining the mechanical lift that transported him from the ship to the ground. She had insisted on riding it with him, even though the ladder was faster. He knew it was so she could watch it in action, but somehow that was more endearing than if she had chosen to ride it to be with him.

Once she was safely on deck, she leaned over the railing and waved down at him. Todd waved back, then stepped carefully onto the bottom rung of the rope ladder. He wove his arm around the next rung and waved his crutch. With a lurch, the ladder began to ascend, snaking back and forth as it did so. Todd grit his teeth against the jerking movement, reminding himself that it would soon be over.

The moment he reached the deck, Katherine took his crutch as Marienne helped him disentangle from the rope ladder. "It's always a fun ride," he assured Katherine, who was staring at his crutch. He rubbed his shoulder before accepting the crutch back, and she frowned at him doubtfully.

"Ah, Marienne!" Robert greeted as he strode across the deck.

Katherine let out a soft "oh" as she saw Robert for the first time. Todd wasn't surprised. Robert had that effect on people, especially women. His hair shone like gold in the sunlight, framing his face as it fell out of the ribbon he had used to tie it back. His lean physique was highlighted by perfectly tailored trousers and vest. His smiling eyes were somewhere between blue and green.

"You must be Katherine." Robert took her hand, bowed low and kissed her knuckles. She blushed and Todd rolled his eyes. "Are you ready to begin your fitting?"

She nodded shyly.

"When will you be ready to discuss payment?" Marienne asked.

"Come by this evening, once I know what I'll be making."

Marienne nodded. "I have other matters to attend to, but I trust you will treat her with utmost respect."

"Do you truly think so low of me?" Robert's tone was light, but Todd saw hurt in his eyes. "I treat all ladies with respect."

Marienne scoffed and turned to leave. "Todd, keep an eye on them. Make sure Robert behaves himself."

Todd gave his captain a jaunty salute, and winked at Katherine. He was also grateful that he wouldn't have to ride back down the rope ladder quite yet.

"Excellent," Robert said with a nod. "I could use some help. *Suis moi.*"

They followed him down into the belly of the airship, through metal hallways with rough floors that gripped the soles of their shoes. Todd found it a refreshing change after the sand outside. Robert stopped in front of a door, grinning proudly.

"Welcome to my workshop." He opened the door with a dramatic flourish.

Todd watched Katherine's reaction as she stepped into the room. She gaped in awe at the shelves that lined the walls. The wraparound windows offered a beautiful view of the bay, but her attention was riveted on the view inside the room. It was as if someone had pulled apart a rainbow and compressed each color into small rectangles as bolt upon bolt of pastels, vibrant hues, and rich jewel tones sat patiently in neatly organized rows. Ribbons stood at attention on spools, a dressing screen occupied one corner, and a small stool waited in the middle of the room. A long table with notches cut into the side held a neat pile of papers on one end and a new model sewing machine on the other. The machine sparkled faintly with the signature sheen of luma. Katherine unconsciously walked over to the machine and began to inspect it, only realizing what she had done when Robert caught her attention by clearing his throat.

She straightened quickly. "I'm sorry."

Todd laughed. "I should have known you would go for the only machine in the room."

"I'll let you look when we are done," Robert promised. He stood beside the stool, a measuring tape draped across his neck. "Todd, would you take down the measurements? There's paper and a pen on my desk."

Todd settled into the chair and wrote Katherine's name at the top. She stood up on the stool.

"Have you been fitted before?" Robert asked.

"It's been a long time," she admitted. "The last time was when I was fitted for this uniform." She gestured to her pale yellow dress with a grimace. She had worn it purely because it was the only thing on the *Vincenzo* that fit her properly.

Robert nodded. "If any measurements I require make you feel uncomfortable, please let me know immediately. Arms by your sides," he directed. He moved behind her and held one end of the measuring tape against the back of her neck, then stretched it down to her ankle. "Neck to hem, 157 centimeters," he called out to Todd, who scrawled on the paper.

"Arm out." He lightly guided her arm straight, measuring shoulder to wrist, then to her elbow, and the circumference of her arm and wrist, all the while repeating the numbers. Todd wrote down each measurement dutifully.

"*Tu es tres petite,*" Robert clucked. "*Une petite souris.*"

"I'm sorry, my French is rudimentary at best," Katherine admitted. "And I've forgotten most of what I learned."

"I said you are very small, like a little mouse."

"I'm sorry."

Todd looked up from the measurement he had been writing down. Her tone had changed; she sounded distressed. Her brow wrinkled and she blinked several times.

"I... I suppose I could eat more," she continued, her fingers twitching. "And try to move around less. I could work as little as possible. That would make me larger, wouldn't it?"

Robert glanced at Todd and they shared a concerned look. Todd stood up from his chair as Robert turned back to Katherine. "I suppose it would," he said slowly. "But I don't recommend it."

Her eyes grew wider, more desperate. She crossed her arms over her chest and pinched herself over and over. Todd rushed to her side. He wanted to take her hands, stop her, but wasn't sure if that would help or make things worse.

"I'm sorry," she whimpered. "I could use rags—"

"Katherine?" Robert's tone was not sharp, but she flinched as if he had raised his voice. He opened his mouth but words failed him.

"I'm sorry." Her chin quivered. "I'm sorry. I'm so useless. Please, just… tell me what you want me to do." Her hands gripped at her forearms tightly, the skin turning red from her pinching. She watched him in anxious anticipation.

Todd watched her, feeling completely helpless.

Robert shook his head. "I don't want you to do anything."

"But I am too small," she whispered.

"I didn't say that," Robert responded. "But I am sorry that I made you feel that way. Who hurt you?" He glanced at Todd as he asked the question.

Todd clenched his jaw and tugged on his curls. Mr. Castle. He knew that Katherine was scared of him, but he had no idea it was this bad.

Katherine looked down at her red arms. "I did." Those two syllables sounded so defeated and broken.

With a sigh, Robert sat down on the floor and invited Katherine to do the same. She obediently sat on the stool, hands tightly gripping her skirt. Todd moved back to Robert's desk and sat down in the chair. He stared at the paper of Katherine's measurements, thoughts racing in a sickeningly familiar dance: *useless, unhelpful, can't do anything right anymore.* He shut his eyes tight against the thoughts.

"May I tell you a story?" Robert asked. When Katherine nodded, he continued, "I grew up in an orphanage. When I was twelve years old, a girl about eight arrived. Her name was Claire and we became fast friends. She was the closest thing I ever had to a sister." He smiled fondly at the memory, but still watched Katherine warily. "After almost a year, she confided in me that she was not an orphan. She had run away from her father's drunken anger after her mother died. I was furious. I wanted to take away her fear, and make him feel that fear instead."

Robert now glanced at Todd, who pretended not to notice. He kept his gaze on the paper in front of him, tugging at his curls. Of course he was furious. Of course he wanted to hurt Mr. Castle for hurting Katherine. And of course Robert saw that. But he couldn't do it. He was useless.

"I was so young, though," Robert continued, "so instead I promised to make her forget the awful times. But she didn't want that." He smiled warmly at Katherine's wide-eyed expression. "She told me something I will remember for the rest of my life. 'I can't forget what he did to me. I never will. It's with me forever. But if you want to help, then fill my future with everything my past lacked. Light, happiness, and love.' I tried my hardest, and I never saw her smile as brightly as the day she was adopted into a loving family."

Katherine looked at him skeptically. "That's very eloquent for a nine year old," she remarked.

"It sounded even better in French," he said with a shrug. Then, with a laugh, he added, "It was over a dozen years ago, you think I remember exactly what she said?"

"You said you will remember it for the rest of your life!"

Robert laughed, and Katherine timidly giggled. Todd watched them with envy and awe. How could they move on so quickly? How could she find such hope in a bright future when her past was filled with such darkness? And how could he even dream of helping her when his own darkness was of a completely different nature?

Robert stood and offered a hand to help Katherine stand.

"I'm sorry for the trouble I've caused," she said.

"My dear Katherine, I never again want to hear you apologize for what happened today."

"I'm—" She caught herself and nodded.

He smiled at her. "Are you ready to continue with your fitting?"

She hesitated. "I know I should."

"If you do not want to, you don't have to," he said gently.

"Then, no, I don't want to be fitted right now. Will that put you behind schedule?"

Robert beamed proudly at her. "It doesn't matter if it does or not. What matters is that you are comfortable and happy. We can continue measurements tomorrow. But since you are here, would you like to help me choose fabrics?"

Todd noticed Katherine's relief at an excuse to stay in the workshop, and Robert's relief at seeing her smile again. But still Todd's arms ached from clenching his fists so tightly, and the back of his throat burned. His anger wasn't completely directed at the man who had hurt Katherine so deeply. Guilt settled heavy on his shoulders as he watched her smile bashfully when Robert complimented her hazel eyes. How had he not seen the scars behind her smile? How could he possibly dream to help her when he had already failed so astronomically? Why could he not help her the way Robert had?

He watched as Robert teased her by suggesting she wear a rich green velvet, and Todd even managed a smile when she laughed at how impractical it was. Perhaps Robert could help the both of them.

CHAPTER 15

The setting sun washed the workshop in a golden glow as Marienne walked in, her heeled boots announcing her presence before she knocked on the open door. Robert sat up from where he had been bent over piles of fabrics, sorting them into different stacks. His aquamarine eyes flickered in alarm to the corner behind Marienne's left shoulder. She suppressed a grin.

You should know better than to leave your gift to me out in the open, she thought. *I should have known it would be clothes.* But she decided to humor him and kept her attention directed at his face. Best not to spoil the surprise.

"Marienne! To what do I owe the pleasure?" He smiled a little too broadly.

She raised an eyebrow. "You made this appointment for us to discuss payment," she reminded. She glanced around, teasing him with the idea that she might look behind her. "And I want to know how long Katherine's wardrobe will take."

Robert frowned. "Today was… unexpected. We're behind schedule, and I'm afraid that means we'll both have to stay a couple of days after the Revel." He shrugged, feigning apology.

She pursed her lips. Every day she stayed put was risky. "Explain."

"Are you aware that Katherine has been through trauma?" He watched her reaction carefully, all levity and pretense gone.

"I am aware that she is an orphan, and lost her father only a couple of years ago. She has not disclosed to me the nature of his death and speaks quite highly of him. I also know that she has been indentured these past two years as a maid at Luma Baron Prescott's summer estate, and would like to free her brother from his servitude."

At the mention of Prescott, Robert's interest piqued, but he shook his head. "This is something else. There was... an incident as I measured her today that uncovered a part of her that not even Todd had seen before. For that I cannot apologize enough." He sighed and raked a hand through his hair. "I spent some time calming her down. I think she trusts me. I hope. We agreed to continue measuring tomorrow, and instead spent our time today choosing fabrics." He gestured to the bolts spread in front of him on the table. "She was very excited to learn about denim."

Marienne blinked slowly. "Thank you for informing me." She might not confront her new mechanic directly—it was not in her nature to pry into the private lives of her crew, as she wished to keep her own past secret. But she would need to be aware of what could set Katherine on edge again. Tailors, for example.

She walked away from the work table to gaze out the large windows at the sun sinking into the sea. She kept her face a carefully constructed mask of polite interest; it was an art she had perfected since childhood. But she knew that her eyes would betray her, and she could not have him seeing the soft emotions in them now.

From the first moment she met Katherine, Marienne had known that she belonged on the *Vincenzo*. She hated her life and needed to escape. Just as Marienne had, and Nyx, and Rose, and Todd. Everyone on the *Vincenzo* had run from something, even down to its very first crew members. A young woman running from an arranged marriage and an ex-Aerocorps amputee whose family had practically disowned him took to the skies and found freedom. Marienne smiled fondly as the sun slipped past the horizon. In the five years since, she had taken on misfits and lost souls to join her little pirate crew. Perhaps her new mechanic could find the same peace in freedom the rest of them had.

Katherine had mentioned how kind Robert had been to her when Marienne asked about the fitting session. For that, Marienne felt overwhelming gratitude to him now. Although she had known him longer than she had sailed the skies, he still managed to surprise her in the most pleasant of ways. But it was time to leave him behind, she realized with a start. For his protection, and her freedom.

"Now," she said at last, "regarding payment."

"I want a hat."

She turned so forcefully that her curls whipped around her face, highlighting her incredulous expression. A smug grin sat on his face as he reclined in his seat. "A hat?"

"A big one." He gestured for emphasis. "With lots of feathers."

She frowned. "I don't have one currently at my disposal. Are you certain this is a fair exchange for an entire wardrobe of work clothes?"

Robert nodded. "Most certainly. You see, it's about supply and demand. I am currently without a large hat, and so demand is high."

Marienne sighed. It was an obvious ploy. By demanding something so ridiculous, he created an excuse for her to stay and see him again. *You can't keep doing this*, she thought. *Stop making me want to stay with you.* "When I am in a position to procure such an extravagant accessory, I will radio you to let you know. It may be best to have James deliver it."

Robert visibly deflated. "If that is best."

"In the meantime, is there anything I can provide as partial payment? I do so hate to leave with an 'I owe you.'"

His eyes drifted to the corner, but he quickly returned his gaze to her. She knew he was hoping she hadn't noticed. "I'll think on it."

Marienne nodded once. "Thank you for your time. And for your help today. I was unaware that Katherine carried such heavy burdens." *But, then again, don't we all.* "She regards you as a friend now. Thank you." She turned to leave.

"Have a drink with me."

Marienne paused. She turned towards the corner where his gift to her sat, but instead looked over her shoulder at him. His aquamarine eyes were wide with horror—though at his words or how close she had come to seeing his surprise, she couldn't tell. How many more chances would she get to simply sit and talk with him? To share a drink, like they had in that pub so many years ago? She opened her mouth, but a knock at the door interrupted her.

They turned to see Todd standing bashfully in the doorway. "I'm sorry, I'll come back later."

"No, I was just leaving," Marienne said. To Robert, she added, "The Revel is in two days. Perhaps I will drink with you then."

As Robert watched Marienne leave, Todd glanced at the corner. "Is this dress for Marienne?" he asked.

"Is that really what you came here to discuss?" Robert felt his mouth go dry and he struggled to swallow. Marienne had come dangerously close to seeing it and spoiling the surprise. He wasn't ready to give it to her yet. Right now it was still a farewell gift, and he couldn't bear to say goodbye to her. If he could somehow convince her not to leave the South Atlantic collection circuit, then the dress would be easier to part with. But she still seemed set on leaving him behind.

"No, you're right." Todd turned to face him. "I want to help Katherine. Like you helped Claire."

"Then why are you here? I am not the one you need to talk to. Only by spending time with Katherine will you know how best to help her."

"That's just it." Todd made his way to the desk and leaned against it with a sigh. "I thought I was getting to know her. We spent so much time together these past three weeks. I can't stop kicking myself for not seeing it sooner."

Robert considered for a moment. "Todd, when I first met you, it had been what, a year since you lost your leg?"

"And six months since my family had sent me away."

"You seemed happy to me."

"But I wasn't," he protested. "Some days were a struggle to get out of bed—physically and mentally."

"And some days you found the sharp scent of atmosphere invigorating you beyond your imagination," Robert countered. "Even in the midst of the deepest sorrows, one will find good days. Katherine has had a lot to adjust to, and we've both observed how machines bring her the greatest of joys. Perhaps whomever had hurt her so deeply had simply flown so far from her mind that she showed no signs of distress."

"But not far enough."

"I'm sorry," Robert sighed as he combed his fingers through his hair.

Todd shook his head. "You couldn't have known. And besides, it's not your fault." His hand clenched into a fist.

"I don't know that she would be ready to talk about who or what hurt her," Robert said cautiously, eying Todd's reaction. He remembered the feeling, when Claire had told him about her father. He had felt it again when Marienne told him about Prescott's inhumane practices. He also understood the helplessness of not being able to act on that anger.

Todd flexed his fingers. "I know." He glanced at the pile of fabric on Robert's desk. "Were you planning on making Katherine a dress for the Revel?"

"I'm certain I could put something together. But it won't be made of denim," he said with a grimace, moving the sturdy fabric to one side.

"But it's so practical!" Todd teased. "Durable and breathable, isn't that what you said?"

"I should not have mentioned it to her," he mumbled. "You were asking about a dress?"

Todd shifted uncomfortably. "I would like to commission one for her. I want her to feel confident, radiant. Like she belongs."

Robert stood and paced behind his desk. "In order to do that, I will need to know more. Tell me about her."

As Todd spoke, his voice grew fond and his cheeks dimpled.

Robert recognized the look in Todd's brown eyes, and a knowing smile spread across his own face. As sure as the moon rose outside the large windows, Todd was falling in love. It was fully dark outside by the time Robert felt he had enough information to create a dress suitable for Katherine.

"Now, you do realize the Revel is in two days?" Robert raised his eyebrows. "There will be a fee for such short notice. And it may delay the rest of Katherine's wardrobe, as well." *Causing Marienne to stay even longer*, he realized. *And the rush fee should satisfy Landreau.*

"I know. Whatever payment you ask for will be more than fair. I'll pay with whatever I can."

Robert struggled to hide a frown. Todd was about as good at holding on to money as he was. *Sorry, Landreau, I'll have to barter again.* The first mate would already lecture him about the payment for Katherine's wardrobe, but he was desperate to try anything to see Marienne again.

Robert leaned against his desk. "Name your firstborn after me."

"What?" Todd's wide-eyed, incredulous expression proved too much for the French captain. He burst into laughter.

"I tease, *mon ami*! I'll think of payment later. For now, I must get to work."

"Thank you." Todd smiled, relieved.

CHAPTER 16

DECEMBER 20, 1904

Katherine turned her face to the mid-morning sun, relishing its warmth. Although she felt closer to the sun when on the *Vincenzo*, the altitude made flying colder than being on the ground. She had noticed that morning that more freckles dotted her nose than had been there a month ago, and her hair had grown past her chin. Mr. Castle would have trimmed it immediately, and sneered at her freckles. She liked how she looked now.

"Thank you for coming with me again," she said to Todd as they walked across the beach to the *Madness*. She walked slowly to stay beside him as he struggled through the sand. "And for… yesterday."

"I did nothing yesterday," he replied bitterly.

He stumbled and Katherine caught his arm. As he straightened, however, she lost her balance and fell to the sand. Todd reached out and helped her up, but she quickly withdrew her hand from his.

Her ears burned like the sun and she crossed her arms over her chest, gripping them tight. She would *not* pinch herself in front of him —not again—but it had been so long since she had fallen in front of anyone. The last time had been in the Emerald Parlor with Luma Baron Prescott. The memory seared into her mind. Her chest felt tight. She walked the rest of the way to the *Madness* in silence, not daring to look at Todd. What must he think of her now?

Once she had climbed the rope ladder, Katherine asked one of Robert's crew members to pull Todd up. As she waited, she spied Robert across the deck and waved at him. He spoke to another man, this one slightly taller and not quite as lean, and a decade or so older than Robert. The captain waved back, and pointed her out to the other man. As they approached, Katherine noticed that this man's short, spiky blond hair looked singed in places.

"Bonjour, Katherine! May I introduce my mentor and friend, James the Lightning-Chaser."

James pushed his goggles further up his head and held out a hand. "Pleased to meet you." His grin pulled up on one side more than the other, and his storm-gray eyes twinkled with either merriment or mischief, she couldn't be certain which.

She shook his hand, which was clad in a leather glove that ended at the knuckles. It was a popular fashion, but she had never understood the impractical design. "I'm sorry, but I've never heard of a lightning-chaser."

James' grin widened with a glint of wild excitement. Katherine decided it must have been mischief she spied in his eyes. "Lightning is essential to luma harvesting," he explained. "It's polarized somehow. Possibly some form of concentrated luma itself."

"That's the electricity you feel buzzing whenever we collect," Todd reminded her as he joined the conversation. She recalled how her hairs always stood on end whenever the *Vincenzo* extended her great wings. "I see you've met James." He nodded to the man.

"Nice to see you again!" James said. "Katherine here was wondering what my profession entails."

Todd laughed. "You mean flying head-first into storms just to make a profit?"

Katherine's eyes widened and she stared at James.

He laughed along. "That's about the front and back of it. It's dangerous work, but necessary to keep luma on the market. Few men are so daring and brave as to capitalize on such adventure!"

A smile stole across Katherine's face as she decided that this man was definitely mad.

Robert clapped a hand on his friend's shoulder. "I'll save some of my best whiskey for you tomorrow," he promised. "But for now, I have a fitting." He held a hand out to Katherine. She glanced towards Todd before accepting it.

Once back in the workshop, Katherine noticed a white shape next to the door. When she turned towards it, she saw that it was a mannequin covered in a sheet, looking almost comically like a ghost. "What's this?" she asked.

"It's for Marienne," Todd said with a smirk. Robert scowled at him.

"Can I see it?" Katherine asked, eyes wide.

"Fitting first!" he insisted. "We've put it off long enough, and if I'm ever going to get it done we must finish measuring."

She pouted as she stepped onto the stool. Feeling like a doll, she bent and straightened on command, trying to ignore the tickle of Robert's measuring tape pulling taut. Todd started to pull faces at her, making her giggle.

"*Arretez-vous!*" Robert scolded, looking at Todd.

Katherine rolled her eyes and started to make faces back. She enjoyed watching how his shoulders shook with laughter, and wished he didn't have to write down the numbers Robert called out. When he looked down, she couldn't see his dimples.

"*Et voila!*" Robert announced. "*C'est finis.*"

Katherine hopped lightly off the stool. "Can I see what you're hiding now?"

He sighed and lifted the sheet carefully off of the mannequin. She moved closer, admiring the beautiful dress. She could easily picture Marienne wearing it and walking with a confident stride, the sheath skirt swaying attractively.

"Is that fabric luma infused?"

Robert nodded. "Please keep this a secret. Marienne does not know."

"Of course she doesn't, it's a surprise." Katherine bent to inspect the shimmering satin without touching it. "You've done a good job. She will look stunning."

"You will, too," Todd said.

Katherine straightened suddenly. "What do you mean?"

"That is… I mean… Everyone is expected to wear their best for the Revel tomorrow," he stammered.

She frowned. "I don't have any 'best' to wear."

"I'm sure that—"

"And even if I did, you didn't mention that it was such a formal event." She crossed her arms over her chest. Her fingers twitched lightly. "I don't really like wearing fancy dresses."

"You don't?" Todd exchanged a panicked look with Robert.

"They're impractical," she said, hoping to hide the panic in her chest. She had begun looking forward to the Revel, but if it was filled with people in formal wear, she knew she would only end up embarrassing herself. She always did. "Are we done here?"

Robert nodded, and Katherine looked at Todd.

"Go ahead," he said, tugging on his curls. "I want to stay and talk to Robert."

She nodded, then turned away so he wouldn't see the hurt on her face. Or how she pinched at the skin on her arms.

The moment Katherine's footsteps retreated down the hallway, Todd burst. "I'm so stupid!"

"Did you know?" Robert asked calmly as he placed the sheet back over Marienne's dress. His mind raced with how to salvage the commission, especially since he had already started on the bodice.

"I knew she preferred practicality, but I didn't think she disliked formal wear. I thought she was just prioritizing her job." He sank back into Robert's chair with a groan. "And I almost blew the secret!"

Robert walked over to his desk and pulled out his sketch for Katherine's dress. He had designed something from a fairy tale, with puffed sleeves and a voluminous skirt all in pastel colors. How could he modify it to better suit her preferences? "She doesn't mind wearing trousers," he mused, glancing again at the bolts of sturdy cloth she had chosen.

Todd shook his head. "She prefers them, actually. But she can also be self-conscious. What if you make her trousers and she feels out of place because everyone else is wearing a dress?"

"Perhaps if I give her options," Robert said. He pulled out another piece of paper and began sketching. "The bodice is almost done, but I could easily turn it into a blouse. Then, making these pieces separately..." He looked at Todd. "I may need you to stay and help, if we are going to complete this in the next twenty-four hours. Consider the labor as part of your payment."

"And the rest of it?" Todd sat up straight, relying on Robert's determination and the promise of work to distract him from his own failure.

"Purchasing autorat traps is becoming a nuisance. I would like an automaton." Robert grinned. "Perhaps you could ask Katherine to make me one."

"I don't know that she would want to do anything I ask her to, especially if she doesn't like the dress," Todd lamented.

Robert tutted and held up a finger. "Firstly, it's an ensemble now. And secondly, I will not tolerate that sort of attitude in my workshop. Think positive! She is going to love it, and you'll romance her by the fire's glow, and she'll say she's decided to—" He stopped himself. He had been going to say *she'll say she's decided to stay on the circuit to be with you.* He cleared his throat. "She's decided to give you something in return and then she'll kiss you."

Todd eyed him skeptically as Robert sat at his sewing machine. "Is there something else you would like to talk about?"

"Yes, this ensemble." He placed the bodice—soon to be blouse— into position under the needle and pushed the lever with his foot. "Fetch me that chartreuse luma-infused organza." Todd stared at him blankly until Robert sighed. "*J'ai besoin de quelqu'un à mon niveau.* The light green, sheer, shimmery one." He pointed towards the correct shelf, then continued sewing.

They would get this ensemble done in time. Not just for Todd, but for himself, too. Even if she never saw him again, Robert wanted Katherine to remember him fondly. Work clothes could be made by anyone, but if he got this outfit right, perhaps she would one day want to see him again. Maybe even make an automaton, and Marienne would need to deliver it. His mind raced like the needle on his sewing machine. Anything, anything, to help him see Marienne after the Revel.

CHAPTER 17

DECEMBER 21, 1904

Katherine sat on the deck of the *Vincenzo*, stroking Nikolai's delicate metal feathers. She longed to open the panel in his chest and look inside at his mechanical workings, but it was locked and Marienne had the key. Perhaps if she could observe many different machines, she could get a better idea of what she needed to make a gift for Todd.

That is, if he wanted her to. She sighed, and Nikolai tilted his head at her curiously. Yesterday, she had expected to have dinner together as they often had, but he barely said hello to her as he grabbed his food and left just as quickly as he had arrived. And this morning she hadn't seen him at all. He usually checked in with her before starting on the day's work, and they tended to eat breakfast together, too. Nyx teased them about how much time they spent together, but Katherine didn't mind. Todd was kind to her, and she appreciated how easy he was to talk to.

So why was he avoiding her?

Nikolai made a whirring coo, and Katherine resumed stroking his head, but her thoughts remained distant. She knew the reason, but didn't want to admit it. Memories from Robert's workshop over the past two days replayed over and over in her mind, no matter how hard she tried to dismiss them. Todd must hate her after how she had behaved. And she couldn't blame him.

"I envy you," she sighed to Nikolai. The falcon automaton looked at her with one glass eye, the luma spark dancing. Automatons didn't have to worry about messing up and people hating them or hurting them. They just did what they were programmed to do.

"Hey, kiddo." James sat heavily on the deck next to Katherine. "You get banned from the preparations, too?"

"I'm useless with everything but machines," she admitted. "Did you forget my name?"

He ran a hand through his already unkempt hair and grinned lopsidedly. "I forgot it the moment I stepped off Robert's ship. Sorry."

"It's Katherine," she reminded him. "What brings you up here?"

"I was looking for Todd," he said, glancing around. "That boy's always fun to swap stories with, and since they won't let me near the food — or more accurately, the alcohol," he winked at her, "I thought I'd catch up with him."

She frowned. "I haven't seen him since last night." Her gaze drifted to the *Madness*, bobbing on its tether only a couple hundred yards away. All of the airships had been moved off the beach to make room for the celebration that night, and now they anchored to sturdy trees in the thick tropical jungle.

"That's too bad," James muttered. He procured a small, silver flask from his hip. Before taking a drink, he paused and grinned at her. "Promise you won't tell?"

"Only if I can get a better look at that design." She had caught a glimpse of what looked like a rat automaton fashioned out of gears and scrap metal, complete with red glass eyes.

He took a swig and replaced the cap. "Got it in Germany."

As he held it out to Katherine, Nikolai flew off her shoulder with a metallic screech and snatched the flask in his talons. Both Katherine and James hopped to their feet, shouting in alarm and rushing towards the automaton. He looked at them for just a moment, head twitching, before he took off and flew over the railing of the deck.

The falcon dove towards the trees and Katherine watched with a sinking feeling, as if he had taken her heart instead of the flask. Her mind reeled and she immediately began to pinch her arms. Marienne had trusted her to watch Nikolai while she helped prepare for the Revel. How could she have lost him? She was supposed to be good with machines! Marienne would never keep her as the mechanic now; this mistake was too big. She didn't deserve to stay on the *Vincenzo* anymore.

James didn't hesitate. He grabbed Katherine's hand and ran with her towards the rope ladder. "After him! We need to get that flask!"

"And Nikolai!" Katherine said as she began to descend the ladder.

"And my grog!"

When they reached the jungle floor, James turned to her. "Where do you think he's gone?"

She shielded her eyes and looked up at the trees. *I can fix this*, she thought, taking a deep breath. *If I fix it and Marienne never finds out, perhaps I can stay.* "He's looking for Marienne. That's what automatons do when they catch autorats—they bring them to their master."

"Great, we have a lead! Where is she?"

Katherine shook her head. "I don't know. All she said was that she would help with the Revel, but that could put her anywhere. The good news is, Nikolai doesn't know where she is, either."

"How is that good news?"

"Because it means that his movements will be more predictable. He'll check familiar locations first. Let's start with the *Madness*." She began to walk through the springy undergrowth towards the airship. But what if Marienne was there, and she saw Nikolai? Or what if Katherine was wrong, and Nikolai found Marienne first?

"You seem to know a lot about automatons." James' voice interrupted her turbulent thoughts.

"Engineer, remember?"

"More than their mechanics, though," he continued, brushing a large bug off his shoulder. "You know what they're thinking."

She paused as a flash of light caught her attention, but it was just the sunlight filtering through the wide leaves. "I find them interesting. Automatons act like real creatures, to an extent, but only because they're programmed to. It wasn't Nikolai's fault he flew off with your flask. He's programmed to attack autorats." *Although it is strange that he would mistake the flask for a real autorat.* She wondered if that was a common problem among predatory automatons.

"If anything is damaged, I expect reimbursement," James grumbled, his stern expression ruined by his goggles slipping down his forehead. He pushed them back up and wiped the sweat off his brow.

Katherine's shoulders slumped. "You would have to talk to Marienne about that, since Nikolai belongs to her. But I wouldn't be surprised if she took the expenses out of my pay."

"I'm more concerned about the liquor than the flask. It was a nice find, but I need what's inside." He grinned at her, but she could not muster a smile in response. "Here we are." He held out the rope ladder for her to climb.

Katherine tried her best to wipe the sap off her palms on her borrowed trousers, but her hands still stuck slightly to the rope ladder. As she climbed, she hoped that Nikolai was here, and that Marienne wasn't.

When she made it onto the deck, she spotted Landreau instructing another crew member to open the cargo door and start taking supplies down to the beach. A quick glance around revealed that no one else was on deck, including Nikolai. Her fingers twitched as she waited for him to finish his conversation.

When at last he turned to her, Landreau said, "Todd isn't here."

Katherine looked at him strangely as James joined them. "I didn't ask about Todd."

"Oh, *bon. Parce que* he is not here." The first mate grinned. "What can I help you with?"

"Have you seen Nikolai?" she asked, trying to keep her voice calm. Landreau looked at her strangely, so she added, "Marienne's automaton falcon."

"*Non*, not today, but I've been busy. Has he run off again?"

"Again?" Katherine glanced at James, who shrugged.

"First time he's gone off with my flask," the lightning-chaser said.

Landreau shook his head. "This happens every so often. I keep telling Marienne to tether him, but she can't stand to keep him tied up. If I see him, I'll let you know."

"Thank you. And not a word of this to Marienne!" Katherine begged.

As they walked back towards the rope ladder, James asked, "What now?"

She thought for a moment. "Has he ever been to your airship before?"

He nodded. "I supply Marienne's lightning, so we meet up every six months or so. Sometimes she'll bring Nikolai with her."

"If a predatory automaton is aware of where the autorat came from, it will go to that location in an effort to sabotage any further luma collection methods. Nikolai associates you as the owner of the rat, and since he knows your ship—"

"That's where he will go!" James exclaimed. "Quick, before he destroys my flask and who knows what else!"

Katherine scrambled down the rope ladder, sharing in James' urgency, but by the time she had reached the ground other thoughts crept into her mind like vines. Todd had promised to help her find Ethan. Would he still honor that promise after what he had seen of her? Had she resigned her brother to captivity after all?

James joined her and they walked through the jungle in silence. After a few minutes, he said, "Alright, kiddo, what's got you down?"

"Did you forget my name again?" she asked quietly.

"Don't change the subject, Katherine," he said, his tone kind. "What's bothering you? Is it Nikolai? We'll find him. And it sounds like this happens, I'm sure Marienne will understand."

"It's not that," she admitted, although the reminder dampened her mood further. "How long have you known Todd?"

James's lopsided smile split across his face. "Got to be going on five years now. I admire the kid. He's been through a lot, but he's always thinking of others and how he can help out. Sometimes he does more for me than my own crew!"

"What is he like when he gets angry?" Mr. Castle seemed nice until he got angry, at which point he could be incredibly cruel. Katherine had made him angry a lot. She didn't want to do the same with Todd, if she could help it.

James thought for a moment. "I can't say I've seen him angry much. The only time I can think of, we were docked in Switzerland, and some boys were throwing rocks at a stray puppy. Todd scooped the puppy up in his arms and lectured those boys so hard they nearly cried from shame. They didn't even speak the same language!" James laughed. "He has a strong sense of justice, and is always looking out for the weak."

Katherine managed a smile. Ethan was like that, too. But James' story didn't match Todd's recent behavior. Why was he avoiding her, if he wasn't angry?

"May I introduce to you *Mjolnir's Child*." James gestured proudly to his airship.

Katherine admired the sleek, functional design of the airship. It was thin and aerodynamic, designed to fly through the most turbulent winds. As she climbed the ladder, she noticed that the hull had been coated in rubber. "Perhaps in better circumstances I can take a more thorough look around," she called down to him.

"Please do!"

Even so, once on deck, she couldn't help but wonder what the instruments next to the cannons could be, and nearly asked when a flash of copper caught her eye. "Nikolai!" she gasped. He stood on the deck, flask still clutched in his talon.

"Aha!" James shouted, but Katherine clapped a hand over his mouth.

"Be careful," she warned. "He might be afraid of you."

"He's a thief," James mumbled behind her hand.

"Let me handle this," she insisted. She could feel him frown, but he nodded. She removed her hand, took a deep breath, and walked slowly towards the falcon automaton. Stretching out a hand, she called out in a soothing voice, "Here, Nikolai. Come to me. You know me, right?"

Nikolai tilted his head, turning it slightly, the luma inside his glass eye flashing as he trained his gaze on James. Katherine didn't dare look behind her to see what he was doing, she only hoped Nikolai wouldn't—

"Captain?"

With a metallic screech, the falcon automaton took off as a member of James' crew stepped out onto the deck.

"No!" she cried. "Catch him!"

James scrambled onto the railing of his ship, taking off his leather jacket as he did so. Katherine fought the urge to cover her eyes, afraid that James would fall back and plummet to the ground. He waited until Nikolai dipped lower to avoid the cables that held the balloon in place, then leapt forward and wrapped the automaton in his jacket. The two of them tumbled to the deck.

Katherine rushed to James' side. "Are you hurt?"

"Just some bruises," he assured her. "Now, I believe this is mine." He lifted the corner of his jacket and pried the flask out of Nikolai's talon. The sharpened metal claws left scratches on its surface.

Katherine eased the rest of James' leather jacket off of Nikolai. The automaton looked at her with a confused tilt of his head. She gently lifted him from the deck and carefully inspected each of his gears and hinged feathers. At last she sighed in relief. "He's unharmed."

"Captain, I must object to such reckless behavior." The crew member who had startled Nikolai stood to one side, frowning.

James rolled his eyes. "Andrew, I know you're new to the crew, but I really don't need anyone scolding me about safety."

"It's not your safety I'm concerned about," the young man sniffed haughtily. "It's the image you present to your crew and clients. Others may perceive you as reckless and flippant, taking time off from collection to come here—"

"Remember your place!" James hissed. Katherine flinched at the harsh tone and the electric charge of conflict building in the air around her. "I am captain here. You don't have to participate in the Revel, since you disapprove so much, but you don't get to decide that for others."

Andrew's mouth thinned to a flat line, then he turned on his heel and walked below deck. Katherine watched him leave, muscles tensed until he was completely out of sight. His words echoed in her mind, but with Mr. Castle's voice: *I object to such reckless behavior.* He would certainly disapprove of the Revel, if he knew Katherine was considering attending.

James lifted the flask to his lips, then frowned. He tilted it upside down. Not a single drop came out.

"I'm sorry, the cap must not have been on all the way," Katherine said.

The lightning-chaser sighed. "I guess I'll have to wait until the Revel." He glanced at the sky, which now turned a shade of pink. "Looks like I won't have to wait much longer. You'd better get back to the *Vincenzo* and get ready. Think you can find the way?"

"If I can't, Nikolai can," she reasoned.

"I'll see you at the Revel, then."

Katherine shrugged. She placed the mischievous automaton on her shoulder, then climbed down the rope ladder. She had already been considering not attending—between not having proper clothes and it being such a formal event, she didn't feel like she would fit in. If she did go, she would want to spend the evening with Todd, but it seemed he didn't feel the same.

Nikolai nuzzled her cheek, and Katherine patted his head. Machines understood her, and she understood them. Perhaps it would be best if she spent the night in the engine room.

CHAPTER 18

"And where have you been?"

Katherine stopped short. Next to the *Vincenzo*'s rope ladder, arms folded and a disapproving frown on her face, stood Marienne. Katherine almost expected her to say she had been looking for her everywhere, or that she had missed curfew. No one had scolded her like that since she had left home, and it reminded her of her housekeeper, Mrs. Thorne.

"James came looking for Todd," she started. "I helped him look, but we never did find him. I brought Nikolai along for the walk." She gave her most innocent smile.

Marienne arched her eyebrows, unimpressed. Katherine knew she was unconvinced. The captain took Nikolai and placed him on her shoulder. "Hm. Well, you're here now. Go on up and get ready. Dinner begins in half an hour."

"I'm sorry, but I don't think I will attend the Revel."

Marienne studied Katherine before responding in a softer tone, "If that's what you want, it is your choice. However, the only available food is down at the beach. You are welcome to request that someone bring you back a serving. It will be delicious," she said with a smile.

With a nod and a small "thanks," Katherine ascended the ladder.

Halfway up she heard Marienne scold Nikolai for running off again, and her grip tightened on the rope. *I'm sorry I lost him.* She had found him again, but fixing a mistake didn't erase it. Sooner or later she would face punishment for it.

When she set foot on the deck, Katherine saw many members of the crew chatting as they waited their turn to use the lift. They all wore fine dresses or suits, and she squirmed uncomfortably. Rose waved at her with a smile, looking lovely in a corseted plum dress. Katherine waved half-heartedly back. *She would bring me food if I asked her*, Katherine realized. But before she took a single step towards Rose, she saw Todd making his way across the deck.

"There you are!" she called. She wanted to rush to his side, but hesitated. Did he want to see her? His shocked expression wasn't reassuring. "James was looking for you," she said as he approached.

"Was he?" Todd smiled without dimples. He wore a green vest that had most likely been made by Robert. "Um, I think you should get ready. I'll meet you down there for supper."

She felt as if she had touched an exposed wire. He turned his back on her and moved towards the lift, not waiting for a reply. Katherine ran down to the engine room. As her footsteps echoed around her, they beat out a rhythm with her pounding heart: *I'm sorry, I'm sorry, I'm sorry.*

I'm sorry, Marienne, for losing Nikolai. I'm sorry, James, for ruining your flask and losing your liquor. I'm sorry, Todd, for... She paused outside the door to the engine room, arms crossed over her chest, fingers pinching. She didn't want to say it, didn't even want to think it, but the words came anyway. "I'm sorry I'm so useless."

As she pushed open the door, Katherine sighed. "I belong in here, where machines make sense." The engine functioned as well as it could—she still hadn't been able to get replacement parts—so all she could do tonight was sit on her bed, alone with her thoughts. She glanced at the workbench as she moved around the massive engine. She supposed she could work on blueprints for her next project, but that would just remind her of Todd. That was too painful right now.

When Katherine turned, she found that the bed had already been pulled out, with clothes laid out on top. Robert couldn't have finished her wardrobe yet, and as she moved closer she saw that only one ensemble waited for her. It was formal more in the quality than the style. A sky blue blouse and matching knee-length skirt sat next to a pair of black trousers. A black and white striped vest lay nearby, neatly pressed. But there was a sheer, pale green swath of fabric that she didn't understand the function of. When she picked it up it shimmered with luma. Next to the clothing was a note from Robert, along with sketches of his vision that cleared up her confusion. The green fabric would belt around her waist as a skirt overlay that reached to her ankles, and she could wear the ensemble with either the skirt or the trousers. She could even leave off the overlay if she wanted.

I hope this is not too formal, and I hope to see you wear it to the Revel. —R

Katherine stared at the sketches. Although Robert did not fill in facial features, he had drawn her hair on the figure. It looked lovely, in all the varieties. Could she do his vision justice? Or would she mess that up, too? Thinking of Robert, she felt immense gratitude towards him. He had been so kind to her, and now he had made her this lovely —yet comfortable—outfit in such little time. He wanted her to enjoy the Revel. She could try. For him.

THERE WAS a dress in Marienne's quarters. She merely glanced at it as she placed Nikolai on his perch next to her piano. Only when everything else was in order did she return her attention to the one thing out of place. An envelope sat next to the dress, but she knew who it was from.

She also knew who had placed it there. Only Nyx and Todd had access to her quarters besides herself. The former was for professional reasons, the latter for personal. Marienne closed the heavy curtains over her windows. In rare moments of fondness, she told Todd he was like the brother she had often wished for as a child. Perhaps if they had been siblings they would have stolen an airship and run away much sooner. Perhaps one of her previous runaway attempts would have been successful. But at times he could irritate her like a brother, too. Such as delivering gifts from a certain French pirate captain.

She studied the dress carefully, rubbing the cream-colored fabric between her fingers. Satin, with the unmistakable shimmer of luma running through it. The sleeves, which would drape scandalously off her shoulders, were rich indigo velvet, puffed slightly with scarlet ribbons set at intervals. It mimicked some of her favorite designs from the past, with a modern sheath cut to the dress body. Marienne smiled despite herself. Robert knew her well. She picked up the envelope and broke the gold wax seal.

Mad Marienne, it began. She appreciated that Robert addressed her as such. He was one of the few people who knew her full name, but when she became captain of the *Vincenzo*, she requested that he never use or divulge her surname. He had always respected that.

If you must change circuits, I know I can't stop you. If this is our last Revel together, let's make it one to remember. —Robert

Marienne glanced at her wardrobe, inside of which waited the gold damask dress she had planned on wearing to the Revel. She had purchased it because the rich gold fabric made her feel as if she was clothed in luma. But Robert, as usual, had outdone everyone else and gotten her true starlight to wrap herself in tonight.

An ache settled in her chest at the last line of the note. She didn't want this to be her last Revel. She didn't want to think of Robert in only memories. A little part of her suggested that she invite him to come with her, sail the world together, but she dismissed it. She knew he would say yes, and she refused to settle down with someone. It had destroyed her mother, and nearly destroyed her. Besides, it would be too dangerous for both of them. Aligning himself with her would make him a target for Prescott, and two ships were easier to spot than one.

She shook her head, sending her curls flying. *Enough of these thoughts.* If she didn't hurry, she would be later than was fashionable, and if she timed it right she would get a clear view of Robert's expression when he saw her wearing her dress. She was determined to enjoy this night, no matter what the future brought.

CHAPTER 19

Katherine breathed a sigh of relief as she made it out of the engine room without accidentally brushing up against any of the machinery. This was the one time she actually cared if she got grease on her clothes, and she would hate for Robert's expert stitching to snag on a loose screw or protruding gear. She stepped out into the golden evening light to see that most of the crew had already made their way down to the beach. Nyx waved to her from the lift, and held open the gate for Katherine to join her

"You look nice!" Nyx said.

"You think so?" Katherine smoothed the over-skirt self-consciously. It was an entirely unique style, and she worried what others may think.

"I wouldn't say it if I didn't mean it," the first mate assured her. "It suits you. Robert's work, right? I thought so," she said when Katherine nodded. "He has a way of knowing just how to flatter someone. He helped me choose what colors look best on me. Not that I care."

Nyx wore large boots, tight trousers, a blood red blouse, and gloves that ended at her knuckles. Over her shoulders and chest, elaborately forged armor of crimson and gold flashed in the dying light of the sun, and a similarly designed plate of armor draped across her hips. A dark hooded cape hung from her shoulders. Her hair remained in its usual spiky tail set high on her head. Katherine found it comforting that Nyx was also dressed unconventionally, but really the armor was the only thing different from her usual outfits.

The lift stopped, and Nyx hopped out. Katherine followed at a slower pace, her steps growing sluggish as she approached the beach. *It's different*, she tried to tell herself. *I'm not a maid. I'm not serving anyone. There are no expectations.*

The sun bathed everything in a rosy light as it sank beneath the waves. Bonfires already dotted the beach, each with four or five driftwood logs placed around them. Tables of food were gathered at the top of a large, flat rock a safe distance away from the surf, and already a long line formed as people waited to claim their portion. Katherine's stomach growled and she hoped that perhaps she would find Robert near the food.

As she drew closer, Katherine caught several gazes turning towards her. Strangers she didn't know from other ships began to whisper to each other. The women all wore corsets and bustles in the popular rust and copper tones. She stopped in her tracks. *It's different,* she told herself as her heart pounded. *They're admiring Robert's work. It's not the same. I didn't do anything wrong!* But her arms crossed over her chest and her fingers began to pinch. *This was a mistake.* She turned back towards the *Vincenzo*.

"Katherine! You've arrived!" Cutting through the crowd like an airship through a cloud, Robert approached her with open arms, a genuinely pleased expression on his face. He stopped an arm's length away to inspect her. "I see you chose the skirt rather than the trousers."

"I thought it was what you would have wanted," she admitted. Her fingers stopped, but her arms stayed across her chest.

"Next time, I want you to choose what you want," he said in a gently stern tone. "I made something extra. May I?" He procured a bow made of the same black and white striped fabric as her vest.

She turned around and let him fasten the bow in her hair. "I feel out of place," she admitted.

"You are a peacock among songbirds." His voice was smooth as he turned her back around and began walking towards the dinner line.

"I don't think I do your work justice." She glanced around at the eyes still trained on her.

"Nothing is fashionable without confidence. The only reason trends are fashionable is because the small-minded are confident that everyone else is wearing the same thing. And if you don't feel like you have confidence, then pretend you do! Now, chin up, shoulders back. Walk with purpose. Be proud of your feathers!"

Katherine took a deep breath and tried to follow his advice. She stood up straighter. She thought of Marienne, who faced every situation head on with a steely glare and a mad grin. Katherine couldn't muster that, but she managed to walk to the food tables without pinching her arms.

The dishes set out for them to use were mismatched, whatever the airships had to offer. Robert picked up a slightly chipped china plate with azure pagodas. Katherine took a tin plate with a dent on one side. She rubbed the dent back and forth with her thumb.

"I'm sorry, but I did ask that you not make me anything for tonight," she said at last.

Robert spooned some pilaf onto his plate. "I was commissioned. I'm being paid for that dress. That being said, I did modify the design once I learned that you were opposed to the idea. And," he pointed the spoon at her, "you had the choice to wear trousers."

She frowned as she took some mashed potatoes. She probably would have felt even more out of place in trousers. She wasn't Nyx.

Robert's voice was soft as he said, "You've had your time as a maid, *ma petite Cendrillon*. Now it's time for your ball."

She stared at her plate. "I don't want to go to the ball," she whispered.

"But where else are you to meet the prince?" He smiled.

Katherine followed his gaze to see Todd standing just beyond the buffet line, already holding a plate of food in his free hand. His wide brown eyes were fixed firmly on her, and he let out a breathless "wow."

She immediately looked back down to her plate, suddenly feeling like she had taken too much food. What would he think if she dropped it? Her heart jumped into her throat as she heard him approach.

"You look beautiful," he said once he was standing behind her.

She didn't know what to say, so she said nothing. He acted as though nothing had happened between them, as if he hadn't avoided her for the past two days. Mr. Castle's voice hissed in her mind: *You hold on to the littlest things. Why can't you move on? Everyone else has.*

"Would you like me to save you a spot by the fire?" Todd asked.

Katherine shook her head. "I'm sorry. I'm going back to the *Vincenzo* to eat."

"May I join you there?"

She shrugged. She didn't know which was worse: to have Todd there, or to be alone. But she didn't want to be at the Revel anymore. *I'm sorry, Robert. I did the best I could.*

CHAPTER 20

$\mathcal{M}$arienne timed her entrance just right. The sun had nearly disappeared over the horizon, washing everything in a rose-gold glow that made her dress shine brilliantly. Robert was walking away from the buffet with his full plate of food when he saw her and stopped short. As always, his face was an open book, and now displayed his breathless admiration. She smirked in self-satisfaction, which turned to a snort as Robert started towards her only to run into James, spilling his drink.

"*Zut! Pardonnez-moi.*" Robert glanced at James' waistcoat and, satisfied that he hadn't spilled on it, nodded. "No harm done."

"No harm done? That was only the finest whiskey!" James gestured with the now empty glass.

"Ah, so the one I brought."

James grumbled as he left to refill his glass. Marienne shook her head in amusement, and partially to shake her thick curls.

"*Vous êtes très magnifique,*" Robert breathed as he turned to her.

"But of course. Why should you expect any less?"

"What do you think of it?" he asked, his gaze traveling the length of the dress. She couldn't be entirely certain that he was checking the fit, but she didn't mind if he admired her figure.

She looked down at the cream-colored satin, shimmering in the evening light and reflecting the glow from the bonfires. "I think it suits me rather well, don't you?"

But when she looked at Robert again, his open expression had turned to a new page, one forlorn and heartbroken. *Don't think about that*, she thought to herself as much as to him. *Don't think about how this may be the last time we see each other.*

"Would you like me to save a seat for you by the fire, while you get your food?" he asked in a subdued tone.

He always asked. Some years she said no, when she felt dangerously close to being attracted to him. But if this was their last Revel, she felt an obligation to be honest with herself. She wanted to spend every moment with him, to stretch out this last celebration together as long as they could.

But she could not be honest with him. "Oh, why not? I'm in a generous mood."

She watched him stride down the beach, even with his shoulders hunched with sorrow he was so very handsome. If she ever allowed herself to tell him how she really felt, she knew that her life would be tethered to his. She would not allow herself to give in to the very thing she had run away from. And now, with Prescott determined to find her, more than ever she could not bring herself to involve Robert.

After tonight, she must forget him.

Nyx strutted down the beach, spirits high. Her stomach comfortably full of delicious pork that had roasted all day in the open air, it was time for some entertainment. Music infused the evening with lilting melodies and rhythms that invited everyone to move in time, but Nyx didn't want to dance. She wanted to fight!

Meandering between bonfires, the flickering flames making the uneven sand somewhat difficult to navigate, she scanned for a sparring partner. Clyde was busy telling some of Robert's crew about one of their latest escapes from an Aerocorps ship, while Beth and Rose interjected with corrections to his more exaggerated details. James walked by and Nyx almost stopped him to ask if he wanted to spar, but stopped when she heard him grumble under his breath about there not being enough liquor. She shook her head and continued; James was grumpy without at least a little drink in him, and sloppy when he indulged too much. She wanted a real fight.

She spotted Landreau sitting by a fire, not engaging in the conversations around him, just finishing the tender, greasy cut of pork on his plate. She bared her teeth in an excited grin and called out his name.

"No thanks," he said without turning around.

Nyx frowned. "Aw, come on! I've got so much energy, I need to move!" She bounced slightly in the soft sand.

"Then run laps around the island, or swim." He gestured towards the dark water gently lapping the shore. "But I'm not about to spend tonight getting beaten up by you again."

"It's only ever bruises," she said, rolling her eyes. "I never hurt you that bad!"

"You wouldn't know how much it hurts because I never land a hit on you!" At last he turned around to look at her. His expression was unyielding. "I refuse your challenge. Now, go find someone else."

"No one else will!" she complained. The agitation in her muscles increased and she shifted her weight from foot to foot.

"James has some new recruits," Landreau suggested, pointing towards a bonfire at the edge of the shore. Nyx followed his gaze, noticing how a small cluster of people huddled close together, yet apart from the rest of the celebrants, their fire one last small pool of light against the encroaching dusk. "*Dieu pardonne moi*, but they likely don't know any better than to spar with you."

"Thanks Landreau! We will spar at some point before we leave!" she promised as she jogged away. He groaned, and she laughed as her feet sank into the soft sand, her muscles straining delightfully in the shifting terrain. She ventured further from the bright, warm concentration of bonfires that illuminated much of the beach towards the one on the edge that sputtered weakly in comparison. The half-dozen men who sat around the small flames that were quickly dwindling into coals were strangers to her, but that wasn't surprising. James' crew tended to have a high turnover rate. She slowed as she approached them, and their muttered conversation ceased before she reached the edge of the fire's glow.

"Hey! I'm Nyx, first mate on the *Vincenzo*. I heard you're new on James's crew."

They stared at her, expressions ranging from wary to distrustful to annoyed. An awkwardly long silence passed, in which Nyx was acutely aware of the sound of the fire popping, the waves lapping, and the distant music.

They clearly didn't want to engage, but her pent-up energy begged for an outlet, so she tried again. "And you are…?"

"Andrew," the one in the middle said, his tone short and terse. None of the others offered to introduce themselves.

"Well, Andrew, I don't know if you've been told, but it's a bit of a tradition during the Revel to set up a friendly sparring pit where anyone can practice combat moves," she fibbed. "You want in?"

He stared at her coldly with pale gray eyes that chilled her. "We have no need to fight, we're lightning chasers."

One of the other men—a large, burly figure that Nyx particularly wanted to skirmish with—leaned over and said not quietly enough, "Are you sure? It could be good practice for—"

"Shut up!" Andrew hissed. He again turned his cold gray eyes towards Nyx. "Our answer is no."

"Fine." She shrugged to hide her disappointment. She couldn't pinpoint why, but she really wanted to punch Andrew. Perhaps she would ask James about him later. "If you change your mind, you can come find me." She jogged off again in search of anyone else who would indulge her.

Todd watched Katherine as they ate their food. She hadn't spoken to him at all, and their plates were nearly empty. She looked at him and opened her mouth, as if she were going to say something, but then returned to her meal. He frowned at his plate. Was it the dress? Did she really hate it after all?

She put her plate on the bench next to her and looked out over the railing of the deck at the stars. Drawing in a deep, shaking breath, she finally spoke. "Please tell me what I need to change."

"What?"

She crossed her arms, fists clenched tight. "I'm sorry. I'm not good at knowing what I've done wrong. It would save a lot of trouble if you just told me."

"Wrong?" he repeated, eyebrows drawing close together. Confusion and alarm swirled in his stomach. "Katherine, you've done nothing wrong."

Her fingers twitched. "Then why have you been avoiding me?"

A jolt of electricity ran through Todd, leaving cold dread behind. With a groan, he buried his head in his hands. "I am so, so sorry, Katherine! I didn't mean to—I mean, not entirely. I..." He glanced at her and saw her confused expression. Straightening with a sigh, he started again. "I commissioned that dress."

She looked down at it. "Oh. I thought Robert was just being nice."

Todd shook his head, then tugged on his curls. "This was before I knew you hated dresses, although I should have guessed. I should have known! And then I almost spoiled the surprise yesterday, so between helping Robert and trying not to spill the secret, I..." *I hurt you, when I should have known better.* "I'm sorry. I just wanted to help you be happy. I guess I did it wrong."

"You want to help me be happy?" she asked, her large hazel eyes staring at him. "Being with you makes me happy. You don't have to get me anything special."

Something warm bloomed in his chest at her words, but he found them difficult to believe. Nobody had wanted him around before unless he could help them in some way. Even Marienne, his closest friend, had only taken him on board because she needed his help to fly the *Vincenzo*.

"Especially," she continued, "a dress I didn't ask for."

"You really don't like formal wear, do you?" He struggled to keep the amusement out of his voice.

"I don't like formal events," she said quietly, staring down at her hands. "Parties, fancy dinners, any of it." She looked like she wanted to say more, but stopped herself.

"Then what do you like to do to celebrate?"

She smiled shyly. "I like to dance. But I'm not good at it, so I don't."

"Would you like to dance now?" Perhaps this would make her happy. But he wasn't going to make the same mistake twice—he would ask first to be sure. "I won't even watch, if you don't want me to," he assured her. He would have liked to see her dance, but this was about her and what she wanted.

Her large eyes were hopeful, but hesitant. "There's no music."

"I can fix that. Do you want me to?"

She nodded, and Todd rushed down to the radio control room as fast as he could. He switched the radio to receive external transmissions, then dialed in to a station that played upbeat, syncopated ragtime music. He routed the transmission to the speakers on the deck, hearing the strains of music drift faintly down the hallway. He made his way back to the deck, uncertain about whether Katherine would want him there or not. She hadn't said.

When he reached the deck, she was already flouncing ungracefully around, almost in time with the music. She paused when she saw him, and he was afraid she would be upset. But she grinned and waved him over.

"Thank you!" she said breathlessly before resuming her childish dance.

Todd moved back to the bench, unable to keep a smile off of his own face. She seemed almost as happy as when she was fixing machines. He had once loved to dance, too, and now longed to dance with her. He felt it as an acute ache where his leg used to be.

CHAPTER 21

Marienne bit delicately into a strawberry, the sweet juice on her tongue curling her lips into a smile. Still grinning with relish, she tossed the stem into the fire and watched it shrivel and blacken. Somewhere in the semi-darkness outside the firelight, a band had started to play a slow, intimate ballad. She hummed along.

Robert stood and offered his hand. "May I have this dance?"

She stared at him, considering the offer. She wanted to accept, but feared that if she did she would never want to let go. "I am not currently in a dancing mood," she said, her gaze drifting to the inky lapping surf, unable to face the disappointment in his eyes. "Perhaps later."

He bowed graciously and sat beside her, the flickering firelight dancing across his troubled face. Marienne held in a sigh. She almost wished she could take back the words, but she wouldn't. She must keep her resolve... and her distance.

"I'm not trying to tell you what to do," he said.

She forced a laugh. "You can't."

"I know. Which is why I don't try."

"But you are trying to convince me to stay in the South Atlantic circuit," she whispered. "Gifts, dances, flattery. I can't be so easily swayed."

"I do those things because you are very dear to me." He turned to her and put a hand on her shoulder.

She shrugged it off. "Every man who has given me gifts, dances, and flattery has only sought to control me. My own father sold me to be shackled to a deplorable man, all in order to increase his already extravagant wealth. Both he and Prescott treated me as a prisoner in my own home. A bird in a gilded cage."

Robert nodded. "The day I met you, I wanted so desperately to help you escape. It tore me up that I failed."

"*I* failed," she sneered. "My escapes always were and always have been my own responsibility." *No one to blame but myself. No one to let down but myself.*

"But you made it," he reminded her. "At last you escaped."

"For now," she muttered. She straightened and shook her curls. "Enough talk of the past. It is gone and there is nothing more we can do about it." *And no more talk of the future. I can't afford to change my course.* "For tonight, let's celebrate the freedom we enjoy among the stars!"

"Couldn't have made a better toast myself!" James entered the ring of firelight, looking more alert than Marienne had expected. He grinned and held a bottle out to her.

Marienne did not think, although she had a brief flash in her mind of her drunkenly agreeing to stay with Robert. She must keep her wits about her. She snatched the bottle out of James' grip and tossed it into the fire with such force that it broke open. The flames roared for a moment before returning to their previous gentle crackle.

"Are you mad, woman?" James shouted.

A wicked grin stole across Marienne's face, which, when combined with the shifting shadows, lent her an unsettling visage. "That is my preferred title." She regained her composure and said, "The evening was getting dull. I wanted to liven things up a bit."

"So you toss the only drink I've been able to hold on to for more than five minutes into the flames?" he complained.

"I'll replace it," she responded airily to cover up her chagrin. He had not been handing her the bottle after all.

James grumbled, "Don't bother." He turned his back and stalked out into the darkness.

Robert studied her with an amused smile while she pretended not to notice. "That was quite the dazzling spectacle. Am I really such boring company?"

"The conversation was getting too personal," she admitted.

"I don't mind."

She opened her mouth to say "I mind," but the words wouldn't come. They hovered at the back of her mouth, weighing down her tongue. The strange desire to continue talking bubbled inside her, but those words refused to budge.

"Where will you go after this?" Robert asked. He leaned back and looked up at the stars, pinpricks of luma hanging in the sky.

"I have business in Paris that I must attend to, but after that I have to leave Europe." She kept her gaze on the fire. "It's a risk going back even for that, but I promised a client before…" She closed her eyes. Why was she telling him this? What was it about the fire and Robert that made her want to tell him everything she felt?

"I'll be in the Mediterranean," he said. "I think I'll go to Italy. You could stop by, if you'd like."

"I can't."

He sat up straight. "But of course you can. We'll have two ships between us, and mine has more cannons than yours. My crew is experienced in fighting Luma Baron ships. We would happily defend you!"

"I don't want you to defend me!" Her catlike green eyes glared at him.

"You would rather run away? You would rather never see each other again?"

She frowned. No, she didn't want that. But what choice did she have?

"If this really is the last chance we have," he said quietly, "please. Will you dance with me?"

Marienne searched his aquamarine eyes. She knew he wouldn't

give up, and her resolve felt as fragile as sea foam. She had already made too many allowances tonight, she couldn't afford another. "No."

He sighed. "I don't understand you, Mad Marienne."

She stared into the fire as he turned on his heel and walked down the beach. "It's easier that way," she whispered. The words fell heavy and dead into the cold darkness between them.

"OF COURSE, Marienne had to be polite to the dock master while we were there, but the moment we lifted off we all laughed about it. To this day we can't mention docking in Glasgow without joking about the toupee that Nikolai mistook for an autorat." Todd laughed at the memory.

Katherine had exhausted herself dancing and sat on the bench next to him. She shook her head. "I just wish someone had told me about his habit of getting into trouble. I thought Marienne was going to maroon me for sure!"

"It's almost a rite of passage at this point," Todd shrugged. "You're not a part of the crew until you've been the victim of some Nikolai mischief. At least the worst of it was some lost liquor, and not an angry dock master!"

She smiled, looking down. "Oh, I suppose we should return these dishes." She picked up her tin plate, dirty with grease and crumbs.

Todd reached down for his own plate, but before he could stand, Katherine took it from him. When she turned, however, she tripped over his crutch and fell to the rough deck. Her plate clattered and rolled away from her, spilling the rest of its contents, but Todd's ceramic plate shattered to pieces.

"Katherine!" He picked up his crutch and knelt down next to her. "Are you okay? Are you hurt?"

She trembled, and her hair covered her face so that he couldn't see it. *What can I do to help?* he wondered frantically. *What should I do?*

She did not respond for a long time. He placed a hand on her shoulder, but she flinched away, so he removed it. At last she said in a tremulous whisper, "I'm sorry." She rose and ran below deck.

Todd struggled to follow. By the time he reached the engine room, the heavy metal door was already closed. He leaned against it, but could only hear the rhythmic mechanical thrum of the engine.

"Katherine?" he called through the door. "Please let me in."

No answer.

Resting his forehead against the warm metal, Todd closed his eyes. What had turned the sweet evening so bitter? "I only want to help," he said, his voice softer. "Let me in. Please."

After a few minutes of hearing only his heartbeat and the engine, Todd turned and hobbled back up to the deck. He replayed the last few moments in his mind, wondering if there was something he had done to upset Katherine. When he reached the deck, he saw Marienne picking up the broken ceramic pieces and placing them on the tin plate.

"Do you know what happened here?" she asked as he approached.

He nodded. "Katherine fell. She's... locked herself in the engine room. I don't know what to do!"

"Give her space for now," Marienne said. She stood and handed Todd the tin plate with the shards of ceramic on it. "She'll come to you when she's ready."

Todd sighed. "I hope you're right."

"Of course I am. Now, if you'll excuse me, I'm retiring for the night."

He bade her goodnight as she went to her quarters. Before he could even reach the lift, muffled piano music drifted from behind her door. "So," he mused, "You had a bad night too."

CHAPTER 22

DECEMBER 22, 1904

Marienne stood at the railing of the *Vincenzo*, watching as James loaded canisters of lightning carefully onto the lift. He managed to fit about a dozen cylindrical canisters onto the platform before stepping onto it himself. The canisters looked deceptively benign, the only indication of the volatile contents inside was a jagged symbol stamped into the leather on one side. As the lift ascended, Marienne watched with bated breath as the canisters shuddered and knocked softly against one another, the leather hardly making a sound while James attempted to hold them all as still as possible. The handful of crew members he had left below with the rest of the lightning shipment also watched their captain travel higher, higher, their expressions filled with anxious anticipation.

Marienne, on the other hand, kept her face strictly neutral.

When James safely reached the top and the gate of the lift creaked open with squeaky hinges, Marienne breathed a soft sigh of relief.

"As exciting as that is, I admit I prefer when we dock properly," James said with a crooked grin. "Much easier transfer of goods."

"I appreciate your willingness to improvise," Marienne said in a smooth tone as she helped unload the lift so that it could return to the ground for another load.

James shrugged as he stepped onto the deck, carrying one of the cannisters. "For the most part they're perfectly safe, but once in a while you'll get a faulty rubber seal. You just don't want to find out the hard way."

Marienne nodded solemnly. "Excuse me a moment while I retrieve your payment." She left James to finish unloading the lightning, the squeak of pulleys groaning behind her as he lowered the lift for the next load.

Nikolai whirred as she entered her quarters, lifting his head from under his wing.

"Yes, another shipment of lightning," Marienne responded absently as she opened the safe and counted bills inside. "The real question is how do I tell James that we'll be changing circuits?" She sighed. It was very likely that she would need to find a new lightning supplier—one who wouldn't mind selling to an illegal harvester. Knowing James had been a stroke of luck, one made possible through Robert.

She slammed the safe door shut and spun the dial forcefully. Nikolai clicked in reprimand, but Marienne fixed him with a steely glare. By the time she left her quarters, she had composed herself, and strode across the deck purposefully towards the lift. Nyx and Katherine had joined James in unloading the second set of lightning canisters and placing them onto a cart to take down to the hold.

"Loose lightning would likely only short-circuit the mechanisms," Katherine was explaining. "We could still manually operate the lift."

"Or you could repair the controls," Nyx offered.

Katherine frowned. "Maybe." She and Nyx walked below deck, the canisters snug and unmoving in the cart.

Marienne handed the stack of money to James. "Here you are."

"Much obliged," he said as he tucked the money into the inside pocket of his jacket.

"At least someone on this island takes actual money," she muttered to herself.

James chuckled knowingly. "He did it again, huh? Boy doesn't know the meaning of the word 'profit.'" He sighed and shook his head.

"And others seem too fixated on it." He glanced over the railing as the lift lowered for the last few canisters.

Marienne followed where he looked. Most of the men working on the ground she recognized, but one glanced up at her, his steely gaze sending a shiver down her spine even at that distance. "New recruit?"

James nodded.

"Oh, that Andrew fellow?" Nyx asked as she and Katherine returned. "Yeah, watch out for him. He gives me the creeps."

"He's too ambitious," James agreed. "But he came so highly recommended, that I signed him on for a year. If I kick him off, the severance pay would make for a hard month. Not to mention he's got a few friends on board who would likely follow, leaving me short handed." He shrugged. "So, I just have to endure it for another nine months. Perhaps by then he'll have saved enough money to buy his own airship like he's always talking about."

The last load of lightning reached the deck and the four of them made short work of loading the canisters onto the cart, which Katherine took down to the hold.

"Your new recruit seems to be adjusting well," James noted.

Marienne nodded, watching Katherine disappear down the ramp that led to the belly of the ship. "I think her joining was a very good thing, for everyone involved."

"Especially Todd." He grinned lopsidedly again.

She hummed thoughtfully. Before last night she would have agreed, but this morning he had been sullen and despondent, holed up in the radio room.

Nyx's voice cut into her thoughts. "With your permission, Captain, once Katherine's done putting away the lightning, I'd like to take her down to the beach for some target practice."

"Permission granted," Marienne said as Katherine walked back out onto the deck, looking as lost in thought as Marienne had just been.

Nyx grinned. "Come on, Katherine! We're going to teach you how to shoot a gun!"

Katherine stopped in her tracks, large hazel eyes wide. "I don't... think I would be very good at that." Her fingers twitched lightly.

"It's a good skill to learn," Marienne encouraged. "Go with Nyx." When Katherine still hesitated, Marienne added calmly, "That's a direct order from your captain."

Katherine sighed, and with a resigned, "Yes, Captain," followed Nyx down the rope ladder.

James waved at his crew to return to *Mjolnir's Child*. "We'll be taking off this afternoon," he told Marienne. "I assume you'll be taking your usual circuit?"

A lump caught in Marienne's throat. "That may change."

James looked at her curiously. "Something happen?"

"I feel it is necessary for a change to be made," she said simply.

He shrugged. "You don't want to tell me, fine. But you know where I'll be, if you need me. Let me know when you need a new shipment and where, and we'll see if we can make it work." Leaning against the railing, he gazed out across the jungle treetops. "I assume you've told Robert about your plans. How'd he take it?"

"Don't you have an airship to prepare for launch?" she said fiercely.

"Yeah, I do," he said, pushing off of the railing and walking towards the rope ladder. Just before he stepped off the deck, he said, "Radio me if you need more lightning. Good luck, wherever you go."

KATHERINE AIMED the pistol carefully at the wooden post planted firmly in the sand.

"Good grip," Nyx coached. "Cock back the hammer, aim, and pull the trigger when you're ready."

Katherine took a deep breath, but her hands were far from steady. Her fingers twitched, and she accidentally pulled the trigger. The shot deafened her ears as a spray of sand flew up far to the left of her target. "I'm sorry," she sighed, clicking the safety back on and handing the gun back to Nyx.

"For what? You had excellent form."

"I missed."

Nyx looked at the offered weapon, confused. "You're going to give up after one failed attempt?"

"I'm just not good at it," Katherine shrugged, looking down at the sand.

"Yet."

Her downcast gaze snapped up to Nyx, who grinned at her.

"You're not good at it yet," she repeated. "It's something my sensei taught me—the man who taught me martial arts," she clarified, seeing Katherine's confusion. "Most combat comes easily to me, but I really struggled to learn this one move. Every time I said I couldn't do it, he added the 'yet.'" She looked at the scar in the sand left from Katherine's bullet.

"I assume you're telling me this because you didn't give up," Katherine said. She still held the gun, but when she looked at it she felt unsure.

"I'll show you!" Nyx said eagerly. "Landreau!" she called to where he sat fishing. "I need your help with something!"

Landreau trotted over. "*Oui*? What can I do for you?"

"I'm showing Katherine a judo move."

"Not again," he groaned.

"We're on sand, so you'll be fine," she assured him. "Now, come try to grab my left arm."

Resigned, he obliged. Nyx ducked under his grip, grabbed his leg, and deftly flipped him over her shoulder. He hit the sandy ground with a *thump* that knocked the wind out of him.

"Are you okay?" Katherine squeaked.

"I will be in a moment," he gasped. "I'm used to it. Honestly, I'm surprised it took this long."

"Only because you wouldn't fight me last night," Nyx said. "But I can demonstrate some more to make up for lost time."

"*Non*, that's okay," he said quickly as he stood and shakily made his way back to his fishing.

"So," Nyx turned back to Katherine. "Ready to try again?"

Katherine frowned. "You wanted to learn that move. I'm not sure I want to know how to shoot."

A somber look settled on Nyx's face. "It may not be a matter of what you want at this point. You've chosen to stay on the *Vincenzo*. As sky pirates, we sometimes find ourselves clashing with the law, or luma barons, or other pirates. They aren't all as friendly as Robert."

Katherine shivered. "How often?"

"Depends on where we are and how recently we got a haul. But when it happens, I want you prepared. You're part of the crew, so it's your responsibility to help defend the airship."

Katherine nodded, but her hands shook worse than before. She clicked off the safety and aimed for the target, but the bullet flew past it and into the water.

A moment later, a dead fish bobbed to the surface.

"Hey, you caught a fish!" Todd said cheerfully, suddenly appearing behind them. "Better than Landreau's done all day!"

Katherine yelped in surprise and dropped the gun. She did not look at either Todd or Nyx as she apologized and hurried away, arms crossed over her chest.

Nyx glared at Todd. "What did you do?"

He watched Katherine leave, a concerned frown creasing his face. "I wish I knew."

CHAPTER 23

DECEMBER 23, 1904

*R*obert hunched over his sewing machine, hemming a sturdy trouser cuff. Katherine's wardrobe was almost complete. He felt the seconds tick away with each pump of the foot pedal, an inexorable finality marching closer with each stitch. The moment he finished the last article of clothing, Marienne would fly away and out of his life.

He wanted to delay that moment as long as possible, but not enough to purposefully sabotage his commission. Katherine didn't deserve that. So he continued, trimming the thread on the finished trouser cuff and moving to the next one. It pained him that the sewing he loved so much brought him closer and closer to heartbreak.

Robert had not seen Marienne since he left her at the Revel. That night had replayed over and over in his mind in the two days since. He had tried his hardest to convince Marienne not to leave the circuit, but it wasn't enough. He didn't understand her logic, but it didn't matter. She had made up her mind, and no force of man or nature could change it.

Except perhaps one. The thought had nagged at him the whole time he sewed, like a stubborn piece of lint that he couldn't remove. Robert loved Marienne—he had known that for a long time. Everyone around him knew it. He had never said it aloud, though. Perhaps if he did…

What would happen then? A frail, childish hope rose unbidden inside him that she would decide to stay, go with him to the Mediterranean, that they would live happily together. Perhaps even admit her love for him in return.

Robert snipped the thread and set the trousers aside, starting now on a blouse. Plain white linen, at Katherine's request. Easy to work in, lightweight to keep her cool in the heat of the engine room. Practical.

Practicality had never been Robert's strong suit. Embellishments and flamboyance were his style. Marienne, on the other hand, was direct, no-nonsense. She tolerated him, indulged him, but loved him? Robert shook his head as he replaced the brown thread in his sewing machine with white.

No, much more likely she would laugh, or purse her lips, and still bid him farewell, leaving him more hurt than before.

And how could he be so selfish, asking her to stay with him like a petulant child refusing to give up a beloved toy? Marienne had already endured too many years captive to men who demanded that she give up her desires because they loved her. He would be no different than Prescott, treating her as a possession.

No, there was nothing to be done. Robert sighed as he pressed the pedal down again, easing the white fabric past the needle. He would simply have to accept a new hole in his heart, a missing piece larger than any other. He had to do the impossible: let Marienne go.

CHAPTER 24

DECEMBER 24, 1904

Katherine leaned against the railing, gazing at the island as if she intended to commit every leaf on every tree to memory. She had only been here a few days, and yet she wished she could stay longer. It seemed a place where the rest of the world held no importance. Everyone else had left once the effects of the Revel wore off, but the *Vincenzo* and the *Madness* had stayed until Katherine's wardrobe was completed.

"I'm sorry to keep you here," she said to Nyx, who stood behind her, practicing with a curved sword.

"You've apologized before and I've told you before that we're happy for a couple extra days of vacation," the first mate said, slightly out of breath. "If you apologize again, I'll assign you extra training."

Katherine frowned, but her face brightened as she saw Robert and Landreau approach the airship, arms full of brown-wrapped parcels. She lowered the lift for them, admiring how convenient it was to help bring on small loads, especially in situations when the ship couldn't fully dock and extend its gangplank. She wondered why it wasn't a standard design as the two men reached the deck.

"Delivery for you," Landreau said as he stepped out of the lift.

"Thank you," Katherine said, accepting the parcels from Landreau.

Nyx sheathed her sword and went to take the bundles from Robert, but Marienne beat her to it.

"I see you have completed your commission," Marienne said, a frigid formality clipping her words short. "Once I find a suitable item that matches your request I will make arrangements so that you receive it."

"If you can't come find me in Italy, I can be patient for the next time we meet." Robert looked so sad when he said it. "For now... *au revoir.*"

Marienne nodded and turned on her heel, walking across the deck towards the stairs that led down to the engine room.

Katherine realized with a start that she wouldn't see Robert for a long time—possibly a year. The revelation hurt more than she had anticipated, and she impulsively set down her parcels and rushed forward to give him a hug. "Thank you," she whispered. "For everything."

"You take care of yourself," he said in a similar tone, hugging her back. When she let go, he smiled, but it did not reach his eyes. "Until next time, *Cendrillon.*"

Picking up her parcels, Katherine trotted to catch up with Marienne below deck. She felt anxious thinking of her captain in the engine room, scrutinizing her work. They walked together in uncomfortable silence down the hallway. As they approached the radio room, Katherine looked down at the floor in front of her until they had passed by.

Once inside the engine room, Marienne pulled out the bed and placed the parcels on top. Katherine followed suit, carefully opening the brown paper of each article of clothing. She would have admired Robert's careful craft if Marienne hadn't lingered, looming beside her.

"As captain, it is my duty to look after the well-being of my crew."

Katherine paused, but did not look at Marienne. Instead, she knelt next to the trunk that sat at the foot of her bed and ran her finger over the brass nameplate, smudging the dust away. The name Nathaniel Higgins had been etched into it. At last she said, "I'm sorry to make you concerned. But I'm fine."

"That's not true." Marienne handed her a few carefully folded blouses, all in neutral colors. In contrast, her jewel-toned eyes were intense. "Robert told me what happened in his workshop. Todd is worried as well."

Katherine opened the trunk. The ensemble from the Revel lay at the bottom. Seeing the luma-infused fabric sent a sharp bolt into her chest, and all she could think of was that shattered dinner plate on the deck. *I always mess up.* She shut her eyes and pinched her arms.

A hand gently touched her shoulder. "It's alright to feel hurt. It's alright to need help."

Marienne's tone was soft, but Katherine broke under the force of her words. Through the tears that spilled out of her eyes and dripped down her cheeks, she croaked, "I'm sorry, I don't understand. You're so kind to me. You and Todd and Robert and Nyx are all so kind to me. I don't deserve it. I'm not good at anything. I lost Nikolai."

The captain shook her head. "I should have warned you about his bad habits. I am to be blamed for that, not you. And you found him." She smiled and handed Katherine a handkerchief. "That's not only important, but impressive! You found him after he flew away."

"I'm sorry," she sniffled as she wiped her face. "I shouldn't be crying."

"Never apologize for honest tears. Have you always held such a low opinion of yourself?"

Katherine shrugged. "Growing up, I was always so focused on mechanics and working with my father that I didn't really care about much else. It wasn't until I became a maid that I realized how useless I was."

Marienne began handing Katherine more clothes to place in the trunk. "When I hired you, I saw in your eyes a hunger for escape. I've seen that look in every member of this crew, starting with Todd and myself. I have never once regretted your presence here. You have loved this ship as much as I have." She paused and looked around the engine room. "You've done excellent work here."

A warmth bloomed in Katherine's chest that made her want to

smile, but Mr. Castle's voice sneered in her mind: *You don't deserve such praise. Not with all the mistakes you've made.*

"I do not wish to pressure you," Marienne continued, "but Todd has been moping around the ship ever since the Revel. You don't owe him an explanation, but perhaps if you could speak to him he would stop haunting the ship like a forlorn specter?"

Cheeks turning pink, Katherine nodded.

"Thank you." The captain stood. "We fly in ten."

As Marienne left the engine room, Katherine sat on her bed, kicking at the floor and thinking about Todd. He was worried about her. How long had it been since someone had concerned themselves with how she was feeling? With a deep breath to help her gather her thoughts and courage, she walked down the hallway to the radio control room. She knocked on the door, feeling her stomach tighten and pressure build in her chest. When Todd opened the door, she froze.

Marienne must be mistaken. Todd didn't care about her. How could he, after she had broken his plate and run away? After she had avoided him for three days? After she had shown him how useless she was?

Todd wrapped his free arm around her in a tight embrace. His cheek rested against her forehead, and she breathed deep the scent of metal and leather. "I missed you," he whispered

"I'm sorry, I shouldn't have avoided you. Please forgive me?"

"Of course!" He pulled away carefully, using her shoulder to steady himself. He moved back into the radio room and she followed. "What happened at the Revel? When you fell, I thought you were hurt, but you ran away. Let me know how to help you." He settled on top of the counter, and Katherine sat in the leather chair.

She wanted to tell him, but Mr. Castle's voice rang in her mind again. *He will hate you if you tell him your biggest failure. He will never look at you the same, knowing how monstrously you mess things up.* She crossed her arms over her chest, fingers twitching.

But Marienne's words overpowered all other thoughts: *It's alright to feel hurt. It's alright to need help.* Katherine placed her hands in her lap. Perhaps talking to Todd would help.

"Do you know how the British Luma Company handles debts and indentured servants?"

Todd nodded. "They'll take anyone over twelve years old to help pay off debts that people acquire when they borrow luma."

"Parents can choose to sell their children's labor to help pay off their debt. My father would never allow that, even though Ethan volunteered. The debt was a black cloud that lingered in the household like coal dust, but we tried not to talk about it. Ethan was the only one who would ever bring it up. Father would always say he was working on it. Then he died."

"How?"

"He got sick," Katherine shrugged. "So his debt fell to us. Our housekeeper, Mrs. Thorne, tried desperately to adopt us so she would take on the debt, but the process took too long. The collectors took us three weeks after the funeral."

"How old were you?"

"Sixteen. Ethan turned eighteen two weeks after being indentured."

"That should release him!" Todd said vehemently. "Especially with you being indentured, they have no grounds to keep him! He is old enough to pay off the debt on his own!"

Katherine shook her head sadly. "We thought so, too, but they wouldn't accept an extension and they didn't release either of us. We were separated. I have no idea where he went."

Todd reached out and took her hand. "We'll find him, I promise."

She nodded absently. That hadn't been her intention in telling the story, but his reassurance felt nice. "I became a maid at Luma Baron Prescott's summer estate. I had no idea what to expect. I had never been away from home before. That first week the whole household was in a frenzy, preparing for a party. It was Prescott's mother's birthday, and they were coming to celebrate with guests, a large dinner, a ball—everything. I was chosen as one of the servers for the dinner." Her fingers twitched lightly, brushing against Todd's palm.

"The first course was soup. I was supposed to serve a young woman, but to get to her I had to go by Mrs. Prescott's seat. She had a cane that she had placed on the floor. I... tripped over it, and fell. The soup wound up all over Mrs. Prescott. The bowl broke on the floor. Mr. Castle was furious. I apologized and cleaned up what I could while Mrs. Prescott went to change. I could hear everything the guests said about me."

"That's horrible," Todd said, squeezing her hand gently.

"It gets worse," she said in a small voice. "When the guests left, Mr. Castle assembled all the servants together and said that I deserved to be punished for my mistake. I wasn't allowed to eat."

A dark cloud crossed Todd's expression. "For how long?"

"It was supposed to be a full day, but then he caught me sneaking some cheese from the kitchen. He called me a little mouse and extended my sentence. It was extended again when I tripped while carrying some bedding up the stairs. He said I wasn't learning my lesson."

"How long?" Todd repeated earnestly, his brown eyes fixed on her.

Katherine hung her head. "Three days. I learned quickly that I wasn't good at anything except machines, and that the more I followed the rules the less I got into trouble. But I still made mistake after mistake, and Mr. Castle always seemed to find me in time to witness it and punish me. He called me Little Mouse. Even the other maids found fault in everything I did."

Todd shook his head. "No one should have to go through that. I'm so sorry. Please believe me when I say that you're wonderful! At machines and so much else!"

"When I'm with you, I feel like I'm enough." She smiled. "You let me make mistakes, and you don't blame me for them. I feel... happy when we're together."

CHAPTER 25

DECEMBER 26, 1904

The bright morning sun reflected off of the railings of the *Vincenzo* while the crew gathered in the cool shade under the balloon. Katherine glanced at Todd, noticing how he frowned. A twist in her gut tried to convince her that she would be humiliated in front of so many people, but she firmly repeated in her mind, *"that's not true."* Marienne was not like Mr. Castle— if she had a problem with Katherine, she would speak of it in private, not in front of the whole crew.

"Does Marienne usually call everyone together like this?" she asked.

Todd shook his head. "Only on rare occasions. Last time it was because we hadn't collected as much as we usually do, and she let everyone know that she was still paying them the same amount. She took the loss completely on herself, despite everyone's arguments." His frown deepened. "If she's calling an assembly, she's got an announcement, and one that's not up for discussion."

Katherine mirrored his expression and turned to look at Marienne, who emerged from her quarters with a stoic face as she gazed out at the crowd. Nearly all the crew stood before her in anxious anticipation—only Nyx, who stood at the helm, was absent.

"I hope you all had a fine vacation," she began, her voice loud enough to echo across the deck. "Our next stop, as usual, will be Paris to deliver our cargo to our regular customers there. However, after that stop we will no longer use the South Atlantic circuit."

A ripple of murmurs coursed through the crowd. Katherine looked to Todd, whose frown had deepened and he tugged on his curls. "What does that mean?" she asked.

"Each Luma Baron has a set circuit, so that they don't interfere with each other," he explained quickly. "We've been using the South Atlantic— the French circuit."

Marienne held up a hand and the low voices stopped. "I recognize that we have been on this circuit for some years now, and it is familiar. We have established good contacts and worked out a route that is relatively free of interference. However, I'm afraid that it has recently become too dangerous for us to continue here."

"She means it's too close to Prescott," Todd muttered. He added to Katherine, "England uses the North Atlantic circuit. Although we haven't had too many run-ins with them, it's only a matter of time."

Katherine's mind spun wildly like an overworked gear. Ethan had been so close this whole time? And yet, now, Marienne wanted to leave the circuit... to leave him behind. She struggled to hear the captain's next words over the rushing of blood in her ears.

"A fresh start elsewhere may be difficult at first, but I believe that it will also come with great adventure and exciting new opportunities." Marienne grinned, but it looked strained. "I do understand that many of you have various ties in this area, so if you wish to disembark in Paris, I will not stop you."

"What circuit will we fly?" someone far to the left of Katherine asked.

"I have not yet decided," Marienne said. "But it will be far away from Europe. The Americas, perhaps, or even to the East in Asia. Those who disembark risk not knowing where to find us again."

Katherine's heart sank. "What about Ethan?" she blurted. Everyone turned to look at her, and she shrank back from the attention. Todd put a hand on her shoulder. Drawing strength from him, she looked at

Marienne. Was it her imagination, or was there sorrow in those green eyes? "What about the people we leave behind?"

"As I said before," she said calmly, "you are free to leave the *Vincenzo* to be with them. I recall telling you that my crew takes priority, and it's too dangerous here for the *Vincenzo* to stay."

Someone else asked a question, but Katherine didn't hear it. She turned and ran below deck, hot anger rising in her like steam, silent screams building inside her. She heard Todd's unique gait following her and stopped in the hallway so he could catch up.

"You didn't tell me that Marienne was a liar!" she hissed.

He stared at her in shock. "What are you talking about?"

"When I first joined, Marienne said that she would help me find my brother. He's indentured to the British Luma Company."

"The North Atlantic circuit." Understanding dawned on him. "If we leave the South Atlantic circuit, you're afraid that you won't find him."

"America or Asia!" Katherine's voice broke and she leaned heavily against the wall. "That's so far. I may never see him again."

"Remember that I also promised to help you find him," Todd said, taking her hand and gently rubbing the back of it with his thumb. "I'm not going to give up."

She shook her head. "I appreciate it, but if we don't find him soon, we may lose our chance forever. Modern radios don't stretch that far."

Frowning, he asked, "If we don't find him before we leave Paris, would you come with us, or stay?"

Pain built in Katherine's chest at the choice she faced. Either way she was leaving behind someone she loved. "I don't know," she whispered. "I... I need some time to think." She walked away towards the engine room, and Todd did not follow.

He watched her as she left, intense urgency building up inside of him. He needed to find Ethan, and soon, or else he risked losing Katherine forever. But how could he find one man in all the skies?

. . .

"How'd they take it?" Nyx asked as Marienne joined her in the control room.

The captain closed the door behind her with a sigh, then waved Nyx away from the helm, taking over steering her ship for a time. It wasn't something she did often, but she needed the distraction now. "It was as to be expected. I have a very opinionated crew."

"You hired them," Nyx said as she settled into the hammock she had strung up at the back of the control room. "Watch out for that fog bank ahead. We'll hit it in about five minutes."

Marienne nodded understanding. When she had first started flying the *Vincenzo*, fog banks terrified her: the way they enveloped everything so that you could not see the prow from the stern, and concealing all other objects in the sky from view. She also had been concerned about the possibility of lightning. But knowledge had given her courage as she now understood how to read the instruments that extended to either side of the helm, keeping her on course and warning her of obstacles along her way.

"Do you think anyone will leave?" Nyx asked as she sharpened a knife.

"Katherine might. She took the news rather hard."

Nyx frowned. "Didn't think she was one who would care where we went."

"She still has family in the area," Marienne explained, not willing to give details. If Katherine hadn't told Nyx directly about her brother, then it was not the captain's place to inform her. "There's a couple others who might take the opportunity to settle down."

"Clyde has a girl in Paris, and Veronica has been complaining about how the thin air affects her asthma," the first mate reported. "I wouldn't be surprised if they stayed grounded." She glanced at the captain. "Have you decided where we'll go yet?"

Marienne shook her head, her curls tangling. "Some days it feels like nowhere will be far enough. Prescott has never been particularly close with other Luma Barons, but they could still be a resource if he thought it was necessary..." Her voice trailed off as her thoughts burrowed deeper into the issue. She would have to gather some information on his relations with the other Luma Barons of the world. Unfortunately the enterprise had touched every inhabited country and spanned over the wildernesses between civilizations. Was there anywhere left in the world where the sky could be hers?

"How long will we stay in Paris?" Nyx asked, inspecting her knife. Satisfied, she sheathed it.

"Ten days."

"Shorter than usual," she noted.

"I would have liked it to be even shorter," Marienne said, "but Pierre couldn't make it any earlier."

Nyx eased herself out of the hammock and stretched. "I'm going to get some food, do you want any?" When Marienne declined, she put a hand on her captain's shoulder. "You're doing the right thing."

Marienne nodded, but didn't trust herself to speak. Doubt flickered behind her green eyes. *Am I doing the right thing?* she thought as the door closed behind Nyx. *I've spent my whole life running away.* Was it the right thing?

Exhaustion enveloped her as thoroughly as the fog bank she sailed into. To run, to leave everything behind, to cut all ties… how long could she keep it up?

"I'm flying blind."

THE RHYTHMIC THRUM of the engine brought no comfort as Katherine sat at the workbench. Her hands moved automatically, tinkering with spare parts and affixing gears to make a small wind-up toy. It was a simple exercise, one her father had taught her years ago when she was first learning the workings of mechanics. But her mind was far elsewhere.

The *Vincenzo* had become her home—the most that she had ever felt at home since her father had died and she had been separated from Ethan. It wasn't just the airship, either— although she loved the machines that surrounded her, humming lullabies as she fell asleep in the warm engine room. She had a purpose here, an important work. She was valued. Warmth bloomed in her chest as she remembered

Marienne's compliment to her: *You've done excellent work here.* She kept the ship flying.

Flying to unknown places.

Cold anxiety crashed into her as she considered the change in circuits. If she didn't find Ethan soon, her chances of ever seeing him again shrank to nearly zero. If she didn't find him soon... Should she even stay on the *Vincenzo*?

The thought stuck like a bad taste in her mouth, and she lost her grip on a gear. It bounced off the edge of the workbench and rolled away, arcing towards her bed. With a sigh, she stood to retrieve it. More than the ship, more than the work, more than the machines, Katherine had come to love the people here. Although Marienne was unpredictable, she was kind. Nyx was forward, but encouraging. Rose was gentle, but firm.

And Todd...

Katherine picked up the gear and stared at it, not really seeing the small metal piece. As she walked back to the workbench, she struggled to find the words to describe Todd. How did you describe someone who lit up the room just by walking into it? Who had made her feel loved, who had helped her truly feel like herself again? How could she bear to leave him? To leave any of them?

They all had helped Katherine feel welcome after leaving the estate, and now she felt happy. She had a family again.

But what about her real family? The only family she had left?

If she left the *Vincenzo* to find him, where would she go? She had no leads, no idea where in the whole North Atlantic circuit he could be. All she knew was that he was on a luma harvester for the British Luma Company. Would that be enough?

You could always come back to me, Mr. Castle's voice hissed in her mind.

Katherine froze, tools in hand, cold dread filling her body. It was true. If she returned to the estate and legally paid off her debt, she would see Ethan again.

She set her jaw and said aloud, "No. I will not return to the estate. I will never go back to you!" A proud smile spread across her face as she imagined the Mr. Castle in her mind shrinking back at her words. He spoke lies: going back wouldn't solve anything. She would be severely punished, and possibly never pay off her debt. It would be years before she saw Ethan if she went that route—years of torment and torture. And she would not put herself back in that situation.

The little wind up toy was complete. It looked like a rabbit, and when she turned the key, it hopped lightly across the table until it bumped into the rolled-up drafts of blueprints she had set aside. Falling on its side, the little legs still kicked and she picked it up, feeling the ticking mechanisms like a tiny heartbeat against her palm; a small, pale echo of the deep, powerful pounding of the engine behind her.

"I can't do this by myself," she said softly, cupping the little toy in her hands. "No matter what I choose, I can't find him on my own."

Once the toy had wound down, she placed it back on the workbench and walked towards the radio control room.

Todd sprang out of his chair before Katherine could knock on the open door of the radio room. She smiled shyly at him. "I need your help," she admitted.

"With finding Ethan?"

She nodded. "I don't want to leave the *Vincenzo*, but I can't just leave him behind. And I can't find him by myself."

"We'll do everything we can to find out where he is before we leave Paris," Todd said as he sat on the countertop, offering Katherine the leather chair. "I've been thinking about what we can do before we dock again. Airship companies will often reserve a range of radio frequencies for their ships, if they can, so that it's easier to contact them. I would be very surprised if the British Luma Company hasn't."

"How do you know which frequencies are theirs?" Katherine asked. She was grateful that he had already been thinking about a solution. More importantly, he hadn't pushed her for a decision about whether she would stay after Paris.

He shook his head. "I'll ask around to see if anyone knows. But even when I do learn the range of frequencies, I'll need to know which ship Ethan is on before I can start calling around. Luma collectors are secretive and cautious. They won't take random calls from unknown frequencies, and if I called every ship asking for Ethan it would raise some red flags."

She frowned. "Would they be able to trace the call back to us? I've heard that such a machine is in development. I don't want to put the crew in danger."

"No, that kind of technology doesn't exist yet," he assured her. "They'll know our frequency, but I can lie about who we are and they won't be able to find our location."

"Will we be able to learn much while we're in Paris? France isn't on the same circuit."

"When there's an emergency, aerospace law requires any airship dock to take that airship and crew, regardless of political or corporate affiliation. Luma collectors are constantly the targets of sky pirates, and since England is so near to France, I'm sure that British Luma Company airships end up there all the time. We just have to ask the right people the right questions. We'll find him," he assured her. "I know we will."

CHAPTER 26

JANUARY 2, 1905

The radio crackled to life, causing Ethan and Aaron to sit up straight. They weren't due for a check-in for another two days. "Who—"

Ethan cut off Aaron's question with a quick *shush*. The new module attached to the radio whirred as dials spun until at last settling to display the frequency that hailed them. A voice piped through the speaker, tinted with a French accent.

"This is Captain Robert of the *Madness*. Surrender your cargo of luma peacefully and we will not harm you."

Ethan swore under his breath. Sky pirates. He ran a hand through his short brown hair and glanced at Aaron, who looked pale and frightened. This was Aaron's first circuit on the *Egret*; he had never seen a battle before.

And it would be a battle.

"I'll have to report this to my captain," Ethan responded into the radio. He switched the transmission from external to internal, and punched in the code for Captain Murdock's quarters. "Captain?"

"I see them, Ethan," Murdock responded. "They've hailed us, I presume?"

"Yes, sir. They're offering a peaceful transfer."

"There will be none of that, you hear?" Murdock responded sharply. "We defend this luma with everything we've got. Alert the crew. We fight."

The captain's voice cut off with a click. Ethan clenched his jaw, then with a shout of frustration, slammed his fist into the counter in front of him. Aaron jumped.

"Ethan?"

"Every time," Ethan muttered. "*Every time* I think I'm close to paying off my debt, this happens!"

"Not if we beat them, though, right?"

Ethan looked wearily at Aaron. He was younger than Ethan by a couple of years, and his mousy demeanor made him an easy target for the rougher crew members. He would be an easy target for pirates too.

"Stay out of the fight as much as possible," Ethan said grimly. "But don't let the captain catch you being a coward. That's the only way to survive." He turned back to the radio and flipped a switch.

"Attention all crew members." His voice echoed in every room of the luma harvester, reverberating through its metal hull. "Prepare for battle. Repeat: prepare for battle. Estimated time until confrontation: ten minutes."

Ethan turned off the radio and leaned back in his chair, glaring as a dark cloud settled over his face. After a couple of deep breaths that flared his nostrils, he stood and walked to the door. Before exiting, he spoke over his shoulder to Aaron, "Don't forget what I told you. It might save your life."

The halls shifted between semidarkness and a wash of scarlet as an alarm light flashed on and off. Ethan stalked to the dorm, passing rows of bunks until he reached his own. He did not acknowledge any of the other crew members preparing themselves and their weapons solemnly. Anger was the primary emotion he felt—even more than the fear of death. A dry, humorless smile tugged one side of his mouth upward. He hadn't felt that fear in a long time. Not since his first circuit, when he hid in the hull behind the luma barrels at the first sign of fighting.

He had watched, horrified, as two sky pirates entered the hold and knocked down barrel after barrel, spilling the precious luma all over the floor. Using a contraption that looked like a mechanical leech, they ripped open a hole in the side of the ship, while a suction tube stretched out from the attacking airship. As the spilled luma flew out through the hole, Ethan had stood up, but his grip on the gun was too weak, his arms shaking too much. They easily wrested the pistol from him and shot him in the leg. He had fainted from loss of blood before his captain found him.

They should have killed me, he thought. Instead they created a determined enemy. He drew his standard issue pistol out of his trunk and inspected it thoroughly before clipping the holster to his belt. He then did the same with the saber he had bartered for. Once he locked his trunk, he marched back through the pulsating red-lighted halls and emerged onto the deck.

The sun had already set over the horizon. Twilight fast turned to night up here, and soon the lingering light that turned everything a hazy shade of blue would disappear. Even with the deck lamps lit, it would be difficult to tell who was ally and who was enemy. Ethan grit his teeth. Captain Murdock was a fool to command them to fight now.

But it wasn't Murdock's fault, Ethan thought as his attention focused on the fast-approaching airship. He drew his pistol, his grip tight as he read the crimson painted letters on the side of its hull: *Madness*. Fitting for such foolish attackers.

A ripple of uncertainty ran through the crew standing on the deck, but Ethan held his ground, glaring at the men across from him. They sneered back. Tense anticipation crackled in the air like electricity before a storm, each man waiting for another to fire the first shot.

A sharp crack like thunder and chaos flooded the skies.

Ethan couldn't tell who had fired first, but he quickly followed suit, shooting at the closest men until their faces were obscured by thick gun smoke. Long metal platforms extended from the pirate ship, safety railings snapping into place on either side. Ethan looked down the length of the deck and counted four evenly spaced gangplanks bridging the gap between the two vessels. He almost smiled; the gangplanks would bottleneck the pirates, making them easy pickings as they crossed to the *Egret*.

A volley of shots forced Ethan to duck behind the side of the ship. He cursed as the sound of heavy boots rang in his ears. They had already begun crossing under the cover of heavy fire. Steeling himself, he popped up above his protection and took a couple haphazard shots at the first pirate crossing the gangplank. If he could drop this one, the body would create a barrier that would need to be removed before they could continue, buying his crew time.

But he only hit the man's arm before he was forced back down by another round of fire from the enemy airship. They didn't use cannons—they couldn't risk the damage to the precious luma. Although some pirates roamed the skies only for destruction's sake, these were after a profit.

He stuck his head out again to shoot at the man, now only two yards from setting foot on the deck of the *Egret* and fast closing the distance. But as Ethan raised his gun, so did the pirate, aiming the barrel and a glare directly at Ethan. With another curse, Ethan ducked back down, grimacing at the sound of a bullet striking too close to his head. He drew his saber and a deep breath, crouching like a cat ready to pounce, only waiting for the right moment.

Feet appeared. He slashed at the ankles. The pirate cried out and stumbled to the deck. Once they were face to face, Ethan shot him. No time to think about it; more men rushed off the gangplank and swarmed around him.

He locked blades with one and shoved the barrel of his gun in the man's gut, but another pirate grabbed him from behind, an arm winding around his neck. Ethan gagged, feeling his veins pounding in his head as blood tried and failed to reach his heart. His grip on his weapons slackened and the darkness encroaching on his vision had nothing to do with the fading evening light.

A terrible, rattling gurgle sounded in his ear and he gasped as his airway suddenly opened again. He kicked behind him and, at the same time, pulled the trigger of his gun. As the pirate in front of him stumbled backwards, another moved in to take his place. Ethan raised his saber, but before he could bring it down a sharp *crack* and the breeze of a bullet skimmed past his ear. The pirate stumbled back, gripping his shoulder.

Ethan turned to see who had come to his rescue. His heart sank as he saw Aaron flash him a superficial smile. He wanted to protect his friend, to usher him back into the radio room, but there was no time. More pirates spilled onto the deck, and the two found themselves fighting for their lives.

Not only their lives, Ethan thought as he slashed at another pirate, then another. They were defending the company's luma, and were expected to pay for it with their lives, if necessary.

Ethan cut down another pirate and a quick glance revealed that the space immediately around him had been cleared. The cacophony of battle still raged around him: the cymbal crash of sword, the staccato fire of guns, the chorus of battle cries from both sides ringing in his ears until he thought he would never hear anything else. Searching for another target, Ethan spotted two pirates heading below decks. His hazel eyes grew wide. The cargo hold.

"No!" he snarled, rushing to follow them. He would not let them get to the luma. He would not let them steal his debt payment away. He would not let Aaron risk his life just so the luma could be stolen anyway.

It wasn't until he was already below deck and heard a second pair of footsteps that he realized he was being followed. He whirled around, gun raised, to see Aaron. Ethan frowned, but all he said was, "Stay close, and let me do the fighting."

Aaron brought his gun up, keeping it at the ready, but said nothing. Ethan sighed. Aaron would be safer down here with him… at least, he hoped that was true. They stalked down the hall, attempting to be as quiet as possible. The red light no longer flashed, leaving the hallway lit by dim electric lamps. *But it's still brighter than above deck,* Ethan noted. He did not envy those who fought in the growing darkness. Perhaps it was for the best that he and Aaron had come down here—they spent most of their time in the radio control room, and so members of the crew may not recognize their faces. In the encroaching darkness, they could easily become victims to friendly fire. He shuddered at the thought and forced himself to concentrate on what lay ahead.

The door to the hold stood crookedly open, the lock blasted off by a point-blank shot. Ethan gestured to Aaron to get down and stay quiet, then advanced. He pushed the door open, grimacing at the squeak of hinges, but the sound was easily drowned by the clang of metal barrels being thrown to the ground. The luma made no sound as it spilled out of the spigots, but light shone from where it covered the floor, reflecting in sparkles on the ceiling and casting deeper shadows into the corners.

Ethan stuck to these shadows as he led Aaron around the barrels that still stood, keeping a close watch on the two pirates. One made his way to the wall, pulling a familiar contraption off his back. A muscle in Ethan's jaw twitched. He couldn't let them steal the luma. Not again.

Just as he aimed his pistol, Ethan heard a thump and a groan behind him. Whirling around, he found himself face to face with another pirate who raised a crimson blade to Ethan's throat. It took him a moment to realize that it wasn't the metal of the blade that had been forged red, but that it dripped fresh blood. Eyes wide with fear, he looked down to where Aaron slumped, blood fast pouring from his side and seeping between his fingers.

"Aaron!" Ethan gasped. His friend looked up at him through heavy eyelids, his lips twitching as if attempting to smile through the pain, but the creases on his face were etched too deep. Ethan felt something inside him break, and something else emerge as if hatching from an egg. He let loose a cry of agony and lashed out at the pirate with his saber.

But the pirate was faster. He didn't slice into Ethan's throat, as he had expected, instead cutting deep the flesh in his right arm. The pain flared next to his shoulder and he dropped the sword in shock. He wanted nothing more than to place his left hand over the wound, but instead he raised his pistol and pointed it at the pirate.

The pirate knocked the gun out of Ethan's hand with a quick flick of his wrist. Another barrel fell to the floor nearby, illuminating their faces. The pirate's blue eyes widened, and a hand flew to the fancy cravat at his throat.

"Your eyes," he breathed. *"Ils sont familiers.* Katherine?"

The rage that had erupted inside of him did not register the shock he felt at hearing his sister's name. Ethan rushed forward, fists raised, ready to fight with what little he had left.

The pirate side-stepped Ethan's charge, then raised his sword and brought the hilt down hard on Ethan's head. The shine of luma disappeared as his vision went dark.

CHAPTER 27

JANUARY 6, 1905

"I think we should ask Nyx to help us find Ethan."

"Why?" Katherine stared at the speaker in the wall, where Todd's voice crackled through and echoed in the engine room. He still sat in the radio room, which meant that she had time to work on her blueprints without him seeing. In the days since Marienne's announcement, she had thrown herself into her work in an effort to distract herself from the hopelessness she felt whenever she thought about Ethan. She knew Todd would have to know about her project soon, but the drafts weren't quite done yet. She wanted the blueprints to be as final as possible before she brought the idea to him, but she was running out of time. "Will she agree?"

"Of course she will! Nyx has some great contacts, and can get a lot of valuable information. She'll have time between sales, and I know she would do it just to help you."

Katherine added a note to her blueprints: *more room around compressed air tube?* "If you say so. I still have a hard time reading her."

"She can take some time to understand," he agreed.

"Have you gained any new information from your radio calls?" she asked, trying and failing to keep her hopes from rising.

"Not yet," he admitted. "I didn't even get a response from the

Madness, which is unusual. I was hoping to also ask what kind of automaton Robert wants."

"Oh, can I help you choose one?" Dozens of ideas flew through her mind in rapid succession. What kind of automaton would suit Robert best? Where was best to acquire one? The obvious answer was Italy, but could she convince Marienne to dock there if they went East? And could Katherine make any useful modifications to it before they gave it to Robert? A pang coursed through her chest as she remembered that it would likely be a long time before she saw him again.

Todd's laugh filtered through the speaker. "I was hoping you would offer! I have no idea what to look for, and could really use your help."

Katherine opened her mouth to reply, but was interrupted by a high-pitched shriek. She cursed with a volume to rival the scream that filled the engine room as Bert flew down from his post and flapped around Katherine's head. He turned towards the wall, where steam poured from a leak in a pipe, the cloud quickly increasing as she grabbed her tools.

"Bert, return to post! Every time I fix something on this rusty flying heap," she grumbled as she patched the leak, "something else breaks! I'm never going to have time to—"

"Katherine?" Todd stood in the doorway, leaning heavily on his crutch as his chest rose and fell in rapid rhythm. "Are you alright?"

"Just another busted pipe." She knocked the offending part with a wrench. "I swear, one of these days I'm just going to let it break down and crash."

"Poetic, given how you got your position here in the first place," he said with a smile. He sat down at the workbench to catch his breath. Katherine watched him carefully with wide eyes. "What else would you do with your time, if not fix the machines you love so dearly?"

She hesitated. The answer was behind him, sitting openly on the workbench. But was she ready? Would this change things between her and Todd?

She sighed. Worrying about it wasn't going to get her anywhere. She walked over to the worktable and searched through the papers until she found the complete blueprint. Bashfully, she handed it to him. Todd's eyes drifted across the page, tracing each line, taking in the individually labeled parts. She watched his expression as his eyebrows drew together and his brown eyes widened. His lips twitched as he barely whispered the words he read: shock absorbers down by the ankle, hinges to simulate joints where the foot connects to the toes, electrical sensors to attach to the leg.

"It's a prosthetic," she said after a while. Her voice sounded too loud over the hum of the engine. "I want to build it for you. To thank you." She smiled, warmth coloring her cheeks. "What do you think?"

At last he lowered the paper. "I would very much like to kiss you." He blushed. "That is… If you… May I?"

Katherine blinked, caught completely off-guard by his reaction. She hadn't considered her blueprints leading to this. But as a warmth spread throughout her body, she realized that his request wasn't unwelcome. She thought about his kindness, his humor, their endless conversations together, and how she always looked forward to seeing him. He was gentle, understanding. She hadn't told anyone else the extent of what she had endured during the time she was indentured—telling him had been enough. He accepted her, and that was all that mattered. As long as Todd was with her, she would be happy.

"I'm sorry, I shouldn't have said that." He stood to leave.

Katherine responded by standing on her toes and kissing him.

Their lips pressed together with the kind of pressure she used when working on the helium purifier: not too rough, in case too much should happen all at once and damage the delicate balance. As they pulled away, she let out a gentle sigh; a puff of steam escaping from the engine's cooling vents. She wondered if machines ever felt like this. Is that why they must constantly be fed with grease and coal and labor? Because once they taste love all they want is more?

They smiled, bashful and nervous and giddy all at once. Katherine's gaze flitted to the blueprints on the workbench.

"Really, what do you think of it?" She picked up the full sketch. "It has a long way to go. There's so much research in the area of prosthetics that I haven't even considered. It won't be possible without luma. We'll need it here, and here, and here," she pointed to different spots.

"I'm sure if anyone could do it, it's you." He placed his free arm around her shoulders. "I can help you. If we get the radio frequencies of some of the top scientists, I can patch you through and you can talk to them."

"Isn't that less-than-legal?" she asked with a smirk.

"That's the perk of being a sky pirate! Everything we do is shy of the letter of the law." He chuckled. "But, I'll follow the rules on this one. I'd deal with an army of irritating secretaries if it means it will make you happy."

"Will it make you happy?" she asked.

He squeezed her shoulders in a hug. "No one has ever offered to build me anything before. And I find that people are usually too nervous to talk about my leg. Or they assume I'm fine with it because I manage." Bitterness colored his words.

"That's not fair," she remarked. "Just because you can manage doesn't mean you're happy with it. But why haven't you gotten a prosthetic before? You've been with Marienne long enough, surely you've been paid plenty?"

"I have a tendency to buy things for people."

She glanced sidelong at him. "Like dresses they didn't ask for?"

"I didn't know!"

She laughed, then launched into a torrent of words about how she would go about making a mock-up out of scraps around the engine room, and how she would take luma instead of her wages for a few weeks, and where the prosthetic would need to attach to the nerve endings on his thigh. He grimaced at that, dreading the painful process. She laughed again, and thought, *I wish this moment would last forever.*

CHAPTER 28

JANUARY 7, 1905

Ethan blinked slowly. At first, all he could think about was the light directly above him. It was brighter than the usual lights on the ship, but not near as bright as the sun. Then he heard the creak of bedsprings, a moan, and all his senses seemed to activate at once. He echoed the groan as pain settled into his consciousness, weighing on every nerve in his body. He ached all over, but the worst of it concentrated in his right shoulder.

Where the pirate had stabbed him.

His eyes opened wide and he tried to sit up, but the pain forced him down. "Aaron!" he gasped.

"I'm here." Ethan turned to see his friend looking back from the next bed over where he lay with a weary expression on his face, but he still managed to smile. "I'm fine. Just a scratch, really. How about you?"

"I think I'm going to be okay." Ethan tried to smile back, although he had no idea how bad his condition truly was.

"I had hoped to see Portugal under better circumstances," Aaron said, staring at the ceiling.

The bedsprings under his head squealed as Ethan looked up at the ceiling again. "Is that where we are?"

Aaron nodded. "Docked for repairs. To the ship and the people. I'm not surprised you don't remember. You've been feverish for days. We'll be going to Paris next, that will be nice."

"Why Paris?" France had its own luma baron, and disputes between France and England over luma territory had been intense in the past.

"Murdock wants to report that ship that attacked us. The captain was French, remember?"

The pain in his shoulder flared. Ethan sighed. "We need to get you a sword as soon as possible."

"Why?"

"A blade doesn't run out of shots."

Aaron chuckled grimly. "How did you know?"

"Because I only had a couple shots left myself, and I had been using my saber as much as possible." He closed his eyes, trying to ignore the pain. "You shouldn't have come down to the hold with me."

"Don't worry about me," Aaron said. "Worry about the captain."

"What happened to him?" Ethan wasn't terribly concerned if the captain had been injured, just mildly curious.

"Nothing," Aaron assured him. "But he's coming this way."

The blood drained from Ethan's face as he heard heavy footsteps and frantic words in an unfamiliar language. He turned so quickly that the pain in his shoulder flared and he grimaced. Captain Murdock stalked down the rows of beds in the hospital, ignoring the nurses who tried to stop him, his glare concentrated on Ethan. Too late to feign sleep, Ethan steeled himself.

The light above him was blocked by the dark face of his captain.

"Hello, Captain Murdock," he said in as polite a tone as he could manage, trying to keep the pleasantries as light as possible. He did not succeed.

"What could possibly have possessed you to go down to the hold with only Aaron at your side, boy?" he thundered. The nurses tried to quiet him, but he glared at them and they scurried away.

Ethan frowned. "Excuse me, sir, but I was trying to save the luma."

"Then next time, fulfill your duty and finish the job! Don't faint in a pool of your own blood and get someone else stabbed, too. I should have left you there to bleed out if I knew you were going to fail me so miserably." He scratched at his thick, curly beard, still glaring down at Ethan.

"With all due respect, sir," Ethan said through grit teeth, trying for all the world to make his words sound sincere. "There was another pirate we had not initially noticed. He caught us with a surprise attack."

"Bah! What use are you?" Murdock scoffed. He turned and paced. "Most of the luma's gone, and we only have six weeks left of this circuit. Not to mention the delay of docking here for repairs and medical attention." He suddenly whirled around, coming so close that Ethan could count the hairs in his beard. "You're responsible for these losses. You went down alone, trying to play the hero, and you failed. All expenses from this disaster will be added to your debt."

Ethan opened his mouth to protest, but Aaron spoke first. "That's not fair! Ethan has been here long enough, he deserves—"

"One more word from you and I'll split the loss, adding to your debt as well!" Captain Murdock shouted, turning to Aaron for the first time. "Do you wish to put that on your mother?"

Ethan looked at Aaron, sorrow in his hazel eyes. He liked the boy, and couldn't bear to see him stuck on this cursed crew longer than he needed to be. Ethan's own sentence had been extended twice—this would be the third time the captain attributed damages to him, and punished him for it. He wondered when his time of servitude would end.

"I deserve it," Aaron said quietly. He attempted a reassuring smile at Ethan, who stared at him in shock.

The captain grumbled. "Fine then. You both have more debt. And if we don't make our quota for this circuit, that will add to your sentence."

Ethan sighed. "Is there anything else, Captain?"

Murdock stared at him for an uncomfortably long time. "No. I'm going to make a note of your account balance. And if you die of infection, that debt will be passed on to your family, just as your father passed it on to you. You have a sister who is also indentured, don't you?"

Ethan's face darkened and Murdock smirked. He knew just how to get to Ethan. The captain stalked back out of the hospital ward. Ethan leaned onto his pillow with a sigh. He thought that by now he would have paid off his debt, but if he kept getting blamed for the work of pirates, that would never happen. And as much as he hated being on the *Egret*, it was worse knowing that Katherine was still somewhere working for the British Luma Company too.

If only he knew that she was safe and happy, Murdock's threat wouldn't hold such weight. If she had paid off her portion of the debt, perhaps she was free. He hoped that what Murdock had added wouldn't be her responsibility to pay off. If only he could talk to her.

"Why did you take half?" Ethan asked, his voice weary. "That was a lot of luma. It could take you years to pay it off."

"Because you've been here long enough," Aaron responded simply. "I can't stand a bully, and you're my friend. I can't let you take all the blame when I was by your side."

"You get used to it," Ethan muttered. Every crew member he talked to said that their debt had been added to at some point. This was the first time anyone had willingly requested to split the amount. "He mentioned your mother."

Aaron nodded, the bedsprings squealing. "She's still alive, but she wasn't making payments fast enough, so I volunteered to work to help pay off the debt. I hope she's okay back home."

Ethan nodded. "I know the feeling. My sister's working at one of the estates. A maid, I think. I just hope they don't put my debt on her."

"What's her name?"

He smiled at the question. Aaron was a kind boy. Usually when the crew members asked about his sister, it was to rile him up. They weren't too careful with what they said, and he wasn't too careful with where his fists landed when his temper flared. But Aaron's tone was sincere. "Her name is Katherine."

"That's a lovely name. I'll pray for her."

Ethan looked away so that his friend wouldn't see his bitter expression. Aaron still wore a small silver cross—Ethan had noticed it the first day he boarded the *Egret*. Once, Ethan had worn one just like it. He had tossed it from the skies long ago.

But now, hearing Aaron's sweet, honest declaration, something stirred inside him. It wasn't guilt for having given up on God, or a reconciliation with religion. It took Ethan a moment to realize it was gratitude. It had been a long time since anyone had been as kind to him as Aaron was.

Katherine sat on the edge of Todd's seat in the radio control room, her heart pounding in anxious anticipation. He sat on the counter, his leg dangling off the edge and his crutch resting next to him. With an encouraging smile from Todd, she took a deep breath and pressed the external transmission button. Static hissed and filled the room.

"You're sure it's on the right channel?" she asked.

"For the last time, yes," he assured her with an indulging smile. "I double checked before you got here. Don't worry, it'll be like that until he turns on his radio. We're just a little early."

Katherine glanced at the clock on the wall in an effort to distract herself from the radio. She had always admired this clock. Its metal hands circled a glass face, leaving the inner workings and gears visible. She liked to watch the parts move rhythmically to the *tick tock* of the second hand, driving the entire mechanism. But now it only reminded her of the fast approaching appointment. Her heart hammered in her chest to an irregular beat.

"Are you sure he has a personal receiving radio? He might only have a transmitting one, to give lectures," she fretted.

"I talked to his secretary, remember?" Todd laid a hand on her shoulder. "It's going to be fine. He personally said he wanted to speak to you."

The static ceased abruptly and Katherine gasped. She looked to Todd, who nodded encouragingly. Tentatively, she pulled the microphone close to her mouth and said, "Hello?"

"*Bonjour*? Allo? Allo?"

"Hello! Is this Professor De Guignes?" She watched Todd as she spoke, uncertain of the French pronunciation even though she had practiced it beforehand. He flashed a grin and she relaxed.

"Ah, *oui!*" His voice crackled over the radio worse than when she had spoken to Robert.

Todd had told her to expect as much. Although they were heading towards France, it was still over a week away, and the elevation contributed to the quality of the transmission. But the professor was in range, which Katherine found to be a relief.

"Am I correct in assuming that I am speaking to Miss Katherine Whitehall?"

"Yes, you are! Thank you so much for taking the time to speak with me."

"Your friend commended you so highly, I simply had to see for myself the mechanical genius!"

She gave Todd a sidelong glance. "Oh, I'm sure he exaggerated on more than one compliment."

"I hope he was telling the truth about your skill in working on a helium purifier while airborne. That's impressive, young lady! They're temperamental machines, and at such elevations any mistake can turn fatal."

"Do you know much about airship machinery?"

Before he could reply, the radio again erupted in static. Todd hopped off the desk and leaned around Katherine, twisting a knob delicately back and forth. "Just a little… ah! There!"

The noise subsided and De Guignes returned. "Are you there?"

"Yes, just a little technical difficulty," she assured him.

"Well, as I was saying, I am no expert in airship mechanics. I have only picked up some things here and there. As you know, my area of expertise is biomechanics."

"Which is why we've called you!" Katherine readied her notepad, now that they were getting to the subject at hand. "I want to build—"

"A prosthetic leg, yes. Your friend told me. Before we proceed, you should know that biomechanics is still a new field. I've been heralded as an expert—bah! There is so much we still don't know! We've barely scratched the surface! We don't even know the long-term effects of luma, much less why infusing metal and wires with it suddenly allows otherwise inert components to behave like a functional limb. Although we are making long strides in this scientific field, there are some things that can only be discovered with time, and luma is still so new."

Katherine nodded. "But, Professor, you are at the front of this field. Even if there is still so much to discover, you've helped speed that process along with your work. Thank you for being willing to teach me."

"There is another biomechanist, an Italian fellow who specializes in limbs."

"Santelli. We tried contacting him last week, but he wasn't willing to teach a woman." She spat the last words, unable to keep the bitterness out of her voice. She hastily added, "Not that you should consider yourself our second choice."

De Guignes chuckled, a strange sound crackling through the speaker. "There is no shame in seeking out the best first. I am aware of Santelli's archaic views." He sighed. "I don't understand how some people choose to close the door of science to half the world's population. Think of the brilliant minds who are denied the opportunity to pursue knowledge! The discoveries and advances that could be made! Such as your design for a prosthetic leg. Come, tell me your plans. We'll see what I can do for you."

Katherine described her blueprint to him, piece by piece, starting at the top and working downward. He asked questions and gave advice, only occasionally suggesting that the design would work better another way. She wrote down everything he said, filling seven pages in her notebook. De Guignes advised her to test the nerves of the subject, as those closest to the amputation site may be too damaged to function properly, and would necessitate a brace further up the leg to attach to healthy nerves. Todd winced, dreading the inevitable pain of his nerves being pricked and prodded. The professor also suggested different metals to use for pieces of the prosthetic, as the strength and composition of each metal would lend unique properties to the piece. Finally, he mentioned that there was one thing that she would need that had not been included on the blueprint: an identification disk.

"I've heard whispers of those," Katherine admitted.

"Still very experimental, but highly effective. The luma would align itself to your friend's biometric signature, allowing the sensors on his nerves to control the rest of the mechanisms. It's the only way that the prosthetic will function like a real leg."

"That sounds expensive," Katherine frowned.

"Oh, did I not mention? I am happy to supply any materials you may need."

She gasped. "That is too generous!"

"I must admit, my motives are selfish," he added. "I would ask in return that you share your notes with me. Sign each and every one—I won't take credit for your hard work. But I am curious to know how this turns out."

"Thank you, Professor." Words couldn't capture how she felt.

"Your friend tells me you will be in Paris soon."

"A little over a week. We'll stay there for about ten days, perhaps more depending on how our business goes."

"Please come find me at the Sorbonne. That's not much time, but I think we could manage to finish the prosthetic before you leave."

"That would be..." Katherine shook her head. She could not believe the kindness of this stranger, and she struggled to feel as if she deserved it. "Invaluable. Your expertise in helping to fix any problems that might pop up is greatly appreciated."

"We shall keep in touch," he promised. "But for now, it has grown late. *Au revoir.*"

The radio clicked, then returned to static. Todd flipped a switch and the room instead filled with the low hum of the distant engine. Katherine stretched, feeling her back pop, then looked at the clock.

"We've been here for four hours?" she exclaimed, looking accusingly at Todd. "Why didn't you say anything? We've likely missed supper."

"I didn't think I could pull you away unless Bert was screaming," he said with a smile. "I did catch Beth as she was heading towards the kitchen and asked her to save us some food. Did you not notice me leave?"

She shook her head. She had been completely engrossed in her conversation. "I got so much valuable information, though!" Flipping through her notebook, the pages were nearly black with her writing. "Oh, I can't wait! Thank you for this!" She jumped up and embraced him.

"I just want you to do a good job on my leg," he teased. As they walked out of the radio room, however, his grin disappeared.

While watching her talk excitedly with Professor De Guignes, Todd admired the spark in her hazel eyes. But a heaviness draped itself over his shoulders. He still had no idea how to find her brother. She was eagerly making progress on this enormous gift for him, and he hadn't even narrowed down the radio frequency range to find him. How could he hope to call himself her friend—or possibly more—if he couldn't keep his promise?

CHAPTER 30

Todd convinced Katherine to eat supper on the deck. Although the sun had already set, he still insisted that she needed some fresh air and to stretch her legs after her lengthy conversation with Professor De Guignes. After Beth served them baked potatoes with a good-natured scowl, they walked out onto the deck. Marienne leaned against the railing, scanning the skies in earnest.

"Is something wrong?" Katherine asked.

"Have you eaten?" Marienne did not tear her gaze away from the sky. The moon reflected in her cat-like green eyes.

"Just starting," Todd reported, holding up his plate.

"Eat quickly, then Katherine, get down to the engine room. It could happen at any moment, and though I don't expect trouble for the engine, it's always good to be prepared."

"Trouble?" Katherine frowned.

Marienne turned to them, a mad grin splitting her face. "What fun would our jobs be without any trouble now and again?"

"Are you certain it's tonight?" Todd asked, concerned.

The captain nodded. "The almanac isn't wrong. I've set aside some containers specifically for tonight's luma." A spark of excitement lit up her eyes more than the lamps on the deck.

"What's happening?" Katherine asked.

"You eat, I'll talk," Todd insisted, sitting down on a bench. "I can eat later. I'm not much use during harvesting."

"There's never been engine trouble during a harvest before," she noted. "What's different this time?"

He looked pointedly at her plate until she rolled her eyes and took a bite. Only then did he continue. "A couple years back, Marienne heard a rumor that luma harvesters never collect during a lunar eclipse. After some… covert investigation, she discovered that the rumors were true." He smiled and added, "That's a story for another time. What we never learned is why. She's been looking for an opportunity to harvest luma during a lunar eclipse ever since. I guess tonight's the night," he sighed.

"You don't seem as excited about it as she is," Katherine observed before taking another bite.

"When we were in England, right before taking you on, Marienne was asking around about these rumors. One man said he had heard a story from his brother in Newfoundland. An airship crashed there, and the locals rushed to help put out the fire and rescue any people and cargo they could. Once the fire was out and the smoke cleared, they saw the red and yellow stripes of Luma Baron Suvari, the Ottoman Luma Baron."

"But that's leagues out of his circuit!"

He nodded. "That's exactly what the locals thought. It was their first time seeing the colors of Luma Baron Suvari in person, but one of them was the head of luma distribution in the area, and so he knew all the stripes by heart. They realized now that, in all the time they had been putting out the fire, they hadn't heard anyone on board. No screams for help, and no bodies around the crash site. Once the wreckage was cool enough, the fire brigade went inside. What they found shocked them to their core."

Katherine stared at him, hanging on his every word, her next bite of potato frozen halfway to her mouth. Todd nudged her elbow to remind her to keep eating. As much as he enjoyed telling the story, she still needed to go to the engine room.

"Not a soul was left on board. No bodies, no indication of where the crew had gone. But, curiously, inside the hold the barrels were untouched by the fire. When the fire brigade examined them, they discovered they were luma barrels, all labeled with the same date of collection. When they reported it to the distributor, he went ghostly pale and ordered everyone to stay away from the wreckage. That date on the barrels had been the night of a lunar eclipse. He radioed for some officials from the mainland to come and dispose of the barrels properly. No one knows why the Ottoman ship was so far from its circuit, or what happened to the crew."

Katherine shivered. "Spooky. But possibly just a local legend?"

"That's what Marienne believes," he said with a shrug. "But I find legends more often than not have some truth to them. We've run into a lot of warnings in this pursuit, but Marienne is convinced they're just hiding something. Nothing will stop her when she's set her mind to it."

"Like that time she tried increasing how much lightning we used," Nyx said, pausing before walking below deck. "It took months for my eyebrows to grow back!"

"I didn't mind it when she tried collecting during a meteor shower," Todd said.

"Except when it didn't yield more luma than usual, and then she spent the next week sulking about it. And it's alright for you, sitting in the radio room all day, but I'm at the helm above her quarters!"

"But her piano playing is so nice," Todd retorted, teasing.

"I know, but it means she's sad and then I can't cheer her up!" Nyx complained. "Anyway, it's time to collect. Katherine, to the engine room. Todd, you helping?"

He shook his head. "I want to stay up here. I can't risk getting in the way tonight."

"You're never in the way," Nyx assured him before she walked below deck, Katherine following behind.

The moon had already darkened around one edge, looking as if someone had taken a bite out of it, when Todd joined Marienne at the railing.

"According to the almanac, total eclipse will only last half an hour." She stroked Nikolai's metal head, his feathers glinting in the moonlight. His deep blue eyes shone with luma, a mirror image of the stars above him. Soon, lightning would pull their light out of the heavens.

"Like Prometheus with fire," Todd muttered.

"What was that?" Marienne turned to him, her cat eyes curious.

"Nothing. Are you going to wait until totality to harvest?"

The captain nodded, again turning her attention to the encroaching eclipse. "We won't know for a certainty that any discrepancies are due to the eclipse unless the entire process is completed during the half hour of totality. If we collected now, there may be some differences, there may not be. I believe any special qualities the luma may have would be diluted at this point in the process." She sighed. "I wish we had more frequent opportunities to experiment."

Perhaps it's a good thing we don't, Todd thought. "What if the luma's completely ordinary?"

Nikolai tilted his head and looked at Todd sharply. Disappointment flickered in Marienne's eyes for only a moment before it was replaced by a glimmer. She smiled too wide, the way she did when she wanted to be called Mad Marienne. "Then the professional luma collectors are superstitious, and we have this night to ourselves. What else could they be avoiding unnecessarily, I wonder?"

Todd smiled and turned his attention back to the darkness swallowing up the bright, silver moon. Marienne always tried to turn situations to her advantage. They had been friends for a long time, but sometimes she still terrified him—especially when she smiled like that. He would follow her into hell if she asked him to, but he wasn't entirely certain if he would do so out of loyalty, respect, or a healthy dose of fear. He did know that she would never ask him to do anything without good reason, and for that alone did he trust her as the last sliver of pale moonlight shifted to an orange tint.

"It's time." Marienne's voice echoed throughout the ship as she spoke into the hand-held portable radio reserved for the captain.

The great bat-like wings spread out from either side of the ship, leather snapping as they unfurled. Todd kept his eyes fixed on the moon as it quickly deepened in shade until the face of it was entirely as crimson as Marienne's hair. She gazed at it too, its deep red light reflecting a striking contrast in her jewel-green eyes. The air crackled with the charge of electricity as it rushed down the metal rods in the wings, causing Nikolai to twitch and ruffle his metal feathers, exposing the hinges underneath. Marienne cooed in a hushed tone, giving him permission to return to his perch. He obeyed, flying through the small open window set high in the heavy wooden door to her quarters, and placed his head under his wing the moment he settled.

Todd rubbed the goosebumps on his arms, knowing the cause wasn't entirely from the charge of electricity below him. The moon had now achieved the color of blood, and just looking at it left a sour taste in his mouth. He instead shifted his attention to the river of light that gathered from the stars and gravitated towards the lightning-charged rods.

"It's red." Surprise colored his tone.

"Fascinating," Marienne mused.

Her eyes remained fixed on the starlight as it condensed into a near-solid glowing vermilion mass. It meandered like a lazy river, and Marienne's lips pursed into a frown. Usually luma was drawn immediately to the lightning rods, swirling into a cone shape as it funneled from the vast sky onto the leather wing. She pressed a button on the radio and said, "Increase lightning levels, the luma's resisting."

Nyx's voice crackled through the speaker, sounding tinned. But Todd still heard the reluctance in her voice as she asked, "How much?"

"As much as you can without hurting anyone. Eyebrows are acceptable losses," she added with a wry smile.

"Yes, captain."

Todd felt the hairs on the back of his neck rise as the crackle of electricity intensified, a sound filling the air like a dozen whips cracking at slightly different intervals. He wondered if the engine was alright, and how Katherine was faring. He hoped she wasn't too bored, but then immediately amended it to a wish that she was safe. One glance at the unnatural moonlight and he gave up wishing altogether, instead focusing on the blood-red luma that at last had reached the airship.

Gleaming particles of light, like grains of sand, floated through the air, washing everything in an unsettling red glow. Marienne reached out, her gloved hand holding a tiny glass vial that caught some luma particles. She flicked the lid closed and latched it, a hasty look at Todd daring him to stop her.

He did not; he knew better. Instead, he observed the luma on either side of the ship with a furrowed brow. "This isn't as much as usual."

Marienne nodded, although her attention seemed fixed on the glowing red light inside the glass vial. She held it delicately in her leather gloves. "It's resisting. I'm sure that's only one of the unique properties of eclipse luma. If this trend continues, we will only collect about one barrel full tonight." She sighed. "I would have liked more. But, I must take what I can get. Beggars can't be choosers and all that."

She reached into her pocket and pulled out a small electric light. Again she glanced at Todd as if expecting him to stop her as she turned on the lamp. He only drew a little closer, pulling on his own leather gloves, just in case he had to intervene. Although luma was most commonly placed into machine parts during production, it could also enhance machinery after assembly, but the effects were lessened. Marienne's pocket light had not been created with any luma, so it was touched with the starlight for the first time as she poured several grains of eclipse luma over it.

Todd gasped as the light shone brighter, throwing the shadows on the deck into stark contrast and competing with the dull red light of the ambient luma still drifting downward. Marienne's eyes grew wider as she stared at the light, the different angles of her face lit up red and white.

"Remarkable," she whispered. "The rumors must be incorrect, perhaps even spread by luma barons themselves. It wouldn't be the first time they lied for a profit margin. Eclipse luma can enhance whatever it infuses by tenfold—after production. This could change the market." She looked at Todd, the light beneath her chin creating unsettling shadows on her eager face. "This could change the world. Todd, we could get rich off of this!"

The light flickered, then extinguished with a little *pop*.

Marienne stared at the light, eyes flashing. She began to pace furiously, rapidly covering the distance between the railing and the shaft of the helium purifier, muttering under her breath. "Why do things always happen like this?" she shouted, and she raised the lamp to throw it to the deck, but paused.

"It seems the eclipse luma has a few more surprises than we expected," Todd said gently, laying a hand on her shoulder.

She brought the lamp to her ear and shook it. A small tinkling sound rang out so softly that Todd wouldn't have heard it if he hadn't been standing next to her.

"It's possible the light couldn't take the intensity of energy the luma was putting out," she said, doubt tainting her voice. She walked to her quarters, leaving Todd alone on the deck.

He leaned against the railing, propping up his crutch next to him. The moon had lightened back to a copper tone, and the lightning had been shut off. Only a few grains of luma still drifted down to the leather wings like flurries of snow. The leather bowed slightly under the weight of the eclipse luma as it trickled down to the hold. Most of the crew, clad in protective leather, would be busily bottling it up into containers. Todd agreed with Marienne's earlier estimation: this amount of luma would likely only fill one barrel.

The captain returned, shaking her head. "I replaced the bulb, but it still wouldn't light. It seems to have simply broken, although I cannot tell the exact cause of failure at this time. I would like Katherine to take a look at it, and see if she can identify the malfunction. I expect to experiment more in the future, but in the meantime…" She pulled out the portable radio. "Nyx, put a special label on that barrel of luma. I don't want it getting mixed up with the others. We will not be selling it in Paris, so set it apart from the rest as much as possible. We keep this luma for ourselves."

"Aye, captain."

Marienne pocketed the radio and held the vial of blood-red luma to the moonlight. Now that the eclipse receded, the half-uncovered moon again shone bright silver. The small glass vial glowed brilliant crimson in her gloved hands as she repeated, "I'm keeping this for myself."

CHAPTER 31

JANUARY 26, 1905

odd's leg bounced anxiously as he sat on Professor De Guignes' workbench. The professor worked with Katherine on the prosthetic, both of them so excited they talked over each other, but Todd worried. They had been at it for eight days now —Marienne would be done with her luma sales tomorrow, and anxiety had permeated the *Vincenzo* like a fog bank. They would leave the South Atlantic circuit in less than two days.

He sighed. Marienne likely still blamed him for Prescott recognizing them, since it was his fault they were in England in the first place. If Katherine didn't finish the prosthetic today, he wasn't sure how to ask Marienne for more time in France.

And they still hadn't found Ethan.

Todd tugged on his curls as he thought again about how to search for him. Whenever Katherine and the Professor hadn't needed him, he had been out trying to gather information about the location of various British Luma Company airships. He had successfully learned the range of radio frequencies the British Luma Company used, but it was impossible to know which one Ethan was on. Nyx had also been hard at work digging for information, but even she couldn't squeeze details out of dead ends. They were running out of time.

A knock at the door shook him out of his thoughts. Before he could slide off the workbench, the professor had opened the door. A student handed him a package. "The disk you made, Professor," he reported.

"Ah, *merci*, Jacques!" The professor beamed as he brought the package back to the workbench.

Katherine eagerly unwrapped it and held it up to the light. The brass disk shimmered with speckles of luma spread across the surface in an irregular pattern. It reminded Todd of a music box disk, but instead of music this one was patterned after his biometric signature. He rubbed his index finger and squirmed at the thought that some of his blood had been forged into the disk.

Put luma into blood and it binds a person to their word, he thought. *Put blood into luma and it binds luma to a person.*

"There!" Katherine exclaimed as she placed the disk into its slot just below the knee joint. "It's done!"

Todd frowned skeptically. The wires and gears were still exposed, leaving them vulnerable to damage. "You sure?"

"We'll add the plating shortly," De Guignes explained. "We would like you to try it in this state so that if there are any further adjustments to be made, we can see them clearly."

With a nod, Todd untied the knot in his trouser leg. He rolled up the fabric so that the stump of his leg was visible. He didn't really like to look at it when he could help it. The scarring was a painful reminder of how useless he had become. Showing others was also difficult, but Katherine and the professor had seen it already as they measured and tested the nerves. He winced at the memory. But Katherine had never expressed pity or even commented on its appearance. Her interest was solely on building the prosthetic, for which he was grateful.

Todd slipped on the protective sock, and then buckled the sensor-studded leather belts across his lower thigh. Katherine helped him ease the prosthetic into place and connect the sensors to the leg. Todd cried out at the shock of pain that coursed through his leg—but, he realized, it went through the whole leg.

Amazed, he tested moving the prosthetic foot. Slowly at first, then faster as it obeyed. He laughed and slid off the workbench, gently placing his new foot on the floor. He felt it. He could feel the pressure of standing on the ground. He leaned to his right, keeping weight on that leg out of habit, but his crutch remained leaning against the workbench. Cautiously, he took a step forward. The leg felt stiff and responded slowly, and he stumbled. Katherine immediately steadied him.

"The foot's responding alright," he reported. "But walking is slower than it should be."

She bent down to inspect the complicated machinery inside. "Take a step."

He obeyed. She carefully watched how the components moved. "I think I see the problem," she said as she straightened. "You can remove just the leg. Keep the sensors on, this shouldn't take long." She took the prosthetic from him and turned back to the professor. "We need to rearrange some things around the compressed air tube. It needs more room than we thought."

As they set to work, Todd couldn't stop smiling and staring at Katherine. She worked diligently, her brown hair tied up in a ponytail and grease streaking her cheeks. She wore her favorite denim coveralls—how did Robert manage to make them so flattering? But most importantly, she was smiling. She was happy.

Watching her work for the past week, Todd had noticed Katherine thrived in this environment. The first day she had dropped a wrench, but she picked it up without even an apology. He hadn't seen her pinch her arms since the Revel. The prosthetic leg was an incredible gift she made for him, but he was just as excited to see her healing.

She was still concerned for her brother, of course, and often at the end of the day when she left the Professor's workshop she would dissolve into anxiety over finding him until she fell asleep from exhaustion. But here, while working on her project, it was like nothing else existed.

"You are truly a master at this!" Professor De Guignes praised, not for the first time. "*Vraiment*, if you ever wanted to leave that airship of yours, you would have a job here assisting me in my work. Teaching takes up time that I would rather devote to experimentation, and if I had you to help me the work would go five times faster!"

Katherine paused in her work, blushing, and looked over to Todd.

He could see it in her eyes. *Ethan.* If she stayed here, she would have a better chance of finding him. A cold lump formed in Todd's throat, but he tried to keep his features neutral. It had to be her choice; he couldn't keep her with him if she didn't want to be.

She turned back to the Professor. "That is an incredible offer, but one I'm going to have to think about some more. We're scheduled to leave the day after tomorrow, so that doesn't give me much time to come to a decision."

"Ah, *pardon*, I understand. But the offer stands whenever you are willing to take it."

She smiled gratefully and returned to her work. After a minute, Katherine set aside a small gear that she had pulled from the inner workings of the prosthetic. "That should be more efficient. Here, try this again."

Todd obeyed, grimacing at the shock of the attaching nerves. This time when he walked, the motion was smooth. He nodded. "Feels good."

She beamed, and the professor exclaimed, *"Merveilleux!"* He removed the leg and they started to assemble the bronze protective plating.

Todd picked up the little gear that Katherine had set aside. "You sure you won't need this?" he asked nervously.

She barely glanced at what he held before waving dismissively. "We reworked things so they function smoother now. It no longer has a purpose, and would only get in the way."

A pang struck through his heart. He had heard those words before, back when he had returned home after his amputation. He slipped the gear into his pocket. *You have a place,* he reminded himself. *You made one for yourself.* He tried to hold on to the excitement of his new prosthetic, but the gear—small as it was—weighed heavily in his pocket.

CHAPTER 32

$\mathcal{E}$than stared out the window, cupping his mug of coffee in his hands, unable to keep the slight smile off his face. He breathed in deeply. Although the deep gray clouds threatened rain on the Paris streets, he was glad to be out of the sick bay and inside the warm cafe. Not to mention out from under the stern eye of Captain Murdock.

He took another sip of coffee. The captain had gone to report the pirate attack to the International Luma Distribution Center, but once the paperwork was filled out the crew would return to what was left of their circuit. Ethan suspected they would take off early the next morning. In the meantime, the crew was free to explore Paris with a rare day off. Captain Murdock knew he was not in danger of losing any of his crew to desertion.

With a frown, Ethan unconsciously rubbed the scar just above his knee. No, he could not run away. But he could enjoy this temporary freedom. Turning his attention to the world just outside the window, he glanced through the reflected golden light of the cafe to the gray street. Only a few souls dared venture outside on such a cold day; their breath steamed in clouds as they hurried from place to place.

Ethan wished that Aaron had come to the cafe, but his friend had chosen to stay on the ship. He sighed, firmly turning his mind away from imagining what sort of torture Aaron might face at the hands of the other crew members. The two of them didn't fit in with everyone else, and Ethan found himself more and more grateful for the isolation of the radio room. He didn't understand how the others could move through life so recklessly, and with such a cavalier attitude. Everything Ethan did was carefully planned and calculated—that is, everything except becoming an indentured servant. His grip tightened, turning his knuckles as white as the ceramic mug. He didn't know how much longer he could stand to remain on the *Egret*.

The bell over the door of the cafe rang with a cheerful tinkle as a couple walked in. A man with curly hair and a shining metal leg, and a young woman with shoulder-length brown hair and large hazel eyes who held his hand. Ethan's own hazel eyes grew wide as he watched her smile. Every detail of her slight frame was as he remembered.

"Katherine?" he gasped. He didn't know he had spoken aloud until she turned to look at him.

The confusion in her eyes turned almost immediately to pure joy. "Ethan!" She ran to him and threw her arms around his neck. "Is it really you?"

"I should hope so," he chuckled. "Or you're hugging the wrong person."

She drew back, hands on his shoulders, and studied his face. He noticed that tears had gathered at the corners of her eyes. "I don't understand," she admitted. "How are you here?"

"I should be asking you the same thing!" He grinned. At the moment he didn't care much about what stars aligned to orchestrate their meeting. He was simply happy to see her.

"Todd!" Katherine waved over the man she had entered with. "This is my brother, Ethan. This is my…" she shifted uncomfortably, spots of color appearing on her cheeks. "Todd."

"Pleasure to meet you." Todd held out a hand. He leaned slightly to one side and shuffled his feet, as if he felt off-balance.

"What are you doing here?" Ethan asked. "In Paris, of all places!"

"Among other things, I came to visit Professor Emile De Guignes, who helped me make Todd's prosthetic leg." She beamed with pride as Todd showed off the new prosthetic. "We finished it this morning and came here to celebrate."

"You built this?" His voice was a mixture of disbelief and awe. "You always demanded that Papa teach you as much as possible, but I think you may have surpassed him."

She shrugged. "The professor helped a lot. I wouldn't have been able to do it without him."

"Don't let her fool you," Todd added, lifting his new leg. "She built most of this in a week. She's done the impossible."

"I'm not surprised." Ethan shook his head, then gestured to the table where his coffee grew cold. "Please sit down. I can't wait to hear… everything!"

"If it's alright with both of you, I think I should return to the ship," Todd said. He looked particularly at Katherine, who agreed. Then Todd leaned in close and whispered something in her ear. She flushed and nodded, then he gave her a small peck on the cheek and left.

Katherine sat down across from her brother, who raised an eyebrow. "Do I need to give him the standard older brother speech? Don't hurt my sister and all that?"

Her blush deepened. "No need! Todd's very respectful. Do you want more coffee?"

"If you insist," he shrugged. "Black, please."

As Katherine walked to the counter to order drinks and pastries, her shoulders slumped. Ethan had always liked cream and sugar in his coffee when they were younger. And when he used to tease her about the boys she liked, she could tease him back. She was elated to find him, but now that he was here, what should they talk about? They had both changed over the past two years—how much change would be too much?

She refilled Ethan's order and asked for some tea for herself. While the lady behind the counter made the drinks, Katherine perused the pastries. A smile stole across her face as she spied small, berry-covered tarts off to one side, hiding behind the croissants. She added the tarts to her order, then returned to the table with her treats.

"Look what I found!" she announced excitedly. She placed the tarts on the table and beamed as Ethan's eyes lit up.

"They're just like the ones Mrs. Thorne used to make," he said. He took one and bit into it, the flaky crust crumbling in his hands. It wasn't quite as good as he remembered, but still the sweet filling brought back countless memories of tea time with their housekeeper. In every one of those memories, Katherine was covered in grease, and left too soon to return to their father's workshop.

"You always ate the last one," she accused.

"Only because you ate too slow," he retorted. He washed down the last bite with bitter coffee. "I wonder what's happened to Mrs. Thorne."

Katherine nodded agreement, watching curls of steam rise from her tea. "I hope she found another family to care for, after Papa died."

They both sat in silent contemplation, remembering how valiantly their beloved housekeeper had fought to adopt them. She knew it meant taking on their debts, but Mrs. Thorne couldn't stand to see them indentured. Katherine could still hear her tutting as she bustled around the kitchen, cursing the scoundrels who wanted to take Ethan three weeks before he turned eighteen. Although Ethan had applied for an extension on the payment, he was denied and the two of them were separated.

"I'd like to find her," Katherine muttered into her cup before taking a sip. "Next time I'm in London." The tea hadn't cooled yet and it scalded her tongue and throat.

"How did you get here, anyway?" Ethan asked. He brushed crumbs off the table and leaned forward, intrigue dancing in his hazel eyes.

Katherine delicately replaced her cup on the table, refusing to meet his eyes. "I'm more interested to hear your story first."

He frowned, recognizing her soft tone and avoiding gaze. She had a secret she didn't want to tell. "Fine, but after I'm done it's your turn."

She reluctantly nodded, trying her best to ignore the twist in her gut. As much as Ethan deserved to know the truth, he wouldn't like it.

Ethan talked until his coffee went cold, and then kept talking and drinking cold coffee until the mug was empty. Katherine excused herself twice to refill her tea, and once to refill his mug. She brought back more tarts. He told her about being a radio operator, vented his frustrations about his captain, and described Aaron to her.

"You'd like him," he said. "He's kind and smart, even if he's a little green. He can be naive sometimes," he admitted, "but he always tries to see the best in others. Sometimes he reminds me of you." Ethan looked down and saw his distorted reflection in his coffee cup.

"He sounds nice."

"He is. But tell me about your Todd! I'm sure he's nice, too."

Katherine nodded. "He was very kind to me when I got my job on this airship. That's how I got here," she explained.

"So your servitude has ended?" Ethan asked, his voice hushed. He didn't dare hope, but the thought entered his mind unbidden: she was free. Perhaps soon he could join her— that is, once he had paid for his latest mistake.

"Um… not exactly," she admitted. Her tone had lowered to a whisper and her eyes darted around the cafe. The handful of guests at the other tables chatted with one another, wrapped up in their own conversations. "I may have run away."

The words hit him as forcefully as a physical blow. His eyes and mouth gaped wide, but no words came. He wanted to shout, to scold her, to tell her what terrible hardships he had endured. At last he said, "How long ago?"

"Two months? Perhaps a little more." She shrugged. "It's hard to tell time on an airship, don't you agree?" Katherine watched her brother carefully as he turned to look out the window. A muscle in his jaw bulged. She sighed. He might as well learn the whole truth at once. "Technically the crew I work for is illegally obtaining luma."

He turned to look at her so quickly that his neck made a popping sound. Katherine winced, both from the sound and from the savage look in his eyes.

"You ran away and joined sky pirates?" he hissed, his voice low and seething. "Katherine, do you know what those people have done to me? Every time they attack our ship and steal our hard-earned luma, more time is added to my sentence. I've been injured by them three times—I've only just healed from the last one!" He gestured to his arm, which still throbbed. "So while I'm working to free us of our father's debt, you run away and join sky pirates?!"

His voice rose, and Katherine looked around with wild eyes. She kept her voice low, in an effort to urge him to do the same. "We don't steal any luma!" she assured him. "We have a ship that collects it, same as yours. It's only technically piracy because Luma Barons—"

"But you still sell that luma on the black market, right?" he said, leaning back in his chair. "No distribution center would take luma from an unregistered airship."

Katherine looked down at the last few drops of tea that had collected at the bottom of her cup. "That's true. But they're nice people!" she tried again. "And I'm the mechanic. I'm doing what I love. You could come with us!" She reached out and took his hand, a desperate smile spreading across her face. "We travel all over. I know how much you've always wanted to! You can help us explore, and find the best places to collect luma!"

"No." Ethan pulled his hand out of her grip. He did not meet her eyes as he stood. "I will not tell my captain of your ship and its deplorable occupation because you're my sister. But I cannot join you. And as long as you are employed by those who attack me and keep me in servitude, you are allied with my enemies. I will not speak to you. Not even when my debts are paid." He paused, hesitating before he left. Quietly he added, "Thank you for the tarts."

The bell rang cheerily as he closed the door behind him.

Katherine sat at the table, feeling gutted. Pain ran up and down her arms, and she blinked, realizing that she had been pinching them. How long had she been sitting here? She stood up and walked out of the cafe, into the rain. She had found Ethan, and then lost him again. Possibly forever. And it was all her fault.

TODD SAT in the radio control room, fidgeting with the small gear Katherine had removed from his prosthetic. She had assured him repeatedly that the leg would function perfectly without it, but that only made him feel worse. Every part had to have a place, right?

He sighed and set the gear spinning on its edge. Sometimes that place was a scrap pile. His mother's voice echoed through his memory: *You'll recover much quicker at your cousin's. It would be better for the family if you left as soon as possible.* The gear slowed and fell down with a soft clatter. Todd picked it up again and inspected it.

Somewhere in this vast world there must be some place it could be used. A gear was inherently useful; it just needed to find the right place to fit. Todd had found his place; he was useful. But Ethan had found Katherine without Todd's help. She was so happy, and that made him happy, but what use did she have for an extra gear? He tugged on his curls.

Would she stay in Paris now? Now that she had found Ethan and knew where he would be, would she take Professor De Guignes' offer and stay grounded to be closer to her brother? Would she throw Todd away like a spare gear?

The door behind him swung open, squeaking on old hinges. Todd tucked the gear into his pocket as he swiveled around, finding Katherine in the doorway. Her eyes were wide and unfocused, tears spilling down her cheeks. Red splotches covered her arms where her fingers still pinched and plucked at her skin. He stood and immediately stumbled, tripping over his new prosthetic.

"Todd?" She rushed to his side, snapping into focus.

"Don't worry about me," he assured her. "What's wrong?"

Fresh tears sprang to her eyes as she took a deep breath that shuddered in her chest. "I asked Ethan to come with us. I hadn't been planning on it. I was just so happy to see him, I never wanted to say goodbye again. And the way he described life on a luma collector sounded so awful! But once he learned what we do he... he..." She sniffled and more tears coursed down her face, too many and too quickly for Todd to wipe them away. "He never wants to see me again!"

Todd pulled her into an embrace and let her sob into his shoulder. He rubbed her trembling back and whispered soothing words into her ear. But his mind was far away from the radio room. Ethan had been found, yes, but now he had hurt Katherine. He didn't have to join Marienne's crew—that was his choice. But Todd made a silent vow to himself and to Katherine that he would make Ethan apologize.

Todd held her closer, wishing he could mend it all right now, dry up every tear with just a few words. But soon he would fix everything. He would not be an extra gear.

CHAPTER 33

JANUARY 27, 1905

Marienne strutted up the gangplank to her airship, thanking the stars above that she didn't have to climb the rope ladder. Sometimes she wondered how it would feel to captain a legally registered airship and always anchor at docks, so she could strut up and down the gangplank at will. But no woman had ever commanded a luma harvester. *At least, not legally*, she thought with a curl of her lips. The package in her hand shifted as a chill breeze wound around her, and she held on to it tighter.

"Captain!" Nyx greeted as soon as she stepped on board. "The last of the luma's been sold. Other than the red stuff, of course. We are ready to fly again on your command."

Marienne frowned, full lips pursed. "I see. Good work." She turned and walked to her quarters.

"Do you have a destination in mind?" Nyx asked, jogging slightly to keep up, even though she was taller than the captain. "You need to choose a new circuit."

Marienne paused at the door to her quarters. Following their usual route would be dangerous, now that Prescott knew to look for the *Vincenzo*, but she still hadn't decided where else to go. It had taken months to establish the black market connections needed to sell her luma on the South Atlantic circuit. Could they still make a profit else-where? She did not look at Nyx as she said, "Prepare to leave at dawn. I will give the destination then."

Nyx nodded, and the captain closed the door heavily behind her. Marienne's shoulders slumped as she sighed. She tried to look intimi-dating and mysterious in front of her crew, but only Todd knew her better than Nyx did. She must know something about Marienne was off, like a piano that hasn't been tuned.

Marienne placed the package on the sofa and opened it. The find had been nothing short of miraculous, and she glowed with pride. Nikolai whirred awake as she removed her coat and scarf, and chirruped a greeting to her. She chuckled. "And a good afternoon to you too. Did you have a restful nap?"

He tilted his head curiously at the package on the sofa, and then fixed her with one blue glass eye.

"It's a gift," she explained. His head shot up, luma in his eyes shining bright. "No, not for you," she scolded. "After docking I'm sure there's plenty of autorats for you to chase. Consider that your gift." She turned back to the package. "No, this is for Robert."

Nikolai's metal head dipped down in disappointment, but he whirred his agreement all the same. Marienne lifted the precious item from its box with great care, afraid of breaking something. She laughed at her automaton's confused clicking. "It's a hat!" she exclaimed.

It was indeed a wide-brimmed hat, although it had taken Mari-enne several minutes of examining it from different angles to recog-nize it as such. For every square centimeter, from the top of the crown all the way down to the edges of the brim was covered in shining, delicate feathers. They were beautiful shades of tawny gold and a brown so deep it almost looked black. She couldn't name what bird they came from, except for two large pheasant tail feathers protruding proudly from the wide ribbon band.

"He asked for a hat with feathers," Marienne explained. "When I saw it in the antique shop window, I knew it was perfect." It wasn't practical for air travel by any means, but he had never been a practical man. She wasn't even certain he knew the meaning of the word. She placed the hat back inside its box, suppressing a sigh.

Marienne found herself thinking about Robert and his invitation more and more since the Revel. She hadn't missed him this much since their first meeting, years ago. But back then she had attributed the longing she felt to the way his tales of sailing the skies had awoken her imagination and given her a destination to escape from her discontent. Could it be the permanence of their separation that now kept her thoughts drifting to how he had looked in the golden firelight, the sincerity in his aquamarine eyes, the feeling of his hand on her shoulder as words close to her heart so easily dripped out of her mouth?

And of course there was the dress. Her gaze drifted almost automatically to her wardrobe. The door hung open so that she could watch the luma satin shimmer as the airship sailed through the skies. Some day she hoped to wear it again; she had enjoyed the puffed velvet sleeves and the way it fit close to her curves—although she would never admit as much to Robert. Marienne closed the door of the wardrobe.

Sitting down heavily on her cushioned piano seat, Marienne stared out of the large window at the gray Paris skyline. She had originally chosen the city for its romance, eager at the opportunity to see the seedy underbelly of the place her parents had praised so highly. But now the city held nothing more than a venue to sell her illegal goods. She wanted to be elsewhere. Somewhere the sun shone brightly even during winter.

Italy. The only other place besides England she had vowed never to return to. Why did he have to be in Italy? She detested the country where she had grown up, but that wasn't the only reason she wouldn't return. Her father still supported Prescott, and hoped to officially secure the alliances agreed upon when she had been betrothed. The men her father had at his disposal who used to thwart her attempted escapes as a teenager could still be utilized to keep her grounded if they found her. The risk was too great.

She swiveled around on the seat and lifted the piano lid, exposing the keys. They lined up like little white and black soldiers, standing at attention for her command. She rested her fingers lightly in position, hesitating for only a heartbeat before playing her favorite song. As the melody advanced, she closed her eyes and swayed back and forth to the lilting notes, her fingers flying and dancing of their own accord. The deep bass notes resonated with the counter-melody as the trilling higher notes moved into harmony.

Harmony. Her mother had tried to teach Marienne the importance of moving in harmony with her husband. *Moving together as one ensures little conflict in the home,* she had recited, though the light behind her eyes had long been replaced by a dull darkness. Mother had moved through life with her gaze fixed firmly on the floor. It was for that reason that Marienne fought so fiercely against anything her father— or any man—had wanted her to do.

Counter-melody. That was what Marienne sought. If you moved in harmony with someone, where was the fun, the excitement? Keeping your fingers evenly spaced to play notes at the same intervals for an entire song only resulted in cramps. It was the exquisite blend of two different, sometimes dissonant melodies that made this song her favorite.

Robert was very different from herself. While she demanded her crew pay for luma with their own wages, he had asked for a hat in exchange for an entire wardrobe. She was calculating, defiant, and meticulous. He was impulsive, reckless, and ridiculous. Was that why she wished on every star in the sky that he was sitting beside her right now?

The song ended and Marienne stared at the piano keys, now silent, again waiting for her to make them sing. Was freedom worth leaving those she loved behind?

She knew. Deep in her heart she had always known what she wanted to do, where she wanted to go. Her fingers twitched lightly, as if they wanted to play another song without her. She again placed them into position and began to play. Once that song ended, she played another, then another, continuing deep into the night. The notes rose to join the stars in the velvet black sky. She played after

Nikolai ducked his head and the luma spark in his indigo eyes dimmed. She played until her fingers ached and her eyelids drooped, and then she played one more song.

In the pale predawn mist, Marienne emerged from her quarters. The cold, almost frozen fog drifted lazily in eddies around her as she strutted across the deck to where Nyx stood ready at the helm.

"Where to, Captain?"

Marienne's lips curled into a smile. "Set our course for Italy."

CHAPTER 34

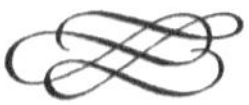

FEBRUARY 1, 1905

*R*obert sat outside, enjoying the warm sun and the sound of the waves lapping on the shore. Syracuse was exactly where he wanted to be right now, lounging outside of a bar with the bottle left on the table for him. In fact, after he had drained the glass he had left it empty and began to drink straight from the bottle. This was how the winter months were meant to be spent, and he wasn't about to let anyone tell him not to enjoy himself. He watched an autorat scurry across the cobblestones and down an alley, sniffing for luma.

Yet he still felt something lacking, like a button missing from his favorite vest. He recalled James, speaking to him outside a bar not unlike this one: "If you chase the horizon, boy, you'll only find yourself further from what you know and drifting in the lonely sky." Perhaps trying to keep Marienne with him was like trying to hold starlight in your hand. She had always desired to be as free as the birds; he had sensed that in her from their first meeting. He had vowed that they would sail the skies together, but now he had missed that chance. He had missed it over and over again.

Robert looked at the bottle in his hand. His eyes felt tired. Actually, all of him felt tired, and the sun still remained stubbornly above the horizon. Six weeks had passed since the Revel, and he needed to accept that Marienne wouldn't join him in the Mediterranean this winter. His mind had already graciously provided him with a lengthy list of reasons why, but top of the list was his greatest blunder.

Why Italy? He kicked himself for it. He knew she abhorred her childhood home. Why would she follow him to the place she despised most of all? It was insensitive of him to demand it of her. Why hadn't he suggested they run away to Spain together instead?

Of course that wasn't the only mistake he had made. He rested his chin on folded arms and traced the curlicue pattern of the wrought iron table with one finger. He wasn't good enough for her. He knew that. Marienne knew it too. Maybe once upon a time she had looked at him with stars reflected in her green eyes and begged him not to go. But that had been when she could still be dragged back home by her parents and James could still rescue him from his own stupidity. That was back when he thought she needed his help to achieve freedom.

Now he would only weigh her down. He was a burden to those around him. Why else would people constantly leave him? He felt each loss acutely, like snags of thread pulling apart the weave of people he loved. But Marienne… this was like shears cutting through the whole bolt.

A metallic screech startled Robert out of his gloom. He looked up, but saw only the blinding sun reflected on metal. Cursing, he rubbed his eyes until he heard a scrape and a soft thump in front of him. Blinking away the bright spots of light in his vision, Robert saw an automaton bird perched on the table. The automaton had knocked over the bottle, which spilled the remainder of its contents on the ground. He hastily picked it up, a string of curses flowing from his mouth.

"Go away!" he shooed the metal bird. Avian automatons were often used as messengers, especially in the artisan country of Italy, but there was no reason he should be receiving a message now. The only person who knew he was here was Landreau, and he would come speak to Robert directly.

The automaton squawked discordantly and began to tug at his sleeve with its beak.

"Hey!" Robert grabbed its head and carefully tried to extract the fabric without damaging it. Before he could, the automaton guided his hand to a paper-wrapped package he had not noticed. Only then did the metal beak open, but the automaton stayed, patiently perched on the table.

Curiosity and bewilderment struggled to the surface of his clouded mind. *A package? From whom?* His fingers fumbled, slow and uncoordinated, as he untied the string, carefully peeled back the wrapping and removed the lid. Inside sat a hat, and next to it, a note. Robert picked up the hat first. It was soft and silky, smooth yet stiff, holding its shape as he eased it out of the box. Two large feathers bobbed from the hat band.

"Feathers…" The whole thing was covered in… "Feathers!" He laughed, placing it on his head. It itched, but he didn't care. "A large hat with lots of feathers!"

How could she have gotten it to him? James wasn't anywhere nearby at this time of year.

Eagerly, selfishly, he snatched the note.

Let's go to Spain. —M

Robert stood, the metal legs of the chair scraping against the stone pavement with a loud complaint that echoed the surprised squawk from the automaton bird. He scanned around the bar, searching the street and alleys for any sign of her. She was here. She was here! Marienne had come to Italy—why? His heart raced as he could only think it was for him.

The automaton bird screeched again, drawing Robert's attention. Only now did he recognize the messenger as Marienne's own Nikolai. "Where is she?" he asked breathlessly. "Take me to her!"

Nikolai took off, flying down the street. Robert ran after him, feet not going nearly fast enough. Marienne had come back! Did this mean that she wouldn't leave him after all? Robert hopped over a small automaton shaped like a pig that was cleaning the streets, eyes fixed on Nikolai as he turned to the east. Or, perhaps, had she only come to give him the hat after all? She hated owing anyone.

But, no, she had made it clear that the Revel was going to be her goodbye. What had changed her mind? He didn't care. Soon he would see her again, and he could ask her in person.

Nikolai darted into an alley and Robert followed, only to find the metal falcon pulling apart an autorat.

"Nikolai, no!" Robert cried. "You're supposed to take me to Marienne!"

The falcon tilted his head, then bobbed it as if chagrined. Robert sighed. "No more distractions," he chastised. "If Marienne's expecting me, you don't want to keep her waiting, do you?" *Unless that's her game —to toy with me.* He shook his head. He wouldn't put it past her. She was a difficult woman to understand.

Nikolai grasped the luma chamber from the autorat firmly in one talon and took off again towards the beach. And, Robert hoped, towards Marienne.

As the cobblestones beneath his boots turned to sand, he scanned the shoreline as Nikolai swooped away.

There she was, looking everything like a dream. The setting sun bathed the beach in a golden glow that seemed to gather and radiate around Marienne, her deep red curls spread around her head like a halo. She wore the dress that Robert had made her, the luma satin sparkling like the sunlight on the ocean behind her. Her lips parted in a smile, and her jewel eyes lit up as she saw him.

MARIENNE ASSUMED another expression as Robert blinked—one more befitting herself as an airship captain and less like a giddy school girl. One eyebrow arched and the curl of her lips turned dry. "You made it after all. And I see you've already put your ridiculous request to good use."

"Ridiculous?" He laughed, but the sound came out breathless. His expression, as usual, was an open book. Elated disbelief registered on every feature, especially in those deep, ocean colored eyes. "This is the most fantastic hat I've ever seen!" He stepped closer and dared to touch her hand.

She did not pull away. Instead she wrapped her fingers around his and whispered, "Let's dance."

"Now? Here?"

She nodded, heart pounding. She hadn't been this nervous since she stole the *Vincenzo*. Robert began to hum and led her in a waltz, their footsteps leaving prints in the sand. Marienne followed his lead perfectly, but her muscles were taut, the movements stiff. As much as she wanted to forget everything around them and savor this moment, she felt conspicuous, exposed. Her father had eyes and ears everywhere, and she had returned to her home country dressed in a scandalously alluring manner to dance to no other music than the humming of an airship captain of ill repute. There was no way this wouldn't reach him. She already had Prescott scouring the skies for her, she couldn't afford to draw the net tighter by involving her father.

"Why did you come here?" Robert asked.

Marienne looked sharply away to hide the shock in her eyes. Instead she focused on the sun sparkling off the lapping waves, the sea birds circling in the air, how the brine-scented breeze played around the hem of her dress. Not only had he stolen the words from her very thoughts, but she didn't have a witty answer at the ready. *I'm slipping.* No, not slipping; she was falling, submerged, drowning in her fear of the men she had run away from for so long. Why did she risk everything she had built by returning to Italy?

The answer was, of course, because she wanted to. That was why she did anything, wasn't it? That had been the ultimate goal, the reason she always ran away. And right now, she wanted to be with Robert. With great effort, she forced herself to look into his eyes, and gasped at their intense sincerity.

Robert loves me.

She had known he did for years. It was why he checked in every so often by radio, why he sought her out at the Revel, why he had made her this dress. But for the first time she understood that this was not the superficial affection of a boy, nor the possessive pride of a powerful figure. His love was adoration, respect, devotion.

He loved her as a man dancing on the beach with the woman he chose.

And she realized that she chose him, too. After all, when she had the whole sky to explore, she had remained in the same circuit as him. When it became too dangerous to stay, she instead had risked everything to be here, in this moment, waltzing in the sand to his humming tune.

For how could she enjoy her freedom if he were not a part of it?

Concern tinted his expression and Marienne realized that she had taken too long to respond to his question. "I missed you," she said simply, the words rushing out of her like surf lapping the shore.

A relieved smile crossed his face, sending a thrill down her spine. He asked in a low voice, "Did you mean what you wrote?"

She turned and looked out over the ocean, unable to keep her features schooled while staring at him. "When we met, you asked me where I would run away to, if I had the chance."

"You said the sky," he responded in a wistful tone.

A smile graced her face, and her eyes looked beyond the horizon to an atmosphere full of possibilities where stars were just beginning to twinkle in the twilight. "But when you pressed further, I admitted that I wanted to see Spain." She turned to him, the mask slipping and her eagerness shining through. "Let's go. Let's go wherever we want, but let's go together."

CHAPTER 35

FEBRUARY 2, 1905

Todd hunched over the radio set, fiddling with the dial, chewing his lip and glancing at the clock. He could spend ten more minutes on his personal mission, but then he had to radio Marienne and let her know Robert wanted to speak to her. That left time for one more radio call.

Discouragement, familiar as walking, settled in his chest as he delicately turned the radio dial another few degrees. The search for Ethan so far had proved fruitless, but he refused to give up. The gear sat heavy in his pocket.

The static on the radio ceased, replaced by a brief, three-note melody, then a male voice said, "State your name and business."

Todd sat up straighter. The voice wasn't Ethan's, but he had reached someone. Perhaps this time they would offer some clue, some assistance. "This is Todd Woolcroft from the International Luma Distribution Center in Paris. I have received a message for Luma Baron Prescott's ship, the *Egret*, but have misplaced my frequency list." It was a weak lie, he knew, but he didn't need them to fully believe him—just enough to get through to Ethan. "Is this the *Egret*?"

"No, this is the *Ibis*." The voice in the speaker took on a wary tone. "The *Egret* is frequency 105.23."

Todd frowned at the list of frequencies in his notebook. He had tried that one already, and it was nothing but static. "Thank you." He shut off the radio and sat back in his chair with a sigh. That was the fifth time he had contacted one of the British Luma airships, only to get a false lead. If too much time passed, there was no telling where Ethan's ship would go. Although the luma-infused radio system had a vast range of communication, there was still a limit. If the ship traveled too far away, Todd would lose his chance to talk Ethan into apologizing to Katherine.

His heart sank. Katherine had thrown herself into her work, studying Nikolai between routine engine maintenance in preparation for creating an automaton for Robert. She insisted that she was fine, but Todd saw the hurt in her hazel eyes. She had begun to apologize excessively again, although he hadn't noticed her pinching. He wanted to talk to her, to comfort her, to convince her that he would make everything alright, but she always excused herself to burrow into her work once more. Perhaps if they stayed here a little longer he could convince her to leave the airship and study the famous automatons of Italy.

Todd switched the radio to internal transmission and punched in the three-digit code to Marienne's quarters. "Captain, are you awake?"

"Barely. Who wants me this early?"

"Robert is asking permission to board."

"Misses me already, does he?" The smile in her voice was audible. "He can board, but have him wait on the deck for me. He can be patient a little longer."

Todd chuckled. "I'll pass the message along."

He again flipped the radio to external transmission and tuned it to the frequency for the *Madness*. After relaying the information to the *Madness*'s radio operator, Henri, Todd turned the radio off. He leaned back and stretched. It was nearly ten in the morning, but he had been up since six trying to find the *Egret*'s frequency. He needed a walk to stretch his leg. *Legs, now*, he reminded himself, laying a hand on his prosthetic.

When Todd reached the deck, he saw Robert leaning against the railing next to Katherine, commenting that her hair had grown since he had last seen her.

"I know," she responded with a smile and a toss of her head. Her hair blew in the breeze, the ends brushing her shoulders. "It's very liberating."

"Do you think you'll ever cut it short again?" Robert asked. "This style is quite becoming on you, but the other was nice, too."

Katherine frowned. "I'm sorry, but I never want to see myself like that again. It would only remind me of… being a maid. I'd like to grow it for the rest of my life, see how long it gets." She looked to the horizon with a smile on her face.

Todd reached out and placed his hand on hers. She hadn't looked this happy for days—what was it about Robert that brightened her outlook in a way that Todd couldn't?

"Katherine," Robert continued in a thoughtful tone, "I saw someone recently who—" He was cut off by the sharp sounds of boots on the deck, demanding attention.

The three turned to see Marienne approaching. Her full lips twitched in amusement as she addressed Robert. "And what is so important that you had to come speak to me in person first thing in the morning?"

He bowed elegantly to hide the amused expression that stole across his face. "*Pardonnez-moi*, Marienne, but we have not yet decided where we will be traveling to."

"That's because someone wasn't offering any suggestions last night. I thought you forfeited your input and we would leave for Spain this afternoon."

"Perhaps we should discuss it at length over breakfast?" he suggested.

"I don't eat breakfast," she said archly. "But I will happily join you for brunch."

"Brunch, then." He grinned and added in a hushed tone, "It's nearly lunchtime anyway."

Katherine giggled, but stifled the sound when Marienne looked at her with an unamused expression. As the two walked down the gangplank to the Italian seaside, Katherine turned and leaned against the railing again. Her gaze floated to where several airships drifted through the sky. They looked so serene, almost lazy, but she knew what intense and sometimes frantic movement of machinery and mechanisms it took to simply keep them aloft, much less moving. The world looked so calm from the outside. If only it was so simple and peaceful.

"What are you thinking about?" Todd asked, leaning on the railing next to her. His eyebrows were drawn together, even though he tried to smile.

She sighed. "I miss Ethan." She felt tears gathering at the corners of her eyes, but blinked them away with a firm determination not to cry. She had wasted too much time already on tears, and it was too beautiful a day—she wouldn't want to spoil it. "The time I had with him was too short, and now I may have lost him forever." Her voice cracked and she looked down at the railing. A curtain of hair fell out from behind her ear, hiding her expression from Todd. Her fingers twitched.

He wanted to comfort her, to assure her that everything would be better soon. But after spending the morning on the radio without coming any closer to success, doubt weighed heavily on his heart. He would not lie to Katherine, and he could not promise that he would find her brother. He realized that his original plan had been impossible. How could he find one person in all the skies?

A drop fell onto the railing just under Katherine's chin. Todd closed his eyes, his whole frame aching with sorrow, his only desire for her to be happy. He gathered her into his arms, and resolved not to give up. As she cried, he determined that no effort would be too great as long as he could see her happy again. He had to keep trying.

CHAPTER 36

Marienne silently noted that Robert fidgeted with his cuff links more than usual as he led her down quaint, sun-filled streets to a small, crowded cafe. She approved of his choice of venue—it was much easier to hide conversations in crowds than in privacy. She observed him carefully as he picked at a fraying corner of the menu, stammered his order to the waitress, and continued to fiddle with his cuff links. She pursed her lips, but he did not look her in the face. As soon as she had ordered and the waitress left, Marienne leaned forward. The table jiggled and vibrated beneath her elbows. A quick glance revealed that his leg bounced uncontrollably against the table, and still his attention was elsewhere.

"Talk."

Robert swallowed hard, his gaze only flickering to her for a moment before turning to a chip in the paint on the wooden table. "I received a radio transmission this morning from an old friend."

"Is it trouble?" She kept her expression carefully controlled, but her heart raced.

"For me only, but it will affect you."

Marienne closed her eyes and pinched the bridge of her nose. Of course it affected her; everything that happened to him from this point on would have an impact on her. Perhaps being together was more of a headache than she was willing to accept. But by that same token, what affected her would now affect him. They needed to talk about Prescott.

"We can't go to Spain."

Her eyes flew open in surprise, and for a moment all she could do was stare at him. At last he brought himself to match her gaze, his sea-blue eyes large and apologetic. She had to admit, a part of her sank in disappointment at his words, but what shocked her was how relieved she felt. There were so many other disasters Robert could have fumbled his way into that a change in travel plans seemed trivial.

But she wasn't ready to admit that she had been worried. "What have you done this time?" she sniffed.

"Well," Robert hummed as he leaned back in his chair and clasped his hands behind his head. "I may have attacked a Spanish government airship. I didn't know they had identified the *Madness*, as it was a rather foggy night. But my friend assures me that I am now wanted in that country." He flashed a bright grin that didn't hide the uncertainty in his eyes.

Marienne sighed as the waitress returned with their food. She breathed in the aromatic steam rising from her coffee and watched carefully as the waitress inched closer to Robert, her shoulder brushing his as she leaned down to deliver his plate of food. He didn't react to the obvious flirtations, and Marienne masked her approving smile with a small bite of her cornetto.

"I understand if you still want to go to Spain," Robert said quietly, staring at his omelet. "I feel terribly selfish saying it is too risky for me to go there when you came to Italy."

"I did take a risk coming here." She carefully chose her words, taking another bite of her brunch to give her time to think. "But I did it to be with you. Now that we are… traveling together, I would never demand that you put yourself at risk merely because I want to go sightseeing."

Robert looked at her, relief and delight painted plainly on his face. "You still want me with you?"

She nodded. "The destination never mattered. I can go anywhere I want at any time." She paused, knowing that wasn't entirely true. "But wherever I go, I want you with me. As long as you're willing to accept the risks. Prescott is still searching for me."

"He won't stop," Robert mused. "Unless we confront him."

Marienne laughed mirthlessly. "Us take on a Luma Baron? That is mad!" She shook her head. "But, I fear that is one thing too mad for me. There's a whole world out there for us to explore. Why would we waste time worrying about him?" She picked up the sprig of mint off her plate and twirled it lazily between her fingers. "Now, as to destinations. Spain has always held my fascination, but it is nothing that cannot be delayed until the political turmoil dies down. Or picks up." She grinned wickedly, then popped the mint into her mouth.

Robert stared at her incredulously. "That's the garnish."

"I know."

"You're not supposed to eat that!"

"It's on my plate," she shrugged. "Why would they put food on my plate if I'm not supposed to eat it?"

"Because it's a garnish!"

A comfortable warmth settled on Marienne's shoulders that had nothing to do with the sunlight. She had come to associate this sensation with the word "home": the *Vincenzo* drifting through a clear sky, sparring with Nyx, reminiscing with Todd, and that campfire at the Revel. This was what she had missed while she was in Paris. Robert's spirit, conversation, humor, presence.

She arched her eyebrows. "If you keep criticizing me, I will fly to Spain and you can follow me or not. But I think we would both much prefer to travel together elsewhere."

"I'm not willing to go somewhere cold this time of year," he said, leaning back.

"Somewhere near the equator, then. That still gives us quite the range. We could go to Africa. I hear Egypt can be quite lovely."

"We've missed the best time of year," Robert noted. "The Nile has already begun to recede. Have you ever been to India?" He leaned forward, a smile spreading across his face. "The jungles are beautiful, and filled with wildlife. The culture is rich and the food exotic. Although," he glanced at her plate, "given your preferences I don't think it will be a problem coaxing you to try new things."

"I have not yet ventured to Asia," Marienne admitted, not even trying to hide the smile that twitched at the corners of her mouth. "India it is, then."

Neither of them mentioned Prescott—there was no need. They could run away together and keep running, perhaps forever.

CHAPTER 37

FEBRUARY 4, 1905

"Have you ever been somewhere so exotic?" Katherine's voice crackled through the speaker in the radio control room.

Todd held his headset to one ear, listening to the static as he moved the dial with as much precision as a thief would a combination lock. "When I was in the AeroCorps there was talk about joining a conflict in Thailand, but I never made it that far." His voice sounded distant and distracted, and he grimaced, but did not cease his task.

"I hadn't even been outside of England until I joined the crew," she continued. "And now I've been to Paris, Italy, an uninhabited island in the Caribbean, and soon India! I wish we could leave today!"

Todd smiled at her chatter. She was in high spirits today, which was nice to hear. "Robert still has some business to finish up," he reminded her. *Good news for me*, he added to himself. The extra days in Italy meant that Todd still had a chance to contact Ethan. Soon they would be out of radio range, and the opportunity would be lost forever. With a renewed sense of urgency, he twisted the dial delicately further, hoping to cut through the static.

"I'm just glad Robert's joining us. I can ask him more about what kind of automaton he wants," she agreed. "I know he wants something to catch autorats, but I—"

The end of her sentence was cut off by a three-note melody. Todd frowned at the sound. They always played right before he connected to a luma collection airship, and each one he had encountered had been different. "Sorry, Katherine, I have a call," he said hastily before shutting off the connection to the engine room. He couldn't let her hear his conversation, even if he hadn't connected to the *Egret*.

"Hello?"

"Have I reached the *Egret*, belonging to Luma Baron Prescott?" Todd tried to keep his voice level and official-sounding, but his heart pounded in his chest.

"It is. Who's asking?"

He ignored the question. "Am I speaking to Ethan Whitehall?"

"No, but I can put him on if you tell me who is calling."

He inhaled deeply, weighing the risk against the reward. "Tell him it's Todd. He knows who I am."

"We aren't supposed to take personal transmissions," the voice on the other end squirmed, hesitating.

"Please, it's urgent," Todd begged, afraid to lose the transmission. "It's about his sister." He tugged on his curls as he awaited the response.

A burst of static that almost sounded like a sigh crackled through the headset. "I'll tell him that you're on the frequency. Please hold."

Todd held his breath and tugged so hard on a curl that a few strands of hair came out, still held firmly between his fingers. After a few heartbeats that felt as vast as a starless night, a new voice came through the headset.

"Why are you calling me, Todd?" The weariness in his voice was evident, even through the crackle of static.

"You need to apologize to Katherine."

"Are you her nanny now?" Ethan sneered.

Todd frowned. "Of course not! But you really hurt her, and I hate seeing her so upset."

"I can't apologize." His tone was flat.

"Is your opinion of us really so low? Do you value your place on that prison ship so much that you wouldn't even consider joining us? Marienne's crew is the most honest I've ever seen, and you would be lucky to have a place on the *Vincenzo*."

"Look," Ethan hissed, "you obviously care about Katherine, but you've made a mistake contacting me. There's more to this than you know. I can't help you!"

"Wait!" Todd shouted, but with a click his headset once again filled with static. His heart sank. He had failed. He pulled the spare gear out of his pocket and threw it across the room.

"Todd?" Katherine's voice crackled through the speaker. She sounded eager. "Are you there?"

He did not answer.

ETHAN LEANED BACK WITH A SIGH, closed his eyes, and rubbed a spot on his temple that had begun to throb. He glanced at the module display, still showcasing the radio frequency that had last transmitted to them. Todd shouldn't have contacted him. And he certainly shouldn't have mentioned the ship and captain's names. It wouldn't be so bad if he could lay low for a few days and avoid Captain Murdock, but at the moment he was watching Ethan like a hawk automaton that has spied an autorat.

The door creaked open to reveal the captain himself standing in the doorway. "Ethan, I hear you're taking personal transmissions. Are you hiding things from me?"

Ethan shot a glance at Aaron, who shook his head. So, the captain was listening to their conversations. "Yes, sir." Ethan had to tell the truth; he had no choice. "It was about my sister, sir."

"What about her? Tell me." He fixed Ethan with a dark stare, and Ethan felt the scar just above his knee begin to pulse.

He took several deep breaths, pushing his hand into his leg, pressing onto the scar, but the pain crept up towards his hip. It burned as it went, and he grit his teeth against the pain and fear. "She's… going to be alright, sir." *Be vague. Answer his questions, but don't give anything away.* It was the only way to protect Katherine. He might not agree with her decisions lately, but she was still his sister. He couldn't have Murdock reporting the pirate ship to the AeroCorps. But could he help it?

One eyebrow crept up Murdock's forehead. "Is she now? I was unaware that she was in any kind of danger. Please, elaborate."

Ethan yelped as the fire in his leg surged into his hip. "She… she was in a bit of trouble when I last had contact with her," he admitted. *Stop prying!* he silently pleaded.

Captain Murdock's voice stayed condescendingly level as he said, "You seem to be in some discomfort, Ethan. Are you alright?" When answered with a glare, he continued. "When did you last have contact with your sister?"

Ethan swallowed hard as the burning sensation crawled up his abdomen. It was searching for his heart, he knew it was. He also knew he could stop it, but doing so would mean betraying Katherine. "I saw her in Paris."

Murdock's eyes gleamed greedily. He had found exactly where to strike at Ethan at last, and went for the kill. "I thought she was supposed to be indentured. Why was she in Paris?"

The pain hovered around his stomach, waiting to see what he would do. If he refused Captain Murdock, he would die. Ethan closed his eyes and offered a silent apology. "She ran away from her servitude." The searing pain subsided, dripping back down to the scar just above his knee. "She now works on an illegal luma-harvester."

Murdock leaned in close, his smile self-satisfied. "What a shame. Did you happen to get the name of the ship? Or its captain?"

Ethan's whole body felt heavy as one last stab of pain in his knee reminded him of the consequences if he lied. "The *Vincenzo,* captained by one Marienne."

Murdock straightened, his expression changing so quickly from shocked to thoughtful that Ethan wondered if he had only imagined the greedy flash in his eyes. "Good job, Ethan Whitehall. Track that frequency. When this is over, you may find yourself rewarded with your freedom."

CHAPTER 38

FEBRUARY 8, 1905

Katherine walked onto the deck, her face and arms immediately peppered with condensation as the airship flew through a thick fog bank. Todd hadn't been in the radio room, and she searched for him among the hazy outlines and muted colors. Anything beyond the deck of the *Vincenzo* was lost to the clouds, though the *Madness* had to be nearby.

She spied Todd leaning against the railing, staring at the pale eddies of mist that formed in the wake of the airship. "How's your leg?" she asked as she joined him.

"Fine," he shrugged. His trousers covered most of it, keeping only the foot exposed, and Katherine had specifically reinforced the weatherproofing on the plating for that purpose. It glistened with the moisture that coated it.

"I wanted to thank you," she said, leaning her head on his shoulder. "Without you, I would blame myself for what happened in Paris. Of course I'm upset about Ethan's choice, but I tried my best. You helped me see that I'm not useless. You helped me see that what happened was Ethan's choice, not my failure."

Todd gripped the railing tightly. "Did you hear any of my external transmission the day before we left Italy?"

Katherine shook her head. How could she have? It was impossible for anyone on the ship to hear an external transmission unless Todd redirected it, or they stood inside the radio room with him.

"I talked to Ethan."

"You did?" she gasped. "Why?"

"I wanted him to apologize for how he treated you." He looked at her with eyes so sorrowful she knew his next words before he uttered them. "I failed."

Katherine felt like someone had overturned her like a box of scrap metal. What she thought she had put away neatly was suddenly before her and jumbled up. She took a deep breath and mustered a smile. "That's alright. You tried, and you did it for me, and that's what matters. Ethan is free to make his own choices, and he's decided to stay away from me." Her voice broke.

Todd gathered her into his arms and gently kissed her forehead. Despite the chilly mist enveloping them, Katherine felt warmth spread through her body.

A sharp whistle and chorus of cheers startled them and they snapped apart. The *Madness* drew up close alongside their ship, close enough for Katherine to see the handful of crew standing on deck— and for them to see her and Todd's affectionate display. Katherine flushed as Robert waved a jaunty salute.

Once the ship matched speed with the *Vincenzo*, a bridge stretched out from the deck with a cacophonous scrape of unoiled metal. Todd moved to where the bridge met the deck of the *Vincenzo* and closed the clamps over the railing, securing it. Guardrails popped up on either side, and Robert crossed. He seemed perfectly comfortable, but Katherine looked down into the swirling misty void, wondering if she could ever bring herself to walk across such a small bridge when a single misstep could mean plummeting an impossible distance.

"You two look cozy," Robert said as he hopped lightly onto the deck.

"That's not what you were wearing this morning," Todd observed, steering the conversation away from himself.

"Indeed it is not," Robert agreed with a grin. Earlier in the day, when he had joined Marienne for brunch once again, he had worn black trousers and a simple white shirt, with a scarf tied around his forehead, the tails of which trailed down to his shoulder. Now the scarf was gone, and he had donned a long, red coat with upturned cuffs. He had changed into brown trousers, and added a cream-colored vest. "What I wore this morning no longer matched my mood, therefore I had to change."

"And us sailing into a fog bank had absolutely nothing to do with it, I'm sure," Todd said with a smirk.

"Absolutely not!" Robert huffed unconvincingly. He looked around, pouting. "I don't understand why it's so cold around Greece today. I came to this part of the world for its reliable warmth and sunshine."

"My humblest apologies for dragging you through the wet and cold fog," Marienne said as she joined them, her tone stiff. She looked Robert up and down, one eyebrow creeping up her forehead, but said nothing about his clothes. "Would you care to warm up in my quarters?"

ONCE THE HEAVY door closed behind her, Marienne sighed.

"What's the matter?" Robert stepped towards her with open arms, but hesitated.

She closed the distance between them, wrapping her arms around his waist and burying her head into his shoulder. He rested his cheek on her curls. Usually when she felt this way, she wanted to play the piano, but now she just wanted to feel him near to her. They couldn't stay like this forever, she knew—neither wrapped up in each other's arms or sailing the skies together. She had to tell him about the imminent danger, the one that threatened to end their short-lived adventures, but for now she just wanted to relish his comfort.

"We're being followed."

"What?" Robert's head snapped up. "But I haven't seen—"

"They're using the fog as cover. Nyx has reported seeing at least one airship, trying to stay just outside of scanner distance, but I suspect there's more. It's been hard with the fog to tell anything about the airships, but…" She looked up at him, green eyes heavy and frightened.

"Prescott," Robert guessed.

"Nyx thinks she saw blue and yellow stripes, but can't be sure." Marienne took a deep breath. "This concerns both of us. Both our ships, and all our crew members. It is up to us to decide what to do."

"We fight, of course!" He pulled away just enough to hold her shoulders at arm's length. "I'm not going to let him take you."

She searched his earnest face. He truly believed that he could protect her, but the memory of the first time he tried to protect her sprang fresh into her mind. She trusted him, of course, but their enemies had always been dangerous and powerful. "We could run," she offered, but the argument was weak, even to her own ears.

Robert shook his head. "If they've caught wind of where you are, it will be difficult to disappear completely. Especially if there's multiple ships following us. Sooner or later we have to stand and fight."

"If anything happened to you…" She tucked a strand of his blond hair behind his ear, her hand lingering. "I don't think I could forgive myself."

"If anything does happen to me, it wouldn't be your fault." His voice was soft, and his face close. "If anyone is to blame for this, it's Prescott. Why does he still chase you?"

"I suppose you're not the only one who I've enchanted." She chuckled mirthlessly.

Robert leaned in and kissed her. Marienne surrendered to the warmth that spread throughout her body, and her hand crept up the back of his neck to tangle in his hair. He pressed her close to him, and she vehemently ignored the imminent threat that screamed at the back of her mind. At this moment, nothing else mattered but every place where their bodies touched.

"Captain?" Nyx's voice crackled through the speaker on the wall.

Marienne peeled herself off of Robert. "Never a moment to ourselves," she muttered breathlessly. She composed herself and pressed the button on the speaker. "Yes?"

Robert's smile disappeared as Nyx said, "They're done playing games. Three ships, gaining fast."

"Alert the crew," Marienne commanded. "We fight."

"I should get back to my ship, and get my crew ready as well," Robert said softly. He stroked Marienne's cheek, then planted one more kiss on her lips. "I will do everything in my power to protect you."

"Thank you," Marienne whispered.

He let himself out of her quarters, and she stared for a moment at the door. Her heart wished desperately that everything was different, but Nyx's voice once again interrupted her thoughts.

This announcement echoed across the deck, pouring out of all the speakers. "Attention all crew members: Prepare for an attack. Team A, you're on cannons. The rest of you, arm yourselves for battle."

Todd trailed behind Katherine as she made her way to the helm of the airship. Nyx spent much of her time at the controls, so she had set her personal belongings underneath a hammock strung up behind the console. Katherine found Nyx rummaging through one trunk, while two others sat with lids opened, weapons spilling onto the floor around her in a mess of leather straps and buckles intermingled with the occasional flash of metal.

"Good, you're here," Nyx said as she straightened. "Todd, I know we haven't had a lot of time to train you on that new leg. Do you think you can manage?"

He nodded. "If it comes to the worst, I can take it off and use it as a club," he joked. Katherine fixed him with a glare and he cleared his throat. "I'll go get my pistol." He turned and left the room, his metal leg knocking against the door with a ringing sound that sent a grimace across Katherine's face.

"Remember what I taught you?" Nyx asked, handing Katherine a handgun.

"Safety off," she recited, pointing to the lever. "Cock, aim, shoot." She held up the gun, bracing her arms the way Nyx had shown her so the gun would stay firmly in her hands. She looked over the top, trying to line it up with some imaginary target.

Nyx nodded. "Good. That's a small one. You've handled it before, remember? Light, not any kick to it, so you shouldn't have too much trouble. And this," she picked a rapier up off the ground, still tucked inside its scabbard with the leather belt swaying as she handed it to Katherine. "I know you've only tried it once, but you need a backup weapon in case you run out of ammo. This is a stabbing sword," she reminded. "No slashing. Speaking of which, I want you to change into the thickest clothing you own. We should have gotten you some armor," she muttered, kneeling down once again and organizing her arsenal. "But at least this way if you get shot or stabbed or whatever maybe it'll keep your innards in."

Katherine's face turned a pale shade of green as the concept of what was about to happen finally settled into her mind as a reality. "Where should I meet you?"

Nyx turned to study Katherine with bright green eyes that flickered in confusion. "You're not meeting me anywhere. You stay in the engine room."

"What? No, I want to come up to the deck to help fight!" she insisted. At least, she did in theory. Her stomach twisted at the thought, but she was determined to protect the *Vincenzo* and its crew. She would protect her freedom.

Nyx stood, looming over Katherine and gripped her shoulders tight. "Listen to me," she hissed. "In a few minutes those airships will catch up to us and they'll stop at nothing to get Marienne. You can bet we'll do everything in our power to prevent that from happening, but we can't do that if someone slips out of the fight and finds their way down to the engine room to sabotage the mechanisms, now can we? I'm not asking, I'm telling you to do an important job. Yours isn't the only life it will spare."

Katherine's knees trembled at the intense expression that almost looked like excitement in Nyx's eyes. She saw a flash that reminded her of Marienne, and she wondered if all sky pirates were just a little mad. She took a deep breath and nodded, ashamed to admit that she was relieved to be out of the main fight.

"Good girl." Nyx slapped her on the shoulder. "Now go. We don't have much time."

Katherine didn't need to be told again. She almost tripped twice on her way to the engine room: once when leaving the navigation control room, and again when she stopped by the radio room. She righted herself and looked inside to find Todd inspecting a gun.

She knocked on the door frame nervously. When he looked up, she saw his expression grow heavier. "Be careful, okay?" she said quietly. She couldn't think of anything else to say.

He put the gun down and rushed to her side, holding her close. She knew he wanted to kiss her, but every heartbeat grew faster and she could not shut out the fear. What if something happened to him in the battle? Katherine pulled away from him.

"Come with me," she begged. "Stay in the engine room. I can't..." Her voice broke. "I can't stand to think of you up there."

Todd shook his head. "I owe Marienne everything. I have to help, especially now that I can."

A sickening realization hit Katherine: Todd could fight now like anyone else because of the leg she had made him. How could she not blame herself if he was harmed?

Todd turned and picked up a portable radio. It was for internal calls only, but also would alert him if an external call came on the main radio. He handed it to her. "If you need backup, just call my name through the intercom. I'll come running, no matter what. I promise."

He grabbed his gun and turned towards the door. His expression was resolute now, but Katherine detected fear in his eyes when he turned to her. "I love you."

She couldn't bring herself to form the words: the weight on her shoulders threatened to crush her lungs. She only whispered as he left the room, "Stay alive."

CHAPTER 40

"What are you doing here?" Marienne hissed as Robert hopped onto the deck of the *Vincenzo*. The bridge from his own airship retracted behind him.

"My crew is perfectly capable of managing a fight without me," he said. As if to prove his point, Landreau's voice drifted through the fog as he barked orders. "I'm staying with you."

Marienne frowned. "We won't be able to trade reinforcements between ships. Not with three of them attacking." She gazed through the fog, but could only see vague, swirling shapes. The enemy airships would be on them at any moment. "But I appreciate you being here. I just wish it didn't have to be this way."

The first airship loomed out of the fog, bright blue and yellow stripes clearly visible along the hull, with silver letters naming it the *Egret*. Each heartbeat brought it closer and her muscles tensed, twitching, preparing for the coming fight.

Her crew gathered on the deck, looking just as tightly wound as she felt—like a spring waiting for release. Marienne lifted her chin and her voice. "This ship is our home! We will defend it and our freedom with everything we have! But those attacking us are indentured slaves!" She pointed her cutlass towards the *Egret*. "Stolen by

Prescott to pay off debts, they do not have the freedom we enjoy. They didn't choose this fight, Prescott did. With no choice, they will fight for causes they don't understand. That makes them weaker than us, remember that! But also," she lowered the sword and her voice. "We have the freedom to choose. So let us choose mercy for these poor souls."

It was a weakness Marienne had tried so desperately to hide, but her crew knew she was soft. She couldn't bear to hurt innocents, and as the *Egret* drew closer she could see the faces of the young men—some still boys—on the deck. *I wish it didn't have to be this way*, she repeated to herself. Bloodshed would be inevitable. But perhaps she could keep the damage to a minimum and still emerge victorious.

It seemed impossible.

Robert leaned in close, his breath stirring her hair as he whispered, "*Je t'aime.*"

Marienne responded in kind: "*Je t'aime.*" Then she blinked the emotion away, for the Luma Baron's airship had drawn up alongside the *Vincenzo*. Another was slinking to the other side of her deck, and the third hung back slightly, just behind. They were surrounded.

From a young age, Marienne had trained herself to control her emotions. She had learned that sometimes it was better to pretend not to feel, or to delay the emotions that boiled up inside her chest like molten lava threatening to erupt from the Earth's crust. She could always sort them out later at a time when she could be alone to think more clearly, or at least to express herself openly. She found the skill particularly useful when plotting another runaway attempt. Or in combat.

An amplified voice addressed her. "Marienne de Santorini!"

She grimaced at the use of her last name, the one she had revoked so long ago.

"That ship belongs to Luma Baron Prescott. If you will surrender it and yourself to us as his representatives, we will not harm you or any others on the ship."

Marienne pursed her lips. A peaceful conclusion? It was tempting, if it meant her crew would be unharmed. But she thought of giving up the *Vincenzo*, and her heart broke. She thought of returning to Prescott, and fear gripped her chest with a tight, icy hand. She looked around at her crew, loyal and willing to fight—even to die defending her. This was her family.

Nyx caught her eye and shook her head slightly, tightening the grip on her katana as she grinned madly. Well, Marienne couldn't deny her first mate a fight when she had gotten all dressed up for one.

"Fire!"

The cannons unloaded first, ejecting heavy ammunition into the hulls of the enemy airships. Metal crunched and screeched as cannon fire ripped holes in the blue and yellow stripes. Marienne grinned. The first volley had been a success, and it was quickly followed by a chorus of gunfire that erupted across the empty space between ships, cannon smoke mixing with fog. The luma harvesters released steam and ducked lower until Marienne's crew stopped firing. They could no longer aim at the enemy without risking falling over the railing.

Marienne cursed under her breath. The balloon of the airship was crafted using a unique combination of metal, rubber, and luma that made it virtually impenetrable to projectile attacks. This not only made the balloon immune to popping, but also provided an excellent shield.

"Lower!" Marienne shouted into her radio. Beth, who had taken the helm while Nyx had her fun, immediately shifted the thrusters. The *Vincenzo* followed the *Egret* down in a controlled freefall that threatened to lift everyone off the deck by a few inches. As the momentum settled, Marienne realized that she had instinctively taken Robert's hand. She wasn't sure why—he couldn't anchor her to the deck—but she didn't have time to think about it now. The *Vincenzo* bobbed level with the luma harvester.

She held the radio to her mouth and projected her voice across the deck, loud enough to be heard by the *Egret*. "You can keep descending if you like, but eventually you'll run out of altitude and hit ocean. After the holes we've put in your ship, I don't think you want to get too close. You've seen a sample of our firepower, so I suggest you surrender now and we can all fly away."

The *Madness* and the other two luma harvesters floated down to the altitude they had stopped at. Marienne held her breath, hoping the enemy captain would take the offer and just leave her alone. But she knew he wouldn't.

A loud metallic *creak* followed by a crash drew Marienne's attention to the other side of her ship. Three bridges had extended from the deck of the second enemy airship and lodged themselves into the *Vincenzo*. She swore under her breath as the *Egret* followed suit. Crew members swarmed over the bridges and onto her deck. She did not need to give the order to attack.

The sharp tang of gunpowder filled the air as the sound of shots fired crackled around Todd. He aimed for the leg of a man standing in the middle of the closest bridge. His intention was not to kill him, only to create a blockade that would slow the others down, making it easier to pick them off. His aim was true, as far as he could tell; the man crumpled. Todd smiled, proud that he could be up here helping instead of confined to the cannons like he used to. He turned to another bridge to repeat the process, only to find it had already been done.

The crews from the enemy airships were larger than Robert had anticipated. They kept coming over the railing of the *Vincenzo* like a swarm of ants pouring out of a hill. Robert shot at them as long as they remained on the bridges, but as soon as one came close enough, he abandoned his firearm for his cutlass.

The cutlass slashed through cloth and flesh, pierced through leather and muscle, and the hilt of it cracked against a skull, each blow forcing another young man down to the deck. But Robert did not aim to kill—he would respect Marienne's wishes as much as he could in the chaos of the fight. He jabbed at shoulders, slashed at thighs, and knocked unconscious those he could.

Nyx owned the battlefield like no one else. She strutted across the deck, firing a rifle until it ran out of ammunition. By that time, she had moved into the middle of the fray. With a wicked grin and a mad glint in her green eyes, she pulled out two katanas, one shorter than the other. She spun in a circle, slashing at those around her until they all fell down. Unconscious, dead, or simply smart enough to pretend to be—she didn't care as long as they were incapacitated.

Marienne didn't always agree with Nyx's fighting style, but the first mate had always told her captain that she would do anything to defend Marienne and the *Vincenzo*. And right now they were overwhelmed; no time to worry about being merciful. She paused for a moment to catch her breath.

A swift kick to her hand and the larger katana flew in the air, clattering to the deck. Nyx turned, an ugly snarl on her face, a growl in her throat. The man wore the emblazoned jacket of a high-ranking airship official. She sheathed her shorter sword, then flexed her fingers. The frown changed to a terrifying smile, and she saw fear in the man's eyes. She relished that expression, grew drunk on it as she punched him in the face. Her custom-made leather gloves extended from her elbows to halfway down her fingers, with bright metal studs that rose menacingly from the knuckles.

The first blow knocked the man down, but she followed him, kneeling on his chest. "I'm going to have to clean these now," she muttered with a roll of her eyes. Her blows did not slow or stop until the man's head lolled, his eyes closed—or swollen shut—and a low moan escaped his throat.

"Stay down," she growled, though she doubted he would get up. Now that he was no longer a threat, she retrieved her fallen katana and plunged back into the fray.

CHAPTER 41

Katherine shivered, even though the engine room was warm enough to make her sweat. The gun shook in her hand as the sounds of fighting echoed above her. The scuffle of feet, the sharp report of gunfire, the heavy thump of a body falling to the deck. Fear and worry mixed together and solidified into a lump in her stomach. She didn't know what was happening. She didn't know who was winning. Worst of all, she didn't know whose bodies made those sickening sounds as they fell above her. She listened hard for the metallic scrape of Todd's prosthetic leg, but could not make it out through the noise.

A new sound caught her attention. It came from the hallway—no, it came *down* the hallway, towards the engine room. Towards her. She trembled all over as she heard two distinct voices, although the words were lost behind the locked door. As they tried the handle and it didn't budge, Katherine took a deep breath, then another. She raised her gun and aimed it at the door, approximately where she thought their head would be once it opened. She inhaled one more time, accepting the fact that Nyx had not lied to her simply to get her out of the fight.

As the handle shot off with a powerful blast, Katherine realized too late that she should have barricaded the entrance. The door swung open. She gave herself just enough time to look at the men's faces and determine that they were strangers before she fired. The bullet hit the door frame with a metallic *ping*. The men looked at her in surprise, but she grit her teeth and tried again. The gun only held eight bullets, and she had already wasted one. As much as she had dreaded target practice with Nyx, now she wished she had practiced more. She felt woefully inadequate, and her lack of ability could doom the entire ship and crew.

The thought of these men trying to harm the engine solidified her resolve, and Katherine tried again. This second bullet hit the first man in the arm as he reached for his own gun. The sight of his blood staining his shirt left a sick feeling in Katherine's stomach, but she couldn't afford to stop and think too much about it. She fired again, this time aiming for the other man, but the shot flew somewhere down the hallway. *Three bullets down.* She chewed her lip. *After this I'll be half gone.*

The second man raised his gun and aimed for her.

THIS BATTLE WAS different from the ones Todd had participated in before. It was the most combat he had been in, even more than his training in the AeroCorps. As he took cover behind some crates to reload his gun and gather his wits, he shivered. Manning the cannons was dangerous, but removed from the violence. This was carnage.

He took a deep breath to steady his nerves as much as he could, then plunged back into the chaotic fighting. Something hard that felt like a boot slammed into his back from behind, and Todd fell to the deck. He quickly rolled over and aimed his gun at his assailant, but stopped just short of pulling the trigger.

"Ethan?" He looked into Ethan's hazel eyes. They looked so much like Katherine's—except for the harsh, angry expression.

"That's for putting Katherine in danger." He loomed over Todd, but kept both his gun and sword at his side.

"What are you talking about? Why are you here?"

"You invited me," he spat. He leveled his sword at Todd's chin, but did not strike as Todd rose. "Where is she?"

"*Todd!*" Katherine's voice rang through the ship and across the deck. Many people around them hesitated slightly in their fighting, but once the others took the opportunity to strike, the battle continued in full force. Except for Todd who ran below deck, not caring that Ethan followed. Katherine was in trouble.

As they ran down the hall, Todd's mind stuck on what Ethan had said. Had he been the cause of this, when he had called the *Egret*? But how? Radios had an enormous range of communication—they couldn't possibly have found them without first knowing where to look. There may be a spy among them, but it wasn't him.

When they reached the door that hung open, Todd only had a single heartbeat to assess the situation. A body lay just inside the doorway—dead or unconscious, he couldn't tell. Just beyond that, Katherine stood with a gun at her feet, timidly pointing her rapier at an unfamiliar man in front of her. He wrenched the sword out of her hand. Todd raised his gun and aimed for the man's chest.

"Don't shoot!" Ethan's voice rasped. Todd turned to see his face chiseled into a grimace. He kept one hand pressed firmly against his leg. "I know this man. Davey!" Ethan called into the engine room.

The man startled, then turned, but did not let go of Katherine's wrist. "What are you doing down here?"

"I've got this," he said, fighting to keep his voice even. "You go ahead back up. I know how much you enjoy hitting things."

"Captain doesn't trust you," Davey said uncertainly. His gaze drifted to Todd, who still held his gun level. "And who are you?"

Todd rolled his eyes and lowered his gun, against his better judgment. "Of course you wouldn't know me. You think the captain doesn't trust Ethan? Then explain to me why he knows who I am and you don't. I'm the one who invited you all here in the first place." He mustered a sickening grin, hoping the ruse would work, and hoping Katherine wouldn't believe it. Even if it did turn out to be true. "Captain wants you back on deck, since you've already taken longer with this simple task than he expected. You've failed, Davey. Do you really want to anger the captain again?"

Davey took one more look between the two men in the doorway, then released Katherine and scampered away, pausing only to pick up his fallen companion. Todd immediately rushed to her side.

"Are you hurt?"

"Nothing more than bruises, thanks to you," she breathed. She stroked the stem of the helium purifier as she walked around the main bulk of the engine, then stopped in her tracks as she saw her brother's pale face. "Ethan! Are you alright?" She ran to him, but stopped short, hesitating.

"I'm fine," he dismissed, but his breathing remained heavy and labored. "Can... Can I stay here with you? It'll look suspicious if I return topside."

Katherine nodded, and turned to Todd. "Will you stay too?" She couldn't stand the torture of not knowing if he had been harmed... or worse.

Todd tried to hide his relief. "Sure, but I'll stand by the door in case someone else tries to come down."

"Sharp thinking," Ethan said bitterly. "Why couldn't you have been so smart three days ago?"

"What do you mean?" He tugged on his curls.

"When you called me, our ship recorded and tracked your radio signal."

"That's not–"

"Not possible?" Ethan sneered. "Perhaps not to the general public, but luma harvesters get privilege. You even gave us the name of your ship and its captain! You might as well have surrendered then and there! Murdock led the attack, but this is your fault."

CHAPTER 42

Marienne bared her teeth in a nasty grin as she spotted him: the enemy captain. At last. He had finally deigned to board her ship; his second mistake. The first was to wear his emblems so openly. He may as well have painted a target across his chest. He looked her way, and as their eyes locked, a smug grin spread across his face. Marienne decided that she wanted to slice that look right off his head.

She took a step forward, but was immediately blocked by a frightened young man with a sword. She couldn't hold back the pity that rose in her chest as they locked blades. His face and eyes were so young, and she cursed Prescott for putting him here. This wasn't his fight.

Marienne backed up and bumped into something solid and warm. A glance over her shoulder revealed Robert's familiar profile. She smiled. His presence so close was more than a reassurance as they fought their respective enemies; it was a comfort. He disposed of his attacker, and Marienne struck at the boy's leg with enough force that he crumpled to the deck.

"Stay down," she advised. Turning to Robert, she reported, "I saw the captain. I'm going after him."

"I'm coming too," he insisted, but paused as he aimed his gun over Marienne's shoulder and fired at something behind her.

"Only if you can keep up," she smirked. Without waiting for a witty retort, she turned and plunged through the seething mass of bodies. She did not use her blade, nor fired her gun as she ran, only jabbed with her elbows, the hilt of her cutlass, or the butt of her gun. She couldn't be certain that she wasn't hitting members of her own crew, but they would forgive her—if they even knew that it was her who had hit them. The chaos around her blurred into vague, human-esque shapes as her vision focused solely on the captain.

He stood in front of her quarters, hands behind his back and that infuriating smile still painted across his face. He let the battle rage around him, as intently focused on Marienne as she was on him. Once she was only a couple of yards away, Marienne raised her sword and, with a fierce shout, charged at him.

The clang of metal shocked her as she stopped, a hand's breadth away from his nose. The enemy captain had raised a sword in defense so quickly she hadn't even seen the flash of reflected light before it stopped her attack.

"Marienne, I presume," he said, his velvet rich voice low and smooth.

"I know why you're here," she growled through grit teeth. "And I swear on my life, I won't surrender!" She pulled her blade away from his and swung again. But again he blocked her strike. Marienne brought her gun level to his face, cocking it with a menacing *click*.

An equally terrifying sound echoed hers, and she felt the pressure of his gun's barrel pressed firmly into her gut. "Listen close and listen well," he hissed. "Prescott wants you, and only you alive. He would like the ship if he can get it, but that can be negotiated. The more you resist, the more your crew will suffer."

Marienne released her blade from his again and turned to survey the battle before her. The captain did not remove the gun. "My crew seems to be holding their own just fine," she noted. Nyx, in particular, used her expert martial arts moves to take down four men at once.

"Perhaps for the time being, but how long can they keep this up?

Are all of them so skilled? And," he leaned in close until his foul breath stirred the hair around her ear. "Can you continue to fight without killing my innocent crew?" He chuckled at the flicker of shock in her eyes. "I've watched you fight, Marienne. You are too merciful for your own good. If you agree to come with me now, we can stop this unnecessary violence."

Marienne's breath came faster and faster as she saw the battle with new eyes. Her crew followed her example, even Nyx leaving the men unconscious or incapacitated rather than deliver a final blow. But it put them at a severe disadvantage, as the attackers had no such qualms. As she watched, Clyde fell to the ground, clutching his stomach where a bullet had struck him. A grave weight settled in her chest as she realized the choice she must make: her own freedom, or the lives of her crew?

If she had the chance to talk to her crew, she knew they would tell her to continue to fight. But was it truly worth it? How could she be so selfish? But if she surrendered, she would be leaving everything she loved behind.

She looked for Robert. He fought a particularly fierce opponent, clad in an officer's uniform. A sad smile spread across her face as she admired how the lamplight glistened off his sweat-covered brow, and how his intense expression spoke of nothing but determination to keep her safe.

If she surrendered now, Prescott would keep her grounded forever. She would never see Robert again. The idea lodged itself as forcefully and painfully in her heart as a bullet. She couldn't leave him, couldn't leave her crew. They were her family, like no one in the world had ever been before. Around her now, they fought to keep her as their captain. She couldn't let that be in vain.

Robert thrust at the man, who sidestepped and swiped at his right arm. Robert cried out, a primeval sound of anguish that echoed too loud in Marienne's skull and twisted in her gut. Blood seeped out, staining the sleeve of his shirt from cream to crimson. He liked that shirt, with its billowing sleeves and deep neckline. Now it had a hole that would need to be carefully stitched shut, and a bloodstain that leaked down his arm even as he clamped his hand over it. She couldn't tear her eyes away from the streaks of red, as if she could command them to stop dripping further and further down.

When would the blood stop? When would people she loved stop sacrificing themselves for her so she could run away again? She had asked Robert to fly with her, and now he was injured. This was her fault; it would always be her fault. Unless she stopped it.

"If you will agree to these terms," Marienne said softly, her words spilling out of her mouth. "You leave my ship, intact and under command of my first mate. You leave my crew alone without any further harm. You leave the *Madness* alone as well. And when I am on your ship, I will receive the privacy and respect I am due as the fiancée of a Luma Baron." She nearly choked on the last words; they tasted like vomit.

"I agree to your terms, as long as no one tries to interfere," he said with a triumphant grin. Marienne felt sick to her stomach. Raising his hands and his voice, he shouted, "Ceasefire!"

CHAPTER 43

Katherine looked up at the ceiling. "It's stopped," she observed. The gunfire, the pounding of running feet, the intermittent thud of a body hitting the deck, all of it ceased like a rainstorm ending. She looked to both Todd and Ethan, but they held equal expressions of confusion. She bit her lip. "There's only one way to find out why." She couldn't quite keep the tremor out of her voice, but tried to hide it by standing up and striding resolutely out the door.

She did not need to turn around to know that Todd and Ethan followed; the sound of their footsteps trailed behind her as they emerged onto the deck. Although perhaps a dozen bodies still remained where they had collapsed—only a couple of them groaning—the majority of both crews stood side by side, weapons lowered, staring at Marienne.

Katherine pushed her way closer, finding a spot where she could see her captain clearly. She was just in time to see Marienne take a deep, shuddering breath and announce, "I'm going with them. I surrender."

Shouts of protest rose from the crew, and Katherine found that she was among them. "You can't!" Her words were drowned out in the muddle of sounds around her.

Robert pushed past Katherine, breaching the crowd. He held his left hand to his right arm, sticky blood gathering between his fingers as he stepped into the empty space cleared around Marienne and Murdock. He stared at her for a long time before he whispered, "Why?"

Marienne responded in an equally low tone. "I'm what they want. If I surrender peacefully, they'll leave everyone else alone. I can't let… my crew. You're hurt." The words stumbled out and she looked at the deck beneath her feet.

Robert studied her face. "Your ship, your crew, your freedom. You're just going to give it all up?" He didn't add the words that burned in the back of his throat like engine steam: *You'll leave me behind?*

"For your safety, yes," she said, straightening and holding her chin high. She turned to Captain Murdock. "Now, if you'll kindly return your crew to your ship and show me to my new quarters, Captain."

"Certainly." Murdock complied with an expression so smug that Katherine wanted to spit at him as he passed.

Robert stood frozen to the spot, still facing the door to Marienne's quarters as Captain Murdock gestured for Marienne to walk in front of him, so that she may cross the bridge to his ship. The other two walkways soon became crowded with young men returning to the *Egret*, but the one Marienne crossed remained clear.

Katherine looked at Ethan, expecting to see conflict in his eyes, but found only sorrow. She reached for his hand, but he shook his head. "I'm sorry," he whispered. He turned and followed the others back to the deck of his own ship.

Katherine's head swam dizzily. She wondered if the engine hadn't been sabotaged after all, and now the ship was falling out of the sky. But, no, everyone else seemed steady and stable, their feet planted on the rough deck. She realized that the feeling was familiar: that of her family being torn apart. She reached for Todd's hand, for something to stabilize her and keep her rooted. Its warmth and gentle pressure brought too little comfort.

Robert turned around. "No." He cleared his throat and said it again, so loud his voice echoed in the immediate silence. "No! You're not taking her!" He strode towards the walkway where Murdock stood halfway between ships. Marienne had already set foot on the *Egret*, her expression pleading as Robert approached.

Nyx joined Robert, towing a young man—barely older than a boy—her arm wound tightly around his neck. "Release Marienne in exchange for one of your own!" she demanded.

The boy looked terrified, but Murdock turned away with a dismissing wave of his hand. "Keep him if you like," he said. "He is insignificant. A worthless comparison." The boy's eyes went wide, and even Nyx relaxed her grip in shock, disgust written on her face.

Robert hopped up onto the bridge. "Marienne!"

Murdock drew a pistol as he turned and fired without aiming. The bullet hit Robert in the chest, knocking him back. He stumbled and fell down to the deck of the *Vincenzo*, where he lay gasping. Katherine rushed to his side, and Nyx released her grasp on the boy, crouching down and placing her hands over the wound. A puddle of red spread out from around her fingers.

Marienne screamed, "Robert!" She attempted to return to her ship, return to him, but Murdock blocked her way.

The bridges retracted with a shriek, and Murdock said in too polite a tone, "Let's show you to your room."

Marienne wanted to feel sick in her stomach, to feel stinging tears in her eyes, to feel her throat constricting and her breath coming in gasps. But she felt nothing. Numbness overtook her mind, her limbs, her heart. Robert was dying. She had surrendered to protect him, had given up her freedom for his safety.

She had lost everything.

CHAPTER 44

$\mathcal{M}$arienne sat on the edge of her cot, staring at her hands. An empty pit gaped in her chest where her heart should have been. Every time she closed her eyes, even to blink, she saw Robert falling backwards, shot. He had to be alive. He *had* to be. She could not abide the thought that he had died. Not when she had sacrificed everything to keep him and her crew safe.

But if Robert… died. What then? Could she bear to sail a sky without him in it? He had been the catalyst that drove her to become an airship captain. What would she do when the color of the sky itself reminded her of his eyes? The luma she relied on shimmered the same golden shade as his hair. How could she survive surrounded by reminders that his death was her fault?

She shook her head. He was *not* dead!

The sharp rap of knuckles echoed hollowly through the room. Marienne looked up as a young man with familiar hazel eyes opened the door and brought in a bowl of thin soup. "Supper," he announced softly.

Marienne took the bowl from him, steam coating her face with condensation. "Thank you," she whispered. Her tongue felt large and wooly in her mouth; speaking seemed an unfamiliar effort.

He sat down in a chair at the foot of her bed and stared at her. She stared back. They had never met, but she recognized those eyes—and the uncomfortable posture. "You wish to ask me something."

His face reddened and he looked away. After a moment of hesitation, he asked, "Was Katherine happy, sailing with you?"

"You're her brother." It was a statement, not a question. Marienne knew she was correct in the assumption. A glimmer of her usual self poked through her despair, like a single star on a cloudy night. "Although I do not know your name."

"Ethan, Ma'am."

"She was happy under my command, as far as I could tell. There were trepidations at first, I will admit, since we technically stole her and she did not entirely trust our trade. But when faced with the choice, she chose to stay. I imagine her love for machines kept her on the *Vincenzo* more than anything else. More than Todd, even."

Her heart ached as she thought about the newest addition to her crew. Would Katherine be alright, knowing that the same man who had enslaved her now had taken Marienne? Was she afraid that Prescott could track her down and take her back to Mr. Castle? Marienne wouldn't let it happen, but there seemed little she could do at the moment.

And what about Todd? He and Marienne had started this journey together. He must feel so useless now. Nyx would surely try to come after her, but she wouldn't be able to do so alone. Marienne hadn't even had time to assess the damage to her ship before she was taken below the deck of the *Egret*. It happened too quickly, and she left too much behind.

For now.

Marienne straightened and took a bite of soup. She had been in this kind of predicament before. The cracks in her despondency widened as she recalled her numerous escape attempts in the past.

Only one of them worked.

Don't think about that now, she commanded herself. *Only one more needs to work, and you won't find it by wallowing in self-pity.* She glanced around the room, which had been a closet only an hour before. Cot, chair, shelves. No windows, door unlocked… for now. She would have to be careful with that freedom, or it could be revoked quickly.

Then there was Ethan. A potential ally, if she could apply the correct leverage.

"At least Katherine is much happier now than she was back in that house where she had been enslaved and abused." Marienne measured Ethan's reaction through half-closed eyes as she took another bite of soup.

His hands curled into fists so tight they shook and his knuckles turned the color of bone. "Who hurt her?" he hissed, glowering at the floor.

"A Mr. Castle, if I recall." *He didn't even question it*, she noted. *He must already distrust Prescott's underlings.* She took a sip of water from a cup on the shelf as daintily as if it were delicate china instead of tin. "Prescott doesn't care how his slaves are treated, so long as they remain in slavery. Cheap labor is so hard to find," she said with a sigh and a toss of her crimson curls.

"Why do you call us slaves?" He glanced at her, suspicion in his hazel eyes.

Marienne suppressed a smile. The suspicion was not directed towards her. She had guessed correctly; Ethan already had doubts about the system that kept him an unwilling laborer for the British Luma Company. Now, she only had to foster those emotions until he trusted her. "I say slaves because that is how you are treated. Tell me, when were you indentured? How old were you?"

"Seventeen," he spat. "Three weeks away from my eighteenth birthday."

She pursed her lips. "Shame, that. And they separated you from your sister." She clucked sympathetically. "How can you possibly attempt an escape if they still have control over her?"

"Every time I made a mistake, Captain Murdock threatened to extend her sentence as well as mine," he said. His fiery words held a tinge of reflection.

Marienne was on the right track, but she had to step delicately. If

Ethan became too angry at the misdeeds of his master, he may do something rash—hot anger burned in this boy. He longed for justice. She wished she could feel like something other than a spider drawing a web around Ethan, but this manipulation was certainly for his own good. And it was refreshing to feel anything again. There was a particular thrill that came with disillusioning those who worked for Prescott. It was her favorite way to undermine his unethical practices.

"How long have you served?" She inquired lightly.

"Just over two years." He sighed, leaning back in his chair. "It seems a lifetime."

"Do you remember the original amount your father owed?"

"How could I forget? 25 pounds."

Marienne frowned. "Between you and your sister, you should have paid that off by now."

He shook his head. "I've… made some mistakes. Those mistakes have been added to my debt. I hoped that I would be personally responsible for paying those off, and Katherine could be freed when she had paid off her half, but I guess it's all on me now." He sighed.

"How much do you owe now?"

"A lot. I don't know the amount exactly, but each shipment we lose to pirates adds so much."

Marienne put down her bowl and leaned forward. "It's more than you think," she whispered in a conspiratorial tone. She smiled sympathetically at his angry expression. "I know, that's not what you want to hear, but listen to me. This whole company is corrupt, straight from the head. I should know, I was—am betrothed to him." She corrected herself with a grimace. "When I was last there—"

"When you stole the airship?" he interrupted.

"It was practically mine anyway," she said with a dismissive wave of her hand. "I just never came back." She frowned. "Until now. I digress. One night, I was eavesdropping at Prescott's study door when he was discussing finances with a member of his company. A shipment of luma had been stolen, and Prescott specifically instructed that the captain should make up the difference by purchasing luma from the black market, and add the cost to the indentured men's debts." She watched Ethan's eyes grow wide. "How many times in the past two years have you been robbed by sky pirates?"

"Five," he answered. His eyes were fixed somewhere distant, his brows furrowed furiously together. "We've sometimes taken on extra luma, but I thought it was from the distribution center. That's what we were told. When I get my hands on those—" His threat was cut short as he gasped.

His hands curled into fists as he winced. He fought to breathe evenly as Marienne watched curiously.

"Are you hurt?" she asked, genuinely concerned.

"It's…" he shook his head, not trusting himself to speak. He now pushed both hands firmly on his knee.

"May I see?"

He rolled up his trouser leg past his knee and showed her the scar. It shimmered faintly.

"Oh," she breathed, flooded with new revelation. Everything clicked into place: how Prescott kept control while being so cruel, why his indentured servants never ran away or mutinied, how luma collection had been kept secret all these years. "You've made a Luma Oath."

"Standard procedure," he hissed as he covered up the scar again.

"All of you? I should have known." She desperately longed for a piano. It was so much easier to plan when her hands were busy. She glanced at Ethan, who seemed to have recovered, except for the pale tint to his skin. "Your Oath prevents you from running away." That made her plans more difficult. It was easy enough to offer freedom to those who wanted it—it was how she had convinced Todd to help her. But if Ethan couldn't come with her, what would he stand to gain by helping her?

"Murdock mentioned that I may have earned my freedom in aiding in your capture, Captain," he admitted. "I didn't trust him before, but now I know he was lying."

Marienne caught his use of her title and smiled to herself. It brought back a morsel of her confidence in an otherwise powerless situation. Of course her weapons had been confiscated, and she couldn't use the crew members to mutiny—not with their Oaths preventing them from harming their captain.

"I should get back." Ethan smiled wryly as he added, "Don't want the captain thinking we're conspiring."

She chuckled as she handed him her half-empty soup bowl. She didn't feel like eating anymore. "Do you still work in the radio control room?"

"No, Captain, I've been moved to the galley. And I don't know anyone who is in there, either. Your crew took my only friend captive."

Marienne recalled the young man Nyx had tried to use as collateral. "I'm sorry."

He shook his head. "Don't be. Although his Oath will prevent him from spilling any secrets, it won't hurt him for being captured. I honestly think he'll be better off as a prisoner on your ship than on this one."

"That's very kind of you. Remember when you're around Murdock to call me Marienne instead of Captain. I don't think he would take too kindly to you calling me that."

Ethan nodded. "Thanks for the reminder. I think we're going straight to England, despite the ship needing repairs. If you need anything on the way, just ask me." He closed the door behind him as he left the small room.

Marienne crossed her arms over her chest and felt something hard under her blouse. With dawning realization, she tugged on the string around her neck and pulled out the tiny vial of eclipse luma. She gazed at its crimson glow, disbelieving. She had forgotten about it; the weight had grown so familiar over the past few weeks. This... this had to be her ticket out! But how, and when?

Marienne pulled her legs up onto the cot and stared at the door. How was she going to free Ethan from his Oath and escape? The truth was, she wasn't likely going to be able to on the *Egret*–using eclipse luma on an airship while it was sailing would be a foolishly dangerous move.

Which meant that she was indeed going back to England. Back to Prescott.

CHAPTER 45

Katherine's shallow breathing sounded loud in her ears as she watched Nyx and Todd move Robert under Rose's careful supervision. Out of the corner of her eye she noticed that the *Madness* had drifted closer. Its bridges lowered to connect with the *Vincenzo*'s deck, Landreau jogging across the platform before it had been fully secured. Panic exploded on his face when he spotted Robert.

"What happened?" he demanded.

"He was shot." Katherine's voice broke. She glanced down at the puddle of blood on the deck and immediately regretted it as her stomach lurched. Her vision swam and she placed a hand over her mouth in an effort to keep from adding to the mess on the deck.

Landreau guided her over to the railing. She gripped it tight, breathing deeper, deeper, clenching her jaw until the feeling of nausea subsided.

"Who shot him?" he asked.

"The captain of that ship. They took Marienne, and Robert tried to stop them." She shuddered as the memory played itself out again in her mind. "He just… shot him."

He patted her shoulder. "First time, *n'est pas?* Stay here and steady yourself. I'm going to go see him."

"I'm coming too." She straightened and faced him, her pale face set in a resolute expression.

He looked at her doubtfully, but did not argue. As she led him below deck, he said, "If you don't mind, I could use your help on the *Madness*. Our humidity condenser and water purifier were damaged in the battle, and our mechanic was injured."

"I want to see Robert first," she said, her voice even. "Then I'll go over and take a look."

The door to the infirmary had been left open, but Katherine did not immediately spot Robert. All dozen cots were occupied with the bleeding, the broken, the moaning. The sound of battle replayed in her mind, turning her stomach as she recalled the muffled thump of bodies falling to the deck and rattling the loose rivets above her head in the engine room.

Steadying herself and her thoughts, Katherine leaned against the wall. Landreau pointed to the nearest cot, and Katherine realized she hadn't seen Robert because Nyx, Todd, and Rose hovered over him, speaking in low murmurs. She pushed herself off the wall and followed Landreau towards the cot.

"—not still in him, see. It went right through. But it's so close to his heart, I don't know what sort of damage he's sustained. It could be as simple as loss of blood, or it could be that his heart has been ruptured." Rose sighed. "But whatever it is, I need room to work, so all of you out!" She glared at Nyx, Todd, and Katherine in turn. "Landreau, you can stay."

Robert took a gasping breath that sounded to Katherine as if it were too wet. Tears pricked in the corners of her eyes as she looked at his face: pale as death and deeply lined with pain.

"Save him," she whispered. "Please, you have to save him."

Rose looked at her with heavy eyes. "I'll do my best."

. . .

Katherine walked over to the *Madness* in a daze, not even noticing the void below as she crossed the bridge between ships. Robert couldn't die. Not like that, not fading on a cot filled with pain and far away from Marienne. She asked a passing member of the crew where the engine room was located and followed his directions down to the inner workings of Robert's ship. Only once there did she realize that she had left her tools on the *Vincenzo*.

With a sigh, she looked around until she found the toolbox left by the injured mechanic. She dug her leather gloves out of her pocket, thankful that at least she had those, and set to work. She wasn't alone in the engine room; two men were busy bolting a large piece of sheet metal over a gaping hole in the side of the ship. It was a temporary fix —real repairs would need to be made soon. It was like putting a bandage over a pierced heart.

She shook her head. *Focus on the task at hand.* The tube that attached the humidity condenser to the outside wall seemed miraculously undamaged, but the purifier unit had been grazed by a cannonball. Exposed wires and gears spilled out of the side of the unit where the metal covering had been ripped off. Mechanical intestines spilling out of torn flesh.

Stop it! Katherine scolded herself. She followed the men to a heap of scrap metal and found a plate that would cover the exposed area. As she set to work, however, her mind wandered. The job was simple, and her hands moved automatically to reconnect and wrap wires, so her thoughts continually returned to the image of Robert laying on the bed, too pale. As she turned to the gears, she removed the ones that had been bent or broken, leaving gaping holes in the mechanisms. Like a friend suddenly ripped out of her life. Where had Marienne been taken? Why did they want her? If the luma harvesting had been the reason for the attack, they would have destroyed the *Vincenzo*, but it was left intact.

Once the gears had been sorted, Katherine noticed the pale, shimmering luma dripping from a punctured tube, like blood leaking from a vein. She recoiled. Taking a deep breath, she reminded herself that this was different, and she had done it before. She patched up the tube, the stardust coating her leather gloves as she did so.

"This is going to need more luma," she announced to the other men in the room. They nodded at her, but were busy patching a hole.

Her job finished, and she stood up. But as she went to wipe the luma off her gloves, Katherine paused. She stared at them for a long time, not daring to look away for fear of breaking the wire-thin concentration she held on the ghost of an idea. It had to work, didn't it? If anyone knew the possibility of success, it would be Rose.

Katherine ran out of the engine room, cupping her luma-coated gloves close to her chest. She wrestled with the idea of saving Robert herself, no matter what the surgeon said, as she flew across the bridge. But what if by trying to save him she made things worse? Even…

No. She would ask Rose first. Luma could be a tricky thing. The night of the eclipse with its red luma had proven that.

Out of the corner of her eye, Katherine noticed Nyx and Todd standing over something on the deck, heads close as they conversed. She did not stop to mention her idea to them; she could not afford to stop. Robert needed her now.

Stumbling into the infirmary, Katherine gulped for breath, her gaze greedily searching for Rose. Instead she found Robert. His shirt had been removed and bandages crossed his chest and shoulder, a dark stain barely visible beneath the top layers. His chest rose shallowly and fell irregularly.

"He's asleep for now," Rose said as she joined Katherine.

"Is that different from being unconscious?"

Rose pursed her lips, and the expression reminded Katherine so much of Marienne that her chest ached. She desperately wished her captain was here.

"He's resting peacefully," Rose said. "Why are you here?"

Katherine peeled her gloved hands away from her chest and showed them to Rose. "Luma. You have to use it. It can save him!"

Rose gripped Katherine's arm tightly and steered her out of the infirmary, shutting the door behind them. "I'm only going to tell you this once," she hissed, her face so close that Katherine noticed a single strand of gray in Rose's dark hair. "Luma is entirely unexplored in the medical field, and therefore entirely uncertain."

"But I've heard of miraculous healing when luma is used!"

"Those rumors are unfounded and we do not know or understand the long-term effects of such a cure. And if I put luma into Robert's wound, would that count as an Oath? Would you have him obey me for the rest of our natural lives?"

Katherine stood speechless. She attempted to stammer an apology, but Rose dismissed her. "Don't tell me how to do my job."

"But he could be dying!" Katherine at last found her voice, even if it did break.

"You think I don't know that?" Rose's eyes filled with tears. "You think I don't care? You think I'm not trying the best I can?" She sighed. "I get it. You want a miracle cure. But it's too early to try something so risky. Robert was only shot an hour ago. Normal medical procedures could be enough to heal him. Please understand that I get to decide how to treat my patient."

Katherine nodded, ashamed. Rose walked back into the infirmary, closing the door before Katherine could follow.

AFTER KATHERINE HAD PROPERLY CLEANED her gloves in the engine room, she returned to the deck to find Todd. She needed his comfort. She found him next to Nyx, who held an unfamiliar young man by the collar of his shirt.

"Who's this?" Katherine asked as she approached.

"The boy I tried to take hostage," Nyx sneered. "Shame your captain didn't value you."

Katherine noticed that his pale expression didn't look so much like fear as pain.

Todd said, "He's not to blame for any of this. You can let go of him." Once Nyx had obliged, he asked, "What's your name?"

The boy hesitated, glancing at his hand before answering, "Aaron."

Something at the back of Katherine's mind sparked, like flint striking steel, but the memory did not ignite. "Did you know Ethan?"

"Yes, I did!" His grin spread across his whole face. "We worked together in the radio control room."

"That's right, he told me about you. He spoke very highly of you, in fact."

"You must be Katherine," Aaron gasped. "You have the same eyes. I thought you were indentured?"

"It's a long story," she said, shaking her head. "But maybe you can help us! You can tell us where they're taking Marienne!"

"I… can't," he said with a grimace. He pressed his right thumb into his left hand.

"Are you hurt?" she asked. She looked at his hand, but saw no blood.

He shook his head.

"Hold on," Todd interjected. He walked forward with a slight limp and a hiss from his prosthetic, and Katherine yelped. "Don't worry, it's just a tweak. You can take a look at it later. Right now…" He took Aaron's left hand and stared at it. A ragged scar ran across the center of his palm, the pale shimmer barely visible in the daylight. "As I thought," Todd murmured.

Nyx inhaled, a sharp hissing sound that whistled through her teeth. "He's taken a Luma Oath. Fool!" She punched the railing of the ship. "Don't you know your palm is one of the most impractical places to cut yourself?"

"Don't yell at the boy, you know it's not his fault," Todd said calmly. "At least you chose a limb."

Aaron nodded. "Some are required to make the Oath closer to their heart."

"A short leash," Todd murmured.

"I don't understand," Katherine admitted.

"He can't tell us anything directly," Nyx said, disgust written on her face. "He couldn't even talk about the Oath until we mentioned it."

"But I was indentured and never had to make an Oath," Katherine said, puzzled.

"It's mostly reserved for harvesters. How else would they keep luma harvesting a secret?" Aaron said. "Can't tell a secret if it kills you."

Todd sat heavily down on one of the benches around the deck and began to unlatch his prosthetic from the harness that connected it to his leg. "It doesn't matter. I know where they've taken Marienne. Nyx, will you bring my crutch, please?" He held the prosthetic out to Katherine.

She took it from him, but didn't move, her gaze fixed intently on him.

Nyx thundered, "Why didn't you say so before?"

"Because it would be impossible for us to overtake them. The *Madness* needs to dock for repairs, and we can't take the *Vincenzo*, because Prescott wants it almost as much as he wants Marienne."

"Prescott, the Luma Baron?" Katherine's head spun as she remembered the day she joined the crew of the *Vincenzo*, and the rage in his voice as he threatened Marienne.

"Marienne stole the *Vincenzo* to escape her betrothal to him. I never thought he would actually manage to capture her." Todd buried his head in his hands. "I don't know what to do."

KATHERINE CLUTCHED the prosthetic as she walked down to the engine room, her mind searching for memories of the luma baron she had been indebted to. He hadn't come to the estate much, and when he did she had been so concerned with Mr. Castle that she hadn't paid much attention to him. The most she had ever interacted with him had been that conversation in the automobile several months ago. She shook her head, reeling at the news that Marienne was betrothed to him.

As she placed Todd's prosthetic leg onto her workbench, Katherine's eye landed on a small metal figurine. She picked it up and smiled at its sleek figure: a stoat for Robert's automaton. She slipped the mock-up into her pocket and went to the infirmary.

Robert still looked ashen, but his chest rose higher and fell evenly, much to her relief. She glanced around and saw that Rose was on the other side of the room, tending to more wounded patients. Katherine pulled the stoat figurine out of her pocket and placed it on the small table next to his bed, next to a book Landreau had dropped off: The Adventures of Squarejaw Jordan.

"What's that?" Robert's eyes opened halfway, his voice rasping out of his throat.

"A promise," Katherine said softly. She tried to smile. "I'm going to make you the best automaton anyone has ever seen. But only after you save Marienne."

"I don't…" he paused, jaw clenched against the pain. "I don't think I can."

Katherine's heart sank. "Don't talk like that! Todd knows where she's gone. We can't catch up to them, but we can rescue her."

Robert tried to shake his head, and struggled to speak. "I can't… Recovery will take too long, Katherine." He looked at her with wide, wild eyes that showed too much white. "Go after Marienne. Please."

"Me? Why?" A shock ran through her body. She couldn't do something so important! She couldn't fight, couldn't save the people she loved. All she could do was fix machines.

"Please," he repeated. "Promise me you'll bring her home." His eyelids drooped and Katherine feared he would slip back into unconsciousness soon.

She thought of Marienne being held against her will, forced to marry someone she didn't love, far away from everyone she cared about. She wondered if Marienne felt as she had back when she was a maid: trapped with no way out. Marienne had rescued Katherine from that life. The least she could do was try to return the favor.

"I promise." Her mouth was dry as she formed the words, and all semblance of courage seemed to have abandoned her.

But a slim smile crossed Robert's face as he closed his eyes and his breathing resumed an even rhythm. Although she still had no idea how to fulfill the promise she just made, Katherine would move all the stars in the sky if she had to, just to see him smile again.

CHAPTER 46

"How far out are we?" Marienne picked the last raisin out of her oatmeal and popped it into her mouth.

"Still over a week, Captain," Ethan said. "It's been slow going with how bad your ship tore up the *Egret*."

She pursed her lips in thought. "If I could just get a message to my crew, they may be able to help in my escape."

"If you have a plan, don't tell me," he said glumly. "It'll just put both of us in danger."

"I don't have much yet," she admitted. "And it would be foolish to try anything while we're still in the air, being surrounded by Murdock's personal army. But it would be nice to have backup. If only you still worked in the radio room!"

Ethan stared at the ground as he said quietly, "Captain, I think we should stop talking to each other."

Marienne glanced at the door. "Do you suspect eavesdroppers?" She wouldn't put it past Murdock to spy on her.

He shook his head. "No, but if Murdock asks me anything, I'll have to tell him everything."

A somber acceptance settled on Marienne's demeanor. "I recognize that you are taking a grave risk in keeping me company. I appreciate all you have done so far, but I cannot ask you to put your life on the line for me."

"But I want to help you," he whispered. "I just wish it didn't involve the possibility of dying."

He thought hard about what he could do that wouldn't violate his Oath, and an idea formed. He cautiously followed his line of thinking, simultaneously remaining very aware of the scar on his knee, in case it protested. Only once he was certain that his Oath would not prevent him from carrying out his plan did he nod.

"Every day there's a list of communications between airships, relaying information to one another. Since radios can only reach so far, we transmit messages to the closest ships, who then transmit to their area, and so on."

"I am familiar with this method," Marienne said.

"The radio operators receive a list of transmissions to send every four hours. I can add your message to the list, but it's a long shot. We wouldn't be able to transmit to your ship—that frequency has been blacklisted."

"That's alright," she said, smiling. "We're not contacting my ship."

JAMES GRINNED as he struggled to keep the airship sailing straight. Winds battered it from all sides, and rain had made the deck so slick that his crew members had tethered themselves to the cables and railings. Lightning flashed in bright reflections off his goggles.

Lightning.

That precious commodity that he risked life and limb and his ship to collect so that he could sell it for a hefty profit. This was what life was all about. Thunder immediately roiled around him, the sound permeating the very marrow of his bones. James never felt more alive than when in a storm. He raised his flask to his lips, but a sudden gust of wind battered against the hull, and he fought to keep his ship steady. His flask, slick with rain, slipped from his hand and clattered to the deck, spilling its contents.

He grumbled at the lost drink, but more pressing matters

demanded his attention. "Activate the rods!" he shouted into the intercom next to the helm. Great metal rods extended from all sides of the ship. Lightning forked out of a cloud and, like a fox that had caught the scent of a rabbit, dove for the nearest metal rod. It surged directly into a leather container coated on the inside with rubber.

Two more strikes of lightning hit and were captured, when a voice crackled through the speaker, pale and faint as it competed with the raging storm. "Captain, we've got an urgent transmission directing us towards coordinates in the Mediterranean."

"It will have to wait," James barked. He did, however, recall that Robert liked to stay around that area this time of year.

"Sir, it came from a luma collector. It's signed MM."

James paused. Under his breath he grumbled, "Got yourself in some kind of mess, did you Mad Marienne?" And if it was somewhere around Robert, chances were he was involved too. He shook his head. He didn't understand why Marienne would try to contact him of all people, but he could not afford to lose this storm.

Still, if she only had time to send coordinates and her initials… It must be serious. He reached for the radio button.

"Captain!" James turned at the voice suddenly behind him and frowned. Andrew held tightly to his rain-slick tether, dark hair soaked and plastered to his forehead. James couldn't read the new recruit's expression behind his dark-tinted goggles, which made him more suspicious. Andrew had a tendency to do everything with a sneer, ask questions too quickly, and poke his nose where it didn't belong. Such as now.

"Captain, those coordinates are in northern latitudes, where storms are scarce this time of year. We will lose valuable cargo and opportunities if we leave this area now."

Behind his goggles, James' eyes flashed. Of course Andrew's argument was sound, as he had just been thinking the same thing. But the boy had been a thorn in his side since he had taken him on, and James leaped at the opportunity to remind him who was captain of this ship.

James punched the intercom button with his fist. "Retract the rods. We're turning this ship around. We're going after our friends."

CHAPTER 47

FEBRUARY 21, 1905

Katherine had spent the past eight days in tense stasis. James had radioed the *Madness* and volunteered to come help, but would only just arrive today. She scanned the skies for any sign of *Mjolnir's Child*, but they had docked near the busy sky port of Athens, and she couldn't pick out James' ship from the others coming to dock. Each day that slipped away she felt Marienne growing more and more distant, her rescue growing more and more impossible. By her estimations, Marienne would arrive in London within the next day or so, if the airship had docked for repairs.

Perhaps, if they had docked for repairs, Marienne had managed to escape and was already on her way back to them.

But, no—if that had been the case, her first course of action would have been to radio them, which meant that the original plan had to continue: the plan where everything hinged on her. Katherine had no idea how to go about rescuing her captain, but James' arrival gave her hope.

Mjolnir's Child descended gracefully and docked next to the *Vincenzo*. A gangplank extended from the side, but before Katherine could clamp it to the railing of the *Vincenzo*, James swung across the gap on a rope, leaping deftly onto the deck.

256

Showoff, Katherine thought with a smile.

"Hey, kiddo!" James grinned. "You ready to go rescue your captain?"

"Ready as I'll ever be," she said with a shrug. "My bag's all packed. I'll go get it."

"I want to see Robert," he said, his tone suddenly somber. "From what Landreau said it wasn't good."

She shook her head. "I'll show you to the infirmary. We'll see if he's awake."

Robert smiled when they walked in the door. "Thank you for coming, old friend."

"Who are you calling old?" James teased, but worry lines deepened around his eyes. "You just rest here. We'll bring your girl home."

"She's not… my girl." His uneven breathing could have been laughter, or it could have been anguish.

Katherine left the room, unable to watch any longer. She desperately wanted Robert to come with them, but he wasn't even well enough to be moved to his own ship. The color had returned to his face, but he couldn't sit up. He still coughed too much and slept too often. To see someone usually so vibrant and full of life reduced to spending all day in bed, using all their energy to rest… it broke her heart.

When she entered the engine room, she found Todd sitting at her workbench. She looked at him quizzically and asked, "Is your leg functioning properly?"

"I want to come with you," he said. "I want to help rescue Marienne. It's my fault she was taken. I need to make it right."

"I don't know what I'm doing," she admitted as she grabbed the travel bag Nyx had lent her. "I don't know what I can do. I feel useless. Again." She sighed.

He put a hand on her shoulder. "We'll figure it out together. You don't have to do this alone."

"I won't be alone. I'll have James," she teased. But warm gratitude filled her heart. She had felt completely overwhelmed with this task. Nyx had to stay with the ship, and so many other members of the crew were injured. The *Madness* still needed repairs, and plenty of members of that crew had been injured, too. Now, with Todd at her side, rescuing Marienne didn't seem so impossible.

"You'll need to ask James if you can come," she pointed out. "He said it would be difficult to fit even me on his ship."

"I know. He took on more crew after the Revel, so he's got a full cabin. But I'm sure he can fit one more. I've already packed, too." He pointed to a knapsack on the workbench.

Katherine buckled on her tool belt, feeling safer with its familiar weight around her waist. She took a deep breath. Time to go.

"THANK YOU AGAIN FOR HELPING US," Katherine said as James led her and Todd across the deck of *Mjolnir's Child*. "I hope we won't be too much of an inconvenience."

"Who ever said I wasn't a nice guy? Friends aren't an inconvenience," he assured them. "And when one of our own is in trouble, we have to do all we can to help them. You know space is tight, so the two of you will have to share a room. Respectable parents and nosy housekeepers would disapprove, so try to behave yourselves, or whatever."

He waved a hand dismissively as he opened the door to what Katherine was certain had been a closet recently cleared of its contents. A single hammock had been strung between the walls. Looking at their bags, she doubted they could fit much else in the cramped room.

"Facilities are at the end of the hall, and meals will be announced. But I do ask that you stay out of the hold," James instructed. His tone was light, but his expression was serious as he added, "We just got a fresh catch of lightning. I would hate for it to get loose and kill one of you."

Katherine stared at him before squeaking, "Sure."

He grinned. "We'll take off in a few minutes." He looked around, eyes wide, before leaning forward and continuing in a hoarse whisper, "Also, be wary of Andrew. I think you met him at the Revel. Don't quite trust the kid, but haven't been able to dismiss him yet."

Todd said, "Be careful, James. Last one you were spooked about turned out to be a luma baron spy."

The captain nodded. "I know. Something is off with him, I just can't put my finger on—" James straightened suddenly, his expression falling away.

Katherine opened her mouth to ask what was wrong, but was interrupted by a *click*. She leaned to see around James, but could not see the face of whoever pressed a gun into the small of the captain's back.

"Is that Andrew?" Todd asked.

"Well, I can't rightly see, now, can I?" James responded. "I don't have eyes on the back of my head."

The boy sneered. "You're a fool to be ironic with a gun to your gut."

James nodded. "It's him."

"Get inside!" Andrew demanded.

James obeyed, genuine surprise on his face. "You're not going to kill me?"

"How would I prove that I'm a more competent captain if you were dead?" He scoffed. "I want to revel in your shame before I throw you off the side of the ship. But for now, I need you out of the way." He shut the door and a key turned in the lock, a deadbolt sliding solidly into place.

"He seems a particular strain of stupid," Todd muttered into the darkness. His hand rested on Katherine's shoulder, which she found to be very comforting in the cramped space.

"That he is," James grumbled.

"I'm sorry, can you readjust your elbow?" Katherine asked. "It's hurting my shoulder."

"Sorry." The captain shuffled in the darkness as best he could. "Better? This room has no light, and was only ever intended for you to sleep in. But it shouldn't take more than a few minutes for my crew to realize I'm missing and come for us."

Something rumbled in the belly of the airship and the closet shuddered, throwing Katherine off balance into Todd's chest. "Was that the engine?" she asked in alarm.

"Of course not. They would never—" James began, but then they felt the unmistakable, stomach-dropping sensation of the ship rising into the air. A string of curses flowed from his lips in a single breath so drawn out that Katherine feared he would lose consciousness.

When at last the captain inhaled again, he said, "Alright, new plan." His voice had a hard edge to it. A loud thump shook the room as he kicked at the door, bumping into his companions in the process.

The door did not budge.

After another unsuccessful attempt, Katherine said, "It will be easier if you let me do it."

"No offense, kiddo, but this door is sturdy and you're just a slip of a thing." He grunted with the effort, the small room not even letting him extend his leg all the way.

"I'm not going to try to break it down," she said, exasperated. "I'm going to remove the knob and lock from the door."

James relented, and they shuffled in the darkness until Katherine stood in front of the door. She felt along it, touching each bolt and screw until she had a clear idea of what must be done. There was no room for error—every second that passed likely took them farther from Marienne. She plucked the correct tools from her belt and carefully extracted each piece from the door, promising James and the ship that she would put them back once all was well.

Once the door swung open, James reached into his coat and pulled out a gun for Katherine, then handed another one to Todd. Katherine inspected the unfamiliar model, certain that she would be able to fire it if necessary, but unsure about how much ammunition it held or how much kickback to brace for. When she looked back at James, he held a gun in each hand. She wondered idly who would have more weapons on their person: James or Nyx?

As they emerged on the deck, James took a quick glance around. Katherine noticed that they were already high off the ground, and the Athens docks faded into the distance.

"We're going in the wrong direction!" James cursed. He stormed up to the helm towards Andrew, who steered the ship with a smug expression. But before he had cleared half the distance, the mutineer aimed a pistol at him.

"You escaped sooner than I expected." He frowned. "I will not underestimate you in the future."

"Give it up," James said, hard lines etched on his face. "You know you won't get away with this, and you're only endangering the people I care most about. That makes me dangerous." He raised both guns, aiming them at the mutineer.

"That's the difference between you and me," Andrew said calmly. "I can no longer allow your emotions to get in the way of this ship and crew's primary purpose. Need I remind you that we are lightning chasers? This time of year there are no electrical storms large enough for us to collect the cargo we need in this latitude, and sailing here is only robbing me and the rest of the crew of what we deserve."

As he spoke, Katherine noticed half a dozen men emerging out of the hatches that led below deck, and surrounding the trio. She tried to point her gun at them, but her hand shook. She couldn't bring herself to pull the trigger.

"Take them to the brig," Andrew commanded in an offhand voice.

James shot, the sound of his bullet exploding out of the gun closely followed by Andrew's cry of pain. Katherine turned to see blood dripping down his arm, his other hand gripping his shoulder.

The memory of Robert being shot flashed before her eyes.

Katherine couldn't breathe. All she could see was the crimson dripping between Andrew's fingers. She didn't notice one of the men lunge forward until he seized her wrist and wrenched the gun from her hand. Too late she tried to beat him off, but her blows didn't seem to affect the large man at all.

Glancing around, she noticed that James and Todd had been similarly overpowered. They stood with grim and glowering expressions on their faces, their hands secured behind their backs as the rebelling crew tied rope around their wrists. Katherine's fingers twitched, anticipating the same to be done to her.

"Take her tools," Andrew commanded.

Her eyes widened in horror. "No!" she protested, over and over, writhing as the brute holding her unbuckled her belt.

"Stand still or I'll make you stand still!" he threatened.

She obeyed, the old familiar fear settling into her stomach and gripping her heart. She stared forlornly at her tools, tossed aside to a corner of the deck as if they weren't the most valuable possessions she owned. How could she be of any use without them?

Once her wrists had been tied, the large man gripped her arm tight. Katherine half-jogged to keep up with his long strides as he escorted her below deck, below the second level, deep into the belly of the ship where dim electric lights lined the walls. She kept her gaze fixed on the back of Todd's head in an attempt to calm herself—though her fingers pinched at each other. As long as they were together, she knew they would figure a way out of this. They could still rescue Marienne.

The brig was made up of four cells crammed into a corner of the ship, two on each side with a narrow walkway in the middle. Katherine noticed that two of the cells were full of about half a dozen men each. They crowded up against the bars as Todd, Katherine, and James were led into view, and shouted obscenities at the mutineers that made Katherine wince. The man escorting Todd opened the cell door and pushed him inside, where he stumbled into one of James' loyal crew members. But to Katherine's dismay, they closed the door behind him and directed her towards one of the empty cells.

"No!" she shouted. "I have to be with him!"

The large hand squeezed tight, and he ushered her none too gently inside the cell and closed the door. As he locked it, she whimpered.

"Andrew's orders," he said with a leering grin that revealed too many missing teeth. "Ladies should be treated special."

James scoffed from the cell next to hers. He, too, was alone.

Once the guards had sauntered back down the hallway, most of the crew members retreated to the corners of their cells. One man untied the knots binding Todd's hands.

"Glad to see you're still alive, Captain," he said casually.

James nodded. "I'm glad to see so many of you here." He frowned. "That sounded better in my head. When did you get locked up?"

"While you were on the *Vincenzo*. They overtook us, one by one." He leaned against the door to the cell, face pressed against the bars and arms threaded through them. "Got a plan yet?"

"I like to have a drink before I make a plan," James sighed.

"Sorry, Captain, no liquor down here. We did hide some weapons in the cells, though."

"By all the stars in the heavens, Newt, why would you do that?" James thundered.

"Because we were suspicious!" he shouted back in imitation. "Andrew has been slinking around for weeks now, recruiting a following for himself. We wanted to be prepared."

"What if Andrew had been caught and thrown in here?" James retorted. His goggles slipped down his forehead, but with his hands still bound behind his back he couldn't fix them.

"We would have moved them," Newt assured his captain. "But the mutiny happened earlier than we expected. We didn't have time to stock these cells." He gestured to indicate the two cells where over a dozen men had been packed together like dogs in a kennel. He then pointed to the two cells where Katherine and James stood alone. "They're all in those."

James glanced around the empty cell. "Where did you put them?"

"Behind the panel with an odd number of screws."

James scanned the metal-plated wall, each panel bolted to the others and to the supporting beams that made up the skeleton of the ship with four screws—except for one in the corner that rattled slightly with the hum of the engine. One extra screw had been added in an attempt to stop the sound. James turned around and tried to unscrew the panel with his hands still tied behind his back.

"Is there a knife in there?" he asked.

"Plenty."

"Good," James grunted. "I would really like to have full use of my hands again." He cried out as he felt his thumbnail crack right down to the quick, a sharp sting in his finger. He gingerly touched the fresh wound and found it wet with blood. Grimacing, he turned to the crew. "Anybody got a coin? These screws are tougher than nails."

Everyone shook their heads. Katherine said bitterly, "All of my supplies were in my tool belt."

"They turned out our pockets when they shut us in here," Newt added.

"Not mine." Todd reached into his pocket and pulled out the small gear, the one that Katherine had taken from the prosthetic—the one that had been a useless extra. "Will this work?"

"Let's give it a try," James said, crouching to the floor near the door of the cell.

Todd carefully slid the gear across the floor to him, a surge of pride swelling in his chest as James fitted it into the screw. He knew that the gear had a purpose. It just needed to find the right time and place.

"We'll get out of here yet!" James called triumphantly as the first screw dropped to the floor with a clatter. In a short time, all of the screws had been removed from the panel, and it fell open to reveal a cache of guns, knives, and swords, all wrapped up to protect them from rust. James chose a short, sharp knife and brought it over to Katherine.

He instructed her on how to hold the knife and placed the hilt in her hands. She shut her eyes tight, praying that the blade wouldn't slip while James adjusted his bound hands over it and sawed the ropes back and forth. With a satisfying snap, he was free.

"You did very well," he complimented. "Now, hold still." He cut the ropes that chafed against her wrists.

Katherine smiled in relief. "Now what?"

"There should be weapons in your cell, too," Newt called. "Odd screws, same as the other."

She nodded, but before she could begin her search, the door at the end of the hall opened. She looked at James with wide eyes, only to find him mirroring her expression. He ran to the corner of the cell, threw the knife inside with the other weaponry, and jammed the panel back into place. But he did not have time to replace the screws before none other than Andrew himself walked into view. He strutted in the dim light, the smallest of smirks gracing his lips. He held a large tray piled high with bread and oranges. A bandage was wrapped around his shoulder, a small spot of dark red visible through the layers of gauze.

"Supper time," he announced. "Ladies first." He brought the tray to Katherine, fixing her with a cold stare. Though his eyes were pale gray, Katherine found them chillingly familiar. They held the same challenge she had tried to avoid for two years: daring her to cross him, to only give him a reason to be cruel to her.

She snatched a slice of bread and an orange quickly. As Andrew retreated, she noticed that her hands shook, and she crossed them over her chest.

"Disgraced captains get second pick," Andrew said, turning to the next cell.

James stood in the corner, his weight pressed up against the wall where half an armory was stored. "I'm not hungry," he said with a shake of his head.

"I insist." Andrew pushed the tray up against the bars. "You must keep up your strength. I will not have you starve yourself before you can see my triumph."

"I won't starve by skipping one meal." James rolled his eyes.

"What's that?" Andrew stared at the tangle of rope that sat at James' feet. He called out to someone who appeared so quickly that he must have been standing just outside the doorway. Katherine recognized him as the man who had so easily overpowered her. He procured a key that shimmered faintly from his pocket and opened James' cell. Andrew handed the tray to the man and picked up the rope.

"This has been cut!" He glared at James, then roughly grabbed his wrist and yanked him away from the wall. The metal panel clattered to the ground, revealing the cache of weapons inside.

James punched Andrew in the face. The mutineer reeled, but his lackey grabbed James' arm in one beefy hand. Andrew grabbed a gun from his belt and aimed it at the captive captain.

As he screamed a tirade at James that was equal parts tantrum and self-praise, Katherine shrank into the corner of her cell. She clutched the orange and bread close to her chest and tried to make herself as small as possible. There was nowhere to hide here. And if Andrew found out there were weapons in her cell, too… She shut her eyes tight as he raised his voice. *Don't think about it. He always seems to know what you're thinking.* Her fingers twitched, scratching at the bread and the skin of the orange, filling the air with the scent of citrus.

The large man opened her cell, and Katherine flinched, but he only shoved James inside before locking it up again. He returned to the other cell and helped Andrew clean out the stash of weapons.

James shot Katherine a warning look, but it changed to one of deep concern when he saw her. She curled deeper into herself. Now he knew how useless she really was.

At last Andrew had removed all of the contraband. He scowled at the loyal crew. "This little stunt has cost all of you your supper," he announced.

Katherine held her portion so tightly that the bread flattened and the orange threatened to pop.

Andrew turned with a smile to Katherine. Cold dread filled her bones at the sight of that smile. "Except for you. You may eat what you have."

James was escorted back to his cell, leaving her alone once again. After Andrew and his guard stormed out, Katherine peeled her fingers away from her food. She looked at it for a long time, not very hungry, but fighting the urge to cram it into her mouth before Andrew could change his mind. At last she sighed. "You can have my orange," she said, rolling it across the aisle to the other cells. "I'm sorry, it's not much, but it'll be easy to divide. And you can have half my bread," she added, turning to James and prying open her fingers to reveal the crumpled slice. "I'm sorry, I ruined it."

"I wasn't lying. I'm not hungry," he insisted. "Go ahead." He watched her curiously as she wolfed down each bite, barely pausing for breath in between.

When she was done, Katherine tried to distract herself from the lingering fear she felt after seeing Andrew. She turned to studying the lock of the cell—or at least, what she could see of it from inside. A hand-sized square panel blocked her view of the keyhole. "What can you tell me about these locks?" she asked James. "That key had luma in it."

"State of the art!" James said with a proud grin. The expression faded. "They're supposed to be impossible to break out of."

"Great," Katherine grumbled. "I'm stuck in here with all the weapons, and no way to get out."

CHAPTER 48

FEBRUARY 22, 1905

Marienne stepped out of the automobile and looked around at the London estate, feeling nothing but disgust. It had been over five years since she had last been here, and it had not changed. She had. Instead of a dress heavy with petticoats and ruffles, she wore leather pants and a coat that sported lapels and tails. Her curls now spread out from her head in a wild halo, when once they had trailed tamely down her shoulders. She felt as if she had emerged from a cocoon and revealed her true self when she had run away from this place, and now they were trying to stuff her back inside the ruined and confining shell of what she had once been.

Antoine Prescott approached her, arms spread and a wide-lipped grin on his face. "My dear Marienne! Welcome back!"

She held up a hand, halting him a single pace away from embracing her. Her expression was stern; the one she had perfected from years of disciplining a crew into following her every order. "Let's get this clear right away. I'm being held here against my will, and will not indulge in anything I do not want to."

He looked at her, baby blue eyes open too wide, feigning inno-cence. "But, my dear, if you disobey me I will destroy my ship and everyone on it." He grinned at the fear that flashed across her face.

"Yes, it was indeed a grave error for you to contact us. You see, we can track radio frequencies back to their source, thanks to modern technology. Now that we have the frequency of… the *Vincenzo* you called it?" He grimaced. "Terrible name. No matter. Once I find it, I will bring it back home, and everything will be right again." He closed his eyes and took a deep breath to calm himself.

Marienne seethed. She had done everything she could to hide from Prescott: changed the name of the ship, painted it a new color, even changed the radio frequency. But it had only bought her time. She was trapped once again.

"Did you know that people have begun to talk?" he asked.

"Begun?" she snorted. He shot her a sidelong glance, but she did not apologize.

He took her arm, and she shuddered as they walked away from the automobile and towards his manor. "Yes, they've begun to talk. Less about you and more about me. I always said I would marry only you, and I must honor that, you understand. But there's been fear that I would not have an heir, and then where would the company go?"

"You have other family," Marienne said through grit teeth as he led her indoors.

"Extended family," he said with a dismissive wave. "They're not fit to run an economic empire, they're parasites! They have no respon sibility."

"So you'll use me to raise an heir who will run the company the way you want," Marienne said, her voice flat. "How unfortunate."

"Perhaps for you," Prescott admitted. He guided her into a plush chair set at the tea table and began to pour. "Do you still take cream and no sugar?"

"Lately I have preferred coffee." She allowed herself a small, satisfied smile when he grimaced. Prescott hated coffee. "But when I take tea, yes. Cream, no sugar." She took the offered teacup and blew gently on the steam. "So you admit that I am to be your prisoner."

"Only because you choose to be," he countered, pouring his own cup of tea. He added three sugar cubes, one at a time, and a splash of cream. "It is not my fault if you do not want the world of luxury I offer you."

"I want the freedom to make my own decisions." Her tone was bitter. "But, since that seems to be as present on the table as coffee, I will take my tea." She sipped from the china cup daintily. "What will happen to those responsible for bringing me here? Murdock mentioned a promotion."

"Oh, yes." Prescott grinned as he placed his cup back on its saucer with a ceramic clink, then licked his fish-like lips. "He will now oversee the routes and positions of half our airships, since he has hands-on experience with that sort of thing. He can direct them to the best sources of luma and out of the vicinity of sky pirates." He looked over the rim of his cup at her as he took another sip, but she ignored him.

"The boy who was responsible for you," he continued. "Ethan, I believe his name was. Murdock tells me he did such a good job caring for you on the ship that I've decided to make him your personal valet."

"I'm too old to have a nanny," Marienne said quietly, then took a sip to hide her smile. The past week, she had been dropping subtle hints to Murdock about how dreary it was to have Ethan watch over her all the time, and how he couldn't possibly let her do anything fun. Her machinations had worked. Ethan would stay by her side. Perhaps together they might just be able to escape.

CHAPTER 49

FEBRUARY 24, 1905

atherine studied the inner workings of the lock. She had been in the cell for two days now, and James was growing impatient. She had insisted the first day that they wait and observe, to know when the guard would come with food or to check on them. If she was caught taking apart the lock... she shuddered at the thought. But now was the longest window of time she had, so she had used Todd's gear to remove the casing and now stared at the mechanism.

For a lock, it seemed needlessly complicated, but for a machine it was rather simple. At first Katherine was disappointed, but then she scolded herself. *Simple mechanics means a simple solution.* Most of it was a hydraulic system to slide the bolt in and out of place. But there was a failsafe that would keep the door locked if she tampered with the hydraulics. Past those, however, was a smaller panel secured shut with tiny screws—too small for the gear to fit into.

"If only I had my tools!" she muttered.

"I've already told you, kiddo," James said from where he pressed his face up against the bars between their cells. "These locks are impossible to pick."

"And I've told you," she responded in a weary tone, "I am not getting out the weapons until I know we can escape these cells."

They had argued the past two days, but any time James insisted that he could overpower any of the mutineers if he had the weapons, Katherine remembered the cruelty she saw in Andrew's eyes. He would find out that the weapons had been in her cell—men like him *always* found out when things were her fault. And she would be punished.

No, better to play it safe.

She straightened with a sigh and rubbed her back. The gear she had been using wouldn't fit into the screws, but if she had a smaller one… Her heart plummeted as she realized where a healthy store of gears and other machinery could be found. "Todd," she said weakly. "I need your leg."

Across the aisle, Todd looked at her. His brown eyes were heavy with worry, and Katherine felt a pang of painful sympathy.

"I'm sorry," she said. "But it's the only way I can keep working on the lock."

He nodded and rolled up his trouser leg, unstrapping the prosthetic, but keeping the brace on so he wouldn't have to reattach the sensors to his nerves later, after she put it back together. It was a miracle Andrew hadn't taken that too, although with his long trousers, it was difficult to tell it was a prosthetic unless he had looked directly at Todd's foot.

Katherine winced as the prosthetic scraped across the floor to her. She held her breath, staring at the end of the short hallway, hoping against hope that the guard wouldn't come investigate. When no one appeared, she snatched the leg and pulled it inside her cell. She used the gear to unscrew the outer plating of the leg, and carefully studied her creation until she found a suitably small piece.

Unfortunately, it was difficult to reach, and she had to further disassemble the prosthetic to obtain it. Each time she removed another piece, she breathed a silent apology to both it and Todd, promising she would repair it the moment she had her tools back.

She delicately opened the smaller plating in the lock, being careful not to jostle the hydraulics too much. Now she fully understood the lock and its luma-infused key. A small disk, like the kind used in fancy music boxes, rested squarely inside the lock. Instead of raised dots and dashes, a spattering of luma sparkled across its surface. Katherine gasped in delight and pulled the disk out, holding it up to James.

"Do you know what this is?"

"Not a clue," he admitted.

"It's an identification disk. These must have cost a fortune, if there's one in every cell." She glanced around, a gleam in her eye dancing like lightning.

"I hope this means you have some sort of plan," he prompted. The other crew members looked at her, faint hope playing on their faces.

"Better." She dug into the prosthetic and eased her solution free. *Professor De Guignes, you are a saint!* "I've got another disk."

The captain squinted at the two disks she held, one in each hand. "They look very similar to me."

"That's a good thing. Identification disks can come in all different sizes, and some are even different shapes. The fact that we have two that are so similar…" She shook her head. "It's more than good luck. Our ticket out of here lies in the difference between the luma patterns."

"Great!" James clapped his hands together in anticipation. "Shove that thing in there and let's get out of here. I have an airship to reclaim."

Katherine shook her head. "I can't."

"What?"

"This disk is programmed to Todd's biological signature, and the lock still needs a key. We'll have to pick the lock, and have Todd touching it at the same time. Otherwise it won't open."

"I can pick locks," Newt offered. "Just need a couple bits of wire."

Katherine picked up some wire from the remains of the prosthetic and slid them over to the opposite cell. As Newt began working on the lock, she also slid over the gears and Todd's identification disk. "Be quick," she reminded, her stomach swirling with pride and anxiety.

James nodded. "We've wasted enough time already. I don't know how far we've drifted from England, or how much fuel we have left after this detour."

Katherine frowned. She was more worried about the immediate threat of the guard. If she was being honest, she had been so focused on her own escape that she had nearly forgotten that she was supposed to be planning Marienne's rescue. Did that make her disloyal, as well as unqualified? Useless, as always.

Her thoughts were interrupted by the cell door across from her opening with a click. Todd gripped the metal bars for support, swaying slightly as the crew members exited. Relief filled her at seeing them pour out from the prison. *I made this escape happen*, she reminded herself. *I can rescue Marienne, too.*

As Newt started on the lock to Katherine's cell, James said, "Will you get the weapons for us now, kiddo?"

She nodded, and used another gear from the disassembled prosthetic to unscrew the corners of the hollow panel. She gently set aside the metal plating to reveal a small cache of guns, knives, and swords. James pressed his face against the bars, watching eagerly as Todd and Newt opened the door to Katherine's cell. She handed a pistol to the captain between the bars, and he inspected it with a mad grin.

"Let's take back my ship."

CHAPTER 50

Rose gasped as she removed the bandage wrappings from Robert's chest. They tried to cling to his skin, sticky with fresh blood that oozed out between cracks in the scab that had formed over his bullet wound. He grimaced as she gently peeled the soiled bandages off his skin, deep lines of pain forming across his brow as she grabbed a damp cloth and began to clean the wound once again.

"*Fait mal*," he grunted.

"I know," Rose said gently. She wadded the blood-soaked bandages into a ball and set them on the small table next to Robert's bed, then soaked a corner of a clean cloth in wine. His breath hissed in through his teeth as she pressed it against his chest. "I know, it stings," she said before he could complain. "But it would hurt more if it got infected."

"Do you have to keep using my best wine?" he grumbled. "I was saving that for a special occasion."

"I think keeping you alive is occasion enough, Captain," Landreau said as he entered the infirmary. "How is he?"

"This is the third time the wound has reopened," Rose said grimly. "I thought it would heal on its own, but I might have to seal it shut."

"Cauterize it?" Landreau asked, concern creasing his brow.

Rose noticed Robert's eyes widen in alarm. She didn't want to upset him, but he deserved to know. "That's not the worst of it. I'm afraid that there has been internal damage, the kind I can't fix." She looked at the captain. "We need to get you to a real doctor."

Under Nyx's direction, both airships had drifted to a remote, secluded location in Peloponnese. Prescott wanted the *Vincenzo* almost as much as he wanted Marienne, so it was only a matter of time before someone came to finish the job, and currently the crew could not sufficiently defend their home. Most of them had recovered enough to leave the infirmary, but still needed lots of rest. Rose had worried that some of the injuries would be beyond her expertise— Robert's at the top of her list. But Nyx insisted that they stay in hiding.

"A real doctor?" Robert smirked. "What do I pay you for?"

"You don't pay me at all," she responded sharply as she dipped the now red cloth into a bowl of water. "I'm not equipped to—"

She was cut off by a deep, wet cough that shuddered through Robert's chest and forced more blood out of his wound.

"That didn't sound good," Landreau noted, looking at Rose.

She pursed her lips. "We've got to get you down to the ground, right now."

"Wait," Robert insisted, though his voice was weak and his breath rattled in his lungs. His green-blue eyes locked on to Rose's in a pleading gaze. "Luma."

She hesitated. "Are you going to swear an Oath to me?" she half-joked, though she couldn't bring herself to smile.

Robert dissolved into a coughing fit that lasted until he gasped for air.

Rose squared her shoulders. "Landreau," she ordered. "Go send a message to James that Robert is getting worse."

"He hasn't replied the past two days," the first mate said, his voice distant as he watched Robert.

"Try again!" she commanded. Landreau shook himself and scampered out of the room.

Once he was gone, she sighed and removed a small vial of luma from where it hung on a chain around her neck. She had taken it in place of her wages the first week she spent on the crew, never intending to use it. She just liked having it for the novelty of holding starlight in her hands. Stories of miraculous healing swirled in her head as she stared at the glittering light: victims of blood loss brought back from the brink of death, mysterious symptoms disappearing overnight, fatal wounds closing up.

Rumors.

But, perhaps, with a kernel of truth to them. She looked at Robert, who stared back at her. A thin layer of sweat coated his face. There was no guarantee a professional surgeon could heal him, and moving him could still cause further damage.

"You're sure you want to do this?" she asked quietly, both to Robert and to herself.

He nodded weakly. "I have to live." His voice rasped in his throat. "For her."

Rose nodded. "If I'm forcing you to make a Luma Oath, don't make me regret it."

Mechanically, as if someone else were performing the movements, she unstopped the vial of luma and poured it onto a fresh, clean cloth. She firmly pushed on his good shoulder until he was laying down, then warned, "I don't know how this is going to feel."

She pressed the luma-coated cloth to his bleeding wound.

ROBERT HISSED as fiery starlight absorbed into the bullet hole in his shoulder. His eyes shut tight against the pain, Rose's face appeared before him. She was looking at him with the same concerned compassion as she had the past two weeks, as clearly as if his eyes were open. The fire in his shoulder surged. Instinctively, Robert knew that if he made the oath to her, the pain would subside.

No! Was that only in his mind or aloud? The image of Rose wavered, but his awareness was drawn acutely to her hands on his shoulder, pressing the luma into his blood. *I said no!* he struggled to form the words, even silently.

Marienne! Robert thought with all the force he could muster while half his attention was drawn unconsciously to the burning in his shoulder. It was growing impatient. His lips moved, but he wasn't sure if any sound came out as Rose's face blurred and transformed. Marienne appeared before him, her catlike green eyes observed him shrewdly, a slight smile playing at the corners of her full lips.

She'll leave you.

He gasped at the memory of the empty loneliness that consumed him in the weeks after the Revel. It slammed into him in a concentrated force, replaying every time she had ever dismissed him, rejected him, left him.

Sooner or later, everyone leaves you.

Dredging through the thick, oppressive misery, another memory surfaced. The smell of salty spray, absent humming without caring if it was in tune, feet leaving prints in the sand as they waltzed on the Syracuse beach. The warmth of it banished the empty loneliness, like a candle in the darkness.

Marienne had come back. She had chosen him. He had to have faith that she would come back again, that she would continue to choose him.

"I pledge myself with an oath on the luma inside me to Marienne."

The luma flared brilliantly and Robert cried out, aloud this time, so sharp it scratched in his throat. He felt Rose jump beside him. The fire in his shoulder subsided, and the luma settled like an ember. Robert's consciousness faded.

CHAPTER 51

"Whatever else you do," Marienne whispered, "live." She stared at the stars twinkling dully above her, her thoughts half a world away.

"What was that, my dear?"

She stiffened as Prescott placed his hand at the small of her back and positioned himself next to her. He looked out the tall window at the half moon that hung heavy and low in the sky.

"Nothing," she said, her voice sharp. Shame burned on her cheeks. How childish of her—wishing on stars! She could not show such weakness in front of him.

"Intermission is almost over," he said in a gentle tone. "We should return to our box."

"What do you care when the show starts? You only came to watch the people," she said curtly.

Still, she turned away from the window with a rustle of skirts and petticoats. They draped off her hips in a tangle of fabric and wires too heavy and constricting for her taste. The corset laced tightly around her ribcage. Admittedly, she looked stunning. She wished with a sigh that Robert could see her, but a gown like this would be far too impractical in the air. And the two hours she had worn it had already been too much.

Prescott took her arm and glided back to their box with her, a smug smile plastered on his face. "How people behave at the theater can be very telling of their character. For example—"

"Some prefer to actually watch the show," Marienne spat. "So far this performance of Barber of Seville has been wonderful."

His mouth turned down as he moistened his lips, and he held the curtain aside for Marienne to enter the box. "You always have enjoyed theater, haven't you?"

"Don't act like you know me!" she snapped. She sat down in the red velvet chair and turned to face the stage, her back to him.

Marienne looked down and fiddled with the engagement ring he had given her. Or, re-given, as it was the same one he had used to propose nearly six years previous. Instead of a diamond, it sported a glass encasement the size of her thumbnail swirling with pale golden luma. The ring had fascinated her when she first received it, as luma was still much of a mystery to her at the time. Now she fiddled with the soldered seam between glass and gold, wondering if she could pry it open. Even that little pinch of luma could prove useful, unlike the crimson contraband she hid under her bodice.

Prescott stared at the back of her head, her rich red curls reflecting golden lamplight. He licked his lips and tried again. "I must watch the other patrons of the theater, my dear." She cringed at his last word. He ignored her display of discomfort and procured a set of opera glasses from his coat pocket. "We must decide whom to invite to our wedding."

"Don't I get a say in the matter?" Marienne grumbled.

"You've been out of the world for some time now," he muttered as he peered through the glasses. "You wouldn't know who has risen in society, and who has fallen into disgrace or poverty. And besides," he lowered the glasses and his voice, leaning in so close that his breath stirred her hair as he spoke, "I hear you've already sent out a radio transmission inviting someone to our engagement party."

Marienne's heart jumped into her throat. She had asked Ethan to send a transmission to James, under the guise of an invitation. She had hoped it had gone unnoticed, but now she knew that had been too much to wish for. "I'm certain that by this point you have tracked the receiving radio frequency that I sent the invitation to."

"I did," Prescott admitted, sitting back in his chair and once again raising the opera glasses to his eyes. "You sent the invitation to an airship."

"And you already know that it was not my airship."

His mouth thinned to a flat line. He did not like it when Marienne called the airship hers, and she knew it. "Murdock tells me that there was a second airship present when he retrieved you."

"Did he also tell you that he shot the captain of that airship?" Her bitter words hissed out of her mouth. The light surrounding the audience dimmed and the lights on the stage brightened, but she turned to look at Prescott.

He suppressed a smile, and continued to peer at the other theater patrons. "Yes, he did. So who, then, did you invite to my party?"

"A friend. A respectable and legitimate businessman, though he may come off as a little eccentric at first. A lightning-chaser."

Prescott lowered the opera glasses and tapped them thoughtfully against his palm. "A lightning-chaser," he mused. He turned to Marienne and studied her intently. "He could prove to be a wonderful asset to the company, if we could contract him. Was that your intention?" His pale blue eyes held nothing but suspicion.

"He is only my friend, and one I would very much desire to be there," Marienne said, her face impassive. "Although, it may be impossible. He usually flies around the tropics this time of year, and I have not yet received a responding transmission."

The orchestra began to play and the curtain lifted. Marienne turned back to the stage, her heart pounding against the rigid boning of her corset. She found it more and more difficult to hide things from Prescott as the date of their engagement ball drew closer and he insisted that she be included in all the planning. He also dragged her to a myriad of social calls that left her wanting nothing more than to tear out her own curls, don a pair of trousers, and run so fast she would never stop.

She missed the sky. She missed the bright stars and the fresh, thin air. She missed her crew, and most of all she missed Robert. As the performers began to sing, Marienne breathed a silent wish, an echo of what she had said earlier: *live*.

CHAPTER 52

odd leaned against the back wall of the brig, the pistol James had given him held at the ready in case any of the mutineers came to cause trouble. James' loyal crew had gone to ambush the mutineers, but Katherine and Todd stayed behind—her to repair all the cell locks, and him because he couldn't fight in his condition.

He glanced at the pile of scrap that had been his prosthetic and frustration flooded his frame, right down to the stump of his leg. He hadn't brought his crutch—he hadn't thought he would need it. For the first time since he had joined Marienne's crew, he was completely and utterly useless.

Not that I've been much help the past few days anyway, he thought bitterly. All he had done was watch helplessly as Katherine struggled alone. The only things he had contributed had been his prosthetic–which was really Katherine's victory, since she had made it in the first place–and the gear. The one she had discarded.

If I'm not completely fouling things up, I'm simply unable to help at all. He sighed as muffled sounds of struggle filtered from above down to the brig: scuffling feet, shouting voices, the sharp crack of gunfire. He didn't want to fight—the last battle had been enough for a lifetime—

but he wanted to do something other than sit and wait for a danger that likely wouldn't come.

Katherine dropped the gear she had been holding, and it clattered to the floor with a small *ping*. Todd looked at it as it rolled away, then at Katherine, who had not moved after it. She held her arms across her chest, her eyes squeezed shut and her whole body trembling.

"Katherine?" Todd moved to take a step, but wobbled dangerously. He frowned. She was only a few feet away, but he could not reach her. He spoke to her gently, "Katherine, focus on my voice. I can't come to you, but you can come over here and I'll hold you, if you think that will help." He wasn't sure how he would manage wrapping an arm around her, holding the gun, and keeping his balance against the wall, but she relaxed as he spoke.

As she timidly padded over, Todd wracked his brain for what had upset her. He had been so focused on himself that he wasn't paying attention to her. What had he missed? He placed his left arm around her trembling shoulders, leaning slightly on her for balance. A loud thump rattled the ceiling above them, and she flinched. Her fingers twitched.

The fighting, Todd realized. "It's okay," he said in low, soothing tones. "We're safe. James knows what he's doing. No one's going to get hurt this time."

Slowly, she relaxed as Todd continued to speak comforting words in her ear. After several minutes, she took a shaky breath and smiled up at him. "Thank you," she said. Carefully, she extracted herself from his embrace and went to retrieve the gear and finish with the lock.

If I'm able to do just one good thing in this world, Todd thought as he watched her, *I want to protect her.* She still flinched at the sounds above, but she was able to continue working. Perhaps one day he could prove his worth by banishing all of the fear from her mind, keeping her safe from anything that would dare to threaten her. As the sounds of battle continued overhead, he grew angrier. Didn't they know how frightened she was? Didn't they care?

Just as she had finished replacing the plating back onto the lock, Newt arrived with the first batch of mutineers, their hands bound behind their backs. Newt procured the key to the cells and threw them into one. Todd's resentment grew as more of the rebels trickled in a couple at a time, each escorted by a loyal member of James' crew. The fighting above dwindled as the number of mutineers diminished, but the embers of his fury continued to smolder.

Those embers flared into flames as the burly man who had captured Katherine appeared. He struggled against the thick rope tied around his wrists as three crew members shoved him into one of the cells. Todd seethed as he stared at those large hands—hands that had gripped Katherine roughly, the too-tight hold on her shoulders leaving fingerprint bruises that she tried to cover up with the collar of her shirt. He watched as the thick fingers writhed uselessly, unable to undo the bonds that rendered him completely helpless.

Todd grinned, satisfied with the justice of the situation. Every single one of these men belonged behind bars, but most especially that one. And Andrew.

Todd glanced around. He hadn't seen the mutinous boy yet. Instead, he watched as Katherine, pointedly looking down, gathered up the pieces of Todd's prosthetic and wrapped them into a bundle with a coat one of the crew members had lent her. She glanced around, apprehensive, unable to bring herself to make eye contact with any of the mutineers. It wasn't over, yet.

Tense silence filled the brig as footsteps echoed down the hall—two pairs of boots approaching. Breaths held suspended, suspicious glances were exchanged on both sides of the bars, feet shuffling as several men prepared for the possibility of another fight. Katherine held her bundle tightly, fingers twitching. Todd placed a comforting hand on her shoulder and tried to appear more calm than he felt.

James himself escorted Andrew into the crowded brig, and his loyal crew applauded. The usurper not only had his hands bound behind his back, but was gagged as well. His cold gray eyes swept the brig contemptuously as he was placed in the very cell James had occupied, all alone. The bolt of the lock slid into place with a solid *clunk*, and the crew began to filter out of the brig. Katherine let out a relieved sigh.

"Found your tools, kiddo," James said, handing Katherine her tool belt. "Before you get that leg fixed, can you take a look at the engine? I can't imagine that Andrew would sabotage it, but it's possible something went wrong anyway."

She nodded, but Todd noticed she picked nervously at the cloth bundle she held, and her eyes darted to Andrew's cell.

"And, Todd," James continued, "My radio operator betrayed me. Can you take over there?"

"Sure thing," he answered absently, his attention trained on Andrew, watching for any movement towards Katherine. The mutineer paced the otherwise empty cell, muttering behind his gag unintelligibly, his cold gaze flickering accusingly towards the others who had followed him.

Todd leaned fully on Katherine for support as they walked out of the brig together. As they passed Andrew's cell, she averted her gaze, her fingers pinching at the bundle of mechanisms. Todd watched with a frown.

Once they were alone in the hallway, Todd said, "Andrew reminds you of Mr. Castle, doesn't he?"

Katherine shrank. "It's the look in his eyes. He knows how to find and exploit weaknesses to get what he wants." She shuddered.

"Well, you don't have to worry about either of them ever again," Todd said, giving her shoulder a squeeze. "It's over now."

"Thank you," she sighed in relief. "I'm glad you came with me."

"Yeah, it's a lucky thing my prosthetic had just what we needed." He wasn't able to keep the bitterness out of his tone.

"Not just that!" she insisted, stopping in the middle of the hallway. She looked at him earnestly. "Todd, you're always there for me when I need you. The worst part of being locked up was that I was separated from you. You know just how to help me when I'm afraid."

For the first time since the mutiny, Todd smiled. If he could continue to soothe her fears, to help her stay happy, perhaps he did have a purpose. *Not an extra gear.* "I'll always be here for you." He kissed her, then they continued towards the radio control room, away from the brig, the danger, the lingering fear that the mutiny had cast over her already troubled expression.

A note sat patiently on the desk in front of the radio, waiting for them. The previous radio operator must have written it down. Todd frowned as he read it.

"What does it say?" Katherine asked.

"It's an invitation to Marienne's engagement ball. It's in a week." He turned to look at her, tugging on his curls. "Her wedding is a week after that."

Katherine's gasp was interrupted by a sharp sound from the radio. Todd sat down in the chair, flipped a couple of switches and said, "This is *Mjolnir's Child*, proceed."

"*Enfin*, I'm through!"

"Landreau?" Todd exclaimed in disbelief.

"Where have you been? I've been trying to call for days!"

"It's a long story. Do you have news?"

"*Oui*, and it isn't good. Robert's getting worse."

CHAPTER 53

MARCH 2, 1905

arienne trudged down the street, Prescott to her left and Ethan to her right. Her valet carried a large, weighty package that she could not help but sneer at. Inside the package, the dress for her engagement ball sat neatly folded. The ball was tomorrow, and a week after that would be the wedding. Time was running out quickly, and she was out on shopping trips with Prescott.

"Do cheer up, my dear," Prescott said with a satisfied grin. "The new dress looks lovely on you. Mauve is the color this season. And the dressmaker said your wedding gown will be ready in time, which is rather impressive given she's had such short notice."

Marienne rolled her eyes and grumbled, "The rush fee was nothing to you. I would accuse you of simply trying to marry me as soon as possible, but if that were the case you wouldn't worry so much about everything being perfect."

His obsession with public appearance, as annoying as it was, had been advantageous to her. Prescott was trying his best to marry her quickly, but it had to be done *right*, and every day they spent shopping and preparing was another opportunity for her to plan her escape.

Prescott licked his wide lips with a frown. "I am a prominent figure in society. Of course it must be perfect."

As they passed the luma distribution center, Murdock joined them, immediately engaging Prescott in a report of the airships he oversaw. Marienne was disgusted that she felt relief at seeing Murdock, but he sufficiently distracted Prescott from conversing with her. *Beggars can't be choosers*, she reminded herself. She tested how diverted the two men's attentions were by slowing her pace so that they walked slightly ahead. Ethan stayed by her side.

Prescott glanced back to check on her, then with a satisfied nod that she was still following, he turned back to Murdock's report.

Marienne allowed herself a smile. She was on a short leash, but she would take whatever morsel of freedom she could.

"Did you see how that shop girl was flirting with Prescott?" Ethan said with a shake of his head. "Shameless."

"She can have him," Marienne snorted. "Unless you were interested in her?" she teased. She laughed at his disgusted expression.

Nearby, the sound of applause erupted, catching Marienne's attention. Her green eyes lit up at the sight of a crowd gathered on the opposite side of the street. They surrounded what looked like circus performers advertising an upcoming show by rehearsing parts of their routine.

"Look, Ethan!" She tugged on his arm and ran into the street, dodging an automobile along the way. Her heart pounded in her chest. *Don't look back; it'll slow you down. Perhaps they haven't noticed, and even if they have, you can lose them in the crowd.* A golden opportunity lay before her; she was not going to let it slip away by doubting herself.

She plunged into the crowd, towing Ethan behind her. The poor boy was still trying to balance the heavy box while she pulled him along. People clapped again as she emerged at the front of the crowd, but she didn't look at the performers. Marienne was on the prowl for the best escape route. She didn't care where it led, as long as it was away.

There! Behind the one-man-band, the mouth of a narrow, dark alley gaped invitingly. An eager grin split across Marienne's face, and she began to edge around the crowd towards the alley. All of her senses were on high alert, trying to detect any indication that Prescott and Murdock had followed her, but the crowd was too noisy, too close, too much for her to discern anything else. It was a disadvantage, but she pressed on.

At last she and Ethan burst free of the warm, excited crowd and emerged into the cool shadows of the alley. Loose newspaper, broken bottles, and decaying wooden boards littered the ground, and the smell of rotting produce lingered in the air. To Marienne it was paradise—a shot at freedom.

"Let's go!" she urged Ethan in a breathless whisper, breaking into a run. She didn't know where the alley would lead her, but if she could get far enough away, she could lose Prescott. Then, as he wasted time mobilizing whatever forces he had at his disposal to search for her, she could find a way out of town. Perhaps on a steamer—he would expect her to go straight for the airships, so he might ignore the sea docks altogether. And then—

"Stop." Murdock's voice was calm but clear, and echoed off the close-set brick walls.

Marienne sneered at the thought of actually listening to him, and continued to run until she heard Ethan cry out behind her. Skidding to a halt, she turned to see Ethan kneeling on the ground, one hand pushing on his knee. The large box had tumbled from his grip, laying in the alley yet still firmly tied shut with twine, sitting placidly while he fought against the luma inside of him. She looked up at Murdock, who stood near the mouth of the alley. He did not advance any closer, only smirked.

"Ethan," he commanded, "take that broken bottle and hold the edge to your wrist."

Marienne's eyes widened. She watched, horrified, as Ethan tried to resist the command. "Don't do it!" she called out, knowing that it was useless. He was not bound to her. The luma would respond only to Murdock.

Agony contorted Ethan's face as he struggled, pushing harder against the scar on his knee, until he screamed in primal despair. As the echoes of his scream reverberated around him, his hand shot out and gripped the bottle by its neck. His breath shuddered as he brought the razor sharp edge that glinted in the dim light to rest against the skin of his wrist, just a slip away from spilling his blood.

Marienne's pulse thundered in her ears, and she struggled to hear Murdock's voice— too calm—as he spoke to her.

"You have a choice, Marienne. Either return with me peaceably, or I order Ethan to slit his own wrist."

Ethan's hazel eyes grew wide and wild, like a horse's when it's broken a leg. He gritted his teeth. He was trapped between the fire waiting to rush towards his heart, and the cold, sharp edge of glass in his hand. His pulse fluttered rapidly against the glass, and he feared that if his heart beat any faster, the pressure alone would press against the edge too hard. He wanted to close his eyes against the thought, but found that he couldn't. He could only stare at Marienne as she decided his fate.

Anguished begging poured out of Ethan without words. Marienne couldn't breathe. It wasn't a decision—not one she was willing to make. And Murdock knew it.

As much as she wanted freedom, she would not accept it at the cost of an innocent life.

And he knew it.

Marienne seethed. How dare he. How *dare* he force her into this position again, to acknowledge that he could manipulate her through her moral code. She longed for her pistol so she could shoot that smug look off his face. That would free Ethan.

"Let him go," Marienne growled. "You know I'll come with you."

As she stepped forward, Murdock said, "Ethan, cut the palm of your hand."

Squeezing his eyes shut against the pain in his leg, Ethan obeyed. Marienne's shouts mixed with his as she dropped to his side. She pulled a handkerchief out of her pocket and wrapped it around his bleeding hand, then glared at Murdock.

He smiled at her coolly. "Don't forget who holds the cards."

CHAPTER 54

MARCH 3, 1905

"Stop pacing, kiddo," James complained. "You're making me anxious!"

"You're not already?" Katherine stopped in the middle of the deck and stared at him in disbelief. "Any one of a million things could go wrong at any moment!"

"If I've told you once, I've told you at least a dozen times," he said wearily. "We've got just enough fuel to get us to the coordinates Marienne sent, and you've inspected the engine more times than I can count. You said so yourself that you found nothing wrong. Why don't you sit down? It should only be another half hour until we reach the ball."

"I'm afraid I'll wrinkle the dress," she grumbled, smoothing a crease from the borrowed gown. James had found it in a storage trunk and deemed it to be suitable for her to wear, even though it hung off her frame in bunches. She draped an ivory shawl across her shoulders to hide how the neckline dipped almost too low.

More than that, though, she had to leave her tools behind on the airship. She knew it was because they would give away her disguise, but without them, she felt utterly inadequate. How could she possibly help Marienne without her tools?

"You look great," Todd said as he emerged onto the deck. His newly repaired prosthetic peeked out from beneath the cuff of his borrowed maroon trousers, and he tugged on the sleeve of the matching jacket. "The color really brings out your eyes, though it's not as nice as the dress Robert made you."

"Doesn't fit as well, either," she grumbled. She turned to James. "I'd rather you burst in with guns blazing than dress like this."

"That was the original plan," the captain agreed, leaning against the railing of his ship and gazing down at the English cityscape, tinted blue in the gathering dusk. "But since half my crew decided to turn against me, we don't really have the manpower to take on whatever security Prescott can afford these days. Infiltration is the best option."

Katherine noted the bitter tone in his voice and joined him at the railing. "I'm sure you'll get to shoot someone tonight," she assured him.

He shook his head. "I'm just dropping you two crazy kids off. I have to go refuel the airship, or we won't make it past the channel. Not to mention I want to get those dirty mutineers off my ship. If I shoot anyone, then things have gone very wrong."

She stared at him, mouth and eyes wide open. "You're not coming with us?"

"Wouldn't it be a bit suspicious for a young woman to be accompanied by two men?" he teased, glancing at her with a smile. "I'll come back for you after I refuel at the nearest station. They'll be able to hold Andrew there until the Aerocorps can get him. Shouldn't take more than an hour."

Katherine turned her attention to the landscape drifting by below her, trying to ignore her pounding heart and the urge to pace again. The city fell behind them, the tall metal smokestacks and coal-thick air giving way to forests of skeletal trees as stars began to appear in the sky. How could she and Todd rescue Marienne by themselves?

A village appeared to her right, the warm yellow firelight spilling out of the windows, painting the frosted ground in sparkling gold. The steeple of the village church rose above the cluster of houses like a pastor giving a sermon. A beautiful stained-glass depiction of

Stephen's vision of God burned with bright colors in the growing darkness.

Katherine gasped and stood up straight, her entire body going numb. The blood drained from her face, and she somehow couldn't remember how to breathe; she could only stare at that window.

"Kiddo?" James asked nervously. He waved Todd over, then placed a hand gently on her shoulder. She flinched away from it. "Katherine, what's wrong?"

"That's Saint Stephen's Church." Her words were slow and heavy; her tongue felt thick in her mouth. She looked at James. "This can't be right."

"You know this place?" Todd asked.

"Don't you?" she retorted, her attention snapping on him. "No, you couldn't. You never left the ship." Her eyes darted frantically back and forth, always returning to the village below them.

"I'm just following the coordinates Marienne gave me," James said defensively.

"I'm sorry, they must be wrong. This is wrong! It has to be." She shrank back from the railing and crossed her arms, fingers pinching through the thick emerald velvet. Her breath came in rapid spurts; her lungs couldn't seem to get enough air. "No, no, no."

Todd put an arm around her. She flinched, but did not move away, though she still pinched at her arms. "Where are we, Katherine?" he asked gently.

She looked up at him, her eyes too large and too bright. "This isn't Prescott's London estate. We're on our way to his summer home."

Todd's expression turned hard as understanding sank into his bones. "Alexander Castle."

"I'm sorry," she whispered hoarsely, squeezing her eyes shut. "I can't go. I can't go back. I can't face him. Not again."

Memories crowded her consciousness, blocking out everything around her: Mr. Castle yelling at her that she was useless; Mr. Castle demanding that she not sleep until her chores were done; Mr. Castle threatening to bind her to him with luma. Mr. Castle... Mr. Castle... Mr. Castle... The weight of them crushed her. She felt so small, so useless. *He was right. I can't do anything.* Her fingers pinched faster and harder.

But there was no pain.

With this realization, Katherine found the strength to open her eyes. The memories dissipated, but hovered at the edges of her mind, threatening to come back. When she looked down, she saw that Todd held her from behind, his arms wrapping around her torso and placed under her hands.

He had let her pinch him instead.

She turned around to see his face. He smiled at her, relief not quite covering up his concern.

"I can't get Marienne out by myself," he said quietly. "And James has to be with the ship, or they won't accept the prisoners. But you won't be alone this time. I'll be there, and Marienne will be there. We can make sure he doesn't find you. Do you think you can be brave?"

Katherine glanced over the railing just as the trees receded and revealed the enormous house where she had spent two long years. Her stomach dropped as if the airship had taken a sudden dive. Every window facing the front lawn was lit up and the faint sound of music drifted on the breeze as the airship descended. She had been a prisoner, tortured in that house. The very idea of setting foot in it again made her want to disappear.

But Marienne was in there. Marienne, who had rescued her from that very house, and praised her for her work on the *Vincenzo*. Marienne made Katherine feel important.

Now her captain needed her. A quivering resolve timidly whispered inside her. It was Katherine's turn to rescue Marienne.

"Let's go," she said before her determination left her. "Let's save our captain."

CHAPTER 55

$\mathcal{A}$s Prescott paraded around the room to speak to each guest, Marienne stayed firmly planted in the corner, alternately observing the guests and her engagement ring. The wedding loomed only a week away. Prescott had brought her to his summer estate to distract her with an unfamiliar landscape, and she hadn't had time to plan any more escape attempts. Guards were set all around the estate. To a casual observer, it would appear as security for the ball, but they had been tasked specifically with keeping her inside.

Just before dinner, three serving girls had helped Marienne into the heavy mauve dress and pinned her curls into a fashionable twist. She tried to speak to them, to encourage them to rebel and escape— after all, they were not bound by Oaths. But their eyes held no interest in her, no light at all. She recognized the hopeless look, and felt it creeping over her now. They had been broken from years of service with no end in sight. Her marriage would be just as stifling.

She scanned the room for any sign of a familiar face, but found none. Even Ethan had been separated from her, ordered to stay in the servants' quarters for the night. She was alone, isolated in a crowd, and rapidly running out of options. She had still managed to hang onto the eclipse luma, hidden safely in her bodice, but what good would it do her? It was a single tool without a purpose unless she came up with a plan.

Her mind remained stubbornly blank as despair set in. Cold dread seeped into her limbs as she realized that she might really have to marry Prescott. She glanced again at the engagement ring, that tiny bit of luma swirling inside.

It reminded her of the sky, and her chest ached at the thought. Her mind turned to Robert, and she silently repeated the mantra she had adopted: *live, live, live.*

"Pardon me, my dear," Prescott said as he approached Marienne. "A couple has just arrived saying you invited them."

Marienne looked past him to the doorway, and a flash of surprise and alarm stole across her face before being replaced by a genuine smile. Katherine and Todd had not been the rescuers she had expected, but for the first time that day she felt hope.

"Yes! I told you I had invited a lightning-chaser." She strode towards them, Prescott trailing behind her. "May I introduce to you, James and Kat of *Mjolnir's Child.*"

Katherine smiled gratefully at Marienne for the nickname, although she felt like they were only delaying the inevitable. Mr. Castle was here somewhere. All she could do was hold on to the thin hope that he was too busy to see her.

Todd adopted his role as James quickly. "Thank you for inviting us! This must be your fiancé."

Prescott shook Todd's hand. "I've heard many interesting things about you and your freelance business. I have some questions, if you don't mind."

"Not at all!" Todd beamed as Prescott led him away. "You won't believe the dangerous adventures I've had!"

Katherine held back a giggle. Todd's stories would keep Prescott busy; she only wished James could see Todd impersonating him.

"What are you doing here?" Marienne hissed to Katherine as she led her to the corner where she had taken up residence. "Don't get me wrong, I'm glad you're here, but why are you here?"

"We came with James. Good idea, getting him on board."

"I sent that transmission nearly three weeks ago! What took you so long?"

"There was a mutiny," she reported. "But we came as quickly as we could." Katherine pushed aside the guilt she felt for wasting a day before opening the locks in the brig. Now was not the time to dwell on past decisions.

"And Robert?" Marienne asked hesitantly.

Katherine shook her head. "Last report wasn't good. He's alive, but having difficulties healing. Rose is doing all she can and more."

From her position in the corner, Katherine looked around, fearing she would find Mr. Castle, but unable to keep herself from scanning the room. Better to know where he was.

"You look nice," Marienne commented. "But your hairstyle is noticeably out of place. Most ladies these days wear it up, and yours is long enough now that we could do something simple with it."

Katherine shook her head. "No, thank you. I'm hoping that I will be harder to recognize."

"But you aren't any harder to spot," Marienne sighed. "This can't be easy for you. I appreciate what you're doing for me."

Pride surged through Katherine, strengthening her courage. "Do you have a plan?"

"Not yet," she admitted. "But I was hoping you could help me. What should I know about this house?"

"Everything is automated and uses luma-based technology, from the lights, to the heating, to all the kitchen appliances. That phonograph over there," she gestured to the machine that piped out elegant music. "All of it is connected to a generator in the basement." She spotted a familiar yellow dress and quickly looked away, using her hair to screen her face.

Marienne carefully watched the serving girl as she made her way across the room.

Katherine continued, quieter now. "The generator controls and regulates everything. It's the source of luma and power to the whole house. I was never allowed to work on it—that was the one machine I couldn't touch, though I liked to look at it as much as I could."

A mad grin spread across Marienne's face. "I have a plan." She glanced over to see that Todd was in the middle of telling a story so engaging that several others had joined him and Prescott. With a satisfied nod, she took Katherine's hand and led her to the card room across the hall.

They weaved past three tables occupied with games of whist and cribbage before settling into a window seat half-hidden by a large potted plant. Katherine remembered the plant, a knot forming in her stomach. She had tried to water it, but spilled when Mr. Castle startled her. He had berated her for the mistake. She shrank back in the seat.

Marienne carefully watched the dimly lit room, and it was only when she was certain that no one paid them any attention that she spoke. "We are going to sabotage the ball, cause enough confusion to cover our escape." She unbuttoned the high collar that choked up to her chin and tugged on a string around her neck until a small vial emerged from where it had been nestled inside her bodice. The contents glowed red.

"Eclipse luma!" Katherine gasped. When she looked at Marienne's face, she understood. "You want me to put it into the generator."

"You said so yourself: heat, light, anything mechanical will break down." She handed the vial to Katherine. "I don't know how long it will be before the luma takes effect."

"James said he would come back in about an hour, when he dropped us off," she said as she placed the vial around her own neck. "We have forty-five minutes left. That doesn't give much time for error."

"Last time I tested it, the light burned brighter before going out. Watch for that as our signal to prepare to leave. Where should we meet?"

Katherine thought about the manor, and which rooms would be crowded or empty during a ball. "There's a laundry that leads outside in the west wing. The lawn is large enough for James to land there, and no one will use it tonight. Will that do?"

"Sounds perfect. Now, I have some people to find." Marienne rose, and Katherine followed.

"Who?" she asked.

"One is your brother," Marienne said quietly as they passed the card tables again.

Katherine fought to keep her composure. "Ethan is here?" she hissed as they entered the hallway. "Why didn't you tell me?"

"Because I knew you'd be quick as a bullet to go off and find him. We can't risk that right now." Marienne stared hard at Katherine. "Leave him to me. You take care of that generator."

Subdued, Katherine nodded. Marienne was right. She had a job to do, and Marienne was capable of bringing Ethan. That was, if he wanted to come. "Who's the other person?"

A wicked glint appeared in Marienne's eyes. "I'm going to free Ethan once and for all."

CHAPTER 56

Katherine strode confidently into the ballroom, the eclipse luma hidden under her bodice and resting lightly against her chest. Marienne's plan was solid; it would work. She just needed to find a way to tell Todd what to expect before she went to the basement. He was still off to one side of the ballroom, spinning stories about lightning chasing to interested listeners, Prescott included. Todd's eyes met hers, and they shared a smile.

Before she could take a step towards him, someone grabbed Katherine's hand and waist, and even as the word "dance?" slipped from his mouth he had already begun the steps to a waltz. Katherine stumbled along, concentrating on finding her balance and the rhythm before she looked up to see who had so rudely claimed her for the song.

She gasped. He smiled down at her with eyes as dark and cold as a starless sky. The expression turned her stomach.

He leaned in close and whispered in her ear, "Welcome home, Little Mouse."

She swallowed hard, acutely aware of how his voice raised the hairs on her arms and the back of her neck. "Mr. Castle," she managed to stutter breathlessly. She couldn't escape the waltz—his hold on her wrist was too strong, his step too quick. And to cause a scene could ruin Marienne's plan. She looked frantically around for Todd, but the ballroom went by in a blur.

"Your hair looked better when it was shorter," he scoffed. "I always told you that. Why didn't you listen? You never listened, Little Mouse, and now look where it's gotten you. You can't even run away properly."

"I'm sorry," she squeaked.

"No you aren't." His voice was low, but a sickeningly familiar gleam lit up his dark eyes. "Not yet."

He spun Katherine around and she blinked, surprised to find that they had moved close enough to the doorway that he only had to nudge her and she stumbled out of the ballroom. As she straightened, she turned to look back into the bright, crowded room, hoping to catch a sympathetic glance from someone… anyone…

Mr. Castle took a firm hold on her wrist and led her forward. "It'll be better for you if you just obey me. How many times have I told you that?"

How many times had he told her that? So many that she found herself nodding. Her heart pounded in her chest, and she felt small, so small. Her life among the stars seemed so far away, like a dream, and his hold on her was real and present. She let him tow her through the hallways to the emerald parlor. They were as far from the ballroom as they could get.

"Sit." He watched as she obeyed, then moved around the room, checking the drawers of the desk and the end tables. "I don't know where you found such a ridiculous and ill-fitting dress, or those ill-mannered airs. Parading around the dance floor like some gentle lady." He glanced at her to be certain that she still sat in place.

She shivered under the gaze of his coal-black eyes. His face was pleasant, and his smile could be called charming. But Mr. Castle's eyes always seemed to find her weakness, something he could exploit. She sat tensely in her seat, her fingers pinching at her crossed arms.

I have to leave, she thought frantically as he resumed his search. *Marienne is depending on me.* She could feel the weight of the eclipse luma against her ribcage, but tried not to think of it. *He always knows what you're thinking.* If he found the luma, all would be lost.

According to the clock that ticked loudly on the mantle, James would arrive in half an hour. But fear held her like a spell to the chair. *Listen to him,* a soothing voice crooned in her mind. *You know it will be easier if you do.* Back on James' airship, she had felt as if she would be crushed by the weight of the memories of Mr. Castle. Now she felt merely numb; a machine that had run out of fuel.

When I follow the rules, I am safe.

"Here we are." Mr. Castle pulled a large pair of scissors from a drawer. As he approached, he shook his head. "I wouldn't have to do this if you had simply taken better care of yourself, you know. I don't know where you got the notion that running away would be better for you. But all will be set right soon." He gathered Katherine's hair and began to snip away all the length she had gained in the past few months, the months she had spent in the air.

Tears rolled down Katherine's cheeks and dripped off her chin as the scissors sliced through her hair. It felt as if they were cutting into her heart. The ends fell away until the last of her rebellion had been cut off.

"There," Mr. Castle said, satisfaction coating his words. "Isn't that better?" He put the scissors down on an end table, then strode around the chair to face Katherine with a pitying expression. "Come now, stop crying Little Mouse. It's time to get you into your uniform."

She stood mechanically, ready to follow Mr. Castle out of the room. But when she looked up, Todd stood in the doorway. A surge of hope caught in Katherine's throat. Mr. Castle's grip on her arm tightened until his fingernails dug into her skin. He opened his mouth to speak, but Todd did not let any words pass his lips before he punched Alexander Castle in the jaw.

As he stumbled back, bumping into the end table, he released Katherine. She rushed into Todd's arms, shuddering breaths wracking her body. She couldn't even manage to thank him. Todd ushered her behind him, protectively shielding her with his body.

"You don't know who you're messing with, boy." A trickle of blood seeped from Mr. Castle's lip.

"Actually, I think I know exactly who I'm dealing with," Todd retorted. His voice was laced with a hatred that shocked Katherine. She looked into Todd's face and saw an unfamiliar loathing etched into his features.

As soon as Mr. Castle stood up straight, Todd kicked him in the chest with his prosthetic leg. A sickening *crack* echoed through the room. Mr. Castle fell to the floor, his face twisted in a mask of pain. His hands fluttered over his chest, afraid to touch and afraid to breathe. Katherine feared that his ribs may be broken.

Todd loomed over him, expression dark but dangerously calm. Mr. Castle cowered at the sight of him. "You're the man who hurt Katherine." He kicked again, another crack of breaking ribs and a cry from the coward on the ground. "And you were going to hurt her again!" Todd shouted, stomping on the man's hand.

Katherine shut her eyes tight against the sound of bones shattering under metal. She did not feel sorry for Mr. Castle; he deserved this. But Todd? His expression of concentrated hatred worried her. She had never thought of him as a violent man before. What else was he capable of?

As Todd pulled a small gun from his pocket, Katherine whispered tremulously, "Please stop."

She hadn't expected it to be audible, but Todd looked at her immediately. For a split second that grotesque expression was aimed at her before it melted away to confusion. "But... he made you suffer! He deserves to suffer, too!"

"I know." She nodded. "But not like this. Not by you."

Todd hesitated. He wanted to be the one to hurt Alexander Castle, because he wanted to be the one to protect Katherine. But those were not the same thing.

"You're right," he said, and he walked over to her, all the fight gone from him. A heaviness settled on his shoulders. He handed her the gun. "Hold on to this for me, please. I don't trust myself not to use it."

Katherine smiled up at him as she took it. Relief washed over her as she saw that no trace remained of whatever violence had possessed him.

A shout rang through the room.

Todd cried out in pain and fell to one knee, clutching at his right leg. Katherine saw that behind him, Mr. Castle had propped himself up on one elbow, clutching the large scissors he had used to cut Katherine's hair. The blades were crimson and slick with blood that spilled onto his hand.

Mr. Castle struggled, but managed to croak, "Look what you made me do." He raised the scissors again, this time aiming at Todd's back.

Images of Robert bleeding out on the deck of the *Vincenzo* flashed vividly in Katherine's head. She couldn't let that happen again, not to Todd. She frantically fired the gun at Mr. Castle, unable to aim too carefully.

The scissors fell as he slumped to the floor, a crimson puddle spreading quickly around him.

Katherine blinked, an awful realization seeping into her body like blood into a carpet. "He's not breathing," she gasped. One shaking hand flew to her mouth, the other nearly dropped the gun. She stumbled back a step. "He's not breathing!"

Todd stood up laboriously and tried to hide his grimace as he placed weight on his bleeding leg. He eased the gun out of Katherine's trembling, feeble grasp and gathered her into his arms. "It's alright," he soothed. "You were protecting us. You protected me."

CHAPTER 57

"I don't think I can make it down there," Todd admitted.

Katherine had helped him down the hallway, his cravat tied around his leg already stained with too much red. Now they stood staring at a steep, dimly lit staircase leading down to the basement.

"I can do this part alone," she said. "You rest here and keep watch. No one should come this way, but we don't know if anyone heard the shot."

"Be careful with the eclipse luma," he warned, his expression grim. "That stuff is dangerous."

"I'll wear gloves if I can find them," she promised.

Katherine descended the steps carefully. The steam from the generator dampened the air, and she heard the scrabbling of rats in the darkness—though she couldn't tell if they were natural or mechanical rats. She clutched the vial of eclipse luma, wondering if the autorats could smell it on her. Could rats smell death?

Her stomach lurched as she missed a step, and Katherine fought back a sob. She had killed Mr. Castle. Guilt and relief, pride and shame swirled in her in a confusing vortex. She stared at her hands, the light from the eclipse luma painting them a vivid red. Her hands, once only stained with grease, were now tainted with blood.

Don't think about it now. She stood up straight, steeling her resolve, and continued down the staircase. They were running out of time.

Katherine crept towards the generator. It stretched across the wall, brass body and pipes gleaming with the shimmer of luma, gauges glowing softly in the dim light. Once, this machine had awed her in its size and complexity, but after her time spent on the *Vincenzo* with its engine, helium purifier, and other complicated components, the generator seemed rudimentary now.

A quick glance around revealed a pair of leather gloves by the toolbox. Katherine tugged them on. They were too large, of course, but she wasn't taking any chances with the eclipse luma. She uncorked the vial and poured the crimson starlight into the chute. It flowed down the funnel lethargically like congealed blood. She shuddered at the image as the luma disappeared into the machine.

The light in the basement shone brighter, and Katherine smiled. A quick response was promising. An autorat crept towards the generator, the sensor in its nose scanning curiously. With a hiss of steam, it scurried away. Katherine climbed back up the stairs slowly, still haunted by images of blood: on Todd's leg, on the carpet, on her hands.

"Good job," Todd said as she closed the basement door. He tried to stand, but groaned and fell back against the wall. "I don't think I can act natural."

"Then let's get you to the rendezvous point as fast as we can," she said, helping him up and wrapping his arm around her shoulders. He looked pale, and his eyelids fluttered every time he blinked. "Just stay with me. James has a surgeon on his ship, and we've only got twenty minutes before he comes."

He nodded, his head lolling. Katherine bit her lip and looked down the hallway. This was going to be a long walk.

.   .   .

Marienne danced with her fiancé out of courtesy, but did not speak to him. He rattled on about "James" and the business deal he hoped to close with the lightning chaser. Marienne schooled her features so that she would not reveal the truth. She supposed that either Todd knew enough about James' trade, or Prescott knew so little, that they were able to converse at length about the logistics of such a deal.

"But he excused himself rather abruptly," Prescott continued. "Said something about that young lady he had come with—Kat, you said? I do hope they aren't up to anything… improper," he said, licking his lips with a sour expression.

Marienne laughed. "You obviously don't know him very well. They will be fine."

"I hope he doesn't get jealous, though." A hint of conspiracy colored his voice as he leaned in close. "I saw Mr. Castle escorting Kat out of the ballroom."

Marienne's eyes widened slightly and a sharp breath whistled through her nose. But she only said, "Is that so? I wonder where the three of them have gone off to." She glanced over her shoulder, craning her neck for any sight of her friends, but saw only strangers.

Suddenly, the lights brightened, throwing harsh yellow highlights across the crowded room. The automatic phonograph picked up speed, turning the waltz into a polka. Prescott frowned and excused himself to go inspect the machine. Marienne hid a smile behind a sigh and said, "If you must, I understand."

As soon as the crowd had swallowed Prescott, Marienne ran the opposite direction. She had to find Ethan and Murdock both, and fast. The eclipse luma left an undetermined window of time before she would be stumbling blind.

Marienne walked into the dining room, where a single young woman in a pale yellow dress was cleaning up the dishes from dinner. "Prescott is asking that all servants help in the ballroom. Something has gone wrong with the mechanics of the house."

The serving girl looked at the electric lights set in sconces around the room. Each of them shone so brightly that she squinted. "I wondered about that."

"Please fetch those who are in the servants' quarters," Marienne instructed. "We need extra help to make our guests comfortable while we sort this out." She hoped that her request wouldn't seem too suspicious. If she had asked for only Ethan, it surely would have alerted Prescott—or more likely, Murdock—that she was up to something.

Once the maid had left with a curtsy, Marienne snatched a sharp knife from the dining table. With one napkin she wiped the grease and crumbs off the blade, and with another she wrapped it carefully before sliding it into her boot.

"You seem lost."

Marienne straightened quickly and turned to see Murdock standing in the doorway.

"I was checking to see if the lights were malfunctioning in here, too," she said coolly. "Strange, isn't it?"

His eyes narrowed. "Yes, it is."

"If you'll excuse me, I need to report this to my fiancé." She moved towards the door, but he did not move to let her pass.

"I know you're behind this somehow," Murdock hissed. "But you won't escape. Remember, Ethan still belongs to me."

Not for long, Marienne thought, acutely aware of the hidden knife resting against her ankle. But this wasn't the place; he could easily grab another knife from the table to fend off her attacks. Now wasn't the time; she needed the cover of darkness to avoid discovery before she could escape. It was a delicately timed plan, and all the uncertain elements needed to converge perfectly for it to be pulled off. She couldn't afford to ruin her chances by being too hasty.

"Let me pass. I need to return to the ballroom."

Murdock stepped out of the doorway, and said, "Let me come with you. We have no idea what else could go wrong tonight."

CHAPTER 58

$\mathcal{E}$than paced the narrow walkway in between the two rows of beds back and forth, only traveling ten steps before he had to turn again. Three boys and two girls sat on the beds, playing a game of cards. They too had been excused from working the ball downstairs, though for them it was a matter of having enough people already that they weren't needed. For him, it was a deliberate attempt to separate him and Marienne.

And that made him anxious.

Ethan rubbed the bandage on his left palm. Marienne would try to escape again. The crowd would provide enough cover, if she could create a suitable distraction. But where would that leave him? After her previous attempt, she assured him that she wouldn't let Murdock hurt him again. But how long would she let him hold her back?

"You're making me dizzy," one of the girls complained with a pout, tossing her blonde hair over her shoulder.

"Come play cards with us," one of the boys invited, patting the bed he sat on. The springs creaked as if calling to him, too. He added with a wink, "Winner gets a kiss."

"I never agreed to that!" the girl countered.

A muffled *pop* sounded from a room somewhere beneath them.

Gunfire. Ethan's expression grew hard as the others stared at him, confused. Of course they wouldn't recognize the sound—they hadn't lived among it for the past two years. Questions hung on their lips, but Ethan flung himself out of the door and ran down the stairs.

Had the guests heard? He strained to listen as he clambered down the narrow staircase, not daring to slow down. The sound of his own feet and heavy breathing echoed too loudly for him to detect anything else. Perhaps the music and chatter were so loud that no one noticed the gunshot.

Was Marienne in trouble? Had she caused trouble? Scenario after scenario played through his mind as he raced out into the hallway.

Ethan looked around uncertainly. He had only been at this estate for a day, and he had spent most of that in the servants' quarters. He glanced out the window and saw the south lawn—the same view from the window he had been staring out all day. The gunshot had been audible, even from two stories above, so the room that it was fired in had to be directly under where he had been standing.

As he turned a corner, Ethan saw a couple walk just out of sight at the other end of the hallway. He hesitated; they could be involved with the gunfire, or they could be enjoying themselves and looking for some privacy. Deciding not to follow them without evidence, he continued down the hall.

The sharp stench of blood wafted out of an open door as Ethan approached. He froze in the doorway, paralyzed by what he saw. A man lay on the floor, his own blood spread around him, soaking into the carpet and staining it with the last bit of his life. His chest lay lopsided, and one hand splayed in a gruesome display of mangled fingers and knuckles. Ethan covered his mouth and swallowed down the bile that had risen up his throat. He had seen bodies before, but those had usually been clean deaths—stabbed or shot, and then left alone. This man had been tortured.

Bloody scissors lay not far away, but that small of a weapon couldn't have been responsible for this amount of carnage. Where was the gun—and who had fired it?

With a conscious effort, Ethan peeled his gaze away from the body on the ground and glared down the hallway. Whoever he had seen walking away must be responsible. As if in invitation, each of the lamps along the walls burned brighter, one by one, the light steadily moving towards where he had seen them. Ethan snatched a letter opener off a desk by the door and tore down the hall, determined to catch the killer.

He didn't recognize the man in the green parlor, but it didn't matter. Whoever did that to a person must be punished.

As he turned the corner, he spotted the couple. They hadn't made it far, and their arms were wrapped around each other. "Stop!" he shouted as he ran closer. He held the letter opener ready in his fist. If they had a gun, he would attack.

They looked over their shoulders in confusion, and Ethan nearly fell as he struggled to stop. "Katherine?"

Her expression melted into relief, and she almost dropped Todd as she turned around. "Ethan! I'm so glad you found us!"

"What are you doing here?"

"We came to help Marienne," she explained.

He held the letter opener uncertainly. "A man is dead."

Her expression fell. "Mr. Castle."

The name sparked in Ethan's memory and anger flared. That was the man Marienne had told him about, the one who had abused Katherine. *He deserved to die*, he thought savagely. But... the torture? Did he deserve that too? Part of him vehemently roared *Yes!*, but another part was still unsure.

"He stabbed me," Todd said, his voice rasping. "Killing him was in self-defense."

Ethan frowned. Blood seeped from the back of Todd's leg, staining a white cloth that was tied around the wound. He would have been stabbed from behind, and the wound was too severe for him to have turned and fired back. Ethan looked at Katherine, but she wouldn't meet his gaze.

Ethan had killed before, during pirate raids on the *Egret*. But it was easy to justify the chaos of battle, the absence of choice with an Oath forcing him to obey his captain's order to fight. He couldn't imagine how Katherine must feel, killing the man who had tortured her for two years, even if only to protect Todd.

"You protected each other," Ethan said at last. "Thank you."

Katherine managed a tremulous, grateful smile. "Marienne was looking for you," she said.

Ethan opened his mouth to reply, but Todd swayed on his feet, his face pale. As Katherine struggled to hold him up, he slumped to the ground. Behind him, Ethan heard footsteps. He turned to see the blonde maid from upstairs approaching him.

"Ethan," she called as he bent down to help Todd. "There's been a call for all hands on deck. We're needed in the ballroom."

"This man is injured," he shouted back. "I'll stay and help him, but please tell Marienne I'm with Katherine, and that Todd is hurt."

She nodded and ran off. Ethan studied Todd's face. Deep lines of pain were carved into his forehead and around his mouth as he grimaced.

"Can you stand?" Ethan asked.

Todd nodded weakly. Ethan helped ease him up, then placed his arm around his shoulder so most of Todd's weight rested on him. Katherine stood on Todd's other side, helping to steady him.

"We've got to get to the laundry," she said, panic coloring her voice. "We don't have much time!"

"Why? What's going on?"

"There's going to be a blackout, and then an airship is coming to take us and Marienne. If we're not there in time, it's sure to draw enough attention that we won't be able to leave."

"Can you lead the way, even if the lights go out before we get there?" Ethan asked. Already, keeping Todd upright was growing difficult. His head drooped towards his chest.

She nodded. "Todd, just hang on for another fifteen minutes. Please."

He managed an insincere ghost of a smile at her before sighing wearily. "I'll try."

"Don't speak," Ethan urged. They walked down the hallway slowly, laboriously. "You know I can't come with you," he said quietly.

Katherine walked silently, struggling as Todd shifted his weight to her. "We know about your Oath," she said at last. "Marienne said she would take care of it. But if you still don't want to... I may not agree, but I understand. It's your choice."

They continued down the hall without speaking. Ethan's hand ached from holding Todd's arm, the cut still fresh enough to throb, but it was the scar on his knee he focused on. He could feel the warmth of luma resting there, dormant, waiting. He couldn't directly harm Murdock, but there was nothing in his Oath about preventing harm from coming to him. If he avoided Murdock until Marienne could free him from his Oath... then what? Would he go with Katherine and Marienne? It would mean running away from his debt as Katherine had.

But when he thought of staying, his stomach churned. Murdock was just one of many luma harvester captains who all treated their crews the same way. Ethan could no longer endure such a life. Even though he was still bound by Oath, Marienne had already liberated him by disillusioning him to the system that held him captive.

I'll go with her, he vowed silently. *If she can free me from my Oath, I'll escape with Marienne.*

CHAPTER 59

*P*rescott kept Marienne close to his side as a current of anxiety ran through the ballroom. He smiled reassuringly whenever any of the guests came to him with questions and concerned expressions, but as soon as they turned away again, he licked his lips with an impatient scowl. One of the guests had offered to take a look at the generator, and Marienne hid a satisfied smile. The luma was inside of it now; there was no stopping the disaster that would follow.

Prescott glanced sidelong at her. "You're not to leave my side again until this is all sorted out."

She stared straight ahead into the crowd of people speaking to each other in hushed tones. "If only you had kept such a close eye on me earlier, you wouldn't be so suspicious of me now—not that it would have made a difference. You can't prove that I'm behind this. Pity."

His face turned a deep shade of red that matched Marienne's hair, but propriety kept his mouth shut as one of the yellow-clad maids approached them.

"Miss Marienne?" She curtsied to her. "Ethan asked me to deliver a message to you. He says he is with Katherine and Todd, and that Todd is injured."

"How badly?" she demanded, fear clawing its way up her throat and straining her words. "Did you see?"

"Not much, Miss. He fell down as I arrived. I think it was his leg, and he looked pale."

Marienne nodded, struggling to keep her expression under control. If Todd's leg had collapsed out from under him, there was a chance that his prosthetic had experienced some mechanical failure. But even as the thought entered her mind, she knew it was not the case. He was pale, and Ethan had stayed to help him.

A glance at the clock revealed that she had less than ten minutes before James would arrive. The lights still burned brightly. Marienne clenched her jaw and silently wished them to wink out so she could escape this place once and for all.

"Thank you, you are dismissed," Prescott said to the girl, although his puzzled expression was directed towards Marienne. She tried to ignore him, but he said slowly, "There's no Todd on our guest list."

She continued looking straight ahead; she could not let him see the scrambling panic behind her eyes. The clock ticked in time with her pounding heart, and she felt every second slip by and fall away, like a fast dissipating cloud. Where was her darkness? "Perhaps it is the name of one of the serving boys?" she said, fighting to keep her voice steady.

Prescott frowned hard and licked his lips, a pronounced line appearing between his eyebrows. "I know that name…" he mused, glancing around the room. "I know…" His eyes widened, then his expression turned steely as he gripped Marienne's arm tightly.

Marienne swallowed hard and schooled her features into a neutral mask. Everything was falling apart: Todd was injured, Murdock still lived, the lights remained brightly lit, James would arrive within minutes, and Prescott had caught on to her scheming. But she could control herself. She could control her expression and her actions. She would not relinquish what little control she had—not now, when everything else was going so terribly wrong.

"You brought him here, to my home, after five years?" he hissed, a few droplets of his spittle hitting Marienne's cheek. "After he stole you away from me?"

She glared at him, ripping her hair free of the myriad of pins holding it unwillingly in place. The curls spread around her face in a fiery halo as she leaned in close, her tone low and threatening. "Let's get this clear once and for all. Todd did not 'steal me away' from you. If anything, I stole him. I took your airship, I learned to captain it, I figured out how to harvest luma, and I willingly gave myself up to protect the family I love. Everything I have done since the day I met you has been a conscious, active effort to stay as far away from you as possible."

One by one, the electric lights around the ballroom winked out in a quick succession of *pops*. The phonograph abruptly stopped its accelerated melody with a sharp squeal, echoed by the panicked shrieks of the guests.

Marienne grinned, her teeth flashing in the darkness like a crescent moon. She purred, "And now you've lost your hold on me once again. Goodbye, Prescott." She wrenched her arm out of his grip, ignoring how his grasping nails tore at her skin, and stumbled out of the ballroom into the hall.

The house had gone completely dark, with only a hint of moonlight shining through the tall windows. Chaotic confusion erupted from the ballroom behind her, and Marienne was confident it would cover her escape.

But there was one more thing she must attend to. She paused between two pools of moonlight pouring in through the windows and knelt down to pull the knife from her boot.

"Marienne." Murdock's commanding voice echoed down the dark hallway, growing louder as he walked closer. "You will return to the ballroom immediately.

"I'm not one of your slaves that you can command into obedience," she hissed. She unwrapped the knife and held it ready, but remained crouched in the shadows. "And Ethan isn't here for you to use against me."

"Prescott has given me permission to use any means necessary to return you to him." His smug tone sent shivers down her spine. He could hurt her now, and he would enjoy it.

Marienne waited patiently as Murdock stepped closer, closer… now! She sprang from the floor, knife aimed at his chest.

He neatly sidestepped her strike, grabbed her wrist and twisted her arm behind her. Marienne gasped in surprise and pain, fighting to keep a grip on the knife.

"Remember, it was I who caught you in the first place," he hissed into her ear. "I, who succeeded when—" His speech was cut off with a grunt as she kicked his shin with the heel of her boot.

She spun out of his grip and held the knife threateningly in front of her. He straightened, meeting her gaze with that infuriatingly smug air. She frowned. It was a mask—it had to be. He backed away from her reach, closer to the windows. She had him cornered. So why was he smiling?

Murdock grabbed one of the curtains and threw it towards Marienne. Surprised, she tried to sidestep the attack, but found herself tangled in the fabric. She could feel it wrapping tighter around her as her opponent trapped her in the curtain. She struggled, but her arms were pinned across her chest, the knife wedged in the crook of her elbow. If she moved it, she risked the blade cutting into her own skin.

"There now," Murdock crooned. "You're all packaged up and ready for delivery."

She heard linen ripping and felt a tug on her prison—he was pulling the curtain down from its rod. She wriggled, but just as the fabric around her loosened, Murdock tightened it again. He lifted her over his shoulder and began walking back down the hallway.

Marienne screamed in panic; she couldn't keep it in anymore. She couldn't fail now! She was so close! Kicking and writhing as much as she could, she tried to free herself from his grasp.

"Come now, stop that," he scolded. "It's unbecoming. Accept your defeat with grace. You know, after this little stunt I may have convinced Prescott to take a page out of his own book."

Marienne paused, a sick premonition settling over her.

He continued. "I suggested that he make you take a Luma Oath. It would be the perfect wedding vows!"

Disgust and rage poured out of Marienne in a yell and she stabbed with all her strength through the layers of linen. The knife bit into her arm, but she ignored the pain—it was nothing compared to the threats Murdock had made. He cried out and stumbled to the ground, Marienne tumbling out of his arms and to the floor. He scrambled towards her, but she had already disentangled herself from the curtain.

They glared at each other in the moonlight, daring one another to make the first move. Murdock lunged forward. Marienne ducked under him and sliced at the back of his calf. With another shout of pain, he fell, clutching the wound. She moved behind him and dragged her blade across his throat.

Marienne left his body in the shadows for someone else to discover. She held the bloody knife in a tight grip as she ran down the hallway. No one would stop her. The low hum of an airship vibrated through the walls of the manor.

James had arrived.

CHAPTER 60

"She did it," Ethan whispered.

Katherine looked at him, unsure she had heard him over the sound of the airship engines. He lightly touched his knee and she thought she saw tears in his eyes. "Ethan?"

He blinked and smiled at her, relieved. "I'm free. Come on, we have to go!" He helped Todd back to his feet. The fresh bandage they had fashioned out of some clean laundry already showed an alarming amount of red.

Katherine opened the door to reveal *Mjolnir's Child* bobbing low, the thrusters straining against the helium-filled balloon to keep the ship close enough to the ground for them to reach the rope ladder. "What about Marienne?" she called over the noise.

"She'll be here," Ethan assured her.

She nodded. They stepped outside, struggling under Todd's increasing weight. "Stay with me!" she shouted to him, her words competing with the roar of the engine. "Don't pass out now!" As they moved closer, the air rushing into the thrusters tugged at their hair and clothing, as if urging them to move faster, faster. She looked at the flailing rope ladder, wondering how they would get a half-conscious Todd up the ladder and to the deck.

"We're almost there," Ethan encouraged.

Once they reached the rope ladder, the end bobbing and weaving as the ship fought to stay put without tethers, Ethan urged Katherine to go first. "I'll be fine, just tell them to hurry!"

She hiked her skirts around her knees and scrambled up the ladder. She couldn't afford to waste a single second. But behind her worry for Todd, another concern throbbed: *Where was Marienne?*

Her hand slipped and her heart skipped a beat as the ladder swung uncontrollably. She held on tight, squeezing her eyes shut until the movement slowed to a more manageable rhythm. She forced her fears out of her mind and focused solely on climbing; this high up, a distraction could turn into a disaster. Marienne could take care of herself.

"You're almost there!" a familiar voice shouted down from the deck. Katherine didn't look up, but she smiled at James' words and felt an extra surge of strength. A few more rungs and strong hands gripped her by the shoulders, helping her up onto the deck of the airship.

"Thank you," she gasped.

"Who's next?" he asked, looking over the edge.

"Todd's hurt, he can't climb," she explained.

"We can't lower the gangplank," James mused, his voice only barely audible over the humming thrusters. "We could use the hammock from your room, if we hook it up to some pulleys. It won't be as fancy as that lift Marienne has, but I think it will do."

"Please hurry!" she urged.

As he rushed away, barking orders to Newt and his remaining crew, Katherine peered over the edge. She waved at Ethan and shouted down to him that everything would be alright, but he shook his head. He couldn't hear her. She frowned and hoped that he would be able to support Todd until James was ready. In the meantime, she stared at the large mansion, now dark, and waited with tense muscles for Marienne to appear. She barely dared to breathe.

"Everything is set and Newt is lowering the stretcher now," James announced, joining Katherine at the railing.

"Thank you," she said, but she couldn't relax until Todd and Marienne were both on board.

"Who's that with Todd?"

"My brother, Ethan. He's coming with us." She glanced down and watched him place Todd carefully on the makeshift stretcher. Once Todd was settled and the stretcher began its ascent towards the deck, Ethan grabbed the rope ladder and began to climb.

"And here comes our lovely Marienne," James said.

Katherine followed his gaze, and her whole soul relaxed with a sigh as she saw her captain running across the grass, her heavy skirts held high around her knees. A bloody knife flashed in her hand. She was not yet a third of the way to the airship when another door opened and Prescott tore after her, surrounded by guards. And he gained.

"Watch it!" James shouted. Before Katherine could react, he had drawn his gun and fired.

Prescott stumbled back, clutching his shoulder.

"What do you know?" James grinned, turning to Katherine. "I did get to shoot someone tonight!"

MARIENNE HEARD THE CLEAR, loud crack of a gunshot over the dull roar of the thrusters. A quick glance over her shoulder caused her to stop dead in her tracks. Prescott touched his shoulder gingerly, his hand soon sticky with blood. He looked at Marienne with wide, blue eyes, his expression wounded more than his body.

A thought struck Marienne as suddenly and forcefully as lightning. She bared her teeth in a ferocious grin, and ran back towards him. Hope rose in Prescott's face—a desperate expression that filled her with disgust. She drew up close to him until they were nose to nose and her green, catlike eyes bored into his. With an ungentle shove on his injured shoulder that caused him to yelp in pain, she forced him down into a kneeling position before her.

Marienne brought the knife up so that it glinted crimson and silver in the moonlight. She stared at the blade, admiring how it winked back at her. Then she brought it down fast and hard, smashing the handle into her engagement ring. The glass shattered on impact, but the force of it also jammed her finger with a loud pop. She ignored the pain, using the tip of the knife to pry the broken glass apart until the luma shone clear in the night air.

She inhaled deeply. Most people didn't notice, but luma had a scent: a sharp tang of lightning with soft undertones of rain and clear air, plus something she could never quite place, something entirely unique. She could smell it now as she opened up the glass container on her finger, although it was faint and a little stale. Oh, how she had missed the scent of the stars! It reminded her of the *Vincenzo*.

Marienne drove the ring into Prescott's shoulder, the luma absorbing into his blood. "Swear yourself to me," she growled.

He whimpered pitifully.

"What's the matter?" Her lips peeled back in a grotesque smile, but her eyes flashed with malice. "You were going to swear yourself to me in a week's time. Till death do us part. Will you not do so now?"

"Not the same," he simpered. "Not with luma."

"Oh?" she mocked. "Not even with your own luma? A gift of love, you called it."

"No!" he shouted, at last finding some shred of courage. "I will not give you such power over me!"

She twisted the ring in his shoulder, and he cried out in pain. The luma was inside his body now, swirling through the blood in his shoulder. "And yet you were eager to exercise the same power over me!" Marienne spat. "You were going to force me to marry you, to bind myself to you by law and by luma! If you are willing to take my freedom—and the freedom of thousands of slaves you employ—you must suffer the same fate. Swear yourself to me, or by all the stars in heaven I will slit your throat here and now!" Marienne raised her voice and her knife.

"You are mad!" Prescott screamed.

Her grin widened as she pressed the blade to his neck. "Yes, I am."

She waited in tense silence, tempted to kill him anyway. It would be so easy. The knife twitched in her hand.

"I swear!" Prescott choked. His lips were dry. "I swear myself to you, Marienne de Santorini."

Twisted satisfaction shone too bright in her catlike eyes. "Do you swear on the luma now coursing through your veins that you will obey my every order, direct and implied, as long as you live, on pain of death by that same luma?"

"I so swear," he rasped, his tone resigned.

Marienne nodded and removed the knife from his throat, casting one last disappointed glance at the unbroken skin. She straightened, her gaze drifting to the house. Guards began to rush out the doors. "Very well. Your first order is to ensure that the departure of this airship is unhindered and uninterrupted. You will not follow it, nor try to determine its location, nor its destination."

"Will you stay?" Prescott asked. "Now that you have all the power you wanted, will you stay here with me?"

She scoffed. "It was never about power. I'll send you more instructions over the radio. There are going to be some changes around here." A genuine smile graced her lips as she allowed herself one final look at the estate. She saw what it could become, with her guidance, and that cheered her.

The guards ran towards her and Prescott, shouting to be heard over the airship that hovered above them. Marienne stared at Prescott until he ordered them to stop. They drew up short just behind him, confused.

Marienne shouted to them, "He is hurt. Take him inside and tend to his wound."

"But Miss Santorini—"

"Let her go," Prescott said, his voice as dry as his lips. He repeated in a whisper, "Let her go."

CHAPTER 61

MARCH 4, 1905

Katherine sat on the deck of *Mjolnir's Child*, the wind whipping through her hair as they sailed over a bay. She forlornly tried to tuck her hair behind her ear, but it fell out. It was too short now to tie back into the style she had grown used to while working on the *Vincenzo*. She buried her face in her hands, afraid of the images that swirled in her brain: Mr. Castle cutting her hair, Todd's violence against him, and the smoking gun in her hands. Always that gun in her hands, and Mr. Castle laying dead, blood pooling around him.

"You couldn't sleep either?" Ethan asked as he sat down next to her.

She sighed as she uncovered her face. Her attention turned to a bird flying through the cloudless sky. "How do you feel, knowing that you're free because someone else is dead?"

Ethan studied her face. "Both Murdock and Mr. Castle abused their power, and hurt those that weren't in a position to fight back. I don't feel bad that they're dead. But it's different for me. Marienne killed Murdock for me, whereas you..." He trailed off as her eyes filled with tears. "I won't say if what you did was right or wrong. That's not my place. But remember why you killed him, why you fired that gun. It wasn't for revenge. You were protecting Todd, and yourself."

She nodded, still watching the bird. She had tried to tell herself that she had only shot in self-defense over and over, all night long. But she still felt such heavy guilt. Would it ever leave her? Would she ever feel like her hands weren't stained with blood?

The bird flew out of sight, and Katherine at last turned to look at her brother. "What will you do now?"

He shrugged. "I'm not sure. I can do anything I want." A smile stole across his face. "That's a big decision after two years of being a slave."

"Do you want to join the *Vincenzo*? I'm sure Marienne would take you on."

He shook his head. "I like Marienne, and I'll forever be indebted to her, but... I don't think I can work on a luma harvester. It's..."

"Too close to what you were doing before," Katherine finished, nodding. She understood.

"But I think I want to keep flying," he continued. "I like traveling, seeing new places."

"James has some openings on his crew," Katherine said with a smile. "If you don't mind the danger of lightning-chasing."

"Maybe I'll ask some of the crew about it. Like him." He waved to Newt, who walked over to them.

"Katherine, Todd is awake," Newt reported. "He was asking for you."

She made her way to the infirmary automatically, feeling a twist in her gut with every heavy step. She wasn't sure how she felt about Todd at the moment. His behavior towards Mr. Castle had frightened her—she never thought he was capable of such violence. But when she had stopped him, he had been stabbed. Should she have let him continue? Was his injury her fault?

She hesitated at the infirmary door, stuck between desire and fear. At last, she took a deep breath and walked inside.

Todd was the only one in the infirmary, and he turned to Katherine with a smile. She attempted to mirror the expression, but failed. His brows knit together in concern.

"What's wrong?" he asked.

"How's your leg?" she deflected.

"I'll heal," he said slowly. "I'll need to rest for a while, and I'll have to use my crutch again until I can put my full weight on it. I'm glad you made me the prosthetic before this happened, or I wouldn't be able to walk at all until I recovered completely."

She nodded, not saying anything. Of course she was relieved to hear that he would be alright, but it didn't erase everything else she was feeling.

"What's wrong?" Todd repeated gently. He reached out and took her hand. His hand was so warm, so inviting. How could he be the same man who had kicked Mr. Castle's ribs in?

"Last night, I… I've never seen you so angry," she admitted. Her face flushed and her fingers twitched lightly, brushing against his palm. How would he respond? She thought she had known him, but he had proved her wrong.

His face darkened. "I've never been so angry before," he said. "Never. But when I saw him, what he had done to you… what he was going to do to you… I lost control of myself. If you hadn't stopped me…" Todd closed his eyes. "I wanted him to suffer. He deserved it. But I scared you. And I used the prosthetic you made to do it."

Katherine nodded slowly. "I didn't like seeing you like that. That was never what I intended when I made it."

"I know." He looked at her, his brown eyes large and pleading. "I'm sorry. I know it's too much to ask that you forgive me right now, but will you let me at least try to rebuild your trust in me?"

She leaned down and kissed him. "Of course," she said with a smile. "It will take some time, but we'll get there again. Because I love you."

Todd beamed and kissed her again. "I love you too."

CHAPTER 62

Marienne leaned on the railing of *Mjolnir's Child*, tapping a pen against her chin. She held a small notebook, in which she had already written a list of changes to make to the British Luma Company through Prescott. The top item on the list read: *Abolish debt payment system and free current indentured servants.* She would reform the company into a respectable business, and reunite families. Like Katherine and Ethan.

Ethan joined her at the railing. The sun sparkled off sapphire water as they skirted around the French coastline. "Those clothes suit you better," he observed. She had changed out of the bloodstained, heavy mauve dress into some spare clothing James had lent her. "Newt says it's not the first time you've worn James' clothing." One eyebrow crept up his forehead inquiringly.

She laughed. "That's a funny story. Involved piranhas." The chilled wind of high altitude whipped through her curls in a comfortingly familiar way.

"Thank you for freeing me," Ethan said.

A smile spread across Marienne's face as she gazed at the horizon. "I could not stand by and watch you remain in captivity when I could help. Especially not after you had treated me with such kindness and loyalty."

She noted with amusement that he scratched at his scar. The luma had dissipated, flushed out of his system, but he couldn't be expected to give up the habit so soon.

"I think I might ask James about getting a position on his ship," Ethan said. "You get your lightning from him, right?"

Marienne nodded. "You would get to see Katherine whenever we trade or celebrate together. James will appreciate your initiative. If he asks me about you, I will give my honest opinion, which is nothing but praise." Her smile shifted and grew wry. "But be warned: James acts more pirate than most of us. He trained Robert."

Robert. Even saying his name sent her heart thumping. Though she had radioed her crew the moment they were out of sight of the manor, she had not yet heard back from either her crew or his. A lump formed in her throat, and she fought to dislodge it. Even as they sped towards him, she repeated her mantra: *live, please, just live.*

"He may act like a pirate," Ethan continued, not noticing her worry, "but his work is honest, if dangerous. I think I can manage a few less than reputable business associates."

"Hey, I'm respectable now!" she asserted, waving the notebook. "All it took was a little luma."

"I'm glad you're the one running things now," he said with a smile. "Someone with integrity finally calling the shots."

"I might need your advice on some of the inner workings of the company," she admitted.

"Anytime, just let me know." He spotted James taking over at the helm and pushed off of the railing. "Except now. I have some questions of my own for another captain."

Marienne turned back to gaze at the water far below her. She wasn't certain what awaited her back on the *Vincenzo*. It had only been a few weeks, but it felt like an eternity since she had seen her crew… and Robert. She had faith that the ship was in good shape; Nyx was an excellent first mate and a competent interim captain. But fear still gripped Marienne's heart whenever she thought about Robert. She almost wished she didn't love him, so that she could stop feeling sick from worry.

Almost.

The next few days would be torture as they flew to meet the *Vincenzo* and the *Madness* in Greece. A wisp of a cloud drifted by, passing along the hull too slowly. The wait to reunite with everyone and everything she cared about seemed too long.

A sudden lurch in her stomach signaled the airship was beginning to descend. Marienne looked to James, who stood at the helm. He wore a giant grin.

"What's going on?" she asked, her heels clicking on the deck as she approached. "We don't need to refuel so soon."

"Change of plan," he announced, still wearing that beaming smile, his eyes glinting jovially. He took a long drink from a flask. "We're going down here. I hope you won't oppose, once you see why." He put on his goggles, the tinted lenses reflecting the morning sunlight as he turned *Mjolnir's Child* south.

Marienne peered over the railing of the airship. The water receded, and now they flew over red-roofed buildings and a small bay that quickly narrowed into a branching river. She wasn't certain where they were anymore. Southern France, where she had spent her summers as a child, perhaps? As the airship continued to descend, a dock grew larger, several other airships already secured and swaying. Marienne gasped, one hand flying to her mouth as unashamed tears gathered in the corners of her eyes.

Side by side, the *Vincenzo* and the *Madness* bobbed as if waving to her.

James lowered the airship to an empty dock. Marienne resisted the urge to throw her arms around him. "Thank you," she breathed. "I… I can pay you for all your help."

He shook his head. "You just make my boy happy, promise?"

She nodded enthusiastically, hoping that this meant he knew Robert was alright.

"What are you waiting for?" he asked. "You've always wanted to see Spain, right?"

"Is that where we are?" Marienne wiped tears from her cheeks, knowing they would only return. As much as she wanted to keep a brave, stoic face in front of her crew, that would be an impossible feat today. But it didn't matter. Tears of joy were well worth sharing.

James lowered the gangplank, and Marienne flew off the airship. Before she could make it back to her own, dear *Vincenzo*, Nyx called her name. She stopped short and looked around.

The first mate waved to her from the doorway of a dockside cantina. Marienne's face split into a huge grin, and her heart felt as if it would burst. She ran to Nyx, and the women embraced, laughing as if nothing in the world mattered but this moment.

"Welcome back, captain," Nyx said as she pulled away.

She led Marienne into the cantina, where the entire crew waited for her. They cheered loudly and crowded around her. Tears leaked freely down Marienne's cheeks now, and she did not bother to wipe them away. She was with her family again.

Another voice called her name, a voice from the back of the crowd, a voice that pierced her straight to the heart. She looked towards him and, unable to contain her joy, rushed to Robert. She stopped just short of throwing her arms around him.

Visible underneath his open vest, bandages still criss-crossed his shoulder and chest. Her hand hovered over the place where he had been shot, shaking slightly. She looked at him.

"You're alive," Marienne breathed.

"More than that," Robert whispered back, as if no one else were in the room. This moment belonged to them alone. "You saved me."

She blinked, thinking of all the times she had wished for him to stay alive. Had he heard them all? Her cheeks colored at the thought.

He noticed and chuckled, tucking one of her curls behind her ear. His hand rested at the back of her head. "I wasn't doing so well," he admitted. "I asked Rose to give me luma, and made an Oath to someone who loves me."

Her face twisted into a horrified frown against her will. "No. That's not..." Seeing the alarm in his eyes, she said in a rush of words, "I mean, I do love you, but—" She pursed her lips and glanced around. Members of both crews were pretending not to notice her outburst, but she saw their gazes flickering towards her from the corners of their eyes.

"Another round of drinks for everyone!" Nyx called out jovially, the words met with a rousing cheer that elevated the room for everyone except Marienne and Robert. "James' treat!"

"What?" the lightning chaser protested as he walked through the cantina door.

As the crowd erupted into laughter and cheerful conversation, Marienne gestured to a small square table tucked into a corner. Robert nodded and followed her to the relatively private and quiet edge of the celebration. Marienne pinched the bridge of her nose as he eased himself gingerly into the chair across from her. *This is supposed to be a happy occasion*, she reminded herself. *I should be overjoyed. Robert is alive, I'm back with my crew, the* Vincenzo *is safe.* But all of that was clouded by Robert's revelation.

"What could possibly have possessed you to swear a luma oath to me?" she hissed, eyes still closed.

"I used to think dying would be easy," he admitted. Marienne's eyes flew open and she stared at him. His melancholy gaze was fixed on the table, one hand resting gently on the bandages under his vest. "A simple release of pain, and you're gone. But, as I laid in the infirmary with nothing to do but contemplate my own situation, it felt too much like leaving. And I couldn't leave. Not yet. Not you."

Emotion caught in Marienne's throat. She swallowed it down with difficulty. "But luma?"

"I wasn't getting better. I knew it, and Rose knew it. She suggested taking me to the ground to see a doctor, but what more could they do that she hadn't already done? I pushed her to use the luma, and she didn't want me to make the Oath to her. My thoughts had always been focused on you, anyway."

"You could have made it worse," she argued weakly. "Luma isn't generally a remedy."

"But it worked," he countered. "It wasn't easy or pleasant. I could… feel the luma knitting me back together." He grimaced at the memory.

"I was still in bed for the better part of this week, Rose taking notes all the while."

"Why didn't you make an Oath to yourself, or none at all?"

He shook his head. "I don't think it works like that. I needed you to want me to live for the luma to take effect."

Her face flushed again as she remembered all the times she had silently repeated her plea for him to live. Marienne looked away, watching the crews enjoying themselves with drinks and good company, teasing and joking and celebrating her return. She couldn't bring herself to share in the joy, not yet. "I never wanted this. Not with you."

She had forced Prescott to make an Oath to her, but that had been a satisfyingly exhilarating experience. She was finally out of his reach, and immense relief had replaced the constant vigilance of watching her back. But Robert...

"I don't mind," he said earnestly, taking her hand. "I know you'll never abuse this power. That's why I trust you."

"You don't understand," she implored. "I—"

"But I do! Marienne, I understand you—"

"Shut up and listen!" she snapped.

"You're not listen— ah!" He gasped and his hand flew to the bandages again, his face lined with pain.

Marienne's eyes stung with the threat of tears as she watched, horrified, at the pain her reckless words had caused him. "I'm sorry! Speak freely! Don't... that wasn't an order!" She grasped his free hand, anxiously watching as his expression softened. Behind her the clatter of voices had quieted as some noticed them in the corner, but she couldn't spare a thought for them.

Once Robert's breathing had returned to normal, he slowly looked up at Marienne, new understanding in his aquamarine eyes.

"We will get through this," she promised, still holding his hand clasped in hers. "Together, as equals." *There must be a way to release someone from a luma oath*, she thought. *I will find it.*

Robert nodded, the lines of pain around his eyes softening.

"Together. No matter what it takes." He smiled coyly. "Perhaps it could be as simple as a kiss from my true love."

"If it was that easy, I think it would be common knowledge by now," she countered.

"Couldn't hurt to try."

With a good-natured roll of her eyes, Marienne indulged him. She kissed Robert fiercely, allowing herself to enjoy this moment. They were together at last! Everything else seemed to melt away and she felt as if she shone with the same golden light as the stars. The future could take care of itself. For now there was only the feeling of his lips pressed against hers and the flood of joy that warmed her entire body. A cheer rose again among the crews, snapping her back into the present, and Marienne smiled so much she had to pull away.

As she looked around, satisfaction radiated from her. She was free now, truly free. Never again would she glance over her shoulder, afraid to see Prescott chasing after her. Robert stood by her side, holding her hand. Her crew surrounded her. The *Vincenzo* waited nearby for her command. No matter what difficulties the future held, she was here, now, happy.

Marienne whispered, "I'm home."

End of Book One

ACKNOWLEDGMENTS

So much goes into publishing a book that even a self-published book cannot exist without the help of so many. First and foremost I must thank my husband Jordan for his invaluable feedback as he read each draft and update, and for his unending support as I pursue my dream. My best friends JD Morris and Miranda Day I thank for constantly listening and offering advice as I talk through whatever scenes are giving me trouble.

Without Vale Prosper, there would be no Marienne at all. Not only did they provide the inspiration for the character, but they also were the first person to encourage me to write, saying they thought I would not only enjoy it but be good at it. Thank you.

I cannot give enough praise to my beta-reader book club: Rachel and Andy Marble, Ellie and Alec Gauthier, and Ben and Hailey Ladner. Your enthusiastic response to my book gave me the confidence I needed to pursue publication, and your feedback helped to improve and refine my manuscript into what it is now.

Sean Wallis is such a talented artist, and I am forever grateful that he was able to bring my vision and my character to life with this cover. To my editor, Melanie Christensen, I apologize for the atrocity of my dashes and thank you for your dedication in fixing them. And to Jamie Hixon, I thank you for formatting my book and helping me navigate self-publishing.

Thank you all who encourage me, inspire me, and enjoy my book.

ABOUT THE AUTHOR

Katelyn Yates grew up in Southern California, then moved to Northern Utah for college. She earned her Bachelor's Degree from Utah State University in English with an emphasis on Creative Writing and a Minor in Folklore. She and her husband live in Cache Valley, Utah, and when not writing she can be found singing, playing games, or cross-stitching.